A VOW OF LOVE

♦

As always, Anne kissed the seal on her husband's letter, then breathed a prayer for him before she broke it.

As she read the bold, familiar script—page after page—its message so positive, so surprising, so full of hope and joy—so welcome, she had to keep drying her eyes to go on.

> *I repeat, dearest Anne, that the danger here has passed. Elijah Clark has been soundly whipped and is no longer a threat to the peace of the colony. With my whole, eager heart, I plead with you to come to me at the earliest possible moment. There is now no reason to wait until June. None whatsoever. You have promised to come and I hold you to that promise. I need you and our children. And once you are in my arms again, we can live each glorious hour as though it will never, never end. . . .*

Still holding the letter, she fell to her knees beside the bed. "Dear Father in heaven," she whispered. "I need him too. . . ."

Eugenia Price

❖❖❖❖❖❖❖❖❖❖❖❖

Don Juan McQueen

BANTAM BOOKS
NEW YORK • TORONTO • LONDON • SYDNEY • AUCKLAND

This edition contains the complete text
of the original hardcover edition.
NOT ONE WORD HAS BEEN OMITTED.

DON JUAN McQUEEN
A Bantam Book / by arrangement with the author

PUBLISHING HISTORY
Lippincott edition published 1974
Bantam edition/December 1975
Bantam reissue edition/May 1993

ISBN 0-553-22853-6

Published simultaneously in the United States and Canada

*Bantam Books are published by Bantam Books, a division of Bantam Doubleday
Dell Publishing Group, Inc. Its trademark, consisting of the words "Bantam Books"
and the portrayal of a rooster, is Registered in U.S. Patent and Trademark Office
and in other countries. Marca Registrada. Bantam Books, 1540 Broadway, New
York, New York 10036.*

PRINTED IN THE UNITED STATES OF AMERICA

RAD   0 9 8 7 6 5 4 3 2

For TAY HOHOFF

♦

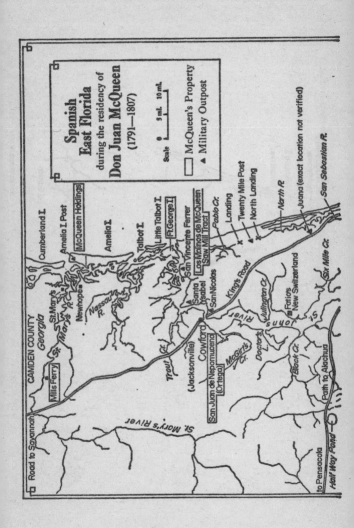

Spanish
East Florida
during the residency of
Don Juan McQueen
(1791—1807)

Scale ● 5 mL. 10 mL.

☐ McQueen's Property
▲ Military Outpost

Road to Savannah

CAMDEN COUNTY
Georgia

Mills Ferry

St. Mary's

St. Mary's R.

Cumberland I.

Amelia I. Post

McQueen Holdings

Newhope

Nassau R.

Amelia I.

Talbot I.

Little Talbot I.

Ft. George I.

San Vincente Ferrer

Los Molinos de McQueen
Saw Mill Tract

Santa Isabel

San Nicolas

Pablo Cr.

Landing

Twenty Mile Post

North Landing

North R.

Juana (exact location not verified)

San Sebastian R.

Trout Cr.

Cowford
(Jacksonville)

San Juan de Nepomuceno
(Ortega)

McGirt's Cr.

King's Road

Julington Cr.

Doctor's L.

Fatio's
New Switzerland

Black Cr.

Six Mile Cr.

St. Mary's River

JOHNS RIVER

Path to Alachua

Half Way Pond

to Pensacola

PART 1

Chapter 1

✦✦✦ "John, I wish you wouldn't refer to your father as 'Don Juan' McQueen! Whoever heard of anything so absurd?"

"He's a Spanish subject now, Mama. I rather like his new name. To my ears it sounds debonair—like Father."

"Well, not to mine."

Anne McQueen watched her eldest son prop his feet on the porch railing and settle into the old rocker to gaze out over the darkening marsh and river—hands clasped behind his head—exactly as his father had always done. The boy, grown as tall as Big John, had been back at The Cottage at Thunderbolt only since early afternoon. Mother and son had last seen each other in England, the day she left him at the Chelsea schoolmaster's house in 1785, seven years ago. Through every agonizing month since Big John went away, she had counted on the joy, the comfort, the security of her son's return. Now, beside her on this unseasonably mild early December evening, sat a cultivated, confident young stranger, as kind and attentive as his father—and so like him in appearance—but with a most unsettling maturity. Even when her husband had acted against her better judgment, he had done so with the near innocence of a child. Her son, not yet twenty, seemed to possess a strength which, instead of reassuring, made her uneasy.

Light was slipping from the sky so swiftly that Anne had trouble seeing his face, but she could feel him studying her.

"Are you sure you're warm enough, Mama?"

"Oh, yes. I sit out here in all sorts of weather. The house is close—and lonely at night with everyone in bed."

"Could you smile, before it's too dark to see your face?"

She patted his hand; forced herself to smile.

"If only you knew how many nights I lay in my bed at old Mr. Butler's house during those first weeks at school in Chelsea and tried to call up the exact memory of your smile."

"You did, son?"

"I'm not the only one. On our way to the new school-master Father picked out for me in Paris a few years ago, we talked about how much we both need that smile. It means you're approving of us. Did you know that?"

"I don't suppose I ever thought about it."

"Right now I think I need to know you approve of me," the boy said.

"You have my approval, John! And my love. You've asked me not to question you about the horror in Paris. I won't. But you were wise to get away from it, especially now that the Marquis de Lafayette is in prison. I'm so thankful to have you home—at last." She cast about in her mind for a more cheerful subject. "Your voyage was far better than Eliza's last year. I still feel ashamed that after all that time away at school in England, neither parent was there to welcome the girl. Of course, I did make an effort—at the wrong dock in Charleston!"

"At least you could make the effort. Papa was in exile."

Anne did not answer. She had never been able to bring herself to accept the word *exile*.

"I hope I've inherited some of my father's spirit," her son went on. "He's painfully lonely for us all in St. Augustine, and yet his letters are downright buoyant. Same humor, never a complaint that he was forced to start life over again at forty—alone."

Anne tensed. Had her husband, through his usual flow of letters, managed to win all of their son's sympathy? Big John was so persuasive that she had come almost to dread his letters, even as she prayed for another by every boat that might bring mail from East Florida. But had she shown no spirit which drew the boy's praise? Not once had he mentioned her courage in the face of the humiliation of his father's debts: the anger of the creditors turned on her when they learned that John McQueen, Esquire, had run away from the Georgia courts to the safety of a foreign land. Was it of no consequence to the boy that his father had turned his back on America—even to baptism in the Roman Church?

God keep me from jumping to conclusions, she breathed. My son did choose to come to me first.

"Has Papa always been so full of hope for the future?"

"Unlike me, yes," she answered stiffly.

Anne wished suddenly for fourteen-year-old Eliza, who had put the two younger children to bed early so that mother and son could spend the first evening alone. She felt irritation that undoubtedly Eliza was closeted in her room now, studying the Spanish grammar her father had sent, already preparing for the day when she would be permitted to visit him again. Struggling against the unexpected strangeness with her son, Anne needed the comfort of Eliza's familiar presence.

The boy's voice was lighter, less marked by booms and whispers, not as musical, yet it made her think vividly of Big John. One had to give attention every minute for fear of misinterpreting a nuance, the meaning of a laugh. At least with her husband, she had always felt certain of her own point of view; not in control of him, heaven knew, but never afraid of his censure. Even after an argument, she had been able to count on his laughter in time, or the sudden solace of his arms. Never mind that the solace was often deceptive and short-lived. It was there.

Now she was on guard.

"Tell me more about your Aunt Wright's family," she said. "Were there lots of parties when you got to London?"

"With Cousin Margaret Cowper visiting from Jamaica, you know there were parties galore."

Anne's sisters, Mary Cowper and Sarah Wright, married to British Loyalists, had been forced to return to England at the end of the Revolution—their husbands'

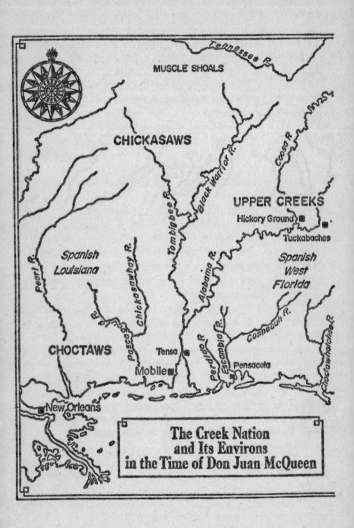

The Creek Nation
and Its Environs
in the Time of Don Juan McQueen

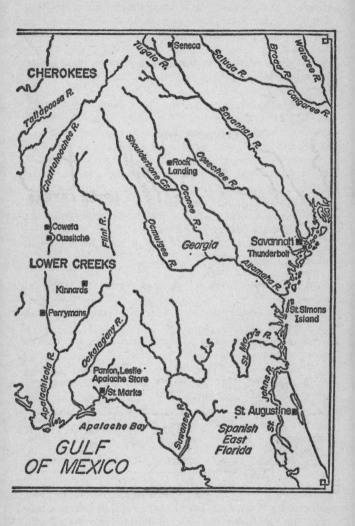

American holdings confiscated. With Eliza, then six, John, eleven, and the infant McQueen children, Sallie, William, and Alexander, Anne had joined them on the voyage. On the same ship were her lifelong friend, widowed Mary Esther Huger, and her only son, Frank. After a visit of several months, Eliza, John, Jr., and Frank Huger were placed in English schools. Anne had not seen her friend or sisters since.

When the Cowpers moved to their Jamaica plantation, she had been grateful that Mary Esther was still in England and could watch over the McQueen children as well as young Frank. Later, when John and Frank went to continue their education in France, Mary Esther sometimes traveled back and forth between England and the Continent. Of course, they all corresponded as regularly as erratic sailings permitted, but Anne was hungry for firsthand news. News which would, at least temporarily, take her son's mind off talk of his father.

"Is Margaret Cowper at sixteen as beautiful and popular as her mother claims?"

After a pause, John said, "Margaret Cowper is the most beautiful creature I've ever seen. And the most sought after."

"Did you escort her to the cotillion your Aunt Sarah gave in her honor?"

"I escorted her—and was permitted all of two dances during the entire evening."

He was silent for what seemed a long time. Then his voice lightened. "My evening wasn't wasted, though. I spent most of it waltzing with Aunt Sarah, who is a delight. Do you know she's genuinely concerned about Father's well-being in what she, of course, calls that 'heathen foreign land'? I admire that. She might have felt he'd deserted you."

Anne said nothing.

"Sarah Lady Wright and Don Juan McQueen correspond often, it seems. Your family in England loves Papa. They worry about him, but no one speaks of him as a failure." In the darkness, Anne felt him turn toward her. "How do *you* think of him, Mother?"

She took a slow, deep breath, then spoke on the sigh:

"As . . . so far away. So *far* away. I'm . . . terribly afraid, too. I've always feared distance between your father and me."

"Mama . . . you do believe he had no other choice except debtor's prison, don't you?"

"Now I do, yes. Since I've acted as his attorney—along with Grandfather Smith and Uncle Aleck—I believe it. My—my head believes it anyway."

John got up abruptly to stand at the piazza railing, his back to her. "Uncle Aleck McQueen!"

"I couldn't have managed without him."

"I can hear him gloat in that mealy, fat-man's voice because his older brother, who outshone him all his life, got into enough trouble for him to come to the rescue!" He whirled to face her. "Mama, why did you let Uncle Aleck get his fingers into our affairs?"

"I had to! Your father had kept so much from me, I needed help, even in finding out the size of the indebtedness. Grandfather Smith is getting old. His heart is so weak, I couldn't put all the burden on him."

He turned away. "I suppose not."

Anne steeled herself; there was no longer any hope of postponing the painful discussion. The boy needed to hear her side of the ghastly story. They must have it out. He appeared as uncomfortable with her as she was with him. "Please sit down beside me again, son . . . please?"

He came back to the old rocker almost reluctantly, Anne thought. Perhaps she would find a way to help him understand. After all, he was away when his father left.

But before she could decide how to begin, he said, "Was it the—the size of the indebtedness that finally convinced you that Papa had no alternative but prison?"

"I admit I was not easy to convince."

"Why? Papa finally told you the whole story, didn't he?"

"Yes, but—"

"Didn't you believe him?"

"In a way, but your father had been talking about the advantages of East Florida under Spanish rule ever since his first visit to St. Augustine back in 'eighty-four, John.

He went down there almost as soon as we were on our boat bound for England."

"Why did he go then?"

"I was naïve and trusting in those days, but as I understand it, the governor of Georgia, John Houstoun, sent him on some sort of mission to the Spanish governor. There had been a complaint from St. Augustine about a few remaining Loyalists crossing the Georgia border to cut Spanish timber illegally. Your father was sent to smooth things over."

"Ah, yes! Where peace and harmony are needed, send Don Juan McQueen. That grew to be a habit, didn't it? Washington, Nathanael Greene, Jefferson—even old Houstoun. When in trouble, send McQueen."

"Your father was always willing, too."

"Spain had just taken back the Floridas then. I wonder what Father liked about the place—beyond the tax-free land grants?"

"I can't imagine, but I've seldom understood his enthusiasms. Knowing his passion for land, I suppose tax-free grants were enough. I do recall his telling me that he actually liked the city of St. Augustine, though. Naturally he was royally received by Governor Zéspedes, entertained—fawned over, I'm sure—by all the officials. After all, even back then, it was no secret that Georgia posed the biggest threat to their vile little government."

"You really despise the Spanish, don't you?"

"I despise all cruelty," she said.

"Let's not argue about that. Go on with your story, Mama. I'm listening."

"Of course, St. Augustine was desperate for settlers. When the British left, the Spanish did not, as expected, pour back into the empty colony. I have no idea what sort of proposal Governor Zéspedes made to Papa, but by the time the children and I returned from England, East Florida was all he talked about. Your grandfather and I managed to get his mind off it after a while. As I recall, he bought those islands on the Georgia coast, Sapelo and Blackbeard—part of St. Catherine's—about that time, so said no more about it. But when all the pressures began to mount for him here two years ago, I—I was sure he was

using the excuse of his indebtedness to—get me to agree
to move down there."

"I see."

"Do you see, John? Do you really understand how I
felt at the thought of leaving the United States—our new,
free country for which your father worked and fought so
hard? Twice he barely escaped with his life when he was
captain in the South Carolina Navy. He was imprisoned
for eight long months by Monarchists! Do you really understand how confused I was? How confused I am still?
How hard it was to believe that indebtedness could force
him to—give up his citizenship in the land he had loved so
much? He seemed terribly worried about the debts and
lawsuits—and yet so eager to try life in that horrid place!
I didn't know what to believe, John. Do you see that?"

"I'm . . . trying, Mama."

The pain in his voice brought fresh pain to Anne. At
only nineteen, the boy could not fairly be expected to understand. He had been away such a long time. And of
course, his father's enthusiastic letters were far more palat-
able than hers, which she knew had been stilted and too
brief because she had tried to shield her son, especially
when eight-year-old Alexander died in 1789. Suddenly,
she seemed no longer able to protect him. Her own needs
ran too deep.

Anne struggled to control her voice. "Papa has always
been a mystery to me. He's still a mystery, but I think I
understand far more now than—than the night he left."
Tears stung her eyes. "The debts were—*are* impossible.
He did face prison. But the night he left, I was too terrified
to grasp that! Too terrified to think. . . ."

The stormy, wild night he left, nearly twenty months
ago, should have grown dim by now.

It had not. . . .

He had already said good-by, his rich voice warm, urgent, trying to reassure her, as she clung to him in the privacy of their second-floor bedroom. Then, for the first
time in all the years of their married life, Big John had
wrenched her arms from around him and walked away, his

boots heavy on the stairs. The front door closed solidly, and she heard him run down the path to the dock.

In a panic, Anne grabbed her thick blue cloak, tied the hood in place against the storm outside, then fell to her knees beside their bed and tried to pray. Thunder and wind shook The Cottage ... the cramped, modest plantation house from which she would probably be evicted, since he had mortgaged that too. She could not reach God. Her pleas went no higher than the ceiling of the once cheerful room overlooking the Thunderbolt River, the marsh and the dock—the familiar dock from which the family had embarked on so many festive trips across this very river to picnic at Oatland Island, another of her husband's plantations; the dock, where this night such strange things were taking place, as Big John worked now in the driving rain, side by side with young Harry and Cletus and Strephon and Black Thomas.

Anne shivered as the battering wind drove near and then sucked away the sound of her husband's voice shouting orders, strained, hoarse, impatient. Impatient to be off on his journey—away from her, their children, their home, their country—to a foreign place where no one loved him.

"Dear God, *no!*" She scrambled to her feet, not comforted. *"I won't let him go,"* she screamed, then caught her breath, startled at her own shrill cry. Sallie and William were asleep across the narrow upstairs hall. They must go on sleeping. Must not find out—not until morning. At least, not until morning. "But I *can't* let him go. I'll stop him. I'll find a way to stop him!"

When eight-year-old Sallie began to call, Anne jerked open the bedroom door, ran down the steep stairs, through the hall and out into the storm. Her cloak, flailing in the wind, caught on a firethorn and almost tripped her as she stumbled along the path.

"John!" Her scream flattened in another crash of thunder, but she kept running toward the wavering flame of his big lantern, down the wet bluff and out onto the dock. John's lantern blinded her, and her head reeled above the sickening motion of the dark water. She strained to make out the forms of the four Negroes already waiting at the oars of the plantation boat—the fourth, Harry, a mere

twelve-year-old boy who had pleaded to go with him. Then she could see her husband's broad back. He was settling the pitifully small trunk with his few belongings into the stern of the boat.

She cried out again.

He turned, strong legs braced, as the boat swung against the dock. "Go back to the house," he shouted. "Go back, Anne!"

"No! You can't go tonight. You'll all be drowned!"

He leaped to the dock and stood staring, not touching her. The open, troubled face was stark. The thick hair whipped around it in long, wet ropes. He was soaked to the skin. For a moment, he stood as though undecided. Then his arms went around her, his big hand pressing her face into the rough wetness of his great coat.

"I have to go."

"No!"

"*I have to go,*" he repeated firmly. "But, Anne, I'm not leaving only in disgrace. Did you hear what I said?"

She clung to him. He rocked her, helplessly.

"Don't lose the sense of being near me—like this," John pleaded. "Remember me with my arms around you, beloved Anne. And don't forget I am not leaving only in disgrace. Spanish Florida is our land of promise! I'll send for you soon. Soon. Believe in me . . . *believe* in me. . . ."

Young John broke the silence. "Mama, I have to know what you write to Papa when he begs you to go to him. I have to know that."

"I—I'm sure I wrote you, son, that I had planned to go with Eliza last year. I was almost packed when your grandfather fell ill."

"I know that. I'm not talking about a visit. Papa wants you to move to St. Augustine. To be his wife again. What do you tell him?"

"Always, always that I *am* his wife. Beyond that, I . . . try to convince him that an impoverished foreign military outpost is no place for a lady and her children. Oh, I know Eliza was captivated, but—you'll never know what a struggle it was for me to let her go alone."

"She had Papa's friend Andrew Atkinson looking after her on the boat, didn't she?"

"Yes, but don't you understand I had to force myself to trust God that your father wouldn't try to keep her once she was there?"

"He didn't try."

"No. God answered my prayer."

"Maybe."

"If we find he can't return safely to Georgia, I'll visit him. I'll have to. I—love your father. Enough to see to the welfare of his children. To assume full responsibility for them."

"But, Mother, does the government of a country where children grow up make that much difference?"

"To me it does." She sat erect. "It once did to your father."

Neither spoke for a time, and during the lull, a marsh hen cried somewhere down by the quiet river.

Finally John asked, "Could your real reason for not going to him be—your parents?"

Anne's hopes for a hint of understanding lifted. "Your grandfather is very frail. I certainly would feel guilty leaving Grandmother Smith with the burden of his affairs, should . . . something happen to him."

John gave a short laugh. "I don't seem to remember Grandmother as being particularly helpless. But doesn't your Bible say a woman is to forsake even her parents in order to cleave to her husband, no matter what happens? St. Augustine isn't a world away from Savannah. You could visit my grandparents."

She had hoped too soon. Her son did not—perhaps *could* not understand her lonely position in all this. What, indeed, had she expected of the boy? Had she assumed that he would share her horror, as did her parents, at the thought of the children growing up as papists? True, she would not be forced to renounce her religion, but in Spanish Florida, unless she attended the idolatrous Mass, she would have no church at all. Did this not bother young John? Had he lived so long in France that he too had turned away from his Christian training? Away from the Church of England? She pushed the thought from her mind, trying to believe that the indefinable barrier she felt between them was the boy's natural grief over his father. Young John could not possibly feel at home with her yet. Not so soon.

She longed suddenly to feel the assurance of his hand, but kept hers folded in her lap. Did her son know how she had resisted when his father decided to move him to the home of a Catholic schoolmaster in Paris? Anne held no love for the Crown of England. She was an American patriot. But at least in Britain, her children were exposed to Christian influence. She dared not ask what he believed now.

What she said next must somehow give the boy hope. She forced a strong, positive tone. "*I am* going to visit him. I've told you, I hate *any* distance between us."

"But when will you go?"

"I don't know!" She paused. "You're a man now, but Eliza and William and Sallie are still children. I *have* to think first of them. Your little brother Alexander died as a child because we didn't have a doctor. There's no doctor at all in St. Augustine much of the time. There's always danger of war. At least they're safe here—though poor. John, no one is safe in Spanish Florida!"

"Where did you get an idea like that? After what I've lived through in Paris, it sounds like heaven. Besides, do you think Father would have permitted Eliza to visit him if life down there is so dangerous?"

"He saw to it that she came during a safe interim. *After* he was back from some wild-goose chase. We had to postpone the sailing for over a month until he'd finished with his adventuring on the high seas—he was chasing an unprincipled pirate named Bowles. On the new governor's orders."

John laughed. "I wish Papa could hear *that* description of William Augustus Bowles!"

"I didn't realize I was being humorous." Anne was thankful for the dark. She must not let him see the way her face changed when she spoke or even thought of his father's life now. In her own looking glass, she had seen the strain appear, the lines deepen around her normally full, generous mouth; had seen age come from the torment of her dark thoughts of his life in the faraway little Spanish city. That he breathed danger in its very air, she had no doubt. Danger not only to his person but to his soul.

All her life, Anne had heard tales of the horrors of St. Augustine, the unwashed, dark-skinned women who gave themselves up to vile Spanish officials whose evil desires were matched only by those of their debauched Catholic monarch! More than that, any Georgian knew that every savage Indian attack of defenseless white women and children settled in Florida was prompted, even directed by the Spanish governor at the Plaza in St. Augustine. The very name of the shadowy city repelled her, and the Plaza—the town square on which, she had been told, the colony's Government House was situated—symbolized more to her than merely the seat of government; it was the headquarters of evil itself.

Still, in spite of all she knew of the officials in East Florida, she had not been surprised that her husband had managed a delightful time for Eliza. After all, the Spanish were clever. Obviously, they had believed General Anthony Wayne's exaggerated letter of introduction, had believed John McQueen, Esquire, to be still so well connected in Georgia that he could surely persuade other influential Americans to settle in the impoverished East Florida colony. He had, indeed, been able to talk his contemporary, Colonel John McIntosh, into accepting land grants there. So it was no surprise to Anne that the treacherous new governor, her husband's friend Juan Quesada, had entertained Eliza with a fancy-dress ball. Neither had it been a surprise that her daughter had *not* been shown the damp, moldy horrors of Castillo de San Marcos—especially its legendary dungeons.

"How do you learn of all this supposed danger down there, Mama?"

"Our newspapers are filled with it! Only last week, I read of a ghastly Creek attack on the St. Mary's. John, an eleven-year-old girl *lived*—after being scalped!"

He reached for her hand. "But, Mama, I've just crossed the ocean with one of Papa's best friends. Mr. Leslie's place is only a short walk from Papa's house. John Leslie's a gentleman. You were acquainted with him before he left South Carolina. Father's friends at Government House in St. Augustine are gentlemen too. You know perfectly well that Georgia newspapers exaggerate everything Spanish!"

"I have another source of information, son. Creek Chieftain Alexander McGillivray still writes to me regularly."

John sat up. "Why, Mama, I'm impressed. I knew you and Papa had known him back in Charleston, but McGillivray's one of the most important men in East or West Florida now. Papa says without him, Panton and Leslie's trading firm *and* Spain's rule in the Floridas—Louisiana too—would crumble!"

"Your father's right. We could make peace with his Creeks if the Spaniards didn't keep them supplied with guns."

"You'd call that making peace? I see the Spanish as *protecting* the Indians. Without that Spanish protectorate, the Georgians would 'make peace' with them, all right." He laughed. "By driving them off their hunting grounds."

The boy was almost totally under Big John's influence. She would have to be more careful. "Just the same, I'm hopeful that Alexander is beginning to change a little in favor of the United States. President George Washington is a fair man, son! Your father has always been devoted to him."

"What has Washington to do with McGillivray changing toward the United States?"

"Well, he did travel, in spite of poor health, all the way from his home on the Coosa River to New York two years ago to treat with the President. I don't think whatever they decided has worked out yet, but I'm hopeful for Alexander's sake. I've been fond of him since he was a boy of fourteen. We still lived in Charleston, you know, when Alexander's Scottish father sent him there to be educated."

"I remember hearing you and Papa talk about him, but I suppose I hadn't connected the name with the now-powerful Creek chieftain." He settled again in the rocker. "I *am* impressed with my mother. The famous chief really does write personal letters to you? Confides in you?"

"For years. I don't tell everyone, of course. He's not

always trusted in Georgia. I make no bones with him about my dislike of his alliance with the Spanish, but Alexander McGillivray, the man, I trust. And pity."

"Pity? Whatever for?"

"The boy's had a sad life. He loved his Creek mother and his loyalist father deeply. His mother is dead now. Lachlan McGillivray, a bitter old man, is back in Scotland, his South Carolina holdings all confiscated. That's one reason Alexander has hated the United States." She sighed. "I suppose I know more about political intrigues than most women. I was brought up to keep abreast of world events. But I don't pretend to know or understand what Alexander is up to. I simply care about his—heart. It makes me sad for him to hate America, even if—"

"Even if the Georgians are after the Creek lands?"

"Yes. But I also worry about his poor health and—his soul."

"His soul? I thought you said his heart."

"Both. He has a Scottish name, but Chief McGillivray is a Creek first, last, and always. He lives by his mother's Wind-clan customs. You see, Alexander has more than one wife!"

John laughed. "Oh, Mother, you're marvelous! I certainly wish I'd known all this while I was still abroad. Frank Huger boasts constantly of his mother's friendship with Mr. Jefferson. But my mother is a friend of a world-famous Indian chieftain! Do you realize that even the London papers carry stories about him?"

"I must say I'm relieved that your opinion of Chief McGillivray is so high, because his letters are my most reliable source of news about the very real dangers in East Florida."

John was silent for a moment, then said guardedly, "Well, I have no opinion of him, really. I merely know he's famous. Or *infamous*, some of my British friends feel. After all, British Governor Dunmore of New Providence was sponsoring your unprincipled pirate, William Augustus Bowles—hoping to throw McGillivray from his Creek throne and put Bowles in his place. The British grieve that Bowles is at last in jail. The Spanish rejoice."

"Your grandfather can explain far better than I about

Alexander's ties with Spain. I know he holds the key to everything for Panton and Leslie. Keeps the Creeks preferring their goods over any other trading house." She sighed again. "Both William Panton and John Leslie were fine Scottish gentlemen once. Heaven only knows what they're like now that they've sold their birthrights for a mess of Spanish pottage."

"I know what John Leslie is like, but let's not argue any more about the virtues or sins of Papa's new government. Tell me something else about McGillivray, the man. Did you and father meet him through family connections in Charleston?"

"Your Grandfather McQueen and Lachlan McGillivray were friends, but Alexander just walked quietly and smilingly into my hyacinth garden one day and said, 'Good afternoon.' My heart went out to him."

"Was I born yet?"

"You were an infant. I'm only four years older than Alexander, but I was touched then by his loneliness for his mother. I'd look at you sleeping in your cradle and pray someone would be kind to you if ever you were lonely. I also felt certain that Alexander was going to be . . . different. Different and important. That took no real insight. His mind was ingenious, even then. He was kind, unusually compassionate for his age. He laughed easily, and he loved to work in the hyacinths with me. My hyacinths were famous, you know."

John sniffed elaborately. "I can still smell them. Weren't they blue? All blue?"

"Yes. Your father brought me some blue hyacinth bulbs just before we were married. I planted them in the front yard of our Charleston house."

"And from then on, blue hyacinths have been your favorite flower. Yours and Father's."

"I didn't know you were aware of that."

"Papa told me."

"I see."

After a while, John said, "So—Chief McGillivray is the real reason you're so afraid of going to my father."

"If any man knows of the dangers down there, he does. Even with all his enormous power among the Indians, they're too widely scattered for Alexander to stay informed of all their savage attacks. There's no possible way he can guarantee that there will be no more bloodshed."

"And you believe the half-breed chief over Papa?"

"It doesn't amount to that."

"I think it does."

"Chief McGillivray is trying to keep the children and me in a safe place!"

"And Father?"

"Your father wants us there with him so much, he's blinded! He's"—her voice trembled—"he's too lonely to think clearly."

"Lonely enough to lie to us about the hardships and so-called evils of St. Augustine life?"

"Oh, son, your father never feels he's lying. He's convinced always, always that everything will turn out fine. That the best is yet to come." Anne was suddenly exhausted, fighting tears.

"It was young of me, wasn't it, not to realize you'd be—bitter," he said.

"I've lived so long on—his dreams, John!" An involuntary sob shook her body. "But I swear to you, I'm more frightened than bitter. I've never been away from him without fear. My particular, hateful, familiar fear of—of *distance* between your father and me."

"Because you don't trust him?"

"Because I love him!"

Young John dropped to one knee beside her chair. "Poor Mama," he whispered. "Poor Mama. . . ."

For the first time in twenty months, Anne McQueen felt no guilt for being weak. For being human.

Chapter 2

✤✤✤   In the night, the weather had turned damp and cool, more the way young John remembered the coast in December. He was comfortable in his greatcoat and muffler on his first morning home, as he drove unwillingly in the ancient McQueen phaeton over the five miles to Savannah.

Even with his father gone and the family living in a house he'd never seen, he had looked forward to being back, to the fun of getting acquainted with his sisters and brother, to leisure time for writing letters, to loafing for a few days. But, beginning last night on the porch with Mama, nothing was the way he had dreamed. To make matters worse, before he was fully awake this morning his mother was in his room, begging him to visit Grandfather Smith today. Not a few days from now, as he'd planned; today.

"I promised him," Mama had said. "I know I should have told you last night, but. . . ."

Maybe nothing was the way Mama had dreamed, either. He had never seen her cry before. The agony of her sobs had not left him. During the years away he had thought of her quiet, haunting beauty—the soft brown hair, the wide-set gray eyes, the gentle, generous mouth—firm but young, even when she was cross. Mama . . . always pretty. Last night when she had wept, the age in her voice shocked him. This morning, her eyes were dark-ringed and swollen. Her terrible pain, he admitted, was somehow surprising. Before, his sympathy had surged toward Papa, alone in a strange place. This had not diminished, but from now on he would have her heartache to carry as well. Her pain and his own, along with the rebellion he felt now as Rita, the aging McQueen roan he remembered from his childhood in South Carolina, trotted stiff-legged, taking him to an encounter for which he was not ready.

"I wish you could talk, Rita," he said to the mare. "I need to talk to someone else who was here before Papa went away."

He loosened his grip on the reins. Rita knew the road from Thunderbolt to Savannah. He didn't. "I'm a stranger here," he said, and the sound of his own voice pushed him back into his familiar world abroad: his rooms at the home of his last schoolmaster, M. Watrin, at Pigne-puce, near Paris ... and back to the first tiny attic hideaway at the Reverend Mr. Butler's place, where his schooling had begun so long ago on China Row, Chelsea. Aunt Wright's home in London had seemed more a part of his world than his own mother's house in Georgia. Not only because the Wrights were gay and light-hearted. He had lived through the build-up of the nightmare rebellion in France. He was not looking for days void of trouble or danger. The serious side of his nature would dry up if life were one continuing soirée. But somehow, danger of the kind he knew in Paris hadn't depressed him. He had often run for his life, had lain wide-eyed in his bed hearing murder happen in the street. Still, that trouble had not scarred him; was not really his.

How could he make his mother understand that, important as it might be, one nation's actions toward another would not matter in the long run? From his studies of history, he had come to see that governments would always wage wars. To him, people mattered, not governments.

And family trouble was worse than war.

He had grown up in the midst of the American Revolution, had lived through the mounting terror in France; England and France and Spain could be at war within a few months. He accepted all that because he could do nothing about it. But kinfolk should not hurt one another! Running through a dark street in Paris from a man gone wild with a musket had been a tough, maturing adventure.

Back in the safety of his rooms, he'd felt like a man for having escaped.

There was no adventure in feeling his mother's pain. Pain she could so quickly end, if only she would.

On the Panton and Leslie schooner during the crossing, he had been eager for the future, ready for responsibility. Now, he was uncertain, needing to run to one of his parents for safety. Neither could help. His father was too far away and his mother too locked into her own grief. The two people who could quiet his doubts were causing them.

"Margaret," he whispered. "Margaret . . . if only you would be serious, I could get away from all this trouble—with you! I love you, Margaret . . . I love you."

His cousin had been so delighted to see him again, when they met last month in London, that it seemed like destiny to John when she chose him as her escort to the cotillion. One glimpse of her, after the years, had sealed his childhood love forever. He had loved Cousin Margaret Cowper all his life. Now, he loved her as a man loves a woman. But she had laughed the afternoon he asked her to marry him.

He could still hear Margaret's laughter and his mother's sobs. He could bear neither.

Last night with Mama, his pain might have shown, but he had not permitted it to show with Margaret that day in the Wrights' garden. Somehow, he had managed to laugh too, and had simply told her that she was still young—perhaps too young to know her own mind—and that he would never give up. He meant it. One day he would win her—by showing her that, if he had to wait for years, he would wait, his hopes firm. He tested those hopes now, after what had happened last night with Mama; tested them again against the dread building in his heart at being forced to visit his grandfather. The hopes held. Margaret *would* marry him some day, if he kept his spirits high.

"Like Papa," he said aloud. He had planned to write to Margaret today and to his father. Since the talk with his mother, he felt he needed to reassure Papa that between them, father and son, everything was still right.

He thought of his father hurrying each day to John Leslie's office hoping for a letter. "If you could see the

man's face," Leslie had told him on the voyage over,
"you'd write more often—all of you. Out of kindness to
me, if nothing more. I'm the one who has to watch that
look when there's nothing for him." John smiled at the rest
of what Leslie had said: "But if there's nothing for him,
the next day he's right back with his hopes higher than
ever!"

Poor Father . . . poor Mother.

He breathed deeply of the piny air and stretched his
legs into the far side of the cramped phaeton. He had gone
off to sleep last night puzzling over the difference between
the way he felt with his mother and the way his friend
Frank Huger apparently felt with Mrs. Huger. Frank and
his widowed mother were friends, able to disagree with
neither feeling any guilt. If Mary Esther Huger had had
her way, Frank would have left school as soon as the
French trouble broke out, to finish his medical studies
back in Pennsylvania. But his friend was still abroad, embarked by now, John supposed, on his pretended pleasure
tour of Austria—dead set on locating the prison where his
idol, the Marquis de Lafayette, was being held in solitary
confinement.

The Hugers and the McQueens had been the first
American colonists to meet the brilliantly uniformed,
nineteen-year-old marquis. Some fifteen years ago, when
the McQueens were visiting the Hugers, Lafayette's ship,
Victoire, ran aground at the small South Carolina creek
near the Hugers' plantation. Patriots Benjamin Huger and
John McQueen had warmly welcomed Lafayette and his
party. For a week or more, John had forgotten how long,
there had been dinners and patriotic functions in honor of
the French nobleman who had come at his own expense to
offer his services and his fortune to General George Washington and the cause of liberty.

What John remembered most clearly were the drums
and the cheers at the Huger dock the day Lafayette set sail
for the north to meet Washington. Frank Huger and John,
both five years old, had been almost too excited to breathe
as they stood beside their fathers for Lafayette's farewell
speech.

But one thing had happened that day to Frank which

had not happened to John: the dashing young Lafayette, just before he stepped into the McQueen boat to return to his ship, had leaned down to pat the chubby cheek of Benjamin Huger's small son. The moment had marked Frank's life. Otherwise, he would now be back in America with John.

Through the years, the friendship between John McQueen, Sr., and the marquis deepened. Young John seldom received a letter from St. Augustine in which Papa failed to inquire after Lafayette. The thought of the courageous, action-loving marquis locked up alone in an unknown Austrian fortress was more than anyone could conceive. How quickly the man's fortunes had changed! Even the French revolutionaries had turned against him, and by the time John left Paris, the mention of the name of the Marquis de Lafayette could send a man or woman to the guillotine.

John had meant to tell his mother of the latest heartache and agony endured by faithful little Mme Lafayette. Her life and the lives of her mother and children were in constant danger because she still proudly refused to deny that she bore the marquis's name. His wife had no idea where they had imprisoned him. Even the American minister at The Hague knew nothing, but Mme Lafayette's faith in her husband did not waver.

At one point last night, John had almost told his mother that if she thought her life was hard, she should consider the tortured days of Mme Lafayette. He was glad today that he hadn't, but his mother revered the marquis so much, it might have helped if he had at least reminded her that Lafayette, with all his nobility and love of liberty, was as human as Papa. The great Frenchman had weaknesses and faults too; did foolish, unnecessarily daring things. Having spent so many evenings at the Lafayette home, John knew that time after time the marquis had left on military missions of his own impetuous making, without even an *au revoir* to his wife. Still, gentle Mme Lafayette had told John and Frank the last time they saw her in Paris that somehow, as soon as the Austrian fortress was discovered, she intended to go—taking their children—to be imprisoned with her husband!

Mary Esther Huger would soon be back in America. Suddenly, he was counting on the traveled, less provincial Mrs. Huger to help his mother see how wrong, how useless it was to allow religious or political prejudice to keep her away from Papa a day longer than necessary.

While two miles of road still lay ahead before he reached Savannah, he took a cigar from his pocket, clipped it with his pocketknife—and then put it back. He carried brimstone matches and flint, but the air smelled too good to fog it up with smoke, even smoke from the fine Havana cigars his father had been sending so proudly from St. Augustine ever since John began smoking. His mother didn't know he smoked, of course, and neither did his grandparents. He laughed. Just as well not to have one now, he thought, picturing his inquisitive grandmother.

Under any other circumstances, he would be eager to see his grandparents again. He'd always been proud of them; especially John Smith, a man common in name only. He remembered his grandfather, slim and erect, making eloquent, penetrating speeches in behalf of liberty for the colonies. He could now look back and recognize that his mother's father had been years ahead of his time in liberality of heart and mind. Yet Grandfather Smith; who seldom spoke at home because Grandmother gave him very little opportunity, could—when he meant business—send a chill through a young boy.

It would surprise some people, he was sure, but he had always been fonder of his grandmother, Elizabeth Smith. At least, more at ease with her. Mainly because she talked so much and generally answered her own questions anyway, there was little need to pay attention.

He knew of no one who didn't respect the John Smiths. He certainly knew of no one who didn't weigh Grandfather's words. But he recalled almost no one who had never looked about for a way to escape the stream of talk—however cheerful—which flowed from his grandmother.

He grinned, remembering that because of her long lectures on the subject, replete with genealogical data, he had firmly believed until lately that he had been born into the two best families in America. According to her, the Smiths and the McQueens left nothing to be desired in the way of ancestors.

He loved the way she looked—rather the way grand-mothers should look, he thought. He could still picture her sitting in her chair—the tapestry wing-backed chair no one else ever thought of using—sun streaking her graying curly hair, the jutting chin up, the dark eyes looking off through an open window—seldom at you—as words poured forth with such absorption in her subject that if a cousin took your place, she seldom noticed. A portly, pleasant, kind lady. Maybe beautiful once. Always immaculately groomed, her dress smelling of potpourri and her breath of cloves. He still hated cloves; Grandmother, who always carried a few dried buds tied in the corner of a handkerchief, had forced him to chew so many of them his tongue burned at the memory.

"Excellent for your teeth and gums, John," she would say with her customary certainty. Then, with equally customary flattery, which she never blinked at using, she would add: "You have such ruddy gums, dear boy, and such perfectly formed white teeth, Grandmother wants you to take good care of them!"

He made a wry face and wondered if Elizabeth Smith still had all her teeth.

They would both be older. He was prepared for that. His grandfather had been ill. "Promise me that you'll do whatever he suggests," Mama had pleaded this morning. "His heart is so weak. Don't upset him." John frowned. What was Mama really saying? He found himself hoping Grandmother Smith would be at home. Not out doing good with the prayer society ladies. Grandfather wouldn't have a chance to say much with his wife beside him.

His dread was deepening, as were the ruts in the old road. Maybe Rita needed him to drive after all. He gripped the reins firmly in both hands, but to be honest, it was more to slow the mare than to drive. He was glad to be alone.

"Rita—do you realize that I'm a stranger here? That everybody's strange to me? Do you realize that I know Mrs. Huger far better than I know my own mother?"

Chapter 3

✥✥✥ "Your grandmother was sorry not to be on hand for this first visit, son, but she's never missed a prayer society meeting when she was to preside, except once while I was sick last year." John Smith chuckled. "The truth is, she jumped at the chance to attend, knowing you'd be here to look after her ailing old husband. She'll be home soon ... help me to my chair, please."

As they walked slowly to the library, the tremor in his grandfather's frail body sent an ache of concern through John. He sat in a chair directly opposite, so that he could watch the changing expressions on the genteel face. No matter what explanations he had been given, it was clear to him that time alone with his grandfather had been pre-arranged. Surprisingly, now that he was here, he did not resent this. Only John Smith's unerring judgment, he supposed, had ever caused him discomfort. Mama is a lot like him, he thought. Both too apt to be right for comfort. But he felt a rush of affection for the old man. And less dread.

Grandfather's letters to John, which had come to Paris more often since Papa left Georgia, had shown no hint of bitterness toward Papa. Not even disappointment. The two men had been friends, and besides, Grandfather had tried to be a father to his son-in-law, whose parents had been dead so long. Still, the old man had seen his daughter suffer for almost two years, and John wondered how much of this would show in his face.

They discussed John's voyage; then he said, "I promised Mother I'd be home for supper. Could we come right to the business of—our family trouble?"

"I think we should do just that, son. So does your grandmother." John Smith's hand shook as he picked up a portfolio from the table beside him and laid it out in his lap. "Knowing you'd want my opinion of what's happened, I collected most of your father's letters for reference. I've felt honored that my son-in-law has kept me informed concerning his dealings down there. But"—he looked straight at John—"before we discuss any of this, I want you to know that I did all in my power to help him before he left. Had we known sooner how bad things were, Aleck and I might have been able to do more. Even your mother didn't know until it was too late."

John's nervousness lessened. Maybe his grandfather intended to help him, after all. He leaned forward. "What happened, Grandfather? He inherited so much land from Grandfather McQueen. I've always taken family wealth for granted. Papa knows good timberland. His friends in Paris—Mr. Jefferson, when he was still minister, and the Marquis de Lafayette—used to tell me that there wasn't a man anywhere with a better eye for timber than my father. I've heard Papa laugh and say he'd lost count of how many thousands of acres he owned in Georgia alone. There's an enormous market for pine and oak and cedar. What happened? How did he get into so much debt?"

For a long time his grandfather looked at him, as though deciding just how much to say. Then, before he finally began to talk, his faded gray eyes fell to the pattern in the library carpet.

"I think perhaps this is one answer to your question, son. Grandfather McQueen died too soon. I knew him. He was a levelheaded though ambitious man. His ambitions, not uncommon in colonial America, where opportunities abounded for a man interested in both trade and land, occupied much of his conversation. Your uncle, Aleck, wasn't old enough yet to travel, but the senior McQueen began taking his son John with him on business trips into the wilderness of Georgia and the Carolinas when the lad was seven or eight. Week after week they traveled together over miles of virgin timberland—Indian country.

"Until the white man came with his saws, taking down a tree was a gigantic task. The savages' method of slow, careful burning until the tree fell took days. Such effort was not expended unless the tribe had real need of the timber—for a canoe or the foundation of a wattle-and-daub hut—or some such. So, Indian land here in the east was thick with timber. Your father learned early of the wealth to be gained from those wildernesses. The boy would listen at night around the campfires to his father's dreams of owning still more timberland. But you must keep in mind that Grandfather McQueen was a mature and sagacious man, in spite of his big dreams. When he bought a piece of land, he knew before he bought exactly how he would cut and transport the wood, exactly where he'd find laborers, how he would meet his payments. Most important, he knew the markets and saw to the operation and management of his own mills." John Smith shook his head. "But the senior McQueen died when your father was only eleven."

"My age when I was sent to school abroad."

"Precisely. Old enough to be excited about the promise of life, but not old enough to know how to handle it without guidance." He coughed painfully, then rested a moment. "I—tend to grow a little short of breath at times," he apologized. "I'm sure it must be difficult for a young lad like you to be patient."

"Not at all, Grandfather. But I think I know what you're trying so carefully to say. Papa's father could have given him the guidance he needed. His mother could not." He smiled. "I've heard a few tales about Grandmother McQueen."

"She—she was eccentric, to say the least. The lady never quite grew up, I believe."

"Did my mother and Grandmother McQueen get on together?"

"Yes." John Smith smiled. "Yes, they did. At the risk of sounding disrespectful of the dead, though, I'll have to say that Grandmother McQueen, though not old, went to her reward at just about the right time."

"I was still a baby, wasn't I? I don't remember her."

The old man nodded. "You see, your mother was so

deeply in love with your father when they were married, back in 1772, she saw everyone—including her mother-in-law—through a romantic, roseate haze. Her mother-in-law was undoubtedly one of the most enchanting ladies any of us had ever met. Pretty, pert, rather like a dainty Irish leprechaun. She was opinionated, as are all Irish Protestants, but Mrs. McQueen appeared to believe with her whole generous though often foolish heart that little mattered in life but gaiety and laughter. She lost two children the very same year her husband died. She wept, dried her eyes—and no one ever saw her spirit flag again."

"Father's like that."

"Indeed he is. And such a trait is both admirable and confusing—especially to a less buoyant, more practical woman such as your mother."

John said nothing, but watched him intensely.

"My daughter," Smith went on, "though tender and really quite liberal by nature, does not, as I'm sure you know, feel that all of life is—an entertainment."

"For her own sake, I wish Mother could be a little less solemn."

"Frankly, your Grandmother Smith and I have always encouraged Anne's serious, thoughtful nature. Mrs. McQueen, Senior, on the other hand, evidently believed that her son John, especially, had been put on this earth to join her in the pursuit of good times and laughter. Not so with Aleck. He, although the youngest, was never, I fear, her favorite."

"That's understandable."

"Perhaps, but Aleck has shouldered the load of our latest McQueen trouble without a murmur of complaint. I agree he lacks your father's charm, but he's a steady, well-intentioned gentleman."

"And dull. Excuse me, sir, I shouldn't be tiring you with my asides on Uncle Aleck, who has never been a favorite of mine either. Please go on."

"I saw your father and his lively mother together only a few times, but discerning folk have paid good money to be entertained by performers not half as expert as they! Did you ever hear about the prank mother and son played when Mrs. McQueen was taking the waters at Chelten-ham?"

"While Papa and Uncle Aleck were in school in England? Sounds familiar. Was that the time they planned behind Uncle Aleck's back for Grandmother to masquerade as a French comtesse in the dining hall?"

The old man nodded, smiling. "Between them they got themselves up in rented or borrowed finery, so that your grandmother looked like their idea, at least, of a French noblewoman and your father, perhaps fourteen then, was resplendent in velvet breeches and lace collar—fitting their notion of the elegant, spoiled son of a comtesse. Well, into the dining salon came unsuspecting, literal Aleck, prompt as usual, for his dinner engagement with his mother and brother. Were they on time? Only a full hour late. And when they did arrive, it was an *entrance*. The velvet-clad son of the 'comtesse' entered fanning her with large, sweeping strokes of an enormous feather fan—and on a silver cord, Grandmother McQueen led a full-grown peacock!"

They both laughed; then John Smith went on, "Poor Aleck, his face afire with embarrassment, ran from the room, without his dinner. They didn't go after him, either. For his lack of *their* kind of humor, he went to bed hungry."

"I'm sorry I missed knowing Grandmother McQueen. I think she and I would have understood each other."

"Oh, I haven't one thing against merriment or antics, mind you. I just wanted to make the point that, had your level-headed, responsible grandfather lived, he might have made a difference. Evidently, only his laudable ambition had time to influence your father. I'm sure it's still a heartache to him, too, but your father was away on a wild-goose chase after land he didn't need when your little brother Alexander died. There was no one to fetch a doctor."

For a moment, neither spoke. Then, a little defensively, John said, "You made your point, sir. But I've always been proud of Father—the way he looks, his manner, his style. My pride in him runs far deeper now that he's—in exile." He paused, watching the old man's face. "You may not understand that."

"Would you like to explain it to me, son?"

"Yes, I would," John said. "Few men at his age could make such an auspicious new start in life, in a foreign land, among strangers. I look up to him now more than ever. I value his still gay spirit. Nothing can defeat him—except loneliness. He's managed with an ocean between us to be a wonderful father to me. His letters always encourage me. Keep up my hopes. He took care to book the best possible passage for me on a Panton and Leslie boat. I already knew it, but John Leslie further convinced me during our crossing together that Papa's an important man in St. Augustine. The governor's favorite, in fact."

"He's doing well, very well. Almost too well."

"How can a man do too well?"

When his grandfather didn't answer, John watched the trembling hands leaf through the bundle of letters covered with his father's familiar, wind-blown script.

"Here," John Smith said, selecting a page from the stack. "Let's look at the facts. Right after his arrival in St. Augustine, and that was in April of last year, Don Juan Mc—that name comes hard to me, though it's no doubt used in East Florida—Don Juan McQueen purchased, at public auction and on credit, of course, as most business is transacted down there, a good house on St. George Street with its large lot."

"I know. He lives there. His property adjoins Government House."

"He also bought another somewhat smaller house on an equally large lot located on Treasury Street."

"Papa rents that one."

"And neither purchase could have been made by a man so recently a Georgian without the bond of an influential Spanish subject. In Don Juan McQueen's case—the most influential Spaniard of all, the governor himself, who quite evidently wanted to be his neighbor. And, as of my latest letter from him dated the twenty-third of October, 1792—roughly six weeks ago—he has been granted, for one service or another to his newly adopted monarch, a total of more than fifteen thousand acres of rich timberland!"

John stared. "More than fifteen thousand acres?" He whistled. "Why, the scoundrel!"

"I'd estimate that in less than two years he already owns almost as much land in Spanish East Florida as he owned here."

John spoke with pride. "He's quite a man, isn't he? I know a little about land grants down there. They're normally regulated by the size of the grantee's family and the number of his Negroes. Papa is alone, with only four of our people."

"Your father's powers of persuasion are well known, son. Still, I doubt that he's talked his way into all that land. He's extremely valuable to Spain now. Governor Juan Quesada is in a most uncomfortable predicament. I hear now and then from young Jesse Fish, whose father, the senior Jesse, lived through the horrendous change-over from Spanish to British rule—and back to Spanish. Old Jesse knew the inside workings of St. Augustine under both governments. It was—and still is—chaotic. Many citizens had built good houses there during those twenty years of British occupancy. Others operated flourishing plantations along the magnificent St. Johns River. When the Floridas went suddenly back to Spain, much of the property transfer was left in the hands of old Jesse Fish and his son, as it had been when the Spanish went."

"But almost no Spaniards returned the second time around, and the Messrs. Fish were in a real predicament."

"I see your father has informed you well. I doubt that anyone will ever untangle the confusion over those British deeds and property transfers. I know my old friend, the elder Jesse Fish, suffered greatly when the Spanish returned in 'eighty-three."

"Father thinks that's probably what caused his death a couple of years ago."

"I wouldn't doubt that. There was very little money exchanged. Later on, many of those houses went for a song to the more enterprising among Dr. Turnbull's Minorcans. Poor Turnbull died, too—in Charleston, this year."

"Of a broken heart, I'd think. That New Smyrna colony was his big dream. Papa writes, though, that at least some of the Minorcans who escaped to St. Augustine are prospering now."

"But in proportion to the city's needs, they're few in number. My point is that Governor Quesada is desperate for new settlers. Worthwhile men who will till the land and harvest the timber. This is only one of the reasons Don Juan McQueen is a valuable man to Quesada. His connections back here could mean more solid American settlers."

"I have a feeling Mama doubts that."

The old man sighed heavily. "Your mother is suffering deep humiliation, son, over what your father permitted to happen. She can't be expected to see all things clearly yet. I don't think his American influence has been lessened to any extent. I confess the man continues to surprise me. I see no possible danger that he'll go unappreciated in St. Augustine. Certainly not so long as Spain holds the colony."

John grinned. "I know his friendship from the old days in Charleston with Panton and Leslie—*and* McGillivray—does him no harm." He thought a moment. Maybe his grandfather could throw some light on the chief's influence over Mama. "My mother believes her Creek chieftain literally keeps the peace down there."

"I know she does. Anne's biased in McGillivray's favor. I'm not as certain as she that the young half-breed isn't a rascal, but I hope she's right. He does seem to keep the precarious peace in both Floridas. His power among his mother's Creek people is growing stronger too. He may well be the balance wheel. He keeps the Indians preferring Panton and Leslie goods. For that reason, he is vital to Spain. William Panton and John Leslie now hold a real Spanish trade monopoly. But your father, for all his trouble in Georgia, is—in his way—almost as valuable as Alexander McGillivray." John Smith closed the portfolio. "Don Juan McQueen is an amazing man, although a bundle of contradictions at times to me. Who else do you know who could be elected judge of the Chatham Inferior Court only two months before his debts drove him from the country?"

"I admire that. I have to. I—hope you do, sir."

"I love him. I both admire him and weep for him. Not

only had he just become a judge, in spite of having been posted for two years as a tax delinquent in four or five Georgia counties, he had—not long before his hasty departure—also accepted the high honor of captaincy of the White Bluff Company, Chatham County Regiment of Militia. Not long before that, I'm sure you know, he represented his district as delegate to the Constitutional Convention. Brilliantly, of course. Your father himself inspired these honors, this trust." He paused. "In like manner, he himself got into—the trouble. I hope I'll express this in the right way, but I want you to realize that your mother did not try to slow him down in his wild, almost insane land speculation until she grew so desperate she couldn't help herself. It was then too late."

"I wouldn't have gone to debtor's prison, though, would you, Grandfather?"

The tremorous old chin began to wag, suddenly out of control. For a moment, he seemed unable to form words. Finally, he said, "I—I don't know, son. I honestly don't know what I would have done. It's no secret that the United States wants possession of the Floridas—and Louisiana. If that happens, no matter how successful he is down there, he'll find himself once again at the mercy of the Georgia courts. The courts of a state in the republic he fought to free—whose laws he helped write." Tears glistened in the old man's eyes. "Your mother's grief may shorten my life. But perhaps I'm even more hurt and puzzled that my son-in-law found it possible to leave America. To turn his back on his American citizenship and his religion. The American colonies had no stauncher patriot than young Captain John McQueen. I find myself hoping that his decision to become a Monarchist again—was hard for him. If it wasn't, I never want to find it out."

By the time his grandfather fell silent, John had felt himself beginning to resist so strongly that he got up abruptly and strode to a rear window overlooking the small city garden. . . . The remaining zinnias stood stiff in a dry-leafed row along the crumbling brick wall. Almost without seeing, his eyes followed the bare ropes of an ancient wisteria vine, twisting up a big live oak as grotesquely as his thoughts. He would not accept a hint of criticism of his father, even from this kindly, grieving old man. Only for his mother was he able to hold his tongue; steeling himself, the young against the old, no longer even hoping to be understood.

"I can see I've upset you, John," his grandfather said, "but in fairness to you, I feel the time has come for me to speak out. You've returned to a situation far worse in many ways than the death of one of your parents. Your uncle and I have done our best to help. So has your mother. But unfair as it may be, the brunt of everything is now on your young shoulders."

John turned to face him. "Before you say any more, sir, you should know that right after Christmas I'm leaving for Florida to live and work. Father has a place for me in the firm of Panton and Leslie. I only came here to Savannah first in order to try to persuade Mother to go, too. We all belong in St. Augustine—with him."

The muscles in the old man's face twitched nervously, but the voice, when he managed to speak again, was even. "And does your mother know this?"

"No, sir. I haven't been able to bring myself to tell her yet. I should have last night, but she was—well, I'd never seen her cry before."

"I see. Then, evidently neither has your mother told you about Oatland plantation."

"What about it?"

"When the lawsuits began to come at him thick and fast, your father—in the nick of time—had the presence of mind to put Oatland Island in Aleck's name. Except for the forty-odd acres around The Cottage, that land is all that's left. It is still McQueen property. No liens against it—" He raised his hand. "Now, before you fly into your uncle for any of this, I promise you he doesn't claim a foot of the land. It will be transferred to you on your twenty-first birthday. But you're free to have it cleared and planted right now. Oatland *must* be planted—this spring, or your mother, William, Sallie, and Eliza will be in want this time next year."

John held himself motionless, the real reason for his mother's pleas exploding in his mind: "Promise me you'll do whatever Grandfather suggests. Don't disagree with him, please!" Mama knew all this and hadn't told him. He turned again to stare outside, feeling too trapped to trust himself to speak.

"I understand your wanting to go to Florida," John Smith went on. "If you go, you'll make your father supremely happy. You will also destroy your mother's only hope for any kind of future security. As Don Juan McQueen, your father is doing extremely well down there, but, according to my understanding, Spanish law forbids his sending money here. He may not have any actual money. Don Juan McQueen's wife—and his children—are in real financial distress. I don't envy you the choice, but it must be yours."

His back to his grandfather, John said: "I'm going, sir. I plan to book passage before I leave Savannah today."

"Then your mother will be entirely out of funds by next year. She used the last of her dowry to diminish his indebtedness. It went a very short way. Oatland must be planted this spring. Your father hadn't cleared a field there in a decade—he hated planting. Uncle Aleck will put up the money for seed, but his own affairs allow no time for overseeing the work. I'm not able to do it. Work must begin now if there's to be a crop next year."

Still not looking at him, John pleaded, "You have funds, sir. Can't you lend us some money even for one year? I have no intention of seeing my mother in want! I'll earn a good salary with Panton and Leslie. I have no plans to become a Spanish subject. I'll be working for men who are still British subjects, after all. I'll be free to send money back here. I'd hoped to work in the St. Augustine store in order to be near Papa, but if the pay's better, I'll gladly go into the Pensacola office. I despise the thought of planting, too. Won't you agree to a loan for one year, please?"

For what seemed an eternity, only the hollow, almost labored ticking of the clock filled the room. After a while, John heard the old man groan as he pulled himself slowly to his feet. Then he heard the shuffling steps and the cane across the carpet onto the bare floor. From the corner of his eye, he could see his grandfather steadying himself on the desk, the lamp stand, and the mantel as he came to stand beside him. The trembling hand on John's arm dragged, a heavy weight.

"Son, if I had the money, there would be no problem. I—didn't intend for you to find this out from me, but shortly after your father left, I had to buy back The Cottage at Thunderbolt so your mother and the children would have a roof over their heads."

"Papa—lost The Cottage *too*?"

"I was fortunate to have just enough cash and securities to redeem it—at public outcry. It was painful for your mother, but at least it was worked out so she didn't have the added humiliation of being evicted from her home."

On impulse, John's arms encircled the thin, shrunken shoulders, ashamed that his parents and he were giving this gentle man so much sorrow. Ashamed for having laid still another strain on the frail heart. But how much did they expect *him* to bear? Was it fair to ask him to sustain and comfort both his mother and his grandparents? Was no one but his father interested in the future of John McQueen, Jr.?

"Why won't she go to him? Grandfather, *why* won't Mama go to live with my father? She could settle everything!" He was still supporting the trembling body in his arms, half afraid to let go. "Has she told you why?"

"Danger, John. You've been away, across the water. We hear almost every day of attacks or planned attacks on Spanish East Florida. Not only by Indians McGillivray can't control; by Georgians. Georgians despise the Spanish Monarchy. They fear it."

"And Catholicism!"

"Yes." John Smith tried to stand erect. "Yes. Your mother too. She can't help fearing that foreign, idolatrous influence on the younger children. On you, for that matter." He stepped back. "Your mother's been taught that way. Right or wrong, she can't help fearing—Rome. I fear it myself. I fear—all evil."

"But Papa went into the Roman Catholic Church because his religious convictions drew him there. Can that be *evil*?"

"We don't all agree that he had real convictions, son."

"I was with him when he risked his life to attend secret Masses in Paris! I *saw* my father greatly moved by the lives and the messages of two Franciscan priests—courageous, good men, both of them. The French trouble was just starting, and only those who were real seekers dared go to those services."

"He never told us any of this."

"Why would he? Papa knows how you feel about Catholics! But I know what I'm saying. I saw his convictions grow—take hold of him. I watched it happen." He laughed drily. "There's one book I'm sure he took with him into exile, no matter how lightly he traveled. I saw the look on his face when Father Seraphim gave it to him. A small book of the Holy Scriptures. The Psalms, I think. I'd bet my life it's beside his bed right now! I—know my father wouldn't make a religious choice just to cull the favor of Governor Quesada! I—I resent the implication."

"What you say is interesting, son. I'll give it some thought. But right or wrong, your mother can't help feeling as she does about the Catholic Church. I taught her to fear it."

"Are you telling me that my mother intends *never* to live with my father again?"

"I don't know. I—don't—know."

Carefully, John guided his grandparent back to his chair, eased the thin legs onto a stool, and sat again in the chair opposite. He was both angry and frightened.

"About the money, son. I just can't lend it to you, because I don't have it any longer. The debts were very large."

John struggled for control over his voice. "So, we're at an impasse."

The old man nodded.

"You can't let us have the money, and I can't write to Father to say I'm not coming. He's been counting the days—like a child. So have I. We even hoped Mama might go too." Both arms hung limply over the sides of his chair. "Papa and I must seem like lunatics to all of you."

"You've decided against your mother then?"

"How can I decide anything? I can't even think!"

"The choice is still yours."

"No, it is not!" He was on his feet. "You've left me no

choice! *I want to go to my father.* That's all I want. But you twist what seems a simple desire into—something heartless, selfish!" He clenched and unclenched his hands. In the strained silence, he pictured his father's crestfallen face when John Leslie handed him the letter saying their plans had broken apart. He saw his mother's eyes this morning, dark-circled and swollen, pleading with him to do whatever Grandfather asked. The older man had not moved except to bow his head.

They're going to beat me, John thought. They're going to beat me because I'm young!

"All right," he said at last. "All right, you win—both of you. I'll stay here one year! But I refuse to write Papa the glorious news! Let him read it in your hand that none of this is my doing. Tell him I wanted to come—*intended* to come—just the way he and I planned."

His grandfather's head rolled back against the chair, eyes closed. One blue-veined hand lifted in assurance. "I'll gladly comply with your wishes. I'll write the letter to your father just as soon as I feel able. We all—we all thank you."

"Only one year," John repeated. "Only until the crop is in. I suppose I'll have to grovel to Uncle Aleck for Negroes."

"That's been arranged. I can lend some too."

His laugh was bitter. "I see it was all arranged, even before my boat docked yesterday!"

"Son, will you come again in a few days? When I'm feeling stronger? I regret that I must lie down now, but I so want to help you understand. If you'll come again, I think I can make you see that with you back home, lifting your load, we'll manage. Hopeless as it all seems today, even your father's disgrace need not be permanent. Such a puzzling man . . . but very worthy. I long to help you understand him."

John had picked up his hat. Suddenly he wanted to throw it across the room. Get out, he warned himself. Get out of this house, fast. He said: "Don't worry about Papa and me. It's—my mother I don't understand."

"I think I can—help—there, too." His grandfather's breathing was labored. "One more thing, son, before you go. You must promise me you will never, never let your mother know that you—planned to leave her—for St. Augustine—now."

Young John had never felt so alone, so helpless, so in need of doing something—anything—to prove that he was still himself.

Without another word, he bowed stiffly and strode from the room. In the wide hallway, he jerked the clipped Havana cigar from his pocket, walked deliberately to the parlor fireplace, and lit it from a spile. When he let himself out the front door of his grandparents' house, he left a cloud of smoke behind.

Chapter 4

✱✱✱ For as long as he could remember, Don Juan McQueen had come quickly awake at first light, his wits about him, cheerfully certain that the day ahead would be good. Should it hold disappointment or trouble, he could decide upon a means of handling the setback later—when the time came.

This bright January morning had begun much like other mornings. Wide-eyed at daybreak, he blinked in recognition of where he was—the dark-beamed, whitewashed ceiling of his bedroom reminding him that another day had begun in the tiny, struggling old city of St. Augustine. After weeks of anxious waiting for some word from his son in Savannah, surely today his luck would turn. No doubt about it: this morning, John Leslie would hand him the long-overdue letter, giving the boy's arrival date.

He stretched luxuriously, savoring the prospect. He was dining tonight with Governor Quesada in the family quarters at Government House next door. An event to anticipate always, but weeks had passed since his most recent peacemaking mission to the hotheaded American settlers between the St. Johns and the St. Mary's rivers. Almost certainly, in view of the increasing problems besetting the governor, the services of Don Juan McQueen would be needed again soon. Time had lain a bit heavily on his hands lately. And of course, another mission for his Excellency would mean still another grant of Spanish land. The more urgent the mission, the more land would be recorded in the neat, upright script of the *escribano*, Señor José Zubizarreta, in the name of Don Juan McQueen.

He took off his nightcap and lay for a few more minutes, hands clasped behind his head, thinking of his eldest son as Juan—no longer John. Juan, Jr., had been a sensitive, pleasure-loving but intelligent lad of sixteen when he saw him last in Paris. McQueen smiled. "Genuinely fond of his father, too," he said aloud to the new day. "Rather looked up to me, I thought." The boy had made an excellent impression on Leslie during their recent crossing. The St. Augustine-based partner of the firm of Panton and Leslie, never easily impressed, now seemed more eager than ever to employ him.

A wren shouted emphatic agreement with his high spirits from one of the remaining orange trees in what had until recently been the Perpal groves across St. George Street from McQueen's house. It was indeed gratifying that the Perpal land now belonged to the Church. He greatly admired Don Mariano de la Rocque's simple drawings, which had at last been accepted by Havana, and since the building of a new parish church would cause untold excitement, he eagerly looked forward to the laying of the foundation.

He was still surprised that Señora Ysabel Perpal had actually offered him all the oranges he could use before the trees had been dug out. Delicious oranges they were, too. It amused him that Ysabel Perpal's oranges, unlike most in St. Augustine, were sweet to the taste. He had felt it symbolic that in spite of their almost constant bickering, she evidently liked him. Although he said little about it to his friend Quesada—since it would not be to his advantage to argue with the governor—he found himself disagreeing strongly when Quesada pronounced the attractive, middle-aged, ambitious señora a devil.

To Don Juan McQueen, keeping a semblance of peace with the Minorcan woman was a welcome challenge. Even when they quarreled, she added color to what might otherwise be a lonely afternoon or evening. His influential Spanish friends and, of course, Governor Quesada were generous with frequent invitations to their homes, but it was true that now and then the presence of wives and children lowered his spirits. At painfully lonely moments, he had taken to visiting fiery Señora Perpal in her house across St. George Street.

She was lonely too. Her husband, in the months in which McQueen had been a resident of St. Augustine, was still merely a name on the governor's census: "Señor Antonio Perpal, absent." Where he was, apparently no one but the señora knew. Perhaps even she did not know. Secretly, he pitied her, but since, like him, she never admitted to loneliness, she had no inkling of his sympathy. Best to leave it that way.

He rather enjoyed their heated arguments over who actually owned his St. George Street house. She had been occupying it when, urged by Quesada, McQueen had bidden it in at the public auction soon after his arrival in the city. Undoubtedly Quesada, favoring McQueen as a neighbor, had pulled some official strings; and the señora and her handful of Negroes had been set out on the street.

That her temper still simmered did not surprise him. He understood the woman's determination to grasp with both hands all she could get from life. Why not? Although a leader among the colonists recruited by Dr. Andrew Turnbull from the island of Minorca for his ill-fated New Smyrna colony, she had endured years of hardship as an indentured servant—years that had broken the spirit and fiber of many less tough than she. But even to those sturdy peasant colonists, life at New Smyrna had finally become intolerable. Ysabel Perpal was still a young woman when she had, along with the rest of her fellow Minorcans—a half-starved four hundred or so—trudged the nearly seventy miles up the beach to St. Augustine, seeking refuge with the last British governor, Patrick Tonyn.

McQueen had known the Scottish Dr. Turnbull in Charleston when the broken doctor had fled there in 1777. Turnbull had told him his version of the failure of the colony, placing all the blame on Governor Tonyn. Lately, McQueen had hinted to the señora that he would be interested in her own story as to why Turnbull's colonists had deserted him, but she had answered brusquely that she meant never to speak of the past.

By the time the young governor, Juan Nepomuceno de

Quesada, took over East Florida from Governor Zéspedes in 1790, St. Augustine was mainly populated by the Minorcan refugees. A few, like the señora, had become fairly successful citizens. He wondered often what Spain would have done without them in East Florida. They still made up the bulk of the population and, being mostly Catholic, had blended easily into the life of the town. True, some were not ambitious like Ysabel Perpal. Many preferred to fish or cut palmetto for a living. The señora, on the other hand, owned not only her present house across the street, but farmland on the outskirts of the city and two small trading ships as well. McQueen found all the Minorcans colorful. He admired their capacity for song and funny anecdotes and encouraged their constantly flaring arguments.

Young Juan will be amused by the señora too, he thought, remembering fondly that he and his son were often amused by the same things. "But the boy will respect her—as I do," he said aloud, and reached into a bowl on his bedside table for one of her oranges. He bit into the skin and let the sugary tang fresh his mouth from the night's sleep.

Except for dinner with official friends or an evening of checkers with John Leslie or Father Miguel O'Reilly, there was little of interest to offer his son in the sleepy, provincial city, so he was glad that the entertaining señora was nearby and that work would begin next month on the new church.

His own Baptism had taken place in the rickety second-floor sanctuary of the Spanish Bishop's Palace on the south side of the Plaza, where Mass was still said. But the people had begun before Christmas to bring in gifts of lumber, lime, offers of free labor—even maize, chickens, and eggs to be sold in order to swell the meager building fund. Because money from Madrid and Havana was always so hard to come by, Rocque, the architect, and Don Miguel Ysnardy, the builder, had wisely decided to erect the new church walls of old coquina blocks. Men were bringing them already, from the ruins of the Chapel of Nuestra Señora de la Leche and of the Tolomato Chapel, crumbling into the Camp Santo Cemetery to the rear and down the Street of the Swamp from McQueen's Treasury

Street property. Once the tedious foundation work was done, he and Juan, Jr., could watch together as the modest building began to take shape.

Surely his son would like this St. George Street house, now well repaired and furnished. Ysabel Perpal, through no fault of hers, had allowed it to run down. Spanish law prohibited repairs on a building still owned by the King. He smiled. Nothing about the señora's actions indicated that she had ever believed the spacious house belonged to the King.

"My hard-earned money bought this house," she had shouted on the morning Quesada's eviction became legal. "I defy you to enter into my doorway, Don Juan McQueen! The stupid census of such a yellow-haired stripling governor does not prove anything to me. From old Jesse Fish I purchase this house, and live in it for the rest of my life I mean to do it!"

Later, on that chaotic morning, Governor Quesada had been forced to send soldiers. Watching them carry angry, shrieking Ysabel Perpal bodily from the house had left Don Juan feeling a bit guilty. Not very guilty. More sympathetic. After all, he too had bought the house—though with money he did not have as yet.

To prove his preference, the governor had even supplied cheap labor for the needed repairs. Two handsomely carved chairs from his Excellency's own family dining room stood at each end of Don Juan's secondhand table. Doña Maria Josefa de Quesada had sent both table and bed linens, and every afternoon the governor himself, often with his eleven-year-old son, Roberto, had strolled across Government House Gardens to inspect the latest renovations.

"My poor health would not have survived that woman a week longer," Quesada would declare. "I was growing old at thirty-two from hearing her complaints—from the crowing of her roosters and the squawking of her hens! No less from her own squawking at dawn because her equally loud-mouthed servants were slow to cook her breakfast. It is now like heaven to have a gentleman nearby, whose yard is once more a garden, not a chicken coop. I have done you no favor, Don Juan McQueen. It is you who favor me."

Legally, McQueen now owned the two-storied residence, but the señora undoubtedly would go right on with her threats of litigation.

Yes, he was fond of this house. Young Harry, who at age twelve had cried to be allowed to flee Georgia with him, now watched over McQueen like a mother. In spite of an occasional jealous rift between Harry and Pedro Llufrio, the Minorcan houseboy, life in the house flowed rather smoothly without a mistress. Black Katrina, dumb but not deaf, left behind by British owners, had learned how to cook Spanish and Minorcan dishes which he relished. He pitied her speechless silence, but her ears caught everything—more sometimes than he intended. He could smell the aroma of Katrina's bread, baking in the kitchen out back. A breakfast of fried meat, hot bread, and tea would be waiting.

A patch of sky visible from his east windows was still red with sunrise. The Panton and Leslie brig, with mail aboard, would not attempt to maneuver the difficult St. Augustine bar until full tide and daylight. For a few more minutes, there was time to anticipate the new day.

He had never bothered to analyze why he had so swiftly fallen in love with the very air of St. Augustine, and continued to love it as day after day he strode purposefully—with or without a mission—up and down the sandy lanes, so narrow a man could almost lean from his balcony and strike or shake hands with his neighbor across the street. Don Juan had no balcony, but the more private side loggia, entered off the street through a high latticed gate, marked his as one of the town's better houses. St. Augustine both satisfied and stimulated him, so long as he kept his thoughts deliberately there—away from his family. His dreams for the future would surely flower in East Florida as never before. That the painful separation from his loved ones would be temporary, he had no doubt. No doubt whatever.

During her visit last year, he had watched Eliza grow to love the little town. "I'll be back as soon as I can, Papa," she had whispered as they embraced at the waterfront the morning her boat sailed. "Don't mention this to Mama in a letter, but I'm a St. Augustinian too, now—like you."

Juan, Jr., of course, would be immediately at home in the city's hodgepodge of foreign cultures. Then—he sighed contentedly—with both his eldest children helping, in no time their mother would agree to a visit. Once she saw his good house, sensed his importance to the government and his standing in the city, dear Anne would again be proud of him. Once she met his friends, she too might even be drawn not only to visit, but to embrace St. Augustine as he had done. Fortunately, thanks to Governor Quesada's leniency, she would not have to embrace the Church. McQueen had done so willingly, gladly—but Anne? He laughed a little. Even his imagination would not stretch that far.

When he had eaten the second orange, he swung his legs over the side of the rope bed, flexed the muscles in his well-formed arms and legs, and yawned noisily. He closed the window and looked around for his slippers. The room, heated by a small Spanish brazier, was damp. The former English owner had added only one fireplace to the house—downstairs. When McQueen's family moved in, he would have the chimney broken open where it passed his bedroom and add another fireplace. Anne hated the cold.

He stripped off his nightshirt and began to slap himself briskly—arms, thighs, and especially his broad, deep chest. "Gets a man breathing properly. Stirs the blood," he had explained to Anne on the mornings when his customary pummeling had disturbed her. *Anne....*

Abruptly, he stopped exercising, reaching for his dressing gown, and sat down on the bed. Anne ... always slow to wake up, preferring to enter each new day gradually, almost as though she feared it—even with him beside her. It still puzzled him that his daily exuberance had seemed at times to annoy his wife.... Was she awake yet today? Did any one of the children have a stomach-ache? Or worse yet, a touch of fever?

Once, soon after his arrival, a month had gone by without a letter from home. But not to hear for more than six weeks, as now, strained his patience; weakened his confidence that they were all right. His son's last letter from England had shown him to be as eager as his father for their reunion in St. Augustine. There had been no rumor of bad weather to the north. Why no word from anyone?

True, he had received a carefully packed Christmas box from The Cottage, but today was the twelfth day of the new year, 1793. He had written at once telling them of his pleasure in their gifts, but not one word had come to let him know that they had received his offerings: a length of fine Irish linen for Anne, a Spanish comb for Eliza, a leather Creek doll for Sallie, an English-made penknife for William; and because they had agreed that Juan, Jr., would stay with the family through Christmas, he had sent his eldest son a heavy gold watch chain. With his own hands, he had also delightedly tucked into the box some Perpal oranges, small packets of sweetmeats, and the rich Spanish *turrón* he loved, heavy with almonds.

"I must be growing old," he chided himself, prodding his mind back to cheerfulness with the thought that, if anyone were ill in Savannah, surely a way would be found to let him know. The silence was to be expected, he supposed, since fewer boats sailed during the winter months.

To further lighten his mood as he washed, he deliberately hummed a risqué Minorcan street song. Better to settle for an indoor bath today; it was too chilly outside for the shower that Pedro had carefully rigged behind a screen of palmetto thatch hung under the loggia stairs.

"When you visit me, dear Anne, we'll try the Minorcan boy's bucket of cold water over your head some fine morning! That will brighten you up so fast you'll have an extra hour of alertness in which to revel in the charm and the sun of St. Augustine."

He often talked aloud, addressing members of his family as though they were there, and suspected Katrina of eavesdropping. Oh, well . . . she undoubtedly enjoyed it.

Razor honed and face lathered, he hunched before the small looking glass to shave. Pulling the blade down along the firm, strong line of his chin, a dark thought struck:

Would Anne ever *want* an added hour here in what to her was a frightening, heathen, foreign land? He shook a blob of lather into the basin and tried to imagine Anne sharing even his amused esteem for Señora Perpal. He smiled at his image in the glass. Only to himself had he ever admitted that Anne's sense of humor left a bit to be desired. But he was rather counting on Father Miguel O'Reilly's Irish charm to win her; at least to convince her that, no matter what she had always believed, Catholic priests were not incarnations of Satan, but good men. Good checker players too, in the case of his friend O'Reilly.

For a moment, he concentrated only upon removing the reddish stubble from his upper lip. That done, he studied his reflection. He would be forty-two this year, yet the teeth were white and strong, the throat still firm, the thick head of hair Anne loved still dark red.

He had spoken to no one, not even O'Reilly, of her lack of understanding, but when she came at last, his friends would all help.

Frowning, he thought, It's been months since I've even permitted myself to dream of her coming here to live with me! How is it I'm dreaming today? Could it possibly mean that when I go to collect my mail, there will be a letter with the news that Juan is not coming alone? That the boy has been able to persuade his mother to accompany him? Indeed, that could well be the explanation for the long silence. She could be planning to surprise me! After all, only her father's illness last year kept her from making the voyage with Eliza.

His body ached at the thought of Anne's nearness again. He had no real reason to believe that she was even considering a visit, but he decided to believe it for right now, anyway, and maybe it would come true.

He dried and folded his razor, splashed his face with cold water, and tossed aside the towel. A smooth shave. Anne loved a man's freshly shaven face. "*Your* face, John," he could almost hear her say. "Not just any man's face. Yours." He looked again at the glass and tried to smile, but the reflection showed a furrow between his brows. He shook his head. A gentleman had to shave. Would the daily chore go on reminding him too painfully of Anne? Would he remember every day for the rest of his life how she had loved the fresh, smooth feel of his cheeks and mouth right after he had rinsed and toweled his face of a morning?

He drew on his smallclothes—a pair of white silk stockings, dark gray knee breeches—and turned his mind to young Juan. Unlike himself, his son was dark-complexioned. The lad's beard could well be heavier than his own when he saw him again, he thought, as he shook out a clean white ruffled shirt. *The long-awaited letter would be there today.* By the time he breakfasted and walked to the Panton and Leslie store on the Bay, the packet of mail from the north would be in Leslie's office. The thought of actually holding a letter from home in his hands again started him whistling.

He flipped his tricorn from its peg on the wall, reached for the door latch, then stepped back abruptly. Forcing himself into a state of hopefully recognizable piety, he rehung the hat, walked deliberately to the windowless north end of the bedroom, picked up his rosary, and knelt at the small private altar. It had been humiliating enough night before last to lose at checkers to Father O'Reilly. He certainly did not intend having to admit to his friend that, in his haste to be about the business of what was surely going to be an eventful day, he had forgotten morning prayers.

Anyway, he thought, settling his knees comfortably on a cushion, Father O'Reilly had mentioned that Padre Narciso Font—newly arrived, young, and solemn—might hear confessions this week before Mass. More reason than ever for a clear conscience.

Unlike Father O'Reilly, a secular priest, young Padre Font was a Franciscan sent from Havana to minister to the Minorcans, whose peculiar dialect he spoke. For two years, since saintly Father Camps had died, the poor people had been without a priest whose sermons they could understand. They had complained that Father O'Reilly not only spoke their dialect poorly, but failed to mourn with them in their homes when death struck.

It was splendid, McQueen thought, for the Minorcans to have Padre Font. He had been drawn to the grave, sensitive-faced young priest. Font had reminded him of Father Seraphim, his Franciscan friend in Paris who had been such a comfort there. But the already mounting Georgia debts which had plagued him four years ago were behind him now, and the more cheerful, less exacting God of Miguel O'Reilly suited his new life far better. This idea of confessing to Padre Font, despite his appeal, for some reason made McQueen uneasy. He dismissed the new priest from his thoughts. . . .

In a manner which he hoped would be well received by the Almighty, he had blessed himself with the crucifix, had moved his fingers along the rosary to the first large bead for the Our Father, and was halfway through the fifth Hail Mary when the somehow haunting, thin face of Narciso Font came to mind again. He prayed faster, pushing aside the surprising conviction that if Anne were to respond to any Catholic priest, it might well be Padre Font.

Working his way diligently along the beads into the third decade, he dismissed both Anne and the young priest by exploring the tremendous potential God was holding out to him in the latest land grant from Quesada—six thousand acres of timberland north of Ortega on the St. Johns River—as rich a possession as the whole of Fort George Island, which he had been granted last year.

As he began the third Hail Mary in the fourth decade, his mind skimmed back over the promising developments which had followed his attempt to capture William Augustus Bowles, the devil-possessed young tool of British Lord Dunmore, governor of New Providence. Since Bowles' marriage to a Creek woman, he had fancied himself able to usurp Chief McGillivray's influence over the Creek nations by setting himself up as head of all the Muskogees. The Indian trade, of course, was Bowles' spur to power— trade which, if taken from Spain's friends Panton and Leslie and handed to the British firm of Governor Dunmore, would wreck the fragile economy of the Floridas and Louisiana.

Now, thanks to McQueen's advice, the East Florida government had simply agreed to let the new Louisiana governor, Carondelet, trick Bowles into prison. It had been risky advice. Neither McQueen nor Quesada knew Carondelet, but his self-aggrandizing actions since his appointment as His Majesty's governor had seemed to indicate that the trick might work. The adventurous Bowles had been offered passage on a Spanish ship to New Orleans for a conference, but he had arrived there a prisoner of Spain. The plan had seemed almost too simple, after all the Spanish and Creek efforts to capture him. But it had worked. Bowles was now in a Madrid prison, and McGillivray's power was no longer threatened.

Merely for this advice, Don Juan McQueen had been given the new Ortega grant. And for only two catechetical journeys into the troubled St. Mary's region in the altogether enjoyable company of Father O'Reilly, he had received a half-dozen smaller grants from the grateful Quesada. All very simple, really. While Father O'Reilly baptized several cracker children, McQueen had not only acted as *padrino*, he had used the occasion to persuade at least two bands of hostile settlers from Georgia to abandon their plans to attack St. Augustine. The Americans, many of them from the Carolinas and Virginia, had never seen St. Augustine's Castillo de San Marcos. Don Juan had only to exaggerate its military capability a bit—to describe its thick, impregnable coquina walls, the damp stone dungeons which would surely await them if they tried anything so foolish as to move against the government of His Benevolent Majesty. If the truth were told, Quesada's military forces were pathetically inadequate, but so far, McQueen's ability to shade the truth had been effective and certainly less costly than additional soldiers.

Dutifully repeating the words of the eighth Hail Mary in the fourth decade, he made up his mind to name the new Ortega acreage for Governor Quesada's patron saint, San Juan de Nepomuceno. This large holding, with its ready access to the St. Johns River near Cowford, could at a future date become his principal plantation. His blood tingled with anticipation, and the Glory Be came out in a strong, fervent voice.

Soon, with young Juan, he would take another trip to Fort George Island. Except for Harry, his Negroes who had left Georgia with him—as well as those he had bought—were there, working on the house he was building on the northernmost end of the lovely wooded island; and he wanted to assure himself as to both the welfare of his people and the progress of the house. Such a journey would interest his son immensely. After a time on Fort George, together they could travel to the new Ortega holdings. He meant to make certain that the surveyor, Pedro Marrot, had been accurate in his measurements of San Juan de Nepomuceno, which lay on both sides of McGirt's Creek and included all of Ortego nearly to Fishweir Creek. Surveyors could grow careless or, worse—in view of the language barrier—could misrepresent. He had learned to be cautious in this respect. If there were to be inaccuracies, they might as well occur in Don Juan McQueen's favor.

Of course, nothing short of an order from his Excellency would pry him away from St. Augustine until young Juan came. Eliza had been back in Savannah ten months. He still missed the child. The thought of seeing his son—grown to a young man—brought almost more joy than his heart could contain.

In spite of eagerness for his mail, he could not resist pausing a moment as he rounded the corner of Treasury Street onto Bay. Long ago he had vowed never to become too preoccupied with success or business to miss each day's exhilarating first glimpse of the blue water of Matanzas Bay, full now with high tide, its surface choppy and golden. What was it about the little city that made its sky seem so high? So free? That gave man and gull a sense of liberty beyond their capacity to use?

Even in Havana, where he had begun his expedition in search of Bowles, the sky had by comparison appeared flat. He had often asked himself about the illusion of the high St. Augustine sky. This morning—a good omen, he was sure—the answer came: not the sky itself; the rooftops! The irregular, uneven lines of the St. Augustine rooftops made the difference. He looked about him and felt pleased with his discovery. A few traditional *azoteas*—flat-topped one-storied houses—left from the first Spanish period, were now mixed and scrambled with peaked and gabled roofs where second stories had been added during the more affluent British occupancy. He gazed back up Treasury Street to the west. A solid line of white-washed garden fences and crumbling plastered walls made a cozy tunnel of the narrow street—of every St. Augustine street. The unmistakable signs of poverty seldom bothered him. He reveled instead in the quaint variety and charm of the town as a whole—lifting even its own sky.

Breathing deeply of the sweet air, he permitted his soul to soar a moment with the glistening gulls, then hurried into Panton and Leslie's store.

Past stacks of yard goods, ship's canvas, skins, and furs, he strode through the large front room directly to a closed door at the rear and knocked. "Good morning, Leslie," he called.

The terse, Scottish brogue of his friend was unmistakable. "You'll find it unlocked, McQueen. Come in."

Swinging wide the heavy door, Don Juan boomed, "Indeed, on such a day as this in our fair city, no man could be in danger with a wide-open door, now could he?"

The men shook hands, but Leslie did not get up from his stool behind the high desk. He finished setting down a few figures, then said, "On any day in St. Augustine, a man can be in danger. Behind a locked and bolted door. But I was expecting you. I left it unlatched."

"You always make me welcome."

"I've had occasion to wonder if you'd ever visit me should the mail be brought up at any other location."

"You're joking, of course."

"Aye." Leslie plunged his quill back in its holder and looked at him. "Some day when I feel disposed—which I don't think I do today—I must ask you a question, McQueen."

"Anything! Anything at all."

John Leslie smiled wryly. "You mean your life is an open book?"

"Of course! Now that I live in this beauteous and bountiful Spanish land, it is indeed an open book."

"Hm."

"Your question. I'm curious."

"I suppose this is as good a time as any, if your answer can be brief. Don't you ever begin a day wanting to kick someone in the teeth?"

"Never! I believe good Christian men should bear one another's burdens, while never unburdening themselves."

"Poppycock. I'm of no mind to listen to your newly acquired piety. I knew you *before* your moment of lily-whiteness." Leslie drummed the desk with his fingertips. "While I'm about it, I'll ask this too. Why *did* you go through with all that religious business? I know I've had nearly two years to ask that question. Suddenly, my curiosity's got the best of me. They wanted you here so much, you could have stayed as an American citizen and a Protestant—with no more than an oath of obedience to the Spanish Crown. Like Panton and me." He raised a hand. "Never mind. I wish I hadn't asked. I don't have time for a sermon. If you prefer the solace of the 'true' church to the company of your wife and family, that's no concern of mine."

Don Juan stared at him. The remark hurt, but he needed his old friend too much to risk upsetting the unpredictable Scotsman. John Leslie was, after all, a part of his own youth in South Carolina. McQueen's father had helped young Panton and Leslie when they entered the mercantile business; had negotiated their use of the warehouse at the old town of Frederica on St. Simons Island, Georgia. Except for Leslie, there were few men with whom he could converse freely in English. He certainly didn't care for young Jesse Fish. In spite of Leslie's sometimes caustic tongue, he felt genuine affection for the slightly built, generous though often puzzling man who was now returning his stare. Better to ignore the cutting remark, he decided. Undoubtedly, Leslie didn't mean it.

"I—uh, shouldn't have referred to your family, McQueen," the Scotsman said at last. "Your personal affairs are none of my business. I just see you come here day after day, so sure you'll find a letter with the news that—*someone* is coming to visit you . . ." He sighed. "I shouldn't have said anything at all. No ill feelings?"

"None whatever." Don Juan pulled up a straight chair, straddled it backwards. "But was there a reason behind your ... remark a moment ago? Have you—had word from Charleston or Savannah—word concerning my family that I—I don't know?"

"No." Leslie stacked some papers. "McQueen, do you actually *know* why you chose to give up both your citizenship and your religion? My question isn't idle. Do you *know* why you did it?"

"I do," he answered simply. "I became a Spanish subject in order to free myself forever of the American courts. You're aware, Leslie, that had I stayed in Georgia, I would now be in debtor's prison. I became a Catholic because—you may not believe me, but I could do that with a clear conscience. And I need the favor and confidence of Governor Quesada in order to build my fortune again. I wanted no barriers. You asked. I've told you." After a moment, he added, "Because I trust you."

Leslie cleared his throat. "Well, I have to admire your candor. I shouldn't have insisted. But now and then I think of you sitting over there in your big house all alone. Life has ... boxed you in, hasn't it? Your wife and family too."

"Not at all! I don't see it that way. Already, down here, I'm a prosperous man, fully able to provide a good life for my wife and children." He emphasized his words with open hands. "Leslie, I do expect her to come—one day. I truly believe she will. She only needs more time. Anne and I love each other deeply!"

"You certainly love her, I'd say. At least, there hasn't been a shred of gossip about you here. Small place like this, I'd hear it."

"I've been true to Mrs. McQueen for twenty-one months and two weeks. Without a glimpse of her. I will remain true. I look forward to the moment when I can tell her that."

After a while, Leslie said, "You're one of the smartest gentlemen I've ever known, John McQueen. As Don Juan McQueen, your luck is rising—at the moment. But your wife is a thinking woman. I remember her well. She's perfectly aware that Spain could get into the war over there between England and France. Could be in it now, for all we know. Then what will happen to what we call the economy of the two Floridas? Do you think there's anyone in

Savannah who can read a newspaper who hasn't learned about the bloody skirmishes on the St. Mary's between McGillivray's Creeks and the crackers? Do you think she didn't hear about Bowles and his wild men capturing our Apalache store last year? Word of the Cumberland fighting is bound to reach Savannah."

When Don Juan said nothing, Leslie went on. "I don't know when I've talked this much, but it's you I'm worried about, McQueen. For your sake, I wish she'd come tomorrow, but I hate to see you go on fooling yourself that a lady like that will ever agree to bring her children and move here. She knows how prosperous both East and West Florida were under Britain. She also knows there isn't a peso rolling around our empty little province now. Man, do you really want her to come here to live?"

Don Juan's eyes misted, but he smiled. "Yes, oh, yes! I can give her security now. She's always wanted me to settle down and plant. I already own thousands of acres of rich cotton and indigo land. I've found my place here in St. Augustine, but if she'd only come, I'd sell the St. George Street house and build her a mansion anywhere she likes. I do expect her. You see, my son went to Savannah first with the express purpose of persuading her."

Leslie stood up. "All right. I'll never bring it up again. And if there's anything I can do to help—"

"There is. You can hand me a letter." His smile faded a little. "Did I—hear? Is there mail for me?"

John Leslie reached into a drawer and took out one letter. "Yes."

"Oh, thank you! Thank you!" McQueen took the sealed pages and stood holding them in both hands, beaming.

"Aren't you going to read it?"

"And deprive myself of the anticipation?"

"It's not from your son."

Don Juan examined the handwriting, frowned, then smiled. "My father-in-law, John Smith. But of course, my son had no time to write before he left for St. Augustine. I'm sure his mother had much need of him." He brightened. "In fact, it's undoubtedly from Anne's father because—well, it's quite possible that they're both coming!" He tucked the letter in his pocket. "Do you have any idea, Leslie, how I long just to—to *look* at them after all this time?"

"I'm a son of a gun! You're really not going to open it, are you?"

"I thought I might stroll across the Plaza and savor the contents—put off the joy a bit—now that it's come at last."

Leslie walked around the desk and laid a hand on McQueen's shoulder. "Man, you're beyond me. I'll never figure you out, but I'll be smart and stop trying. My wife says I'm two people at once. You don't stop with two, do you?" They shook hands. "Now, get out of here and read your letter. I've got work to do."

"So you have," McQueen agreed. "And I must see to preparing my house. We'll talk later about when young Juan starts to work for you. But first, his room—everything in my humble abode—has to be as comfortable as I can make it—for my son." His smile broadened. "And maybe for my wife!"

"Don't forget to read the letter before you kill the fatted calf. We don't have any cattle to waste."

Don Juan set his chair back against the wall. "You were born expecting so little, Leslie!"

"But without your chances for disappointment."

Halfway to the door, McQueen jerked the letter from his pocket and broke the seal. "Here—I'll scan it now, just to prove to you that at least my son is on his way!"

He was aware that Leslie waited, but without another word, averting his stricken face, he refolded the letter, turned, and walked from the office, closing the door carefully behind him.

Chapter 5

✦✦✦ B y late afternoon the sky, which this morning had been high and blue-domed, was
stirred to angry gray. Fronds of the tall palms outside in
Government House Gardens rattled like pelting rain, and
thunder—rare in January—shook the old building's loose
windows. No rain was falling yet, and until the first drops
blew down, Governor Juan Quesada refused to close himself in. Breathing was difficult enough for him at best.

Dwarfed by his high-backed chair, the yellow-haired
governor watched lightning streak the sky and only half
listened as his official secretary and military aide, Irish
Captain Carlos Howard, paced the private office giving
one of his lengthy "talks." Quesada tried to remember that
the brilliant older man tended to pay more attention later,
if allowed to finish a "talk" without interruption.

"So, Excellency, to summarize," Howard was saying,
"we are in immediate need in two directions. I must go no
later than tomorrow to the St. Mary's River frontier. If our
reports are true—"

"They *are* true," Quesada interrupted. "The devil
Georgians are at this moment massing on our border!"

"Too many this time, obviously, for even the golden-
tongued McQueen to pacify. Military intimidation alone
will quell this outbreak. As commander of His Majesty's
Hibernian Regiment, only I can handle this matter."

Quesada nodded. "Tell me something which I do not
already know, Captain Howard."

"Of equal importance—perhaps of more importance in

the long run—is your need of a personal emissary to Chief McGillivray. You may not be convinced that he has made a secret treaty with Governor Carondelet, but I am. Since I must go to the St. Mary's, my deep concern is your Excellency's choice of an emissary to the mestizo chief."

"That is also of deep concern to me."

Howard stopped pacing. "But I'm afraid you're considering Don Juan McQueen!"

"*Sí.*"

"I thought so. Such a decision will be a mistake."

The governor spoke excitedly. "Why should I not send Don Juan McQueen, who has so far been successful in persuading the ungrateful *americanos* of their good fortune to be living on tax-free land under the loving protection of His Benevolent Majesty?"

"Dealing with Chief McGillivray is a far different matter. I beg you not to send McQueen!"

"You have not told me *why*."

"Because he talks too much!"

"Nonsense. So do you."

Howard leaned across the governor's desk. "We no longer deal with the thoughtful, reasonable Esteban Miró as governor of Louisiana. This Carondelet, his successor, is a different kettle of fish! McGillivray is so beholden to him for having tricked Bowles into prison at last, who can say what manner of deal they have made? I have no reason to doubt Carondelet's loyalty to Spain, but his sudden, half-cocked decisions—all of them acted upon without consulting your Excellency *or* the governor of West Florida—have to be considered. Even with Bowles no longer dividing the Creeks, we still must pamper McGillivray."

"Remind me of something which I do not already know—too well," Quesada repeated wearily. "I trust Carondelet no more than you trust him. I trust no man whom I do not know."

"My point exactly. His intimacy with McGillivray makes our position here still more uncertain. I don't like the rumors of McGillivray's many trips to see Carondelet in New Orleans. Such secret meetings are an affront to you, Excellency. The chief has never once visited St. Augustine since you took office. You should be insulted."

Quesada rested his head in his hands, but said nothing.

"Now that we know the new French minister, Citizen Genêt, is due to land in America sometime this spring, we had better be more than insulted at McGillivray's independent dealings with New Orleans. We had better be fearful of them!" Howard raised his voice. "Mark my word, East Florida—not Louisiana—will be Genêt's first target for conquest. We will need McGillivray's help."

"I mark also the word of Don Juan McQueen, who agrees!" The governor was almost shouting. "Don Juan has heard from Charleston that the French are recruiting already among the Catholic-hating *americanos*—promising them large sums of money for their cooperation in the overthrow of my government! But Captain Howard, why do we shout? The thunder outside is not that loud." He held up a restraining hand. His voice dropped to a whisper. "Now, do not give me a further talk concerning the importance of our buffers to the west and to the north. I know. The most disastrous blow that could befall us would be the defeat and dispersal by the *americanos*—with or without French help—of all the Indian tribes. As Don Juan McQueen wisely says, 'We need the Creeks to keep the crackers off our backs.' He is right. We must not have the Indians embroiled in some secret warfare to the west at Carondelet's urging. Peace is our goal. Spain's policy has always been to remain on the defensive. Carondelet appears to relish *attack*. For all we know, he may right now be convincing McGillivray that his big war chief, Louis Milfort, should lead the savages into war against the greedy Georgians pushing to the west, until they are whipped back to the lines set by the British. They will never submit to that. And East Florida cannot afford war!"

Carlos Howard was smiling.

"So, smile," Quesada said. "I am now giving my talk to you, *amigo*."

"With which I am in full agreement, Excellency."

"*Gracias*. Your agreement gives me much comfort. We do not need offensive war to the west or to the north. So far, between Don Juan McQueen's powerful persuasion and your military skills, we have managed to ward off an assault on St. Augustine. But unless McGillivray's big war chief keeps active to the east—not to the west—keeps troubling the Georgians with savage raids, they—and Genêt—will have time to mass still more troops against us. This time, their numbers could be too great."

Quesada settled down to a more comfortable position in his chair, his eyes fixed on the flailing palm fronds. "This bluffing we do cannot go on forever. I need a safe buffer between St. Augustine and the Georgia border. An almost empty land is not safe. I am not yet willing to relinquish my dream that through men like Don Juan McQueen we will one day settle the empty land with at least partially agreeable, more enterprising *americanos*. I have much to offer Don Juan. He also has much to offer me."

"It isn't my desire to tire you, Excellency—"

"Then, do not."

"But may I suggest that we take one problem at a time? I can handle the trouble at the St. Mary's frontier, I'm certain, and be back here within eight or nine days. Then, without one day of rest, I will gladly begin the journey to the Coosa River or wherever McGillivray might be found. I trust only myself not to anger him."

"I am gratified by your generous offer, Captain Howard," Quesada said, "and there is no man I trust more than you. *But*"—he slapped the desk—"there is not time! Carondelet precipitated the costly Cumberland war and McGillivray helped. This is against Spanish policy. I cannot wait for you to return from the Georgia frontier. I am the governor and I choose not to wait. My mind is not yet fully made up, but Don Juan *is* under my consideration for this difficult mission to the Creek chieftain." After a moment, he added, "He is under consideration because—I trust him."

The governor watched as Howard walked slowly to the high window overlooking the Plaza. It had begun to rain. A gust of wind spattered drops on the captain's shoulders, darkening his blue jacket. "Do not be noble, Don Carlos. Your uniform is getting wet," Quesada said pleasantly. "You may close the windows."

His secretary latched the leaded casings, dimming the rattle of the rain and the palms. Juan Quesada studied the erect, slender back of the man who had sailed to St. Augustine with old Governor Zéspedes in 1784, to face the almost hopeless task of resettling East Florida for Spain. For nearly a decade, Carlos Howard had served Zéspedes faithfully and well, as he now served Quesada.

I must not be unfair with Howard, he thought. I could not function without this man. More than that, I must not cause him to dislike Don Juan McQueen by showing too much deference to McQueen. "You see, Captain," he said patiently, "Don Juan McQueen and I understand each other."

Howard strode back to the desk. "You force me to tell you something I had long ago decided to forget. You recall, I'm sure, Excellency, that toward the end of Governor Zéspedes' tenure here, he sent me to see to the well-being of Chief Alexander McGillivray during the long weeks in which he treated with President Washington in New York. Back in the year 1790, just before your arrival."

"*Sí.* McGillivray himself is said to have believed that your presence there—reminding him of the long years in which his people have profited by Spanish protection—prevented the *americanos* from cheating him still more."

"One night, after dinner at the home of the American President," Howard went on, "I chanced to be in conversation with Mr. Washington, Mr. Jefferson, Mr. Knox, and Chief McGillivray—the guest of honor—when the name of John McQueen was mentioned."

"So? They were all friends of his. Don Juan has been a friend of Washington long before he became *el presidente*. As a Revolutionary general, he entrusted McQueen with highly secret negotiations—even to the Marquis de Lafayette in Paris. Do you not believe I know of Don Juan's history?"

Howard went ahead determinedly. "Although these gentlemen—McGillivray in particular—seemed to hold McQueen in high regard, even affection, you force me to tell you what one man said of him that night."

Quesada tossed back his hair. "I am tired, *amigo*. What happened two years ago in New York is of no interest to me—except, of course, to go on praying that McGillivray will never honor the treaty made then with the hungry *americanos*."

"I intend to finish the story, Excellency. My conscience, as your advisor, demands it. These were the gentleman's words concerning McQueen: 'The man is perfectly able to persuade paint to peel from a wall. But, if you confide in John McQueen without using extreme caution, beware! He might just as well be asked to hold a live coal in his mouth as to keep your secret.' "

"*¿Eso es todo, mi capitán?*"

"Isn't that enough to cause you to think twice before trusting him with a man as astute as McGillivray?"

"I am thinking many more times than twice! The emissary I send will not go with a secret I do not want divulged. I need someone to discover a secret for me." The governor tapped the tips of his slender fingers together, a half smile on his face. "I think, more than ever, that I relish the thought of the mestizo meeting his match at the game of live coals with Don Juan."

The restless thunder rumbled low in the distance now. The quick, hard storm was passing. Only a drizzle of rain fell beyond the heavier streams still draining from the roof. The room was damp and close. "You will kindly open the windows, Don Carlos?"

Cool air, freshened by the storm, felt good. The governor smiled. "*Gracias.*"

Howard spoke from the open window, his back to Quesada. "What makes you think, Excellency, that McGillivray would tell McQueen anything? According to John Leslie, even the chief's closest friend, William Panton, knows nothing of this secret agreement with Carondelet."

"It is worth a chance. Don Juan McQueen has known the half-breed longer than Don William Panton. They have been friends since McGillivray was educated in Charleston before the American war with Britain."

"But the chief is now a member of the firm of Panton and Leslie. Why, if he hasn't told Panton, would he be likely to tell an old acquaintance? William Panton is like a father to Alexander McGillivray."

Quesada sighed. "We are dealing in mere speculations. I do not have the heart, I do not have the strength for more."

Howard crossed the room, bowed and picked up his plumed hat. "The decision is yours, of course."

"So it is. I promise to make it before you leave for St. Mary's tomorrow."

"In time for me to assist you when McQueen is given his instructions—should you decide to send him?"

"The governor is able to instruct any emissary he sees fit to send."

"If your Excellency pleases, may I at least ask your opinion concerning a few of my own unanswered questions?"

"Provided you keep my headache uppermost in your thoughts."

"Why is McQueen's wife not here with him? How long can a man live without a woman—*if* they are close as McQueen insists? How long can she live away from him—without persuading him to desert us as abruptly as he appears to have turned, for such a flimsy reason, against the United States?" Before Quesada could answer, Howard added with quiet sarcasm, "Except, of course, his burning passion to be transformed overnight from a Protestant American patriot into a Roman Catholic Monarchist!"

"Do you not believe he had to escape the Georgia courts or go to debtor's prison, Don Carlos?"

"I'm not sure. If his letter of recommendation to your Excellency from General Anthony Wayne was in any part true, McQueen's influence in Georgia should have made some more convenient arrangement possible."

"Before you go, Captain—and I hope that will be soon—consider what your questions indicate: that Don Juan McQueen may be holding in his mouth a few live coals of his own. Which he need not spit out for you! The answers you seek concerning his wife are his private affair!"

"I don't agree. McQueen's wife is a Georgian! Spanish East Florida is in more danger of attack from the state of Georgia than from anywhere else. His friends and family are still there. Doña Ana McQueen's influence over him becomes, under these conditions, a direct concern of His Majesty. McGillivray is now in the pay of the United States too, don't forget. Oh, he'll never admit it to us, but you and I know that the chief will remain our friend *only* as long as the Creek nations benefit from Spanish largesse. McQueen's American friends are, many of them, merchants. Nothing would please any American trading firm more than to crush Panton and Leslie's monopoly on our Creek trade! I beg you to believe that Chief McGillivray is *not* trustworthy. If McQueen's American connections appear to offer him more than ours. . . ."

"Enough!"

"You will question McQueen before making a final decision?"

"In my way. But he is my friend. Bear that in mind, *por favor.* I do not make friends with His Majesty's enemies! I respect Don Juan McQueen's privacy and his personal problems. If I decide to send him, I also assume full responsibility for my act."

When Howard said nothing, Quesada got slowly to his feet. "*Adiós*, Don Carlos. The rain has stopped. You will not now get wet crossing the Plaza. I am going to my private chapel to pray for your release from skepticism . . . for my release from the pain in my head . . . and to lay Don Juan's poor live coals at heaven's door. He is not the happy, carefree gentleman he appears to be. Nor is he the scoundrel you suspect."

Chapter 6

✴✴✴ Don Juan McQueen had scarcely noticed the afternoon storm. The evening world outside his house would be quiet now, refreshed by the rain. For once, he could not respond.

From Leslie's office this morning, he had not strolled home, as he usually did, along the Bay and across the Plaza. Instead, the hated letter in his pocket, he had hurried back up Treasury Street, then through an alley, his head down, praying with every step that he would meet no one he knew. Even he could not have managed a cheerful conversation—with Señora Perpal least of all—and so when she appeared coming toward him he had hidden behind a heavy clump of palmetto at the rear of Don Bartolomé de Castro's place until she was out of sight.

He had not eaten since breakfast. Through each of the day's long, agonizing hours, there had been nothing but the unacceptable fact of his disappointment. Always his spirit had managed to open to at least one ray of hope. This time—nothing.

The letter from his father-in-law, written from a sickbed, now lay in a drawer of his desk, but each quavering pen stroke was burned into his mind:

> It becomes my sorrowful duty, John, to inform you that your son will not be coming to St. Augustine for at least a year. If he had not made the responsible choice to plant your Oatland land, Anne and the children would have nothing in their future but want. I

have not told you before, but all my available securi-
ties have gone into the settling of only a small number
of your debts. I long to help you and your family, but
I am too weak, and now, too poor. These feeble lines,
which have been slow in coming due to another attack
with my heart, fulfill a promise I made to your son.
The boy refused to tell you himself, so deep is his dis-
appointment. But he has acted like a man. . . .

That was the line that wounded . . . *he has acted like*
a man.

Don Juan half sensed the coral glow of the sun setting
over the marsh and Campo Santo Cemetery behind his
house. The whitewashed parlor walls were turning softly
pink . . . one of his favorite times for a stroll, especially after a rain. The idea did not even take form in his mind. He
sat, as he had sat through most of this ugly day—legs
sprawled, shoulders slumped—unable to think beyond that
hurtful line. And biting at the edges of his mind: *guilt.*

"Oh, God," he whispered. "Is that what guilt is like?
Have *I* not acted like a man?"

For nearly five years back in Georgia, as his debts
piled up, he had known anxiety, even shame. He had admitted both, of course, but only to himself. A gentleman of
honor goes on, with courage, with strength; never burden-
ing his family or friends with his troubles. "Have your cry,
John," his spirited little mother had admonished. "Admit
your broken heart, but only to yourself. Then go right on
spreading cheer! The wheel of Providence turns . . . the
spoke that is uppermost will be under . . . trouble always
goes away."

The walls of his parlor had never seemed to close him
in before. A large, airy room, spacious enough for a tall
man to stride about in comfort. He pulled a deep breath
into his lungs, feeling he might smother if something
didn't happen soon to make this trouble go away. To help
him out of the—yes, box. He let the breath go sharply.
John Leslie had been right. Life had boxed him in. . . .

How sharp was the old gentleman's knife, finally un-
sheathed! The last thing he had been led to expect from

Anne's father was a wound like that, leaving him helpless against the new, bizarre burden of guilt.

"Anne, I did everything I knew to do before I left Georgia," he spoke aloud to her. "How did I know old M. Duplessis was going to sicken in the climate of Effingham County and toss ten thousand acres back in my face? How was I to know that my influential friends in Chatham, McIntosh, Glynn, and Camden counties were going to renege on their promises and post me as a common tax delinquent? Had I any way of knowing my Sapelo and Blackbeard timber would rot at the docks because the market was not there as I believed?"

He was on his feet, pacing the long room, his voice rising. "All I've ever wanted, Anne, was to regain the pride you once had in me. All I've ever wanted was to make enough money, acquire enough land to give you and the children more than your hearts desired! I didn't mean for things to turn out like this. I didn't. Anne, I'm *angry* at your father . . . do you hear me? Angry—not guilty—angry!"

He dropped into the rawhide chair, his body limp, his eyes closed against the pain. "I need my son," he whispered. "I need my son here with me. . . ."

All day long, he had struggled to hold back thoughts of the bright happy plans he had made for the two of them: long talks in this very room, in which Juan, Jr., could bring him up to date on events abroad—in particular, the latest news of his old friend Lafayette . . . hard, invigorating horseback rides along the waterfront at dawn . . . dinners together at Government House and at Leslie's place. . . . And the sheer joy of pride in his son before his St. Augustine friends. They would have lolled together on street corners, two close companions, reveling in the music and dancing and brawls of the Minorcans. Father and son would have made trips up the St. Johns, where the boy could have seen for himself the extent of the valuable land grants and helped him inspect the progress on the new Fort George house.

A sob—uneven, rough—shook him. He crashed his fist against the chair arm.

It would be at least a year now before he could enjoy

the expressions of respect and pride on his son's face as day by day young Juan discovered exactly how important his father had become to the government of East Florida.

"Have your cry, John. Have your cry . . . then go on spreading cheer. . . ."

His mother had expected too much. He could do neither.

The clock had struck seven when he heard his Minorcan boy, Pedro Llufrio, cough for his attention.

"*Sí*, Pedro? What is it?"

"I have just spoken to the governor," the boy said. "His Excellency had sorrow to hear my message that you could not come to his family tonight."

"Oh. All right. Thank you."

"He send you this letter, but you cannot read in the dark. Do you not know it is growing dark, Don Juan?"

"So it is. Light my desk lamp, then give me his Excellency's note."

He only half saw the boy bring a burning spile from the fireplace, but when the lamp flared, Don Juan managed a smile. Important to hide his feelings from Pedro because of the boy's infernal questions.

Pedro stood scrutinizing him, his arms full of small logs from the hamper. "You are truly ill, Don Juan? Or playing a game with his Excellency?"

"I—I'm just tired. Build up the fire and go to bed."

"I do not become tired," Pedro said over his shoulder as he arranged pine splinters on the dying fire. "Do you know why?"

"No."

Pedro dumped two oak logs on the flaming splinters and turned to him, beaming. "I do not get tired because of you!"

"*Gracias*. But I'm in no mood for riddles tonight."

"Always I feel good—never tired, no matter how much I work. You make me feel good."

"I—do?"

"*Sí*. The answer to my riddle is that I am the one lucky

enough to work for Don Juan McQueen. No other Minorcan boy. Me."

"Good. Good."

Pedro was still beaming proudly. "Not every man holds in his hands, as you do, a letter by the hand of the governor! You are important, so I do not get tired. I feel good all the time. Better than Harry. Black Katrina, she nod yes. She feel good too."

"That's fine. Now, *buenas noches.*"

"Don Juan McQueen—you do not read the message from his Excellency?"

"So, that's it." He broke the seal and scanned Quesada's small, angular script. "All right. I'll read it to you. Nothing important, really."

"*¡Gracias!*"

"'*Mi amigo,* Don Juan,'" he read. "'Do not be ill in your lonely house without care. Send back Pedro to me if you have any need at all.' And it's signed, J. Quesada. Now—will you go to bed?"

The boy shook his head wonderingly. "No Minorcan works for the friend of Governor Quesada but Pedro Llufrio. Only Pedro." He held out both hands. "*Por favor,* Don Juan, let me do something more for you tonight?"

He sighed. "Very well. Run upstairs and bring me the book on my bedside table."

Pedro frowned. "You—read a book to get well? To become rested?"

"Maybe."

He had come to be almost superstitious about the small, leather-bound volume of Psalms, a gift from the first clergyman who had ever stirred in him a recognizable longing to know God as more than a comfortably distant deity. He rubbed the soft leather, tracing the imprint of the tooled gold cross. His thoughts called up the penetrating but loving eyes of Father Seraphim, the brave Franciscan priest who had given him the book, blessing it and McQueen. Over a year ago, his son Juan had written that the gentle young man of God had been killed attempting to take food to an old woman through the embattled streets of Paris.

He crossed himself. Father Seraphim would be much at home in Paradise, he was sure, because the young priest had lived so close to God on earth. As did the Franciscan, Padre Narciso Font. Don Juan still felt a special power in the prayers of a Franciscan.

If he should pay Padre Font a visit tonight . . . and request that it be kept secret, he was convinced that it would be. He dismissed the idea. His heart was heavy enough. The spiritual intensity of the small priest—even the thought of the deep-set, compassionate eyes—would add to his burden.

He needed his son . . . he needed his wife. He also needed to be at ease with himself again. Free of the wound from John Smith's letter . . . the alien guilt gone, so that he could once more know peace within his own thoughts. He needed liberty to hope and believe again that the bright promise of his life in East Florida was real.

At random, he opened the book. To be truthful, he had kept it nearby mainly as a talisman, but perhaps a bit of reading now might rid him of the alien mood . . . might return him to his accustomed buoyancy and faith. Might give back his courage.

He read aloud: " 'Rebuke me not, O Lord, in thy indignation, nor chastise me in thy wrath. For thy arrows are fastened in me. . . .' "

He clapped the covers shut. He waited, then opened the book again, his hands trembling, and scanned the first passage that caught his eye: " 'Give glory to the Lord, for he is good. For his mercy endureth forever. . . . They cried to the Lord in their tribulation and he delivered them out of their distresses . . . he satisfieth the empty soul, and hath filled the hungry soul with good things. . . .' "

For a time, he stared at the page, then laid the volume aside.

Pacing the floor again, he tried to recall one certain Scripture which Father Seraphim had given him. In the midst of a checker game the other night, in fact, he had prodded Miguel O'Reilly concerning it. But since only the word "rest" had stuck in McQueen's mind, his friend had laughingly assured him that the day would come—*if* he attended every divine service—when he would surely hear the passage again and recognize it.

"At the moment," Father O'Reilly had added, grinning his dry, confident grin, "what you need is to be awake. Tonight, at least, you've been resting too much!" Then the sandy-haired priest had jumped a king from corner to corner of the board, beating Don Juan soundly.

He sat down, gripping the arms of the chair until his fingers ached. Would he ever again be lighthearted enough to spend a pleasant evening with Father O'Reilly or Governor Quesada or Leslie?

He held his breath against surging sobs ... then collapsed into such agony that he did not hear the hard, broken sound of his own weeping.

Nor, some minutes later, did he hear the loggia door open and then close.

Having dismissed Pedro, who had trotted beside him all the way through the dark streets to the McQueen house, brown-robed Padre Narciso Font stood alone in the shadowy entrance to the dimly lit parlor, and waited. He had already retired, the old weakness heavy again upon him, but Pedro Llufrio's pleas were irresistible. Unless the boy was lying, Don Juan McQueen, a child of God, needed him. If Font's illness worsened as a result, at least he would have tried, with his last ounce of energy, to please God.

The priest's frail body trembled as he stood still, unnoticed by the man sprawled in a chair. His head swam. The Minorcan boy had made him walk too fast. Pedro loved Don Juan McQueen. A master is good to be so loved by his servant, he thought, studying McQueen's tear-blotched, tormented face.

The room was airless. He raised a hand to slip back his cowl and saw the shadow of his quick movement cross the white ceiling. McQueen had seen it too. There would be no more time to steady himself by even one short prayer for strength.

The priest stepped unsteadily into the circle of flickering light. "Your servant boy, Pedro, fetched me, Don Juan McQueen," he said. "I come in Christ's name, but I do not wish to intrude. I wish to help."

He watched the heavy-shouldered man get slowly, silently to his feet, staring, as though he were looking at a ghost.

"I am not your parish priest. But I—come in God's love."

McQueen bowed stiffly, pressed fingers to his eyes, then said, "I'm sorry my boy disturbed you at this hour, Padre. I'm—quite all right."

Narciso Font moved toward him. "The boy knocked at the door of my room. He was upset that you, whom he respects and loves, should weep. We cannot be sure God did not send Pedro Llufrio."

"I—see. Well, then, by all means, sit down."

Narciso Font perched like a frail bird on the edge of the chair McQueen offered. If it was true that God sent him, he must wait until God gave him the words to speak to this influential and troubled man. His orders were to minister to the Minorcans in St. Augustine. Not to prosperous gentlemen such as Don Juan McQueen. To hear of such a night visit could well annoy Father O'Reilly. But the Minorcan boy had run to *him*, explaining that if there were tears, Father O'Reilly hurried away when possible. God certainly knew of his priest's predicament at this moment. He would wait for God's direction.

McQueen spoke first. "I—I lost control of myself. I shouldn't have."

"We all do that."

"Yes, of course, but to have roused the boy—it was inexcusable."

"Are you unlike the rest of us in the human family, that you need never to weep?"

The young priest sensed that McQueen might break down again at any minute. Waiting seemed almost cruel. But he had no idea, as yet, what to say next.

After an awkward span of time, McQueen got up from his chair and moved heavily to a desk, where he picked up a book—with reverence, Font thought—and placed it in the priest's hands.

"Another Franciscan gave that to me once," the big man said softly. "I—tried to find courage from it tonight. I failed."

Padre Font opened the book to the title page, then closed it. "This is a handsome volume, but in English. I cannot read it, except to recognize that it contains the Psalms. Many men find courage there. Especially during my long, difficult voyage to this strange land—lonely for my family—did I search the Psalms for courage. Still, more often I seek courage from the words of Jesus Christ."

"Oh? Oh, yes, of course."

"What do you mean, by 'Oh, yes, of course'?"

"Why, I—don't know what I mean, Padre. Nothing, I guess. Forgive me."

"I have no reason to forgive you. But—has Christ?"

McQueen returned his gaze, but said nothing.

"We do not always know the real nature of our needs. Is it truly courage you need, Don Juan?" Without taking his eyes from his host's face, Narciso Font went on: "I know of your high standing in the city. I am only the Minorcan priest. I also know of your friendship with Father O'Reilly, who is more familiar with your needs than I. But it is I who sit here in your house now. What I say to you will, so much as it is in my power to know, come from God. Should my words offend you, I will leave. Is that understood?"

McQueen nodded. "Say—anything you care to, Padre."

Narciso Font held up the book. "I do not know which Psalm you read," he said, "but a portion of a Psalm of David comes to my mind." He crossed himself and felt his forehead wet and cold from the weakness. "Listen, Don Juan McQueen." He began to quote, just above a whisper. " 'I am weary of my crying; my throat is dried; mine eyes fail while I wait for my God. . . . Oh, God, thou knowest my foolishness; and my sins are not hid from thee. Let not them that wait on thee, O Lord God of hosts, be ashamed for my sake. . . .' "

The young man squeezed his eyes shut in a desperate effort to stop the dizziness and prayed within himself: *Oh, Blessed Jesus, I cannot think of more to say to this trou-*

blẹd man ... I am ill ... I am helpless without thee, Oh, Lord God!

When Narciso Font opened his eyes, McQueen was on his knees before him, his head bowed. A fresh surge of weakness engulfed the priest, and with effort he raised his hand and let it fall gently in blessing on the thick, dark red hair. Then words he had not planned to say poured from his lips: " 'I am become a stranger unto my brethren, and an alien unto my mother's children. ... Let not the water-flood overflow me, neither let the deep swallow me up. ... Deliver me from all my transgressions. ... Hear my prayer, O Lord, and give ear unto my cry; hold not thy peace at my tears: for I am a stranger with thee. ...' "

He waited. The kneeling man did not move.

"Forgiveness, Don Juan McQueen," he said, his voice barely audible, "is a gift of God to all who seek it. The word *guilt* is almost in my mouth, but I—do not know. I only know guilt to be a heavy burden." He waited again, then whispered, "Our Blessed Savior said, 'Come unto me, all ye that labor and are heavy laden, and I will give you—*rest*.' "

McQueen looked up. "That's it!" he said. "That's the passage I've been trying to recall." He got to his feet. "Say it again, Padre. Repeat those last words!"

Narciso Font felt the room begin to rise, then plunge sickeningly, once, twice—like a tiny bark on a heavy sea. He grabbed for McQueen's strong hands.

"Padre! Are you ill?"

Before he could answer, the young priest fainted.

Chapter 7

✤✤✤ The clock in the downstairs hall at Government House struck two. Doña María Josefa had been sleeping soundly for hours. Beside her in their bed, Quesada had not closed his eyes. The young governor was nervous. Since fever had begun to attack him in St. Augustine, Dr. Travers had urged him to sleep long hours. He still believed Don Juan McQueen to be the best man for the mission to McGillivray, but tonight he was haunted by Captain Howard's suspicions. It angered him that he could resist Howard face to face and then later, too often, found it hard to remain firm.

He clung to the pride in his own ability to make independent decisions, yet he was dedicated to being a good and wise governor. His intention had never been to ignore the advice of his elders. Father O'Reilly agreed with his choice of McQueen, but the name of John Leslie had crossed and recrossed his troubled thoughts as the night wore on. Would Leslie also agree? If so, he felt he could put aside Carlos Howard's disturbing questions. Either way, he would still be free to act upon his own best judgment. Leslie would not relish being awakened at this hour, but on occasion one could take advantage of being governor.

Avoiding any quick movement, since the towering wooden headboard was apt to squeak, he eased himself to a sitting position. Doña María's breathing was slow and regular. So as not to be recognized should he meet soldiers roaming the quiet streets, he decided against his officer's uniform and in favor of a cloak, a pair of gray breeches, and a full-sleeved white shirt. He could not think where clean stockings were kept, so slid bare feet into slippers and made his way noiselessly toward the door. He threw on the cloak, let himself out onto the balcony which led to the outside stairs, and closed the door without a sound.

In the courtyard, he stood watching her window. If he had roused her, she would light a candle and he could hurry back, explaining truthfully that matters of state weighed so on his mind he could not sleep, and that he was going for a stroll in the gardens. Well, almost truthfully. He would, after all, have to walk through his gardens in order to reach McQueen's loggia gate, and cutting through the McQueen property was the shortest way to St. George Street.

The house of Don Juan McQueen was in darkness, except for what appeared to be a dim glow from the bedroom. Tonight had been the first time the *americano* had failed to keep a family dinner engagement at Government House. Quesada had missed him and breathed a prayer that his illness would be brief.

I could not function without the official services of Captain Carlos Howard, he thought, as he started up the narrow street, but Howard is too much older, too rigid in his judgments for personal confidences; for unburdening the heart. Only with Don Juan McQueen can I do that.

He remembered that 1790—the year before the surprising Georgian arrived—had been almost unbearable. Under Howard's tutelage, Quesada had felt more like a schoolboy than the governor. Now he rather commended himself for standing so firmly against the captain yesterday afternoon during the storm. After all, Howard knew as no other man the perplexing, many-faceted political intrigues which had built up in East Florida since the Spanish return.

Carlos Howard, who had made the sea voyage from Havana with Governor Zéspedes, had not only assisted in ridding the colony at last of the stubborn British residents, but had watched and participated in Spain's all-important trade accommodations with young Chief Alexander McGillivray and the British firm of Panton and Leslie— accommodations which had permitted the half-breed chieftain to rise to enormous power among his savages. No one understood McGillivray's mind, his duplicity, his puzzling compassion, as did Howard. Common sense would surely decree that he was the plausible man to send now to McGillivray. Quesada could even see the logic in Howard's questions concerning possible American chicanery involving Don Juan McQueen. Howard's suspicions made sense, although Quesada did not for one minute believe that McQueen meant His Majesty's government any harm.

Juan Quesada had come to recognize the potential of a new kind of diplomacy in his neighbor—a refreshing honesty and good will which he intended to make use of. Not that he considered McQueen to be without guile. A guileless man could not long survive in Spanish Florida, and McQueen was flourishing. But at least, he could be certain that McQueen would never offend the unpredictable Creek chieftain by a fit of pique. Carlos Howard might, merely through confidence in his own unshakable viewpoint.

The governor covered the block to Treasury Street without meeting a soul, then stopped to look back at the McQueen house. From where he stood, the light in the bedroom showed plainly. His neighbor, too, was awake. Perhaps he should retrace his steps and question Don Juan himself. Was he awake at this hour—ill perhaps—because of loneliness? Quesada prayed daily that not only the son but the wife and other children would soon live in the St. George Street house. Did McQueen need the sound of another human voice tonight? His voice? He hesitated. His present dilemma centered in the big man. Tonight was surely not the time to succumb to the warmth of friendship. Tonight he must act the role of governor, not free to go to a friend in need.

He straightened his slender shoulders and hurried toward Leslie's place on the Bay.

In the second-floor living quarters above the Panton and Leslie store, John Leslie set a steaming cup of tea beside the governor's chair.

"If I have a single accomplishment, Excellency," he said, "it is that I still know how to brew a cup of tea. I hope you won't mind if I have a glass of *aguardiente* instead. Tea keeps me awake."

"Perplexity keeps me awake, *amigo*. I am imposing upon you before I must. Before I sleep, I am in need of information concerning the past life of Don Juan McQueen. You knew him when you were both British subjects—American colonists—*si?*"

Leslie nodded.

"Do you trust him?"

The Scotsman half smiled. "I'm not by nature a trusting man."

"This is precisely why I am here tonight."

"McQueen manages most of the time to convince me, at least of his intentions. I confess his perpetual enthusiasm tires me, but he means everyone well. A gentleman. He convinces me that his often foolish heart is—"

"*¿Es bueno?*"

"Good? I suppose that's the word. I'm deeply sorry for him right now."

"Why?"

"Don Juan's heart was set on his son's visit. He expected the boy to live here and work for me. Evidently a letter from his wife's father bore the news that young John is not coming."

Quesada set down his cup. "So that is the reason McQueen did not dine with me tonight! I had not even thought of such a tragedy. Why is it the son will not come?"

Leslie shrugged. "I can't answer that. The look on McQueen's face when he scanned the letter was my only clue. He didn't say a word. Just turned and walked out of my office."

Quesada sighed. "My heart aches for him. But, you see? Don Juan McQueen does not always—talk too much!"

"Anyone who claims he does is not familiar with him—as he really is. He talks a *lot* but, if you've noticed, on subjects he thinks will make his listeners happy. He likes to please. But he keeps things inside. These days, he calls it 'bearing a man's own burdens' or some such pious phrase."

"You made the ocean voyage with the son. Was he ill?"

"Not at all. My guess is that Mrs. McQueen refused to permit the boy to visit here."

Quesada raised his hand. "*Un momento*. I want to hear all you know about Doña Ana McQueen, but first, was Don Juan's father a strong British Loyalist?"

"As I recall, yes. But he died the year before Britain came to power here in Florida. Long before the American Revolution. I haven't thought much about it, but had he lived, the senior McQueen probably would have settled here under Britain. As Panton and I did."

"Then, how did it happen that later on Don Juan became such a burning American revolutionary?"

"I've never been quite sure. Families split often over the issues of that day. Especially in South Carolina and Georgia, where McQueen lived, many people held strong Loyalist sympathies. Even when remaining loyal meant breaking up close-knit families. Offhand, I'd say Don Juan was stirred to the side of American independence by his wife's father, John Smith."

"The man who wrote the bad news to McQueen about his son?"

Leslie nodded.

"Tell me about this Señor John Smith."

"He's a Scotsman like me, but unlike me, he had—still has—strong patriot beliefs. Smith gave up a lucrative plantation near Charleston before the war and moved to Tory Georgia because he thought he could do more for the cause of independence there. Then when young John McQueen met his daughter, he fell so deeply in love with her he'd have done anything—joined any cause—to persuade her to marry him."

"Ah! Now, what of Doña Ana McQueen? You know her?"

"Not as well as I know him, but her American patriotism cost her some heartache. You see, her two sisters, Lady Wright and Mrs. Cowper, were married to Tories. Actually, Basil Cowper had once been a patriot—until Savannah and Charleston fell to the British. He switched back then, assuming the colonists had lost the war." Leslie refilled his glass. "Excuse me, Excellency, but this matter of loyalty is not always the measure of a man or a woman, is it?"

"To me, at this moment, it has to be!"

"Don't forget, Panton and I are still British subjects"—he bowed, smiling—"in spite of our close and enduring and valued accommodation with Spain."

"You and Don William Panton are most unusual," Quesada replied, also smiling. "Expedience can alter many things."

"As in the case of McQueen?"

"*Sí.* Men of good will often have to accommodate each other. I find myself forgetting that you and Panton are still British subjects." He winked. "Except to be glad, of course, when I see your schooners sail into St. Augustine from Nassau and London bearing high-quality British goods with which to keep McGillivray's spoiled savages happy!"

Leslie laughed. "You're free to make all the jokes you like about the peculiarities of our trade agreement, Excellency—as long as you joke only with me. I don't care what anyone thinks. But never joke with Panton. His British conscience, while not strong enough to have prevented our accommodation with Spain, is too strong for levity. I, on the other hand, freely admit that the firm of Panton and Leslie would now be only a bittersweet memory without your government."

"In like manner, Spain's colonies here would now be back in British hands without your firm."

"The truth is, of course, that we'd all be in a dangerous fix without Chief McGillivray! With his rival, Bowles, finally in prison, Alexander McGillivray is the man we have to guard with loving care. He is going to be more and more important to us all as the years go by."

Quesada leaned forward. "The time has come for me to tell you frankly why I have broken into your rest, *amigo.* Captain Howard is needed at once, as you know, to put down more treachery by the Georgians at the St. Mary's River."

Leslie nodded.

"In his position as commander of the Hibernian Regiment, only Howard can go. Yet—I dare not wait longer to send an emissary from this Plaza to discover the truth concerning a rumored secret agreement between McGillivray and Carondelet. Both have ignored me for months." He paused, watching Leslie. "I am considering Don Juan McQueen for this important duty."

John Leslie sat quietly for a moment. "McQueen, eh?"

"You do not seem surprised!"

"I'm—thinking."

"Captain Howard is suspicious because Doña Ana McQueen is not here too. He also suspects that Don Juan might be an agent for an American trading firm with plans to influence Chief McGillivray—and thereby to overthrow Panton and Leslie."

"Well, Excellency, it's surely no secret that the United States would relish the collapse of my firm and your government. The suspicions are typical of Howard's logical mind."

"But do you *agree* with him?" Quesada's hands moved anxiously. "Do you agree with Captain Howard?"

"Not at all," Leslie answered, his voice still calm. "I can't tell you why, but I don't have a single doubt about McQueen's loyalty to you. Howard's suspicions are brilliant, but this time I think he's wrong."

Quesada sank back in his chair, waiting for Leslie to finish.

"For one thing, McQueen almost worships that son of his. He would never have asked me to place the boy in our firm if he had any thought of crushing us."

"Unless, of course, the son is also an agent."

"You don't believe that any more than I do, Excellency."

"One more question, *por favor*? Do you consider McQueen to be free of his American ties?"

"Yes. Except for his wife and family—all of whom he fully expects will join him here one day. I don't; I don't think she can ever bring herself to live in a Spanish Catholic land. But he believes she will; he has to. I honestly think he might—he might do away with himself if he ever had to give up hope that she will come."

"So that is it—she fears a Spanish Catholic land."

"In my opinion, yes."

Quesada got to his feet. "*Gracias, amigo.* I will go, and we will both sleep a little before the sun comes up. I am now clear in my decision. Don Juan will journey in my behalf to McGillivray. Perhaps an important mission such as this will ease the disappointment in his heart because Doña Ana McQueen has not permitted his son to come to him."

Chapter 8

✦✦✦ Narciso Font opened his eyes to a strange room filled with sunlight. Beside the bed, McQueen sat, still dressed in the clothes he wore last night.

For a long moment they exchanged smiles; then the young man asked weakly, "You—carried me to this room, Don Juan?"

"You're light as a bird. You slept. Most of the night—right here in my bed. It's a new day, Padre. Life is hopeful again."

"You—did not sleep?"

"I didn't need to."

McQueen wrung a towel from a basin of cool water and put it on the priest's forehead. Font lay motionless for a while, then tried to sit up.

"I—cannot impose longer. I must go back to my own room."

"After what you did for me last night? Nonsense. You'll stay right there until I say you're strong enough to walk."

"Gracias." He sighed and lay back. "The bed is good."

"After all," McQueen laughed softly, "you're a Franciscan! Franciscans are not proud men. Enjoy the comfort of my bed as long as you need it." The smile widened. "Even our Lord was buried in a borrowed tomb, wasn't He?"

Font tried to smile too. "Your—new spirit today is more—than medicine to me."

"I feel like myself again. All thanks to you, Padre."

The ill young man lifted one pale hand and whispered, "All—thanks—to our Blessed Savior. Not—to me, my son."

McQueen's voice grew tender. "You can't be much older than my son, Juan."

With all his being Narciso Font longed for the strength to converse with this kind man, but the sunlight had suddenly begun to blur to an ugly green-gray . . . his eyes no longer focused, and each breath became an agony.

"Would a cup of tea give you strength, Padre?"

He shook his head. "No," he gasped. "But—*por favor*, Don Juan McQueen—I long—for—one thing."

"Anything! Pedro has gone for Dr. Travers. He'll be here right after he's through at the hospital."

"It—will—be—too late. I need—Father O'Reilly."

"But you slept so well. . . ."

"*Sí*. And—I will—sleep better if I have heard—you say one thing. . . ." The numb, dry lips labored to form the words. "I—*am* young. A young, inexperienced priest. But, I would—find great peace, enough to last—forever, if I could hear you say that—you *are* my son—in Christ."

Font could no longer see the face of the man whose presence so filled the room, but he felt the strong, warm hands close firmly over his . . . and from a great distance, he heard a quiet, steady voice say:

"I *am* your son in Christ, Padre Narciso Font."

Chapter 9

✳✳✳ Young John sat at his grandfather's old desk in the library of the Smith home. He hadn't slept last night for worrying because his father had received no personal word from him. Until today, he had not trusted himself to write.

I still don't, he thought, but neither can I keep Papa wondering a day longer. He picked up a quill and began:

Savannah
14 January, 1793

Dear Papa,

I certainly did not expect to be writing to you on this date from Savannah. If I'd had my way, we'd be together right now at your house. I did not write sooner because I was too angry, too bitter. But I realize it is not fair to you or to Leslie to be kept in the dark as to my side of this unhappy affair. I don't really have a side, to be truthful. I just go about the dreary business of clearing Oatland and avoiding Uncle Aleck—when possible. Since we are using ten of his people and he is advancing money, I will undoubtedly have the dubious pleasure of his company more often than I like.

We are all well except Grandfather Smith, who is so ill he may never leave his bed again. Mother is beside herself with anxiety. I drove her and Eliza here for church services today and Mama has spent every *available minute at Grandfather's bedside. She is there now, as I write. We'll stay the afternoon and I hope to see this long overdue letter on a boat bound tomorrow for St. Augustine before we begin the drive back to Thunderbolt. Mama tells me that she has been accustomed to writing to you once a week, but if she has written since I've been back, she had been most mysterious about posting the letters. So far as I know, only Grandfather wrote, keeping his promise to me.*

He laid down the quill and reread what he had written. Very little of what he felt. He thought of starting over in order to omit anything about his mother, but decided against it. He had never had to be careful with his father.

I wish I could say something about Mama that would encourage you, but I don't understand her any more, if I ever did. I pity her and I am doing all I can to help. But only for this year. By this time in 1794, I will be living in Spanish Florida with you—and that will be none too soon.

My Grandparents' old Hannah horribly scalded her arm this morning and Eliza, under a steady stream of instruction and encouragement from Grandmother, handled the whole tragedy with nobility. Grandmother is as always regal and loquacious and seems determined to stiffen my sister's spine for facing life. I'm still terribly fond of Grandmother and find her as fascinating and irritating as ever. Of course, she is never finished with stiffening her daughter's spine either, but Mama, like her father, lacks the old lady's spirit, though even at thirty-eight, she still excels in beauty. Eliza does not equal her there, but I am genuinely fond of my sister. Young Sallie looks like you and William eats every minute except when sleeping.

I find Thunderbolt and Savannah so provincial that every remembrance of my days in Paris is painful, and at times I wonder if I ever really stood on the Pont Royal looking into the Seine at the lights reflecting from the Tuileries' many windows, or wandered the wide avenues without a care in the world. Was there ever a colorful place on earth like the track and stables at Auteuil? Needless to say, I am not reminded of the thundering French thoroughbreds while jostling along these roads behind old Rita. I can speak to no one but Eliza about these matters of importance and even she cannot join me except in admiration and envy that they have been a part of a life I once knew. Just to be able to write as I have to you has helped. In my next letter, I'll try to explain a little of what is happening at Oatland Island but, fail or succeed as a planter, I am leaving Georgia for Florida at the end of this year. Until then, my heart and desires are there with you. If I could say it better, I would.

Y'r Affectionate son,
John McQueen, Jr.

P. S. Between us, nothing has changed. I have great pride in you, but none in myself for having failed so far to convince my mother that she is wrong to stay here.

Chapter 10

✳✳✳ John Leslie shifted the thick, soft bundle to his left arm and knocked sharply on the door of Miguel O'Reilly's coquina house at the head of the Lane That Leads to the Marina. In a moment, he heard quick footsteps along the inside hall, and the door swung open at the hand of Father O'Reilly himself.

"Come in, Leslie, come in," the lanky, gray-robed priest said pleasantly. "So, a letter from McQueen's son came at last, eh?"

Leslie followed his host through the dim, narrow alcove and into the study. Without a word he took a letter from his pocket and laid it, along with the bundle, on the desk.

"Poor McQueen would have given his right arm for this letter before he left a month ago," O'Reilly said. "But—what's this?" He bounced the burlap-wrapped package on his hands. "Don't tell me Havana finally saw fit to send me a new habit!"

"It's not for you. From Havana, all right, but—the package is for Padre Narciso Font."

"I see. Late, as usual, hm?"

Leslie nodded.

"Ill-starred young man, Font," O'Reilly said, taking the chair behind his desk. "His untimely death will undoubtedly kill his widowed mother back in the old country. He was all she had. His being sent so far from his home village on the island of Minorca nearly broke both their hearts. Oh, I believe the woman does have an older daughter, but—" he touched his cropped, sandy-gray hair. "Not all there, as I understood from Font." O'Reilly set the bundle aside. "I may be killed off too, once more trying to satisfy those Minorcans of his. I've aged ten years in the month since that boy died!"

Leslie grinned knowingly. "McQueen explained your problems with them. You don't make enough noise for the Minorcans, especially when one of them dies. Seems they don't care for the idea that you administer whatever it is you administer—then go your way."

"Exactly. If I don't stay the night—wailing and mourning—I have no pity in my heart. Confound it, Leslie, I just don't indulge in displays like that. Neither would you." He picked up the letter, examined the return address, turned it over once or twice, then laid it on the desk again.

Leslie eyed the desk. "I'd give a farm in Georgia to know what's in that letter, Father."

The priest grinned. "Really? I didn't know you owned one. That rather makes you an enemy of the Plaza, doesn't it?" O'Reilly opened a desk drawer and placed the letter carefully inside. "I promised Don Juan I'd read it—if it arrived," he said thoughtfully. "In some ways, I wish I hadn't promised."

"I'm just nosy enough to want to know why he asked you to read it."

"Well, he thought perhaps, during his absence on the governor's mission to West Florida, his Excellency might be sending him some message or other by horseman, and—"

"You could then make sure his letter came too."

"Yes, but more than that." O'Reilly's angular face grew solemn. "Any journey is a dangerous journey. I'm to read his son's letter, so that should something happen I'll be better able to write to the boy. Long ago he made me vow I'd communicate with the family in the event of his death." The thin mouth tensed. "Leslie, I'd give almost anything not to like that man so much!"

"You do, though. So do I."

The priest nodded. "I wish I were free to let you read it too. I doubt that McQueen would mind, but—"

"Forget it—except, I would like to know when—and if—young John is coming. I can't hold his position open forever."

"Then I'll read it now. Business is business." O'Reilly took out the letter, broke the seal, and read silently, his expression grim. He replaced the pages carefully in his desk.

"Not coming?"

"Yes. Yes, he says he is—but a year from now. Will you be able to wait that long for help in your office?"

"In a year I may not have enough St. Augustine business to need a clerk. Panton can always use him in Pensacola, though."

"It will crush McQueen if the boy has to live in West Florida."

Leslie stood up. "By the way, about that package for Padre Font, I can see to returning it to Havana, if you like."

O'Reilly thought for a moment. "I—uh, hadn't intended to tell anyone this, but I see no harm. Young Font, for the few months he served here, often had to wear his frayed Franciscan habit still damp from washing. He had only one. He's buried in it. Kept expecting a new one, but you know how slow Havana is. Well, when McQueen saw Narciso Font was dying, he sent his black boy, Harry, to fetch me, and I administered last rites. Font had barely enough strength left to whisper that—when and if this new habit got here—he wanted Don Juan to have it."

John Leslie stared. "McQueen?"

"It shocked me too. Unlike us secular priests, Franciscans own nothing, you know. The boy's only property consisted of his rosary, crucifix, the habit he wore—and this one long overdue from Havana. The rosary and crucifix go to his mother." He touched the bundle. "This new Franciscan habit goes to McQueen—as soon as he returns."

Leslie scratched his head. "I'm a son of a gun! How do you suppose young Font happened to be at McQueen's house that night anyway?"

"Who knows? Don Juan had to leave so quickly on his

official journey to McGillivray, I had no chance to find out. I suppose he'll tell me some day."

"I wouldn't bet on that."

O'Reilly smiled. "I won't. But like you, I might be nosy enough to ask."

Chapter 11

✳✳✳ Near the terminus of the trail which he had traveled from the City Gate at St. Augustine to a point some two miles from Pensacola, Don Juan sat propped against a live oak and sharpened his one remaining quill. A bottle of ink stood on the ground beside him and a sheaf of waterlogged writing paper. He whittled idly, smiling to himself at the sprawled figure of his boy, Harry, sound asleep near their tired horses.

The quill suited him at last. He dipped it and began to write.

9 February, 1793
On the Trail, West Florida

My Dearest Wife,

When you will receive this scrawl, I cannot say, but surely from Pensacola, William Panton will have some conveyance heading in your direction. Since I wrote briefly before my hasty departure from St. Augustine on 17 January, I write again to spare you worry. The boy Harry has been attentive beyond his years, but is near exhaustion now. Harry and my Indian guide and I are all much in need of rest. It is sheer joy to be but 2 miles from the comfortable home of W. Panton. My guide has ridden ahead to inform Panton of our arrival. As always, when there is spare time, I write to my beloved Anne. If only I could follow this letter, my

*joy would be complete. Our journey has been rough
and unusually slow. Winter rains have been an almost
daily trouble and twice, hastily put-together cane rafts
have broken apart in mid-stream.*

*Sooner or later, I will be face to face again with our
friend, Chief McGillivray, with whom I am ordered to
confer. If I am successful, I shall surely be rewarded by
his Excellency. There! Did the mention of Quesada
make you frown? Never mind, you are beautiful even
then, Mrs. McQueen.*

*My sorrow that our son could not join me is deep,
but I laid my heartbreak before the God we both worship and (I am smiling) He did not seem to mind that
I held a rosary in my hand and knelt before a crucifix.
(Smile, again and do not think me irreverent, which
God knows I am not.) At this moment, basking in a
beauteous Florida sunset, I am filled with faith and
hope. Even far from you, my spirits cannot stay earth-
bound. But I could not live if I failed to believe this absence only temporary.*

*Ah. I hear a horseman, undoubtedly from Panton in
welcome. I shall add to this before a way is found to
send it. When you receive it at last, my heart will be in
it—so look carefully.*

He was stuffing the writing materials back into his sad-
dlebags when a portly, middle-aged Negro rode up. It was
Panton's servant, Pompey, whom Don Juan hadn't seen
since they were young men back in South Carolina. The
cheerful, sensitive black man had come to British Florida
with Panton and Leslie some eighteen years ago and
would surely know the whereabouts of McGillivray. Panton was known to be close-mouthed at best, but he undoubtedly confided in Pompey to some extent. Pompey
had already become important to Panton years ago; important in the way Harry was going to be to McQueen. A man
tended to tell his most faithful Negro much that he would
not consider telling his closest white friend.

Don Juan welcomed Pompey with a warm handshake,
and after some talk of the old days back in Charleston,

they woke Harry and began the leisurely ride over the two miles to Panton's house.

"I notice you don't call Chief McGillivray anything but Mister Alexander, Pompey," he said casually, as they trotted side by side along the sandy road.

"No, sir. He still just Mister Alexander to me. Come to be Pompey's boy. Mister Panton, he love him too—like his own son."

"I've traveled all this way to find Alexander. Where is he?"

The smile left Pompey's face. "He be at his place on Little River, far as we know. His favorite wife—the children's mother—she die not long ago. Poor boy, he can't stand to go back to Hickory Ground on the Coosa—where they was so proud and happy."

"So, you think he's with his other wife, John Cunnell's daughter?"

"Somebody got to look after him. He be sick so much. Got gout so bad he walk with a cane now. Him not thirty-four year old."

They rode a distance in silence, then McQueen asked: "Do you have any idea how often McGillivray goes to New Orleans, Pompey? Does Panton say much about Governor Carondelet?"

The smiling black man looked at him for a moment, then shook his head. "You better ask Mister Panton your questions, sir. Pompey's job is just to look after him—not to mix in. Now, if you ask me is my master worried about Mister Alexander, yes, sir. He worried about him."

"His health?"

"His health and them other things too. Them government things I don't mix into." Pompey glanced back at Harry and called teasingly, "You got it in your head yet, boy, when to keep your mouth shut?"

Harry grinned. "What do I say to him, Don Juan?"

McQueen laughed. "You see, Pompey, what a smart young fellow I have?"

They urged their horses to a gallop and headed, without any more talk, for Panton's modest house, in sight now on its bluff overlooking Pensacola Bay.

* * *

That night after dinner, when Henrietta Innerarity, Panton's sister, had excused herself, the two men remained at the table. Panton, glad for a visit from a gentleman with whom he could really converse, refilled Don Juan's glass, then replaced the wine decanter in its silver stand.

"You'll excuse me," Panton said, "if I don't join you in a second glass? I'm still a temperate Scotsman."

"May you ever remain such a sober complement to your somewhat less temperate partner," McQueen laughed.

"I don't know, if I had a wife who lives on rum, as Belle Leslie does, I might drink more too. His letters haven't mentioned her in a long time. Is she—as bad as ever?"

"As far as I know, nothing's changed. In a way, Leslie's loneliness is worse than mine."

"Should you pay me the honor of a return visit in the next couple of years," Panton dismissed the subject, "I'll be able to entertain you more comfortably in a new brick house. This one's too cramped. We're in the wilderness here at Pensacola, but for business reasons, I do a lot of entertaining—traders, chieftains and their braves, Indian agents. I need a large house, and I intend to build one right out there on the bluff the other side of my garden. My clerks can use this one then."

"Pompey tells me you keep room available always, though, for Alexander McGillivray."

"Did Quesada send you this way to see Alexander?"

"He did. Do you expect him any time soon?"

Panton, although he had always liked McQueen, meant to proceed cautiously. As important as he knew Don Juan to be at the Plaza, McGillivray's influence over the five so-called civilized tribes was of far greater value, not only to the firm of Panton and Leslie, but to Spain. Alexander's power over the Creeks, Cherokees, Choctaws—even the renegade Seminoles around St. Augustine—had little to do with the fact that, except for the Cherokees, the tribes spoke a related Muskogean language. Actually, Alexander spoke his mother's native tongue poorly. The savages simply trusted him and needed him as a man. So did Panton.

"Do I expect him any time soon?" He shook his head sadly as he repeated McQueen's question. "Pompey's told you Alexander's sick with grief. His life's been hard of late. So many demands on his time—people all the way from colonial governors and influential men like you to widowed old squaws pulling at him for help. He did have one fairly happy period last year at Hickory Ground on the Coosa with Natonka, then she died. Afraid I don't look for him any time soon."

"I marvel then that he's been able to make so many visits to Carondelet in New Orleans."

Panton studied McQueen's broad, strong-featured face, then asked, "How did you know about those visits?"

"The East Florida governor is young in years, but the system of Indian agents under his rule has never been so efficient as now."

"Is that thanks to Quesada or Captain Howard?"

"Perhaps both. By the way, Howard was commissioned a full colonel last month and placed in command of our main frontier post at San Vicente Ferrer on the St. Johns. Colonel Bartolomé Morales took his place in St. Augustine. An enormous loss to us at the Plaza, but too much new treachery is spreading along the Georgia border for a lesser man than Howard."

Panton smiled. "I thought you had the Americans under control up there, Don Juan."

"Well, I feel confident, at least, that Colonel John McIntosh is finally convinced he'll fare better by—uh, use of my more civilized methods at the Plaza. Like the whole McIntosh family, he hates anything Spanish. But he is ambitious to increase his Spanish holdings. I flatter myself that the man's fond of me. Stays at my house when he's in St. Augustine."

Panton went to the sideboard for cigars. "If the prospects weren't so dangerous, I'd have found it amusing when I heard that McIntosh had actually become a Spanish subject. If you've prevailed on him to behave, you've managed a miracle."

"I'm hopeful. He's the only American of influence I've been able to persuade to settle with us. If he has the good sense to drop his grudges, he will become the kind of settler Quesada needs. I can't say as much for some of the others. His Excellency is so eager for citizens, *entre nous*, he's often far too quick to trust their motives."

"Wasn't Richard Lang in the post Howard has just been given?"

"He was, temporarily, after his predecessor was murdered. Lang's a good example of what I feel to be the governor's misplaced trust. Lang and another fellow named John Peter Wagnon. After Lang swore his false allegiance to Spain, he was granted land on the St. Mary's River. But Quesada permitted Wagnon to buy a small house inside the city walls! Wagnon brought in a friend of his named William Plowden, and his Excellency went so far as to grant Plowden permission to build a large home right on the Calle de la Marina." McQueen frowned. "All three men bother me, although I'm not yet sure why."

"Might those men and others like them from Georgia be inclined to join with the French should the rumors of Citizen Genêt's planned attack on us come to pass?"

"Who knows? No trouble yet, so far as we know. Until there is, I mean to trust the governor's judgment."

"You're in Florida to oblige, eh?"

"Indeed, yes. And I'm convinced that Quesada is far stronger, far wiser than his beautiful face and golden hair indicate. I much prefer a governor with the ability to trust to one who has faith in no man." Don Juan took a moment to light his cigar, then said, "Quesada is deeply hurt because McGillivray has never called on him."

"I've heard the governor's sensitive to the point of touchiness at times. But Alexander has not been well these past two years. Not since the long journey to New York to treat with Washington."

Panton felt suddenly defensive. What no one in St. Augustine seemed to understand, he thought, was that Alexander was first of all a Creek. He neither feared Quesada nor, at the moment, needed anything from him. Carondelet, on the other hand, was the governor of the colony through which the Mississippi flowed. It was there that the Americans were most likely to cause trouble, since what they wanted above all were navigation rights on the big river; and Alexander knew this very well. No wonder he spent his energy—little enough at best—with Carondelet.

Still, Panton had to admit that of late he had begun to be somewhat uneasy himself. It would have been natural for Alexander to come to him in his grief. He had not. But—he pulled his thoughts back to the moment—why specifically had Quesada sent McQueen now? Did his Excellency have wind of the rumor which had begun to disturb Panton too? The gossip among the Indians of a secret treaty between Alexander and Carondelet which might throw trade to an American firm?

"Did your governor send you all the way over here, Don Juan, only because he's miffed at Alexander's neglect?"

"We've known each other a long time, Panton. Why beat around the bush? The rumor of a possible secret treaty between your chieftain and Carondelet has reached the Plaza in St. Augustine. You've written nothing to Leslie about it. Quesada is worried. We all are."

"What makes you think Alexander would do a thing like that without consulting me first?"

"I suppose the fact that he holds a general's commission in both the Spanish and American armies—and accepts monies from both governments. In addition to his long absence from East Florida."

"Do you know for certain that he's been to New Orleans lately?"

"No. Do you?"

"I had a short letter from him three weeks ago, but it contained only complaints about his failing health and his heartache. The kind of letter a son writes to a father." He paused. "I might as well confess I've heard the rumor too. There is an American trader in the vicinity trying his best to horn in on our business. Traveling from town to town. But I trust Alexander. He'd scarcely cheat himself, would he? After all, the boy's a member of our firm." Panton smoked in silence for a moment. "Being a bachelor in my late fifties, I find my life centering more and more in Alexander. The lad grows dearer to me every day. Of course, my sister helps me here, but the rest of my family is far away. Odd, I suppose, that this unusual lad should have become so important to me—all aside from his value to the firm."

"And you to him."

"Oh, yes. Our regard is mutual."

Panton had no reason to doubt that McQueen knew exactly how he and young Alexander McGillivray had come upon their initial interest in serving each other insofar as the Indian trade could be brought to benefit—and be benefited—by Panton and Leslie's accommodation with Spain. After all, McQueen's father had helped the partners get started in business just before his death.

William Panton had found young McGillivray, deserted by his father's British sympathizers during the American Revolution. When the Americans had eventually confiscated Lachlan McGillivray's wealth, Alexander, not yet twenty, brilliant and promising, was without friends, family, or property, save a few Negroes. By then he'd come back to Florida to his mother's people—through her blood, a chieftain—to find the Creek nations threatened with destruction by the Georgians, unless he agreed to cede the better part of their lands. Thanks to the good services of Spain, then as now in desperate need of British goods, Panton had the fortune to point out a mode by which Alexander could save his people's lands, Spain's economy, and the firm of Panton and Leslie. Spain gave McGillivray arms in exchange for the Indian trade.

"So far," Panton mused, "our plan of serving each other has succeeded beyond expectations. It's true, we began our dealings on a purely business basis, but the longer we've known each other, the stronger our friendship has become." He sighed. "I esteem him greatly, McQueen. I'm deeply concerned about him now. If, on your way back through Pensacola, you're unable to bring me word of his improved health, I intend to go to him. Should anything happen to him, all that you and I hold dear in the Spanish colonies will eventually be destroyed. Without him, by one means or another, the Americans will devour us. At least, that's my prediction."

◆　　◆　　◆

Sometime that night, Don Juan was roused from sound sleep by noises which he could not quite identify. From the road below, he could hear slow-moving horses and what sounded like a chorus of low, staccato moans. And across the ceiling of his room, a wavering red glow began to spread. He leaped out of bed, his first thought of fire.

At the open window, under a sheen of full moonlight, he could see flaming torches flanking the path of a long, straggling line of men on foot, advancing slowly, to the rhythm of their chant, toward Panton's house. Four horsemen headed the strange procession, and four men on foot carried a litter, their steps slow and careful. On the litter, under a pile of skins, lay a motionless figure.

McQueen splashed his eyes at a basin of icy water, pulled on his breeches and shoes, and grabbed his heavy jacket.

Back at the window for another look at the mysterious predawn visitors, he saw William Panton run down the lane to the road where the caravan had halted.

After a moment, McQueen removed his slippers and trousers, tossed the jacket aside, and crawled quietly back into bed. Panton would want to be alone with his visitor. As surely as though Pompey had announced it, McQueen knew that the man on the litter was McGillivray.

11 February, 1793
Panton's House, Pensacola

My dearest Anne,

Two days have passed since I have had an opportunity to add to this letter which will be sent fav^r Captain Carson sailing with the tide within the hour. I will pray that in my next, there will be encouraging news concerning your beloved McGillivray, who is here, but very ill. True, my own journey has been shortened by his unexpected arrival, but I regret to say that in the company of nearly 200 devoted Creeks, he had to be carried from his Little River plantation. His children's mother is now dead and in his sickness and grief, he has come to Panton to get well in both body and spirit.

When not abed, he sits hour after hour staring into the fire. He appears older and surely is ill beyond the gout which plagues him. He drinks tafia all day and coughs unbearably.

My mission is to confer with him, but thus far, I have not had the chance to speak of anything beyond the affection in which we still hold him. He has, however, sent word that we will talk tonight if he is able. The Chief has lost neither his humor nor compassion. With all his much learning and diplomatic skills, he remains a warm-hearted lad, who wishes to be remembered to you and to know if your favorite flower is still a blue hyacinth. I assured him that it is, at least, to the degree that I am still your favorite husband. (Smile.) Never as copper as his Creek brothers, he is indeed pale now, but, his presence as charged with dignity as ever—a gentleman of great courage, whose mind snaps and crackles like summer lightning. In one way, he is still the Creeks' estechacko (well beloved) but it is easy to understand why his people have elevated him to Hoboi-Hili-Miko—the Good Child King. He is a child and he is good. He is also a crafty—though gentle— ruler.

The tide serves, I am told, dearest wife, so with deep regret I must end this. I send my love to you, to our children and your parents, and ask you to believe me to be your faithful and loving husband always—

John McQueen

McGillivray's shadow, against the whitewashed wall of his room at Panton's house, bulked large in the light from the fire and one lamp which burned on a table beside his bed. To Don Juan, the half-breed, who had managed to breakfast with them only this morning, now appeared shrunken, the deepset, once expressive eyes blank, the high, wide forehead and straight nose more imposing than ever.

McGillivray had motioned Don Juan to a chair, but not one word had passed between them. "Don't try to get him to talk," Panton had warned. "Just sit there beside him until he speaks to you—if he's able. He seemed to want to see you. But don't press him."

Waiting, never easy for Don Juan, was more difficult than ever, as the silent minutes passed, the chief staring at the ceiling as though alone in the room. Don Juan, uncomfortable in a straight wooden chair, crossed and recrossed his legs, hoping the chair's creak would rouse McGillivray. It did not. He cleared his throat. Still no movement from the man propped on the bed, beyond an occasional shifting of the swollen bandaged feet under the fur robe which covered his body.

Don Juan's thoughts went to Anne, who had loved this powerful man when he was a boy, lonely, withdrawn, and openly disdainful of his father's Charleston acquaintances who meant to befriend him. Only Anne had found a way into the arrogant heart of the lad who, although brilliant in his studies, had seemed to despise civilized society. Because of Anne, he, too, had been tentatively admitted to the lad's affections, but now, as more minutes passed in strained silence, Don Juan wondered if the worsening illness had caused even that memory to slip from the once shrewd mind.

As the sunken eyes remained fixed on the ceiling, Don Juan got to his feet and walked the length of the room. At last, back in his chair, he decided that an offer of help could not be interpreted as "pressing." Softly, learning forward, he whispered, "Is there anything at all I can do for you, Alexander?"

McGillivray moved his head on the pillow until he could look straight at McQueen. "Yes," he said. "You can—call me—Alexander again. I have not been called Alexander, except by Panton, since Charleston, when you and Miss Anne—were my friends." He smiled, as though amused at himself. "I—was never a real warrior, you know. I fear no man at the bargaining table, but—even great diplomats are—seldom called by their first names."

"Miss Anne and I are still your friends, Alexander."

McGillivray nodded and went back to staring at the ceiling. McQueen knew it was no secret that the Creek leader hated, even feared actual fighting. He had had no choice but to seek a strong, daring war chief. He had found him in the adventurous Frenchman Louis Milfort. McGillivray's expertise at the bargaining table was no secret either. More than two years ago, when he had treated with the American President, it was McGillivray who had been mainly victorious. Not only had he refused to give up most of the lands falsely claimed by Georgia, over President Washington's disapproval; he had managed not to comply with even the few concessions he had made. The line which would set the boundary forever between the United States and the Spanish colonies was still not run. The Americans still did not have access to the Mississippi, and it appeared that temporarily, at least, both Jefferson and Jay had given it up.

Cunningly, the chief had maneuvered himself and his people into a position where Spain and the United States were now vying with each other for his favor. Each government had made him a general, and given him expensive gifts, had offered trade benefits, and had promised still more gold to the fewer than five thousand armed Indians scattered in small villages throughout the disputed lands. For nearly a decade the Indians, though in no true confederation—held together only by McGillivray's power over them—had been rather contentedly under Spanish protection. But in view of the steadily mounting pressure from the Americans, nothing would please Quesada more than for McQueen to return with some form of guarantee that McGillivray, for whatever reason, was still loyal only to Spain.

"Quesada sent—you to—find me, Don Juan?"

"Yes, Alexander. He did."

"You may tell your—offended young governor that—there is no chicanery with the Americans. Not at Spain's expense, at least." His body jerked. "I hate Americans! Do not speak of them. I grow too angry."

Before Don Juan felt it wise to address him again, McGillivray turned himself so as to look once more straight into the other's eyes. "Tell me, how—do you—live without the beautiful—Miss Anne?"

"I—don't live, Alexander. I exist, because I have to." Then, he surprised himself by blurting, "But you could help me!"

"Yes." The word was hard, deliberate. "Yes, I could."

"Will you? Please?"

"You're not a fool, man! No one—is safe in Florida."

"But I can build her a fine house somewhere near the Spanish fort of San Vicente. I'm a man of property again. There will be still more as the years go by. She's—as wretched as I—with the distance between us."

McGillivray's laugh was bitter. "Of course she is. An empty bed—is a man's worst enemy. I know that now. A woman's too, I don't doubt." He struck the fur robe with his open hand. "My love is gone forever from my bed!"

It had been in Don Juan's mind to persuade Alexander to write to Anne, but for tonight, he would not persist. Because of his own sorrow, the chief *had* understood. There was hope, at least. He stood up. "You must sleep now, Alexander."

"Yes." Then, looking at McQueen again, he smiled almost wickedly. "One thing more: you may go back to your yellow-haired Excellency and tell him that—Chief McGillivray—has made no secret agreement—of any kind—with the governor at New Orleans."

"Why, Alexander, you fox—that's exactly the reason he sent me to find you!"

"Of course. And—I don't blame his Excellency—at all."

Rain came down so heavily the next day that all thought of beginning the journey back to St. Augustine had to be abandoned. Harry helped Pompey. The ill Alexander saw no one but Panton. Don Juan read and prayed.

The burden of his prayers was Alexander's recovery. Not only for the colonies' good; for his own. Despite the gloom in the household, and despite Alexander's own statement that no one was safe in Florida, Don Juan could not stifle a growing certainty that the understanding he had received of his need for Anne did contain an unspoken promise that Alexander would urge her to come.

He had prayed for Narciso Font that night; the young priest had died. But since that death, his prayers had seemed somehow to be more than faithfully spoken words.

Perhaps they would reach God in time to help save McGillivray. . . .

The first piercing howl must have knifed him from a deep sleep, because Don Juan had no memory of going to the window. At the second prolonged scream, he stared down into the writhing, milling mob of half-naked figures, his eyes riveted on the one brave who bore a flaming pine torch, its flame spitting under the still falling rain. A third wail dissolved into a chorus of moans and slow, measured whoops, as the Indian with the torch swung it three times about his head, then doused it in the watering trough at the foot of Panton's lane.

The house, so far as he could discern above the racket outside, was silent. Then he heard someone mounting the stairs. The slow, heavy steps stopped at his door. As he waited for the knock, he knew that Alexander was dead.

He stayed, of course, for the burial in Panton's garden—a mixture of Masonic ritual, for Panton's sake, and primitive Creek rites. Henrietta Innerarity stopped all thoughts of departure early the day after the burial by informing him that he dare not leave for four more days.

"With Alexander gone," she said, "we need Creek loyalty more than ever. By leaving, you would insult the nearly two hundred savages who brought him here. They believe Alexander's spirit is still here, will be for these four days. Your departure on a mere journey would be unpardonable!"

The first night of the four, he slept almost none. Then, as Henrietta had implied, on the second and third nights, some sleep came, in spite of the mourning Creeks' steady wails and cries of anguish. "There will at least be no drumming," Mrs. Innerarity had said. "But you'll learn to sleep over the noise, because they will stop shouting now and then, to chant. . . ."

By the fourth night, McQueen could indeed, discern rhythms—intricate and primitive—relentless, filled with sorrow . . . without hope.

At breakfast, the morning he was to leave, Henrietta Innerarity, her eyes as weary as his own, told him what the chants meant.

" 'Our sun has gone out ... our Child King is dead.' *Hopúewv Meeko Pvsvtke. . . . Hiyáyvke Yomúckē-omē*. Of course, that's a free translation, but no matter. It means— their hope is gone."

He and Harry and the Indian guide rode slowly through the throng of Creeks also packing to leave. Saying good-by to Panton had been difficult, almost frightening; his grief ran deep, and so did his fear for the future of Spain's colonies without McGillivray.

Don Juan had not written to Anne. That could be put off until he was back in St. Augustine, rested from the ordeal. There were no pack trains and no ships anyway. Treachery among the Indians—expected to develop with McGillivray dead—had already begun.

PART 2

✦✦✦✦✦✦✦✦✦✦✦✦✦✦✦

Chapter 12

Papa, my dear Sir,

I have given orders for the day's work and now write quite alone in the kitchen of the somewhat repaired Oatland house. I deem this letter of the utmost urgency and importance and so will go directly to my new information concerning Citizen Genêt and the French, as soon as I say that my mother is stricken with genuine grief over the death of McGillivray. Something tells me that part of her sorrow is due to an unspoken hope that one day the Chief might have managed the safety of those who live—and those who visit—in East Florida. Still, even McGillivray could not have eased her fear of living among Spanish Catholics.

Otherwise, except for Grandfather Smith, we are all well.

In need of a new wagon, purchased (I choke on the thought) with funds borrowed from Uncle Aleck, and longing to hear French spoken again, I made the journey to Charleston for the tumultuous reception April 8 for Citizen Genêt, the new French minister plenipotentiary to the U. S. It is no secret that Genêt's plans (the French consul, Mangourit, has been recruiting for months) are directed toward the Floridas and Louisi-

*ana. Which fact is cause for rejoicing to everyone I
met in Charleston. Such men as General Elijah Clark
of Georgia and your friend Governor Wm. Moultrie of
S. Carolina, are most favorable to French conquest.
Frontiersmen feel that their future success and bliss
would be secured if only Genêt's bold plans can oblit-
erate Quesada, etc. Governor Moultrie invited me to
dine and sends sincere regards to you, now his "beloved enemy." He appears to believe also that he can
best serve the U. S. by using the forces and funds of
France to accomplish what the Federal Government
has refused to do—i. e., put down the Creeks and de-
molish Spain in the New World.*

*It is well that Quesada has protested to the Ameri-
can Congress concerning the number of armed French
vessels now using "neutral" U. S. ports.*

*Ridiculous rumors are rife in Savannah that
Quesada pays a fee for every American scalp brought
to the Plaza by an Indian. Hatred for both Creeks and
Spaniards is red-hot here, although President Washington vainly tries for control, to his own detriment with
Georgians, who behave and talk as though their state
is a separate nation.*

*Madrid must already know of the French threat to
the Plaza, etc., since Spain and France are now at war.
I will keep you informed to the best of my ability,
penned up as I am at Oatland much of the time. I am
like a man without a country these days, but in a measure, Spain's ally, for love of my father. One fact seems
clear—St. Augustine itself is Genêt's first target. He
could be hampered, of course, by a shortage of war
ships due to the conflict with Spain abroad.*

*Since Mama reads both Savannah and Charleston
papers, from mounting fear she will, I am sure, try the
harder to keep me here. I suppose, not without reason,
but I have lived with danger and I am coming before
the year ends.*

*Your obedient and loving son, who proudly signs
himself,*

Don Juan McQueen, Jr.

P. S. I forgot to say that poor Lafayette is still in prison and of course, the American papers agitate for his release. Also that Gov. Moultrie is now in danger of debtor's prison, which fact may be one of his reasons for throwing in his lot with Genêt.

Don Juan read the letter in Leslie's office, then without a word handed it to his friend. Pride in his son's courage and good sense was almost overshadowed by the news— all bad. His heart ached for Lafayette, rotting in an Austrian prison simply because no one was thinking clearly in France any more.

Looking out over Matanzas Bay as Leslie read, McQueen was gripped by a fresh surge of panic because McGillivray was dead. True, a little of his own shame had been lifted at the news that the governor of South Carolina might also be threatened with debtor's prison. He had always been fond of Moultrie, but at least, Anne might see that her husband was not the only gentleman caught in the trap. Still, his son's letter troubled him.

There was no doubt in his mind that the French would make use of an American trading firm as a spearhead for the East Florida invasion—a firm able to divide the now leaderless Creeks with expensive gifts. Leslie's latest word from Panton was that so far, McGillivray's war chief, Louis Milfort, had managed to prevent all but a few Choctaws from shifting their trade away from Panton and Leslie to the still nameless American firm at work in Louisiana. Anyone knew that Carondelet would protect the peace of Louisiana first, and should Milfort not contain the Indians there, Carondelet's only choice would be compromise with the enemy firm.

Don Juan's father had taught him well as a boy that all governments rose or collapsed on the issue of trade. He knew little about Citizen Genêt, but thought him stupid to have landed first in Charleston—an insolent snub of President Washington. From all he had been able to find out, most citizens active in the new French Republic were headstrong, cocksure of the rightness of their cause. After all, the French temper, out of control, had turned against even Lafayette.

A long-awaited appointment as captain of the Rural Militia and another large tract of good Spanish land on Pellicer's Creek now belonged to Don Juan, because he had been able to report to Quesada that there had been no secret trade treaty between McGillivray and Carondelet. Of course, the assurance held little relief now that the chief was gone. The disturbing news in young Juan's letter might indeed make the governor ill.

"I'm a son of a gun," Leslie muttered, rattling the pages as he refolded them. "That's all I can say—I'm a son of a gun!"

McQueen pulled up a chair. "We do have an ally, though, in young Juan."

"It would seem so. The only other bright spot I see is Citizen Genêt's banner-waving in South Carolina before he'd even presented his credentials to Washington. The President won't care for that, will he?"

"He will not. And Juan is right in his estimate of Georgia. Washington is dead set against any state acting as an independent nation." McQueen's face brightened. "Washington may indeed be our hope. I'm positive the President will never permit Georgia or South Carolina to cooperate with this hairbrained French plan."

"None of that, man! I've got far too much on my mind for a sudden dose of your infernal optimism. I couldn't care less about the hotheads in Georgia, but we do have to grant that they've gained almost nothing from being a part of the United States. I could wish they'd all drop off the edge of the earth, but"—Leslie counted on his fingers— "one, Washington has steadily refused to help them get back their runaway slaves in our colony. Two, he's also failed to satisfy their bloody desires to punish the Indians, and three, not one Federal troop has been dispatched to overthrow Quesada. I don't think Georgians give a fig what President Washington says or does!"

"One thing at a time, Leslie! We were talking about Genêt. The President despises sly, impetuous tricks. When he learns of Citizen Genêt's Charleston festival, he'll be highly incensed. Particularly when he finds out M. Mangourit has already begun to recruit."

Leslie raised an eyebrow. "You mean the President

may begin observing his so-called neutrality declaration?" He flipped his hand at young John's letter. "Those French ships could not be putting in at American ports without Washington's knowledge!"

"I'm aware of that, but don't forget that Jefferson is the main agitator for the overthrow of Florida. The Secretary of State and the President are not hitting it off too well these days. I may never see Washington again, but I'll always believe him to be a man of wisdom and reason. I agree he has compromised his neutrality stand, but Genêt's flurry in South Carolina *could* stiffen his spine."

Leslie tossed back the letter. "McQueen? Do you ever get the feeling that we're—trapped here in East Florida?"

Don Juan looked straight at him. "Yes. But I drop the feeling every time it comes—like a hot potato."

"I'm not amused. Panton and Leslie could be bankrupt within a few years. You know Genêt and Mangourit are going to need mountains of supplies from some American warehouse *near* East Florida. Which American merchant is going to be handed the plum? Who's going to have the soul-tingling joy of putting Panton and me out of business?"

McQueen got to his feet. "If I knew that, then I would indeed be as important to his Excellency as I—dream of being, wouldn't I?"

"With your new commission as captain of the Rural Militia, you may get more opportunity than you really want to prove your importance—if your son's news is true. I'll stop talking now. I not only depress myself, I know you're panting to show the letter to his Excellency. Mind a word of advice before you go?"

"Not at all."

"Colonel Howard's still here, doing some other translations for the governor. He won't go back to San Vicente for a day or so. I suggest you permit him to translate the entire letter for Quesada—including the references to your wife. It just might be beneficial—if anything is ever going to benefit any of us again—for Howard to see for himself that Mrs. McQueen is still in Georgia for no reason other than her downright *fear* of all things Spanish and Catholic.

It's more important than ever now for Howard to trust you as captain of *his* Rural Militia."

About midafternoon, Carlos Howard knocked at the governor's door, then walked in, a sheaf of papers in his hand. "Your translation of the letter from Don Juan McQueen's son, Excellency," he said, with more than usual deference.

"Oh, *gracias*. It is good you are here so that I will have an accurate translation." Quesada flipped through the pages. "But you may go now, Colonel. I want to read alone, in order to make my own judgment."

"Of course, but if your Excellency will grant me a moment—"

"I am in no mood for one of your talks. Later."

"I have no talk to make. But I do have an apology. I intended only to be doing my duty when I suspected Don Juan McQueen's presence here some months ago. I now see I made an enormous mistake to doubt the gentleman's motives."

Quesada looked up in surprise. A slow smile spread across his face. "*You*—made a mistake?"

"*Si*. I beg you to overlook my questions concerning McQueen's wife and his son Juan. Since translating this letter, I, too, hope the young man will come soon. We need him. So far as any American settler can be trusted, I believe McQueen and his son to be trustworthy."

The governor threw back his head and laughed. "Do you know what I am thinking, Don Carlos?"

"I can imagine."

"I am thinking two thoughts. One, that I have never liked you so much before, and the second, that"—he sighed—"it has been a long, long time since I have heard any good news—about anything. Your approval of Don Juan McQueen is good news. *Gracias*. Had you not already been promoted to the rank of colonel, I would this day request it!"

Howard bowed, then started to leave.

"*Un momento, amigo*. Don Juan McQueen waits in the courtyard. Perhaps, now that you are his friend too, you will not mind asking him to watch for me on my balcony. When I have finished with my study of this letter, I will want to converse with him."

"Before we speak of what your son has written, Don Juan, may I express my deep regret that Doña Ana is—afraid of life here with us?"

Don Juan smiled. "You're kind, Excellency, but I haven't given up. As soon as some of our present difficulties die down, she'll come—at least for a visit." The smile faded. "You see, Doña Ana loves me. It's just that she can't—"

"Solve the mystery of you?"

"*¡Sí!* And I don't feel at all puzzling!"

"To me, you are clear—like water. But now tell me, did Colonel Howard have a few words of his own to say to you down in the courtyard?"

Don Juan's smile returned. "The colonel was most gracious. He now appears to like me as much as I've always liked him."

"*Muy bien.*" Quesada pulled the translation toward him. "So, to your son's excellent letter. Until he visits here, I am at a loss as to how to show my gratitude. For the present, I have three questions to ask of his father."

"At your service, Excellency."

"First, since you have held residence in both South Carolina and Georgia, do you expect Mangourit to be able to raise a large force?"

Don Juan thought a moment. "If I know some of our settlers between the St. Johns and the St. Mary's, I feel certain that Mangourit is already informed of the inadequacy of our defense forces. St. Augustine citizens Plowden and Wagnon know our military shortcomings."

Quesada nodded. "I am aware you do not agree that they should have been permitted to settle here."

"But I count on their underestimation of Colonel Howard. I count also on the French bravado, which I know rather well. This is a wild guess, but I'd say, for an attack on the Castillo, they'll attempt to mass no more than five hundred men."

"Then I will demand one thousand additional troops from Havana." The governor shrugged. "Not that I will receive them soon—if at all—but with your son's letter enclosed as proof of our need, I will make my demand. Now, to my second question. When, in your opinion, will they attack?"

"Your Excellency flatters me! I have no idea."

"But you are a military man of experience from the American Revolution, Don Juan. Even Colonel Howard cannot know the habits of *americanos* as you know them. Consider the stubborn natures of the Georgians, the distance between settlements, the time required not only to recruit but to bring together their forces, and give me your opinion. One year from now? Spring of the year 1794? I am not well. I refuse to be disturbed in advance of real danger."

"Excellency, much will depend upon how Citizen Genêt is received by President Washington at Philadelphia. Mangourit's funds will have to come from France by way of Genêt. In fact, I have grave doubts that the President will permit a French invasion to take place."

Quesada struck his desk. "How can he stop it? Can he find a new magic to wield over South Carolina and Georgia? South Carolina Governor Moultrie is in sympathy with Genêt! A least, your son believes so. From my unhappy dealings with Georgia Governor Telfair, I make that judgment for myself. He has no respect for the President!" The slender, nervous fingers toyed with a quill. "It is well to hope, Don Juan, but I need your estimate as to when they might be prepared to attack us."

"I fail to see how an outright attack could take place before next spring, but my son does promise to keep us informed."

"The third question then, is: Which American trading house will be employed in their plans?"

"Leslie asked the same question. I've been turning the matter over in my mind since. I could hazard another guess, but better still, I'll write at once to young Juan. He'll certainly try to find out for us."

"You will, of course, use extreme care in your choice of conveyance of such a letter."

"Captain Andrew Atkinson has offered to deliver a packet of letters for me in person to my family. Next week. The man's loyalty to you has never been questioned." McQueen grinned. "He's also most interested in taking over the management of Fort George Island for me, now that my house there is finished."

"Bien." Quesada stood, his hand extended. "Do not weary of hearing, Don Juan, that you are a gift from heaven to me." The men shook hands warmly. "Shall we place a little wager on which American trading house it may be?"

"Gladly. My guess is the Georgia firm of Hammond and Fowler. The Hammond brothers, Sam and Abner, would risk their lives any day in order to break Panton and Leslie's Spanish monopoly."

"So, the terms of our wager will be that if you are proven right, you may select two hundred acres of land anywhere in the colony."

"If I'm wrong?"

"Then—nothing. Nothing, that is, but my continuing gratitude and friendship." Quesada walked with him to the door. "You will convey for me my gratitude to your son, Juan. And for the hot summer months ahead, we will try to find a breeze, enjoy many family dinners together—and wait. A long time, I hope. Without a miracle, it will take a long time for Havana to send troops. Spain's war with France causes the impoverished little colony of East Florida to matter less than ever before."

"Ah, but we have cause for hope, there, Excellency! The same war is also on the French government's mind. Genêt's little scheme may fall by the wayside too, you know."

Chapter 13

✦✦✦ Early in the summer, the papers on a valuable timber lease at Mills Ferry safely in his pocket, Don Juan sat across a narrow table from U.S. Indian Agent James Seagrove in a crowded tavern at St. Mary's town. He owed the good fortune of the new lease to Seagrove and so had invited his old acquaintance to share a meal, although along the Florida-Georgia border, they were, in a sense, adversaries.

"I'm glad the lease worked out for you, McQueen," Seagrove said, as they waited for their food. "Old lady Drayson's a smart woman and her son's a hard worker. With your shipping and market connections, there's no end to the money you can make there. Maybe enough to cause you to favor a move back across the St. Mary's to Georgia yourself some day."

"Never!" McQueen laughed. "But that isn't news to you, *amigo*. No one on either side of the river questions the loyalty of Don Juan McQueen to His Catholic Majesty."

He broke off until the tavern owner set dishes before them and left. "As I was saying, Seagrove, I like living in St. Augustine and relish ownership of all my tax-free Spanish properties. I not only intend to remain for the rest of my days, my persuasive powers will go right on being directed at calming every Georgian of my acquaintance settled on Spanish land." He cut into a slice of ham, piled it with hominy grits. "I miss my wife and family, but God has blessed me with many warm friends in St. Augustine. For a lonely man, I enjoy a good life."

"You don't really mean to sit there and tell me you like those Spanish people, do you?"

"Indeed I do!" He lifted his mug of ale. "To you, *amigo*, for the favor of that splendid new tract of Georgia timberland! I assure you no one on your side of the St. Mary's will ever know."

Seagrove shook his head in amazement. "You must lie awake nights dreaming of timber! I had no idea you'd be crazy enough to come all the way up here to lay your hands on that Drayson lease—flat in the middle of the Creek wilds."

"Why not? It's an enormously good *sitio*. I mean to make a small fortune from squared timber cut from those magnificent trees! *Gracias, mi amigo. ¡Muchas gracias!*"

"Lay off the Spanish phrases for tonight, eh? At this juncture, they turn my stomach. Since McGillivray died, I've got enough trouble with those savages without any reminders of the foreign culprits who keep them stirred up against me."

"Nonsense! His Majesty's officials do no such thing."

A commotion at the front of the long room caused both men to turn around. A roughly dressed, middle-aged drunk with frizzled, pale hair had climbed onto a table and was railing at a group of patrons also in varying stages of drunkenness.

McQueen turned back to Seagrove, amused. "Except for his spicy language, that fellow sounds like a cracker preacher."

"That's another thing, McQueen. How do you stomach all that Catholic business?"

The din in the tavern lessened suddenly and the speech maker raised his voice so that McQueen found it unnecessary to respond.

"I'm here to tell ya true," the man bellowed, "that if ya got any idea atall which side yer bread's buttered on, you'll sign this paper I got chere an' throw in yer lot with the French at the behest of that great Revolutionary general and 'Merican patriot, 'Lijah Clark! Sign up tonight an' help Clark rid our land of them evil-doin', hell-bent Spaniards once an' fer all!"

"I had no idea Elijah Clark had men recruiting here, Seagrove," Don Juan whispered. "Did you?"

"Old Clark's got blood in his eye."

"Against my friends in St. Augustine? Or does he still hate Indians as much as ever?"

"Both. Makes my job unbearable at times. I try to keep some kind of sanity among the Indians. First thing I know, old General Clark's massacred a stack of them."

McQueen recalled a dinner engagement at Elijah Clark's house back in the late eighties, when the revered American general had spoken harshly against Alexander McGillivray. Clark was an Indian trader, and, by some means which McQueen had now forgotten, McGillivray, just rising to power in the Spanish colonies with Panton and Leslie, had cut Clark out of Mobile. From that time, General Clark had been more an Indian fighter than an Indian trader. His eyes that night at dinner in Savannah had shot sparks as he recounted the way his heart pounded with something akin to ecstasy each time he led his Georgia Militia in a good, bloody skirmish against the hated savages.

The fiery recruiter was shouting again: "We won't take no more pushin' roun' by no Injuns nor no dirty, rotten Cath'lics, will we? They ain't a red-blooded 'Merican who's gonna take hit no more. An' thanks to our staunch friends over there in Paris, France, we got our big chanct. When we was fightin' the lousy British monarchy for our liberty, who hepped us? France! Who hepped Pres'dunt Washin'ton more than any other man? A Frenchman named Lafayette! Who sent us money? France! That's who!"

"But so did Spain," a man shouted back, egging him on.

"Not much, not very doggone much!" The orator lowered his voice confidentially. "Them Spaniards was jist atryin' ter git back here an' git a toehold agin in Floridy. What little they done, they done fer theirselves. The way a black Spaniard'll do ever' time! Now, look—some of ya lives over acrosst the St. Mary's on land they give ya—but kin ya sell yer goods at a fair price to folks on this side of the river? No! Kin ya send money to yer' 'Merican relations? No! Black Spaniards is robbers an' crooks an' murderers! Our friends—mebbe the onliest friends we got, is them liberty-lovin' Frenchmen! Why, they's a United States merchant ship anchored right out there in the St. Mary's harbor this minute—an' hit's got a genuine French privateer's commission! We're gonna see action, so I'm here to say ya better git on the 'Lijah Clark-Paris, France side tonight!"

Don Juan leaned across the table. "Is that true, Seagrove? Is the ship out there? Or is he bluffing?"

"McQueen, you know I'm not free to answer that. I'm not too much in favor of all this French recruiting—I'm not sure I trust either Genêt or Mangourit—but that's none of my business. If you were still an American citizen, I'd give you my opinion on the ship's commission. Much as I like you, I can't. You know that."

"Then, I'll ask Elijah Clark's cracker preacher."

"You'd better not! He's not only drunk, he's low-down. I know his folks. They'll use those long fingernails to claw your eyes out and never give you a backward look!"

But Don Juan was already strolling casually toward the front of the tavern, where a handful of men were lining up to sign the recruiting paper. The Clark man looked up, bleary-eyed and flushed, when McQueen tapped him on the shoulder.

"I heard what you said about a French privateer anchored out there in the harbor."

"I meantcha ter hear!"

"I declare," Don Juan went on, "I believe the French mean business—about helping America."

"Course they do!" The man stepped back to get a better look at Don Juan. "You from roun' here? You got Spanish land crosst the river?"

"Yes, I own land over there."

The cracker grinned. "Then I'm jist the man y'er alookin' fer. You ain't too old to fight—" He banged Don Juan on the chest. "You got the build an' the—uh, fancy manners General Clark likes to have aroun' to perk us all up a little. Effen you got Spanish land, you know them Augustine dogs!"

"Could I buy you a drink of rum?"

"Shore! Ain't never said no yit."

"I'd like to hear more about that French privateer."

"Don'tcha do it, Ike," another man shouted. "Don'tcha drink his rum—that feller's a black Spaniard!"

The drunk recruiter swayed backward in surprise. "He shore don' look like no furriner."

From the corner of his eye, McQueen saw Seagrove leave the tavern by the side door.

"That there's Don Juan McQueen! He done turned all the way traitor fer free Spanish land!"

Don Juan glimpsed the hairy fist in time to dodge. The wild swing sent the drunken man sprawling. There was a roar of laughter.

McQueen looked carefully around the circle of gaping faces—long enough to be sure that the suspicious settlers, Lang, Wagnon, and Plowden, were not among them—then walked back to his table, picked up his tricorn and left.

Chapter 14

✳✳✳ Pedro Llufrio, excited that guests were coming to dinner, scurried about the parlor helping Don Juan rearrange the furniture.

"Here, Pedro, let me help you with that heavy chair. I want it near the window. Señora Perpal will sit there—and tonight, whatever might make Señora Perpal happy, we will do."

Together, they lifted the chair to a position Don Juan approved. "So," he said, looking quite satisfied. "Now, the smaller one over here, for the señora's visiting daughter, Juana. Can you manage that alone?"

Pedro stood beaming. "For you to entertain Minorcans in this house—even the prosperous señora—I could move the Castillo!" He flexed his biceps. "Alone—with no help."

His employer surveyed the room. "Now, let me see— I'll sit there on the love seat, facing them. Flowers! Do we have some nice sprays of orange blossoms within reach, Pedro?"

"Oh, *sí*. If not, I climb the trees."

The boy started for the door, then hurried back when McQueen called. "Sit down, son. We have time before the ladies arrive. I want to talk to you."

"Sit—in your parlor?"

"Why not?"

Pedro eased himself onto the smaller chair, his brown eyes shining. That this important gentleman would ask him to sit down in his house was almost more than he could believe. Still, he had long known that he did not work for an ordinary man. Don Juan McQueen was a man of surprises.

"Tell me, Pedro, where is Señora Perpal's husband, Antonio? Do you know him?"

"No, sir. I live fifteen years, but I never see him. It is a mystery where he is all the time."

"You're fifteen, eh?"

"*Sí*. But stronger than fifteen."

"Sixteen or seventeen years ago, your people took that long walk up the coast to St. Augustine when the New Smyrna colony collapsed. Has your mother ever mentioned whether or not Señor Antonio Perpal came too?"

"No. *Mi padre* also does not know of him. Nobody mentions him." Pedro jumped up suddenly and peered slyly at Don Juan. "You—you are thinking—thoughts of a man—about Señora Perpal?"

The moment he'd uttered the words, Pedro could have bitten off his tongue. Never had he seen such a look of surprise and pain, then—sadness. The boy felt sick. The last thing in his life he would want to do was to cause pain for Don Juan McQueen!

His heart eased a little when the familiar, reassuring smile returned.

"Get out of here, boy!" McQueen whacked him affectionately on the bottom. "Go get those orange blossoms and stop letting your imagination run away with you."

At the door, in spite of his relief, Pedro had to say, "*Perdóneme*, Don Juan. Pedro is—sorry."

After Harry had served dinner—Katrina's excellent shrimp pilau—Don Juan escorted Ysabel Perpal to the parlor and seated her in the large chair by the window.

"*Gracias,*" she said, smiling up at him. "I am more sorry than before at the absence of my daughter. Juana has been cheated of this elaborate courtesy."

"You flatter me, señora."

She held her hand to the open window. "I remember well the good breeze here."

He was determined, if possible, to keep his guest off

the subject of the St. George Street house. Tonight, he had far more urgent matters on his mind. "May I serve you a glass of wine, señora?"

"No, no, no. I have long ago learned to keep a clear head in conversation with such a clever man as yourself. *Gracias, no.* But you can tell me why I am being treated as *Doña* Ysabel Perpal—not merely a señora." The dark eyes flashed. "You are up to something, Don Juan."

"Up to something? Yes. A pleasant evening in the company of two lovely ladies. That was my plan. Now— one."

"Wh-ht!"

He had grown accustomed to that "Wh-ht"; one of the most eloquently demeaning sounds he had ever heard, or experienced, was her "Wh-ht!"

He settled into the smaller chair. "That two civilized people can share a quiet evening like this, so near the barbarism on our border, is a wonder," he began. "You really can't imagine how primitive and rough and sordid life is on the St. Mary's these days."

She leaned toward him. "I have experienced more barbarism and violence and rough life than you will ever learn about, Don Juan! Do not try to make pleasant talk of such things with anyone who struggled at New Smyrna." She flipped her hand. "I will not listen. Nor will I tell you the truth about New Smyrna and the loathsome Turnbull. So do not pry again."

McQueen laughed. "You're not only a handsome woman, señora, you're a most stimulating human being."

Her face softened a little. "It is well to be considered—a human being. So, we do not talk of what is past. *Ahora es ahora.*"

"Perhaps that's one of the reasons I find you good company," he said. "I, too, believe now is now, and that we should grasp the moment."

"*Bueno.* The moment is here—I am here. What do you want of me?"

"Would you believe me if I said I trust you?"

"No."

"Then, would you believe me if I said I need your— advice?"

She shrugged.

"I'm not sure Governor Quesada takes the imminent danger between the St. Mary's and the St. Johns quite seriously enough, but—"

"Your yellow-haired patron at Government House takes as important only himself!"

Don Juan had no intention of allowing her to get started on Quesada, whom she had naturally despised since the day his soldiers carried her, shouting threats and curses, from this very house. "You have a right, of course," he said, "to your own opinion. But his Excellency has nothing to do with what I want to discuss with you."

"Then I will listen."

"There has been for months, as you know, what amounts to an undeclared war between the Creeks and the Georgians along our border."

"With Chief McGillivray in his grave, there will be nothing else forever. He was smart." She touched her forehead. "More than both governors together—even old Zéspedes. I listened when McGillivray came often long ago to make talks at the plaza. He, too, did not bother with your yellow-haired Quesada."

"I'm sure you've also heard rumors of a French-American invasion."

"Such will never take place."

"Why do you say that?"

"Chief McGillivray once said—and I always remember—that 'the protection of a great monarch is to be preferred to that of a distracted republic.' Both of Spain's enemies are 'distracted republics.' The French and the *americanos*."

Her excellent mind continued to amaze him. He could see no way in which the formerly indentured servant girl from the Island of Minorca could have obtained an education. Yet he never failed to feel that he was matching wits with a cultivated woman.

"I sincerely hope you're right, señora," he went on, "but my son's reports of French recruiting to the north are being backed up by the latest intelligence from Colonel Howard at San Vicente. Our American settlers between the two rivers would help us fight the Creeks, God forbid, but few have given the slightest obedience to their vows of allegiance to His Majesty. Still fewer pay any mind at all to our trade laws—and the real danger lies there."

She laughed. "You do not believe I know that? You do not believe my two merchant schooners sail always in danger from piracy?"

"There—you've led me right into what I'd hoped to discuss with you. You see, it's been my good fortune to have signed a lease on some rich Georgia timberland about thirty miles up-stream from the port of St. Mary's—the Drayson tract. A place called Mills Ferry. As you well know, here in the province we all need some ready cash."

Her laugh was short but agreeable.

"My new lease," he went on, "is dense with giant pines which, when marketed as squared timber—on either the British or Havana market—will produce a good profit. That is, if I can find a—uh, reasonable means of transportation."

"From your days as a Georgian, you have friends among the St. Mary's settlers—like me, owners of ships."

"True, but under the present troubled conditions up there, señora, I—am in no position to trust them!"

She began to smile. "What you say also is that you are unwilling to do business with them at—their prices."

McQueen laughed. "We *are* having a most enjoyable evening! I declare I find you excellent company."

"A woman likes to be flattered," she said evenly, "but if we transact business together—even at a lower price than you could get from the *americano* pigs—do not think for one minute that I will end my lawsuit for this house!"

He nodded solemnly. *"Le comprendo, señora."*

Until now, her threats of litigation had only amused him. Tonight, there was pathos. At least, it struck him that way. Where *was* this lonely woman's husband? Was she, perhaps, a widow? Her innate dignity had somewhat quelled his curiosity, but he did need to be sure that she was in sole charge of her shipping business.

"Señora?" He kept his voice low. "A moment ago, you said, 'If you and I transact business together—even at a lower price—' Does that mean you're interested in my shipping contract?"

"*Sí*. I am interested."

"And—the decision is yours to make?"

"Who owns my schooners?"

"Well, you are Señora Perpal. I've seen the governor's census. But your husband is listed as living in St. Augustine too, though . . . absent."

"*Sí*. Absent."

She lifted both hands ever so slightly, dismissing the subject of her husband. He thought the long, tapering fingers surprisingly graceful for a woman who had worked so hard. He had noticed her shoulders before, not heavy, but strong . . . shoulders to rest a man's head and heart. Why would Antonio Perpal remain absent from the bed of such a woman as Ysabel? He forced himself to look away.

"Well, then," he said a bit nervously, "as soon as I learn just how much squared timber I can expect, we'll complete our business arrangements. Do you agree?"

The arresting eyes—almost black now—moved from his face to his hands, then back to his face. He could feel her awareness of him. Their glances caught and held . . . then, Ysabel Perpal got up.

McQueen stood too. "Must you—go, señora?"

"*Sí*. At once."

"We'll—have more business to discuss, you know," he said lamely. "You'll come again?" He bowed over her hand.

"*Gracias*, Don Juan McQueen, for the hospitality— and the bow." A soft smile crossed her face. "Do you know you are the first gentleman ever to—bow to me?"

Chapter 15

✤✤✤ The hard ride home from Savannah on the afternoon of November 7 was one young John knew he could never forget. Colonel, a gift from Grandfather, handled like a charm, but the exhilaration of a first ride on a new mount was missing. His grandfather had died yesterday, in his arms.

Pounding around the big curve below The Cottage, he felt ill with dread. The duty of telling his mother would fall to him, as did most hard things these days. At least Mary Esther Huger was there to help. The courageous little widow was not only Anne McQueen's best friend, she was John's too.

"Eliza's with her now," Mrs. Huger said, as she joined John on the porch that night.

"I'm glad you're with me."

"*Merci, monsieur.* So am I. Anyway, that girl Eliza has the gift of comfort. Unlike you and me, she doesn't have to talk a lot, either."

"Has my mother cried yet?"

"Yes. And she's upset with herself for running away when you told her your grandfather was dead."

"I think I was relieved."

"Oh?"

"Mother expects us all to be so strong, I'm ashamed to say I almost get angry when she—isn't."

He felt the quick, reassuring pressure of Mrs. Huger's

hand in the darkness. "You just don't know your mother very well yet. There's really no reason why you should. You grew up with me."

Neither spoke for a time; then John said, "Just before he died, Grandfather told me he was proud of me."

"So am I."

"He also warned me that I must—keep my head. Not only for my parents' sake, for mine. He didn't mention my leaving for Florida—one way or the other."

"Your grandfather was a wise man."

"I *am* going. Before the end of this year. Not for a long visit, as Mother thinks. To stay."

"As you should."

"Do you mean that?"

"Indeed, yes. It's time you prepared for the work *you* want to do. You've been a good manager at Oatland Island, but if you hate planting, you shouldn't plant. Your cotton sold at prices high enough to hire an overseer next year. It's your right to go to your father—and his right to have you with him. Anne has the other children."

"But won't she think me—callous to leave so soon after Grandfather's death?"

"Dear boy, there are times when we must be willing to be misunderstood." When he didn't answer, she asked, "Would it help if I stayed on here—well into the new year?"

"You know it would! But—you've said your place in South Carolina is falling down from neglect."

"So it is. But with Frank still abroad, heaven knows where, I have no one depending on me. Besides, there isn't a house on the face of the earth as important to me as your mother and you."

"I wish I did know Mama. I will say that being with her this year has helped me understand my father better."

"That's interesting."

"There's something about Mother that makes a man long to look after her—even to spoil her; and yet, there's that—high wall." He laughed a little. "A man keeps trying to climb over it. You get the idea that if you could—then, somehow, you'd know your own worth. Does that make sense?"

"To me it does."

"If only she knew this about herself! Do you think she *can* understand if I tell her I'm going to live in St. Augustine?"

"I wish you'd told her before Grandfather Smith died."

"But, *chère amie*, you know she'd never have written that letter to Papa if she'd thought I was going for more than a long visit! I was so happy when she offered, I—couldn't tell her. The fact that she was the one who wrote will probably make him happier than the news that I'm coming."

"You do know your father."

"He and I have spent our lives trying to win her approval. Why, the man's hopes will soar at the sight of her handwriting—approving even a visit." A mirthless laugh caught in his throat. "I know I should have told her the truth, but—but once again, I'm trapped between them. And I'm tired of it. I'm already sick to death of trying to stretch myself to protect them both." He paused. "Sometimes, the thought that it might go on for years is more than I can face!"

"Things will look much brighter once you're with your father."

On a heavy sigh, he said, "How true. But, believe me, this will be the longest month of my life—waiting for the day when I can get on that boat."

Never quite content to dwell only on the things of the Spirit, Father Miguel O'Reilly had a lot on his mind, as he busied himself in the upstairs living quarters of his house on Hospital Street at the head of the Lane That Leads to the Marina. Don Juan McQueen was due soon for an evening of checkers. A fire blazed merrily in its brazier, and on the sideboard stood wine and a bowl of McQueen's favorite sweet. The checkerboard was laid out: twelve red men stacked at one end, twelve black at the other. But tonight the priest did not look forward with his usual zest to the company of the American. Funny, he thought, as he blew dust off the portions of the table not covered by the checkerboard, in spite of McQueen's loyalty to Spain, most persons still thought of him as an American. The more so tonight, annoyingly, because O'Reilly's own mind was troubled.

This afternoon, he had dropped by Government House to give spiritual comfort to Quesada. The beleaguered young governor had assured him that he *had* received help, but Miguel O'Reilly himself hadn't stopped worrying since. Far easier to tell someone else to trust God than to do it. Without doubt, the French and the Georgians were planning to attack East Florida. McQueen's infernal hope that his son's report last spring might be false both irritated and infuriated O'Reilly. Of course, he was well aware that Don Juan's hope sprang from the wishes of his own heart for peace. The man was unbearably lonely for his family. The wife, quite obviously, would not come down even for a visit, if the rumors about the French were true. Still, the son was expected before the year ended. Little more than a month remained.

The letter of warning from young McQueen, along with later word from Howard on the frontier that Elijah Clark and his Georgians were massing along the Oconee River, had been enclosed by Quesada and sent off to Havana, with a strong plea for additional troops and arms. The reply from Captain General Las Casas, which Quesada had shown him this afternoon, was the source of the priest's troubled thoughts: Las Casas quite agreed that East Florida was in grave danger, but because of the war with France, Havana was unable to send a single soldier!

The military situation in the colony was wretched, even for peacetime. Morale was unspeakable among the soldiers in St. Augustine and on the frontier. Active men could not subsist on lard soup and a cup of beans twice a day. Colonel Carlos Howard had been forced to appoint three new officers last week on account of desertions, and not one was qualified. No member of the Third Cuban Battalion had been paid in over a year. How could Quesada—even were he in good health—be expected to sail a tight ship of state under such conditions?

In the event of trouble, more than concern for the safety of his parishioners bothered O'Reilly. Not belonging to any order, he was free to buy and own property. His holdings in the city were growing. A successful French-American attack could ruin him.

Well, McQueen was due. Unless something had gone wrong, the big man could be striding down Hospital Street now. At least, there would be no need to pretend with McQueen. He was one parishioner with whom O'Reilly could speak freely. No man in St. Augustine was closer to the governor than McQueen. Most likely he knew already that no help was coming from Havana.

On the balcony, his gray robe whipping in the cold wind, he raised his hand in greeting. Don Juan, already this side of the Military Hospital, saluted jauntily and broke into a run.

"I've just come from the governor's office," McQueen said, warming his hands over the fire. "He sent for me to be present when he questioned three militiamen just arrived from the frontier."

"Our own, I suppose."

"Afraid so. Howard arrested them for known dealings with Richard Lang and two disloyal citizens of St. Augustine."

"Wagnon and Plowden?"

"The men refused to divulge any names beyond Lang's. For which refusal, his Excellency added one month to the time they will spend here at the Castillo."

"You look disgustingly cheerful, Don Juan, to have brought such gloomy news," the priest scowled. "In view of the fact that the men undoubtedly entering the moldy walls of the fortress at this moment will have ample opportunity to corrupt those already settled in, I find your good spirits rather obnoxious."

McQueen sat down across the game table. "Come now, Father, there is always a bright side to everything. I bring good news as well. Two pieces of good news, to be exact."

"Which do you choose? Red men or black men?"

"I'll take the red tonight. Black suits *your* mood. But let me tell you what's going to happen in a little over a month from now."

"Your son is really coming?"

"Indeed he is. Early in December." McQueen took a letter from his pocket. "Look! But as important as the arrival of my son is the fact that his mother wrote the letter to tell me. There it is. In her own handwriting. And she seems happy that the boy's coming!"

O'Reilly stopped scowling. "Ah, that is good news. Good news! An answer to our prayers, eh?"

"More than an answer. I felt certain Juan would come eventually, but not in my wildest dreams did I expect his *mother* to make the announcement."

"Will he stay?"

McQueen winked. "My wife says he's paying a long visit. Juan and I have other plans. He goes to work for Leslie early next year, after we've traveled a bit—gotten acquainted again. But for this moment, it's more than enough to know that, in spite of my father-in-law's ill health and every burdensome thing I left behind, she *approves* his trip." He toyed with the stack of red checkers. "I've . . . *lived* for the sight of that boy."

"Perhaps you and he are better men for the trial of these long months of waiting."

"I know my son has been magnificent."

"So has his father." O'Reilly began to set up the board. "Too bad conditions aren't more tranquil for his arrival, but I daresay the young don't dread danger as we do. You may move first, Don Juan."

"Before we play, Father, there's one more piece of news. Perhaps not so encouraging at first thought, but it could throw some light on our immediate threat from the frontier—if indeed it is a real threat."

O'Reilly only looked at him.

"After my talk with his Excellency just now, I'm convinced that he finally suspects the truth about William Plowden and Robert Wagnon. Once the militiamen under arrest mentioned the name of Richard Lang outright, he had no choice but to agree that you and I had been right about him all along. They spoke only of two St. Augustine citizens as being involved along with Lang in the French-Georgian alliance, but the prisoners had no sooner been marched from his Excellency's office than he informed me that I am to leave at once for Alachua to confer with Chief Paine."

The priest thought a moment. "I see. Wise, of course, to be sure Paine's Seminoles are still with us, especially since they're only fifty miles or so from the city—but what does the chief have to do with Wagnon or Plowden?"

"The governor quite rightly believes that any white man suspected of dealings with the enemy will sooner or later make contact with Paine's Indians to the west of us. I am to inquire about Wagnon and Plowden. He feels that no attempt will be made to overthrow us without Indian aid in the fighting."

"His Excellency continues to amaze me, for one so young—and unwell. He's right, of course. When will you go?"

"Tomorrow morning. If Wagnon and Plowden *have* conferred with Paine, they'll be arrested. The trip's a gift from heaven for me, frankly. It will pass much of the time until young Juan arrives."

"So it will. Uh, by the way, should you see that rascal Job Wiggens when you take his ferry at Picolata on your way to Alachua, will you remind him that he's a very bad Catholic? Hasn't been to Mass for months."

"Of course. That is, if it appears wise."

"Wise?"

"I mean to question Job closely too. If Plowden and Wagnon are making trips to see Chief Paine, there's no other way to get there except by that ferry. I wouldn't want to anger Job. He'll close up like a clam."

"You, son, are a more faithful Spaniard than you are a Catholic."

They concentrated on their game in silence for a time; then, after jumping not one but two of McQueen's men, the priest leaned back in his chair and asked mischievously: "What if Job Wiggens tells you that your old American comrade, Colonel John McIntosh, has been seen around the St. Johns with the Indians—or with French sympathizers? Would you report that to his Excellency?"

McQueen's startled frown dissolved into a smile. "Does no one trust McIntosh but me?"

"No one else with a brain in his head—so far as I've heard. *Would* you tell the governor?"

"Forgive me, Father, but I don't have to decide that tonight. Therefore, I'm going to forget you even mentioned it. Your move."

"I just jumped you again."

"Oh, so you did."

Chapter 16

✳✳✳ Astride his broad-backed mare, Elena, on the second day of the return trip from Alachua to St. Augustine, Don Juan emerged from the high pine forests east of Cuscowilla and rode out across gentle sand-hill country. Half Way Pond lay just ahead.

On this first day of December, the usually cerulean blue pond was gray and choppy. At the water's edge, he dismounted, spread his heavy jacket over the sweating animal, and led her to drink. To stir his blood against the cold, he jogged a quarter of a mile or so, then walked slowly back to where Elena grazed.

His long, arduous ride to Alachua without a servant had, as Quesada hoped, impressed King Paine. The Governor himself could not have been received more warmly by the giant chief. Affable, tough King Paine of the Seminoles was important as a Spanish ally. True, he had been suspected of stealing on occasion, and no one doubted his genius for capturing and holding runaway slaves from Georgia—a constant harassment for his Excellency in his dealings with Governor Telfair. But in the main, the chief had been a trusted friend to the Spanish.

Only once had McQueen dared broach the subject of the runaway slaves, suggesting that the return of only a few might help ease the tensions building along the border. "My black-skinned people want to stay here," Paine had snapped. "I do not force them! They stay. They know the brutal Georgians—and so make their choice to remain among the Seminoles." Then the chief had narrowed his black eyes in a crinkly smile. "Consider how poor you would be in St. Augustine without the fine horses bred here by my black people. Look at your mare. Was she not raised on the 'Lachua plain?"

True enough. At least, Don Juan knew of no other horses to compare with the animals bred by King Paine's runaway slaves. His prices were fair too. The powerful Indian had even been known to give extended credit in exchange for Quesada's willingness to ignore Georgian demands for the return of their Negroes. Credit was allowed, also, because of lavish gifts to the Alachua Seminoles, who had journeyed regularly to the Plaza to collect their bounty.

King Paine, as had his uncle, Chief Cowkeeper, before him, found it profitable to remain loyal to His Spanish Majesty's colonial government, and Paine had shown full respect for McQueen as Quesada's emissary. Both Negro and Yamassee Indian slaves had served McQueen in the same obsequious manner in which they attended their fiery-eyed Seminole master. Indeed, Don Juan had found his visit entirely pleasant.

From his first sight of the green Alachua plain, he had been made welcome by Indian women and children straggling along beside him as he rode into the town. Young men had then conducted him royally to Paine's large house, where he gripped forearms with the chief, smoked a pipe in good cheer, and drank thin drink. The sumptuous meal that first night—venison stewed in bear oil, hot corn cakes, milk, and hominy—had lasted for hours. But most important, McQueen would be able to assure his Excellency that all was well between Paine and the Spanish. A lesser Alachua chief, Bowlegs, just returned from the Alabama region, vowed that there, only a few of the still grieving McGillivray Creeks had even considered turning away from their Spanish protectors.

If Paine had told the truth, there had been no visits to Alachua by Lang, Plowden, or Wagnon. In a way, this was disappointing, since their immediate arrests might at least have slowed the traitorous activity against St. Augustine. But he was much relieved to be able to report that indeed there had been no communication with Paine by Colonel

John McIntosh. Truthfully, Don Juan was not as certain of
the innocence and reliability of the McQueen family friend
as he pretended. The best he could do was to continue to
use his persuasive powers on Colonel John. So far, they
had seemed to work.

Of course, he had not yet been able to question ferry-
man Job Wiggens, the taciturn Negro slave owner at
Picolata. One of Wiggens' salves had poled McQueen
across the St. Johns en route to Alachua, with the promise
that Wiggens himself would be on hand for the return trip.
If Wiggens kept his word, the ferry would be waiting on
this side of the river.

Beginning to chill from the wind off Half Way Pond,
he selected a shallow crossing and hurried back to his
mount. His jacket, still warm from the horse's body, felt
good as he guided the mare across the pond and on to the
path through the pine forest on the other side. With luck,
he would make the fourteen miles to the St. Johns before
dark and spend the night at the ruins of old Fort Picolata.
The remaining sixteen miles from Picolata to St. Augustine could be covered before noon tomorrow. Young Juan
would arrive within the week, and there was much to do.

Job Wiggens, a free Negro in his mid-fifties, picked up
a little hard cash—difficult, at best, to come by, even for
the owner of a large plantation—as operator of the only
ferry across the St. Johns River in the vicinity of St. Augustine. Wiggens seldom poled the raft himself, since his
ferry was used mainly by Indians and a trip across the
wide St. Johns was hard. Figuring that he had done more
than his share of hard work in his life, one or more of
Wiggens' slaves handled the crossings unless, as on this
evening, his passenger was a man of influence at the
Plaza.

Since the days of old Governor Zéspedes, Job had
been paid a yearly stipend by the Spanish government for
his ferry service. The stipend, he felt, was far too low, so
he welcomed this chance to address himself to the favorite
citizen of the present governor.

McQueen'll be so glad to see me already here and

waiting on a cold day like this, he thought, as he tied his ferry to the dock on the west side of the river, he's likely to agree to whatever I ask. Especially if his trip has been successful.

Bundled in a bearskin coat, Job squinted against the brilliant winter sun, dropping now above the wide river, and felt sure that the horseman galloping toward him over the flat, treeless path would be Don Juan McQueen. When the rider waved and shouted cheerfully, he knew he was right. Job, mainly a silent man, liked McQueen's talkative company. It saved a lot of effort.

McQueen, a heavy growth of reddish beard on his face, did not disappoint Wiggens. The big man hadn't stopped talking from the moment he rode up to the ferry. With the request for more money in mind, Job had brought a blanket for the horse and a bundle of hay. Don Juan, rubbing down the mare as he talked, seemed pleased by the show of concern.

So far, Job Wiggens thought, so good.

Finally, about midstream, McQueen began to run down a little, and Job figured it was time he got in a word or two.

"Sounds like you're carrying a fine report back to the governor," he said, putting aside his pole which no longer touched bottom.

"On the whole, yes. But my report won't be complete, Wiggens, until you tell me what you know."

" 'Bout what? And for how much?"

Don Juan took five pesos from a pouch and handed it to him. "Here," he grinned. "That's a lot of money in East Florida."

"Depends on what you want to know, I reckon."

"Are you acquainted with two men from St. Augustine named William Plowden and Robert Wagnon?"

Job nodded.

"They've been seen leaving the city headed in this direction. Have they used your ferry lately?"

"Nope."

"Well, have you seen them in the last month or so?"

"Yep."

"But they didn't cross the river?"

"Nope."

"Now, look here, Job, you've got the money in your pocket. These men are under suspicion. What do you know about them?"

"What they under suspicion for?"

"Why, for being tied in with the French-Georgia plans to attack us!"

"I figured that's what you'd say."

"If I knew how to handle this lopsided raft of yours, I'd pitch you overboard! What were they doing here?"

"Come to talk to me. I'll tell you about what for a price."

"How much more?"

"A hundred pesos extra a year from the Plaza for ferrying their Indians."

"All right, I'll take it up with his Excellency at our first meeting, I promise. Why did those men come here?"

"To sound me out."

"About what?"

"This and that."

Don Juan again took out his leather pouch. "Here, you old robber"—he opened his bag—"see for yourself. I've got ten pesos."

"Reckon that'll do for now."

Wiggens pocketed the money, picked up a heavy paddle, and began to stroke across the current.

"I'm waiting to know what they wanted, Job."

"Soon as I get us past this deep place."

After several minutes with the paddle, Wiggens laid it down, plunged the long pole back into the murky water, and, working quietly against the river bottom, said: "Wagnon and Plowden ain't sure which way to come at the city when they take it. Wanted to see if I'd take charge of transportation here. Ferry and horses."

McQueen grabbed his shoulder. "What did you tell them?"

"Nothing."

"Well, knowing you, I guess I believe that. Listen,

Wiggens, may I tell his Excellency that you're with us—against them?"

"Providing."

"The additional hundred pesos?"

Job nodded.

Don Juan took off his riding cap and ran his fingers through his thatch of hair. "Well, his Excellency authorized me to deal with King Paine in any way I saw fit—so, I'll promise the money. You'll get it, *if* you conduct yourself as a man in the pay of His Majesty's government."

They shook on it; then Job busied himself with guiding the clumsy raft into the dock.

His ferry solidly secured, the black man watched as McQueen led the weary horse across a wide plank onto the bank of the river. He didn't bother to ask, but Job wondered if the American-turned-Spaniard had ridden the whole distance from 'Lachua today. The heavy shoulders were slumped, the usually springing gait slow. He also wondered how old McQueen was. He looked fifty. Reckon he's not, though, Job decided. They say his oldest son's just turned twenty.

"You planning to sleep here at the old fort, Mr. McQueen? You're welcome at my place for the night."

"Thanks. But that's another five-mile ride. I'm suddenly dog tired. Think I'll just make camp over there behind the ruins. No quieter place on earth these days than a deserted Spanish fort, eh?"

"Ain't deserted no longer. They's a couple of soldiers on duty there now. Lookouts. But they won't bother you. Too mad at Colonel Howard for giving them this lonesome duty. They just come today. It was them told me about your son."

McQueen whirled to face him. "My son! What about my son?"

"Nothing, except he's supposed to be in St. Augustine."

There was no hint of weariness in the hand that gripped Job and turned him around. "In the name of heaven, man, why didn't you tell me this before?"

"You didn't ask."

McQueen tramped up and down, his eyes searching the

sky. "Clearing. Should be a full moon," he mumbled to himself. "Sixteen miles more ... three hours ... I can make it in three hours, if I ride hard!"

Without another word, the big man leaped into the saddle, urged his horse up the sandy riverbank into the forest, and galloped off.

"Crazy fool," Wiggens muttered. "Crazy fool of a man. Kill himself and that fine mare too." He jingled the pesos in his hand. "If he'd had more cash on him, I might have told him Colonel John McIntosh's been by here several times."

Chapter 17

✦✦✦ Under the white moon, the path was visible all the way, but Don Juan struggled to focus his wind-burned eyes. Still west of the San Sebastian River, he was so exhausted that only anticipation kept him conscious. The mare would have to bear him safely over the last familiar miles to the city. Her instincts—for the road and for her rider—were true. As though aware of his dependence and urgency, the horse scarcely slowed when they reached the river before plunging in the dark water to carry him to the other side.

Over the thundering rhythm of the pounding hooves, he gripped the mane and shouted: "Elena! Go, Elena! My son is waiting for us!" Her stride lengthened and between his knees he felt the stretch and buck of her body, the heat of her blood rushing with his.

At the St. Augustine City Gate a little before nine o'clock, he reined in the foaming horse, gasped out the password . . . and waited for the sleepy sentry to appear.

His head reeling, he managed somehow to hold Elena to a trot down St. George Street and around to the stable at the rear of his lighted house. Riding into the black shadows of the trees, he called, "Juan? Juan! Are you here?"

As he handed the reins to Pedro, a tall, broad-shouldered young man burst from the house and ran toward him across the garden.

McQueen slid, exhausted, into his son's arms.

Young John had slept very little. Each time he dozed off, he would come wide awake. This morning, he was still thinking about last night's reunion. He had never loved Papa so much. The bearded, tired, happy man had, for once, been lost for words. Unashamed, the two had hugged each other again and again, his father repeating his name—*Juan*, not John—as though to convince himself that they were together in St. Augustine at last.

In the two days since his arrival, while his father was still gone, John had seen for himself that Pedro and Harry all but worshipped their master. So there was no need to be embarrassed at any show of affection. Harry had even offered to shave Papa at midnight, when he kept apologizing for his disheveled appearance.

That was the way with his father, he thought, as he got out of bed a little after dawn. Everyone who took time to know the man loved him. Even Grandmother, who disapproved of almost everything about him these days.

From his room, he looked across at the foundations of the new church. "Just like Catholics," Uncle Aleck had snorted, "to build an expensive church while their parishioners starve!"

At least, John could forget his uncle for a while, except to be glad he was near Mama, especially now that Grandfather Smith was gone. His father still didn't know. "Since you're going so soon, I won't write of it," Mama had said. "Tell him face to face. It will lessen the shock."

While he shaved, John decided never to let her find out that Papa had made that foolhardy ride because he couldn't bear to wait one more night to see his son. Protecting her from worry had become a habit.

His father would surely still be sleeping, he thought, stooping a little before the looking glass to comb the tangles from his black, wavy hair. He had heard Pedro's answer to Katrina's tattoo—a pewter spoon tapped against an old piece of iron that hung on a rope by the back door. For a woman who couldn't speak a word, Katrina seemed to run a smooth household. He supposed one of the servants would take Papa's breakfast to his room.

His fingers trembled as he forced a shirt button through its buttonhole. He was tired too. The trip down by small boats, borrowed horses, and on foot, had not been easy. But when Mama so quickly agreed, he had refused to wait for passage on a ship. He trembled also from excitement. Now that Papa was home, he could begin to believe that he was here at last.

Carefully, so as not to rouse his father, John eased down the outside stairs to the loggia and stood looking at the yard. There was a well in the center, and around it the winter remains of a vegetable garden, bordered by trees—lime, orange, fig, and shaddock. Beyond the McQueen wall loomed the large, gabled Government House, topped by its wooden lookout tower. Papa was deeply attached to the young governor. John expected to like him, too, but would wait to form his own opinion.

The sweet aroma of Katrina's baking hung in the cool, still morning air, but he decided to sit a while on the rim of the well and think. His salvation, during the monotonous months of work at Oatland, had been retreats into the familiar world of his own thoughts, especially dreams of Margaret.

This time, his mind went first to the messages for Quesada with which he had been entrusted by Colonel Carlos Howard when he had spent the night en route at San Vicente on the St. Johns. Colonel Howard had welcomed him, not only as the son of Don Juan McQueen, but as a reliable means of getting the vital news to his Excellency.

A recent examination of Howard's Spanish Rural Militia had turned up man after man secretly aligned, even at this early date, with both the French and the traitorous Georgia settlers in East Florida. Pacing his quarters, Howard had declared that no man could be expected to defend the frontier against attack when numbers of his own troops sympathized with the enemy. The colonel had also insisted that young John find a way to convince Don Juan that his trust in John McIntosh was indeed misplaced.

The only smile John remembered seeing on Howard's taut, intelligent face came when the boy had produced a clipping from the *Charleston City Gazette and Advertiser* with the news that the French and Americans would attack the port of St. Mary's first. John knew, of course, before

Howard mentioned it, that such an attack would require French ships of war, so far held back from Genêt because of the complaint filed against him last month in Paris by President Washington. Still, the news article had given Howard some idea of where the plans were focused, and he had smiled his approval of John's wisdom in bringing it along.

John had learned much from Howard concerning the tangle of almost nonsensical intrigue along the border among the Indians, Spaniards, Georgians, and now the French. He felt confident that he would be able to transmit the messages accurately to Quesada, but persuading his father to doubt a McIntosh would be harder.

Both Colonel John McIntosh and his cousin, John Houstoun McIntosh, had been McQueen's lifelong friends. The two families were still close. The elder McIntosh, Colonel John, had become a Spanish subject and had accepted tax-free Spanish lands because Papa had talked him into it. Howard's words came back: "The difference between your father and Colonel John McIntosh is as wide as the ocean! When Don Juan McQueen swore allegiance to His Majesty, he meant it. Unfortunately McQueen refuses to accept that difference."

John, Jr., had grown up knowing the McIntosh family and had been told from boyhood that the McIntoshes "are our kind of people." He smiled, remembering how he and Eliza had giggled because Grandmother Smith pronounced the name as "Mack'ntush"—in her lingering British manner, so as to give the cherished family name still more elegance.

"The McIntoshes have never gotten along with the Spanish," Grandmother would declare, "and they never will! After the way those heathen treated Grandfather John Mohr McIntosh when he fought at St. Augustine with General Oglethorpe, how could they stomach Spaniards? Only the McIntosh breeding enables any member of the family to be civil to a Spaniard to this day! To think of John Mohr McIntosh, the fine, courageous scion of the Scottish McIntosh chieftains, wasting away in a moldy Spanish prison!" John Mohr McIntosh had not entirely wasted away, though, because he'd eventually returned to

Georgia in plenty of time to saturate the minds of the younger men of the family with hatred for anything Spanish.

John had, in fact, been surprised when his father wrote that Colonel John McIntosh had indeed become a Spanish subject. At any rate, as soon as Papa felt up to talking, John meant to tell him only that rumors on the frontier were rampant concerning his old friend. His father could make up his own mind in the matter.

John smiled. He had been so occupied with Spanish Florida this morning, he had not yet thought of Margaret! Thank heaven, he would be able to speak freely of her from now on. With Papa, he could be himself.

A ray of Florida winter sun reached down through the clouds and warmed his face. The problems at Thunderbolt and Oatland, the heaviness which had hung over The Cottage even before Grandfather died, had already begun to dim. He could think of the seemingly endless year there now as a long stopover on the journey from Paris to St. Augustine.

He stood up and stretched both arms above his head. If Papa's all right this morning, he thought, I'll tell him about Grandfather. Then—life can begin for us. Feeling a pang of hunger, he headed toward the kitchen, but before he'd crossed the garden, a familiar, cheerful shout stopped him.

"*Buenos días*, son!"

He looked up to see his father at the top of the stairs— shaved and fully dressed—waving both hands.

"*Bonjour, monsieur,*" John called back.

"If you're half as hungry as I, or half as glad to see me as I am to see you on this beautiful morning, then we have quite a day ahead!"

His father ran lightly down the stairs and embraced him. The sound of one pair of clapping hands caused them both to look toward the back-yard kitchen. Black Katrina stood in the doorway applauding—her strong features aglow with joy.

♦   ♦   ♦

Before they finished breakfast, the pale December sun was buried by clouds which at midmorning began to drop a steady drizzle of rain.

Settled across from his son in the parlor before a fire, Don Juan said softly, "You're here."

"Yes. I'm here. I'm—home."

McQueen felt tears smart his eyes. To have the boy call St. Augustine "home" was almost too good to be true. He should respond with some joyous phrase. None came. Had Anne known all this time that their son had not been at home with her? If so, she had surely suffered. "It's— hard," he said, "to love someone as much as I love your mother."

"Yes."

"Well, now," McQueen tried for his customary buoy-ance, "I was too done in last night to talk much, but today you must tell me all about her. Does she speak of me?"

"All the time. But—I don't think she understands you."

McQueen thought for a moment. "I wonder if you're right about that. Your mother's a surprising woman. At times, I half fear she may understand me too well." His thumb rubbed the turned leather of the chair arm nerv-ously, round and round. "Do you realize that I don't feel guilty for—all those debts? Heartbroken . . . often ashamed . . . but not guilty."

"I'm glad. It wouldn't help."

"I—tried in Georgia, son. I failed."

"I can't agree with that, sir. You had bad luck."

A twinkle in his eye, McQueen lifted his teacup as if in a toast to himself. "I'm not failing here!"

John smiled and lifted his own cup.

"You haven't really told me how she is, son. She's so faithful with letters, but your mother's always tried to pro-tect us from worry. I long to know all about her."

The boy took a deep breath. "I'd have told you last night, but you were so tired from that long ride. Grandfa-ther Smith died."

McQueen set down the cup. For a long time, he stared at the tabby floor. "Your—mother?"

"Shattered, of course, but she insisted that I come on here as I'd planned."

Don Juan jumped to his feet, caught suddenly by anger that Anne should have to endure this grief. She had always been too close to her father to be comforted by the thought that he had lived a long, happy life—longer than permitted most men. The thought stabbed: because of me, she's lost young John too!

He turned around. "I—I didn't mean for things to be this way, son. I didn't. . . ."

For a moment, he thought the boy seemed to struggle with something inside himself. Then John began to smile, got up, and came to stand beside him.

"I stayed with Mother when she really needed me—needed a man to do what a woman couldn't do. I think you need me now more than she does, so I'm here."

Chapter 18

Fort George Island
18 December, 1793

My Dear Eliza,

There are no words to express my sorrow in the loss you have all sustained by the death of that good man, your grandfather. Before young John and I left St. Augustine I tried to describe my feelings in a letter to your mother, and it is my hope that in sharing this one as well, she and your grandmother may realize my own grief and concern. Grandfather Smith and I disagreed on religious matters in recent years, but I believe he is now in a place of fullest happiness and in possession of the whole truth, still hidden from us on earth. He knows, as we cannot, that God's blessing is for all who follow with sincerity of heart. Your dear mother will not agree, of course, but when, by God's mercy, I some day also reach heaven, I expect to find that Grandfather Smith and my late, saintly young friend and spiritual guide, Padre Narciso Font, have become close companions. Your old papa is not a theologian, but he is a man with love in his heart for God and most people. I loved John Smith.

No words can tell of my joy at having your brother here. Except to sleep, we have not been separated for more than half an hour since his arrival. He delights me exceedingly and has gained the esteem of all my *friends—even my neighbor, Señora Perpal—by his excellent conduct and engaging manners.*

Colonel Carlos Howard, in command at San Vicente Ferrer, a cynical man by nature, entrusted John with messages of the utmost secrecy, which he delivered admirably to his Excellency during our first meeting at Government House.

There is much talk of trouble from Georgia these days, but assure your mother that John and I are in no danger and that if anyone can restore peace to our frontier, the skillful Colonel Howard will succeed.

John has shown me the drawings you sent and I commend you. I hope you are continuing your lessons on the pianoforte as well, and I long again to hear you play "Sweet Robin." Should Aunt Cowper and Cousin Margaret visit you, no one would be happier than your papa. Be sure to convince them that I sincerely love them as I most certainly love all of you. Be as happy one and all, as I wish, and then you'll have no reason to complain.

> *Yr Affectionate Father,*
> *Don Juan McQueen*

P.S. From my new house here at Fort George, early in January, your brother and I will pay respects to a few Georgia acquaintances among the settlers along the St. Johns, weather permitting, and will return to St. Augustine before the February rains begin.

Eliza finished reading the letter aloud and sat looking expectantly from her mother to Grandmother Smith, hoping one of them would say something nice about what he'd written.

"Good long letter," the old lady said. "Ridiculous idea, of course—your grandfather and that priest—friends in heaven!"

Mama went on darning.

Grandmother had decided to spend a few months at The Cottage, and her presence kept them all on guard. Especially Mamma.

"Papa liked my drawings."

"Yes, he seemed to, dear," Mama said without looking up. "One of us must write to him soon, so he'll know Aunt Cowper and Cousin Margaret are definitely coming."

"Big John might well expect trouble from Georgia," Grandmother said, tapping her fingers, looking off toward the river.

"I thought you agreed Americans are growing weary of all this French interference." Mama smoothed William's darned sock over her knee. "That the President is not going to put up with it either."

Still looking out the window, Grandmother said, "I'm not speaking of a major attack directed by the French government itself, Anne. I do agree that the *better* class of Georgian is sick of Citizen Genêt. But who can tell about those crackers down there? Or about the patience of fine Georgians like Colonel McIntosh who have accepted grants and live daily under murderous Spanish rule? Mark my word, those dear folk are not going to simmer down until the United States owns the Floridas!"

Mama laid aside her sewing. "But you did hear Mary Esther say this morning that the talk in Savannah just yesterday was that the big danger *is* over. That France simply has not sent any warships to support an attack."

"I know, I know, I know, I *know*." Grandmother repeated the phrase in the singsong way which meant that she alone did know. "I also know what you're thinking, Anne. Your sister Mary will soon be here to stay behind with me. You've been planning to go down there for a long time. But, so soon after my recent tragic loss, I can only quiet my nerves by trusting your good sense." She turned brightly to Eliza. "Now, child, show Grandmother that new drawing you've been working on today."

Don Juan McQueen and his son had been on Fort George Island for almost three weeks—the happiest days Don Juan could remember. They would have to move on soon, but their time spent with Atkinson inspecting the great stands of timber and watching the Negroes prepare the fields for spring planting had been exactly to his liking. He had waited a long time to share the wooded, fertile island with young Juan.

Most of all, he had enjoyed their afternoon walks alone along the river bluff beyond his house. Fort George Inlet, the stretch of wide water which had been day-sky blue when they began their walk an hour ago, was now glowing pink. The sun no longer blinded them but hung, a huge cloudless ball, deepening minute by minute from rose to rose bronze.

Young John pointed to it. "Want to clock old Sol again on his way down?"

"Of course!" Don Juan took out his watch, eager to play the little game they'd begun before Christmas, while visiting San Juan de Nepomuceno, his Ortega property. A boyish grin on his face, he began to time the sun—the swift descent from the instant of its first flattening against the horizon of pines and sand dunes. One minute . . . two minutes . . . three. He looked at John, who smiled back as though the speed of the sinking ball was a phenomenon known only to the two of them.

"Three minutes and thirty-five seconds," Don Juan said softly, when the last bright edge had vanished.

"Almost a minute faster than last night, eh?"

They strolled arm in arm toward a grove of live oaks and cedars, draped with barely moving mauve moss, their trunks picking up the afterglow.

"Which do you prefer?" John asked. "The light from the sun or the color it leaves behind?"

He laughed. "Oh, I'd choose the color any time!"

"I should have guessed that."

"Now, what do you mean?"

"Just what I said. Mama would choose light. She has to see ahead."

"Which is better, son?"

"Neither. Or both."

"Would you choose light or color?"

The boy stopped beside an oak, pulled a fern frond from its huge trunk, and began to twist it in his fingers. "I'd want to choose color. I'd probably choose light, for fear of being wrong. Margaret would choose color—as naturally as you did."

"Ah! Then you'll make a perfect couple. I've always believed the very differences in our make-up caused the strong attraction between your mother and me." He grinned a little. "Of course, those differences have caused—discomfort too."

His son was not smiling. "Papa . . . don't give up. Don't ever give up!"

"I don't intend to."

"Neither do I. Not with Margaret or with you and Mother."

They turned back in the direction of the pleasing, compact, two-storied wood-and-tabby house. At the veranda, John said, "You know, if the Cowpers do come to Savannah, I'll have to go back for a visit. Even if I've already started work with Leslie. I have to see Margaret again."

Such a thing had not occurred to Don Juan. He was too stunned to say more than, "Of course."

John touched his arm. "Now, don't look so crestfallen. There's another reason I want to go. Haven't you noticed a difference in Mama's last two letters? Oh, nothing definite, but now that I've been here—and especially with the rumors that the French government is not going to support that much heralded attack on us—I think I can persuade her to come back down with me for a time. Margaret and the children too."

Don Juan sank into a veranda chair, put his head back and closed his eyes. After a while, he whispered, "If I thought you could convince her, son, I'd—let you leave tomorrow!"

"Don't get your hopes too high."

Don Juan looked at him with a quick smile. "I'll do my best not to. But let's cross over to San Vicente as soon as the tide suits in the morning. Who knows? Colonel Howard may have some good news—about something. If there's a chance she might come, something good just *has* to turn up soon!"

Before noon the next day, John watched his father climb ahead of him up the steep bank of the St. Johns below San Vicente Ferrer, and found himself pressing to match the long strides.

"I swear to you, I could have paddled that canoe another ten miles," Papa called over his shoulder. "Harry says I've put on a little weight since your mother saw me last, but I say it has added endurance!"

The sinking feeling that he might have given his father false hope came again. From the moment on the veranda last night, Papa's dreams had continued to soar. How much higher can they go? he wondered, as they came in sight of the shingled roofs and brick chimneys of the taller outpost buildings. He'd forgotten, if he'd ever known, that his father's dreams could sail to the moon on the merest shred of encouragement. Nothing would do but that they confer immediately with Howard on the latest developments, if any, among the troublesome settlers. John hadn't been long in East Florida, but he already sensed how slowly events moved. There could well be months of relative peace, but suppose Howard had bad news?

What would happen to Papa's soaring dreams?

"I've quartered you gentlemen together here in this smaller cabin for two reasons, warmth and privacy for us to talk," Colonel Howard said that evening, settling himself in a chair before the tiny fireplace.

John watched his father's face. Papa actually seemed to be expecting good news.

"Have you visited any of your old Georgia friends between the two rivers yet, Captain McQueen?"

"No," Papa answered. "Juan and I have been inspecting my various holdings. So far, Ortega and Fort George."

"Fine. Don't stop anywhere else. Is that understood?"

His father frowned a little, but nodded.

"It's absolutely essential that you not be seen by anyone in this area," Howard went on. "Is that clear, Captain?"

"Yes, Colonel, but why? His Excellency seemed eager for us to—do a little spying among the settlers."

"His Excellency hadn't seen these." Howard took two letters from his uniform jacket. "One arrived yesterday, the other today. Your visit here is perfectly timed."

"Good," Papa said, suddenly all business.

Howard held up one letter. "Here, gentlemen, is a request from one Abner Hammond for permission to enter East Florida. He'll have that permission tomorrow at Saint Mary's. But—with a condition. His request was to visit his father-in-law, near the St. Johns. Hammond can cross our border, provided he goes straight to St. Augustine first. I made the condition so that when he reaches St. Augustine Quesada can, if he chooses, arrest him."

"On what grounds?"

Carlos Howard held up the other letter. "This. A sworn statement by one of our more supposedly loyal but suspicious settlers, Reuben Pitcher, who evidently hopes to save his own plantation from what he insists is danger of immediate attack upon all American settlers *not* in sympathy with the French cause."

"Excuse me, Colonel," John interrupted, "but I thought you said this Reuben Pitcher is suspected of disloyalty to Spain?"

"He is—but he's the kind to turn against his fellow Georgians settled here if he thought he had to in order to save his skin."

The boy looked at his father, who asked: "What's in the sworn statement, Colonel?"

"Pitcher's story of what he believes to be the details of Sam and Abner Hammond's plan to attack our border, burning the properties of all loyal Spanish settlers. Pitcher also enclosed names of those who will take part in the attack."

McQueen slapped his hands down on both knees. "Well, then, my son and I will be able to verify his list without being seen widely in the area. First thing in the morning, we'll ride to John McIntosh's place. He's our best bet."

Howard jumped to his feet. "That's the last thing you will do, McQueen!" He held the list of names under a lamp for them both to see. "His Excellency and I know of your strong family ties with McIntosh, but—from this point on—for any *loyal* subject of His Majesty's East Florida government there will be no meetings whatever with any man on this list . . . except as an arresting officer."

John went to the lamp table with his father to study the

list. The third name from the top was that of Colonel John McIntosh.

After looking at the paper a long time, McQueen straightened to his full height and said soberly, "I am a loyal subject, Colonel. I believe the years have proven that. I am also only a captain in your Rural Militia. I take my orders from you."

Howard folded both letters and handed them to young John. "If you're stopped on your way back to St. Augustine, these must not be found on your father," he said tensely. "My orders are, Captain, that you return at once to Government House and place them in his Excellency's hands. The final decision concerning the arrests of all these men will be his."

John put the letters in his pocket. "I'm sure you know McIntosh makes business trips now and then to St. Augustine, Colonel," he said, watching his father as he spoke. "And most of the time, he stays with you, doesn't he, Papa?"

His father's face was hard as flint. He nodded.

"I do know," Howard clipped his words. "How you withdraw that hospitality, Captain McQueen, will be up to you. But you have been too loyal to risk showing him even one small sign of friendship now. It would set very poorly with Quesada."

"Is that an order, Colonel?"

"It's an order, Don Juan. And a friendly warning. I doubt that you've ever seen his Excellency in one of his— spells. Even though he's a Spaniard with yellow hair, his particular demon, when aroused, can chill a man's soul."

Chapter 19

✳✳✳ As soon as the tide served the next morning, Colonel Howard—more relaxed, young John thought, since Papa's uncompromising declaration of loyalty—walked with them down to the San Vicente dock, where Harry waited in the canoe.

"Two Seminoles will meet you at the Pablo Creek landing with horses," Howard said. "You know the route, McQueen, but this time begin looking for the Indians once you've left the St. Johns and headed toward the Pablo Creek headwaters. The men will be mounted and leading your horses. If you see more than two Indians, conceal yourselves and the canoe and wait. My agent has sent word that they are to ride with you overland as far as the North River landing, where a boat of some description will be waiting to take you on to the city."

Papa, his manner brusque, saluted and said only, "Your word, Colonel, is my command."

"One thing more," Howard went on. "I urge you to converse with *no one* along the way, Don Juan—friend or stranger. It could be downright dangerous for you. If news of Reuben Pitcher's list of names has leaked out, any number of your old Georgia friends could try to stop you from reaching St. Augustine."

In the canoe, Papa had been almost too silent. Except to point out a flock of painted vultures in flight to the west, he had said little. Harry, more accustomed to his master's moods, seemed not to notice, but the silence made John uneasy. En route to San Vicente from Fort

George yesterday, the talk had flowed—with his father finding more reason with every stroke of the paddle to hope that Mama would visit him.

Howard's orders had changed everything. This was a side of his father which the boy hadn't seen: the enterprising, ambitious resident of Spanish East Florida, plainly excited by another chance to serve Quesada, but buried in his own thoughts. He had not been curt or unkind. Still, the apparent preoccupation with the colony's fresh troubles somehow shut out Mama, too.

All the way up Pablo Creek, they watched for the Seminoles. The marshes were flat and empty, the woods quiet. But as the canoe neared the headwaters landing, two mounted Indians were waiting with the promised horses.

"So far, so good," his father said, leaping from the canoe before Harry had a chance to beach it. "If we're to make St. Augustine before dark, we've no time for small talk with them. Unless I'm mistaken, they won't speak much English anyway."

For more than two hours, they rode hard, the Seminole guides ahead, Harry hanging on behind Papa with relative ease, John alongside. At a point halfway to the North River landing they reined in the horses for a rest, and as John dismounted, he saw the older of the two Seminoles approach Papa. Then, as if on a prearranged signal, Indian-fashion, the two men grasped forearms.

"You have served us well," McQueen said. "What may I do for you?"

Tears welled in the Indian's deep-set eyes. He stood erect, still grasping McQueen's arm. "You see Chief McGillivray dead. Me touch you."

Even the unpredictable, renegade East Florida Seminoles had loved McGillivray! When McQueen asked which man could take the chief's place, the Seminole answered: "No man. Indians lost."

McQueen began trying to reassure him that the Spanish were still their protectors, but the Seminole backed away. He sat on the ground a good distance off, in company with the other guide, and buried his head in his hands.

After the horses had grazed a while, both savages

leaped on their mounts and kicked them to a frenzied gallop. The two McQueens and Harry followed, but Papa signaled that they should make no real effort to catch up—only to keep them in sight. They had gone less than a mile when the Indians pierced the afternoon quiet with sustained, earsplitting screams.

There was no chance to ask his father's opinion, but it seemed to John that, owing to their having met the man who had seen their leader's dead body, the Seminoles were at last able to vent their long-pent-up grief.

A few times during the hard ride, John rode abreast of his father, attempting at least to exchange reassuring smiles. Harry waved, but, except for one glance, his father kept his eyes straight ahead, his face almost as inscrutable as the Seminoles'.

At the North River landing, where they were to continue by water, the Indians, leading the extra horses, rode slowly back in the direction of Pablo Creek—without so much as a wave of a hand.

Harry handed the water jug to his master.

"Thanks, Harry," Papa said, wiping his mouth on his sleeve after a long drink. "Help yourself, son."

John took the jug, but was too disturbed to drink when his father turned abruptly and walked away behind a big sand dune, out of sight.

"Go on, drink," Harry whispered, smiling. "He do that sometimes. Don't pay him no mind."

"Is he—all right?"

"Sure. He just got something big bumpin' his brain."

Harry, seemingly as much at home beside the empty, desolate river as in the St. George Street house, found himself a shelter from the cold wind, lay down, and went promptly to sleep.

John still stood, trying to figure out why, since last night when Howard had shown them the letters, he had felt a troubling distance open between him and his father. The almost primitive exchange with the Seminole had somehow widened it. His mother's words, repeated often during the year at Thunderbolt, came chillingly to mind: "I've always feared *distance* between your father and me!"

A gull screamed somewhere out over the wind-whipped river, and John, too, felt afraid. My father's at home, he thought, in this wilderness. He's comfortable, even with the savages. He doesn't seem alarmed at all that there's no boat in sight, that we could be stranded here.

Worse than that, it was not like his father to go off alone, without at least a pleasantry.

He shivered. As far as he could see, there stretched a world without one familiar landmark—gray water, sand dunes, scrub pine, and Spanish bayonet—vast and cold and desolate.

On his way to St. Augustine from Georgia, John had quickly felt a part of the beauty and the hardships of East Florida. What had changed? Weren't the important letters for Quesada in *his* pocket? Hadn't Howard spoken as freely to him as to his father? He tried to belittle his own perplexity. In spite of the warm letters, did his mother now feel rejected by this man, *Don Juan McQueen*, the loyal Spanish subject, apparently as much at home resting against a sand dune as in a chair in his own parlor?

John's legs felt weak. He sat down on the open river-bank, unable to put out of his mind the moment when—the two men grasping forearms—a strange, almost eerie merging of spirits had taken place between the influential, landed gentleman and the grieving, ragged Seminole.

For the first time the boy found himself able to accept at least some of his mother's fear of the distance.

He was twenty, but only now were his parents becoming man and woman, separate from him. His thoughts tumbled. Could it be that the vast loneliness of this isolated river landing had brought his father a fresh surge of longing for the woman he loved? For Mama? How had Papa—as Don Juan McQueen—managed without her?

He shivered again from the penetrating cold, but also from a sudden notion that perhaps his father *had* managed—by having other women.

How naïve not to have thought of that before. "Don't be too patient with Margaret," Papa had once said laughingly. "After all, a man has to be fair to himself too." Suppose, at this moment, the stranger behind the sand dune needed to talk with him as someone other than a son. . . .

Compelled by the idea of such a possibility, John loped across the stretch of soft, sandy ground to the far side of the high dune—then stopped short. Papa . . . was on his knees, a rosary in his hands, his eyes closed.

John was still standing there wondering what to do when his father looked up. "So—there you are," he said as he scrambled to his feet, stuffing the rosary into his pocket. Then the big man laughed.

In that instant he was so much himself again, John laughed too. "Papa, you don't have to hide from me. I'm not Mama, you know."

His father's laughter drained away, but a strong arm went around John's shoulders. "Now and then, son, I—think I can't bear another day away from her." He pulled the rosary from his pocket. "This helps."

They smoothed a place in the sand and sat down together, their backs against the steep dune.

John asked, "Are you—worried because our boat isn't here?"

"Not at all! I've often had to spend the night in that cove down there because of some mixup in transportation. I'm on familiar ground here, you know." He patted the sand. "Ground I love—ground I'd like to own some day. Of course, the bar at St. Augustine makes for poor shipping. Better profits in land nearer St. Mary's deep harbor. I predict," he went on, as spirited as ever, "that his Excellency will reward me with any grant of available land I choose, once I hand him the papers you're carrying!"

"Any particular piece in mind?"

"Of course! I've just been waiting to perform a service of some special value before submitting my request. I've picked out two thousand beautifully situated acres right on the St. Johns, within three or four miles of our fort at San Vicente. Adjoining my Saw Mill Tract. The most outstanding tract on the river, in my opinion. And the safest, with the military so nearby." He was quiet for a time, then he said, "My dream is to build your mother a mansion on that land. I've even given it a name."

"Before you own it?"

"In my dream, it's already mine."

John longed to put his arms around him and tell him that he understood the dream, that he felt young and ashamed for imagining he had been shut out. But pity for this lonely, striving man was so painful, he could only ask, "What will you call it?"

His father locked both hands behind his head and leaned against the dune. "Los Molinos de McQueen," he said proudly. "The Mills of McQueen. Of course, your mother has always wanted me to settle down and become a successful planter. Los Molinos de McQueen is large enough for both indigo and a timber operation. There's a sawmill already set up, in fact. Left over from the British occupation."

"Papa?"

"Hm?"

"How—do you get along—without my mother?"

"I don't very well, son."

"I knew you'd say that, but—you've been away from her almost three years!" John hesitated, then plunged ahead. "You—*have* to know—other women, don't you?"

The huge body straightened so suddenly that John felt a pang of fear, but Papa's look was more troubled than indignant. Then the familiar endearing smile lighted his face. "I don't blame you for asking, but—no, Juan." He raised his hand. "Before God, no!"

Harry's shout sent them to their feet and running to the river's edge. A tiny sloop—not a canoe but an honest-to-goodness boat bobbing on the choppy waters of North River—was sailing toward them.

"Ah-ha!" Papa roared, waving both arms. "Look what's coming! How's that for excellent service and pure luxury? No more paddling. A sailing vessel to take us right into port at what my wife is disposed to call a primitive little military outpost!"

Chapter 20

✵✵✵   The outside staircase at Government House was so familiar that McQueen could run all the way down without a thought of the steps. Less than fifteen minutes ago, his hopes higher than the blue St. Augustine sky, he had bounded up those steps and into the governor's office, the two letters from Howard in his pocket.

Now, stiffly, too stunned to notice where he was going, he started back down. At the landing, his boot slipped and he pitched heavily all nine steps to the ground.

How long he lay sprawled in the courtyard, he had no idea. He sat up and tried to settle his tricorn on his head. The pain was excruciating. Blood was dripping from a torn finger on his right hand. He learned of his wrenched knee when he began to struggle to his feet.

What a spectacle I've made of myself, he thought, bracing his trembling body against the stair post. The sight in one eye seemed to be blurring as he peered—hopeful of seeing no one he knew—across the governor's garden, the shortest way home. He wiped at the eye with his uninjured hand. His eyelid was sticky with blood.

He flexed his knee. It might be best to try to walk a bit, no matter how painful the effort, before going back to his house where young John waited to celebrate what they had thought would surely be a new grant. McQueen had even set the wine to cool on the loggia in the crisp January air. If, after a while, he could manage to walk in without a limp, the boy would be less alarmed.

He massaged the throbbing knee and discovered that the fall had snapped the band that held his knee breeches in place. A comical sight he must be—bloody head and trouser leg hanging—St. Augustine's most influential gentleman, after a call on his friend and benefactor, Juan Quesada! He was too injured in both body and spirit to be amused; too shocked, still, to believe what had taken place in the governor's office—just minutes before the plunge down the stairs.

Braced against the post, he tried to reconstruct the nightmare moments in the familiar room. His Excellency had been so happy to see McQueen, he had embraced him. "Welcome back to St. Augustine, Don Juan," he had said, and then, in a pleasant stream of both Spanish and English, had inquired after young Juan and their journey and had ended his warm speech by extending an invitation to father and son for family dinner that very evening.

Then McQueen had handed him the two documents, proud to have once more been able to serve. . . .

Too shaken to stand, he eased himself onto the bottom step, his hat dangling from one hand, his head pounding. He was not at all certain that he could walk home without help, and even if he could, how could he regain enough composure to face his son? Without Quesada's favor, his life lay in ruins—his dreams of the mansion for Anne at Los Molinos, young Juan's future with Panton and Leslie. Even the grants he already held could, if the governor chose, be taken back.

He buried his head in his hands to shut out the memory of the changed face—the icy eyes—the madman's scream with which, without warning, his Excellency had dismissed him. As clearly as though he still stood before the wide desk, Don Juan could see the pale, patrician face twist from that of a welcoming, gracious friend to the mask of a stranger. Quesada had asked him to read aloud both letters and every name on the list. At first, the governor had seemed so gratified that such valuable information had suddenly fallen into their hands that Don Juan's thoughts, as he read, were already on his request for the Los Molinos land.

Seconds after McQueen read the name of Colonel Mc-

Intosh, the fury had exploded. The small, clenched fist had struck the desk, and Juan Quesada had begun to shriek. "Get out! I cannot look more at you. You are—one of them! All Georgians are rotten—rotten! Scum of the earth! My patience is at the end ¡*Vaya!* Do not return!"

McQueen swiped at his wet cheek. Not blood. Tears. His valued friend, his human savior, Juan Nepomuceno de Quesada, whom he loved, had ordered him to leave! He sat shaking his head, trying to clear it. Maybe, he thought, just maybe the fall down the stairs, the blow on his head had affected his memory . . . perhaps none of what he seemed to recall had really happened.

He pulled himself stiffly to his feet and stood looking up at the governor's windows. Suddenly the balcony door jerked open and Quesada's white face stared down at him. McQueen tried to smile when, for an instant, the hard mask appeared about to soften. Then the uniformed figure vanished as though it had never been there, and the door banged shut. It was true. He had not imagined it.

Slowly, he dragged himself across the courtyard toward the Plaza. The risk of meeting someone who would recognize him was far greater there, but work on the new church had stopped for a month for lack of funds, and the building site would be deserted. He headed for the privacy and the shelter of God's house; portions of four walls were up. A few moments' rest there alone, a prayer for help and comfort, and he would surely feel equal to going home. The shadowy interior of the unfinished sanctuary would be the place to sort out his thoughts, to devise an acceptable story for his son. He would, of course, tell the truth about the fall down the Government House stairs. He was almost glad that he had fallen; his injuries would divert young Juan's concern from the interview with Quesada.

The Plaza was empty save for a lone woman. His lacerated eye was swelling, but from a distance she appeared to be no one he knew. At least, he could be certain that no official's wife would be out on the streets alone at this hour. The ladies would all be taking their siestas.

Then, the woman began to run toward him, her long red skirt flying. When she called his name, he knew he was trapped. It was Ysabel Perpal.

He must have slept for more than three hours, because when he opened the one eye which would still open, a lamp burned in what was obviously the señora's bedroom and the sky outside was dark. His twisted knee ached; his head throbbed. He was alone in the room, and in Ysabel's usually noisy house, there wasn't a sound.

He eased himself up onto the edge of the bed and tested his leg. He believed that, with effort, he could walk. At the señora's looking glass, he saw that the blood had been washed from his head and face. The torn finger had been cleansed and bandaged. Then he began to remember the woman leading him gently into her first-floor bedroom, where with the utmost care she had lifted his legs, one at a time, onto the bed and removed his boots.

Still peering at his battered face in the glass, he remembered also the high flush of color in her cheeks as she worked over him, sponging blood from his heavy, matted hair and massaging his knee with goose grease. His mouth still tasted bitter from the draft of boneset tea she'd forced down his unwilling throat.

"It will ease pain of the body," she had said. "Drink it. You are filled with pain."

Why had she refused to get young Juan to take him to the Military Hospital? Why had she put herself to so much bother? Where was the señora now? Where was Juan?

He found his tricorn on a wall peg, slipped into his heavy jacket, and limped across the room in his stocking feet, hat and shoes in hand.

"You are awake?" Ysabel called from the alcove.

He opened the door and smiled weakly, embarrassed by her intense scrutiny.

Finally, she asked, "You feel better?"

"*Si*, señora. Thanks to you. You're most kind, but I must hurry home. My son will be worried."

Her short, husky laugh was almost tender. "You will hurry to no place. You will do well to walk. I have been to your house. Juan knows you are cared for." Her face grew solemn. "He worships you as one should worship only God."

Don Juan tried a small, appreciative laugh, but his whole face hurt. "My son and I will find a way to thank you properly, señora," he said and started to limp past her in the direction of the street door.

With one swift motion, she flung a bright shawl across her shoulders, then placed her strong arm around his waist to support him, her body warm and firm against his. Slowly, they moved toward the door, but before she led him into the street, the señora looked both ways, then laughed. "There is no one in sight to gossip that his Excellency's favorite *americano* is being led home—drunk—by a Minorcan peasant!"

This time, her flippant mention of the governor left him with nothing humorous or even appropriate to say as he shuffled across the dark street beside her, trying not to remember the agony with Quesada.

At his gate, she said, "And do not thank me . . . you are a lonely man, with no wife to bind your wounds. I have known joy to serve you."

He tried to bow.

The señora propped him against the gatepost, jerked the bell, shouted for John, and vanished into the darkness.

McQueen rationalized that he had not really lied to young John when he explained that the governor that day had felt too ill for conversation. He had, in fact, almost convinced himself that, indeed, his friend must have been so nervous from the repeated attacks of fever that he had simply been unable to control his anger once he actually heard the names of the disloyal settlers.

His son seemed to be satisfied with the story, although he felt the boy studying him during the long evenings when they both pretended to be reading. He was not certain John believed that only his father's body ached. When possible, he tried to keep John talking on other subjects and so had learned in detail of the renovations at Oatland, of Grandfather Smith's last moments, and of how Eliza disappeared each night into her room to write to her idol, Cousin Margaret, or to study the Spanish grammar he'd sent, preparing herself, John insisted, for the day when she could visit St. Augustine again.

An unnatural gloom hung over the St. George Street

house. His injuries were healing almost too fast. Once he was able to be out and around the city again, everyone would begin to notice that his visits to Government House had stopped. Ordinarily, Don Dimas Cortés, Don Gonzalo Zamarano, Colonel Morales, and surely his new business agent, Don Bartolomé de Castro, would have stopped by to wish him a speedy recovery. Of the men he knew, only Father O'Reilly and John Leslie had come. Of late, even Leslie had not been there.

His deepest hurt had been the continued silence of Quesada himself, who heretofore had always walked through Government House Gardens if he knew that Don Juan had even a slight cold.

The señora, who did come twice a day, had, like young John, made no further mention of the governor. None, that is, except yesterday afternoon, when she arrived with a basket of oranges on her arm.

"You will taste more sweetness in these, Don Juan, than in all the fruit of his Excellency's sour trees!"

As he watched her peel the largest orange for him, he mused, "I don't know how to begin to repay you for your kindness to me—and to Juan."

"Wh-ht!" She popped a juicy piece into his mouth. "Far better to have a woman come to call than the highest officials in the presidio. No?"

Dr. Travers, the royal surgeon at the Military Hospital, had urged him to exercise the injured knee by walking. Instead, he sat hour after hour in the shadowy parlor and brooded over the irony that his once valuable influence with the Georgians along the frontier had now become his downfall. For years, it had been Don Juan McQueen who had kept them convinced that it would be to their advantage in the long run to remain quiet; to leave well enough alone; to take full advantage of their fertile, tax-free Spanish land.

Round and round in his mind the questions rolled: What had changed? Why had his Excellency turned against him? Had he not been the one to bring the incriminating evidence? Had he not chosen loyalty to His Majesty above loyalty even to his old friend McIntosh?

John had begun work with Leslie four days a week.

The house seemed empty, but at least for the hours the boy was away, there was no need to pretend that he had no fear of losing all he had gained in East Florida—even the dream of Los Molinos de McQueen.

Once, he had almost asked Father O'Reilly's help. Quesada, a religious man, was devoted to the priest. If anyone could convince his Excellency that McQueen was still his obedient servant, the priest could. But his friendship with O'Reilly had been more social than spiritual. The humiliation of such a plea was more than he could face.

Prayer did not help. Time after time he had knelt on the painful knee, begging God to wipe out the governor's injustice, pleading for the whole hideous episode to be blotted out, the friendship restored. Once, at his private altar, he had even put his deepest fear into words: "Blessed Savior, save me from ruin—a second time!"

During his latest visit, Father O'Reilly had seemed rather pointedly solicitous of McQueen's gloomy state of mind; but once more they had talked around the real trouble, and Don Juan's only thought, when O'Reilly left, was of the broken, dead body of the Christ and the gray, dead face of Narciso Font.

On a windy, chill February morning, young John, unable to face another hopeless day, woke up determined to find help from someone. For a month he had watched his father suffer from far more than the fall down Government House steps. The man was in pain from trouble too deep, too tormenting to discuss even with his son. For a few days after the accident, John had expected to be told what had happened at the meeting that day with Quesada. But the weeks had dragged by, and now he knew only that something must be done.

I'm tired of it, he thought as he left the house an hour before he was due at Leslie's office. It was hard with Mama, but it's worse somehow with my father. He seems so much more helpless. . . .

On impulse, he crossed the street and knocked at Ysabel Perpal's door.

"*¿Su padre?*" The woman didn't even say good morning.

He followed her inside. They stood facing each other in the tiny parlor. "Señora, what's wrong between my father and the governor? Have you heard any rumors?"

Her face darkened. "Juan Nepomuceno de Quesada is—evil! He has turned his demon onto that good man—at last."

"But why? *Why?*"

"Because he is crazy! A brilliant, weak, ambitious, crazy man who can love only himself. A ship fitted together as Quesada is fitted together would not float!" The expressive clasped hands tipped to one side. "Such a ship would list—and sink."

"But the papers we brought from San Vicente were so valuable to his Excellency and to the colony, my father expected—" He stopped, unsure of how much she knew. "Señora, if certain men whose names were on those papers had been arrested, a lot of his Excellency's troubles with the Georgians would have been lessened."

She smiled crookedly. "How do you know they were not arrested? There are more Georgians locked into the Castillo now! Your father has not heard?"

John stared. "No one's told him anything! Not even Leslie. It's as though they've all turned against him."

"The men of the city, they *know* Quesada. They fear the devil in him. Even Father Miguel O'Reilly would not dare to cross him!"

He started for the door. "So, my father suffers alone—in the dark."

The señora nodded. "In the dark. But—try to wait. Quesada is too ill to govern." She held up a warning finger. "He will some day be well, or—he will be recalled."

"Either way, it could be too late for my father."

"We can pray, *niño.*"

Head down, John walked slowly up St. George Street. The señora could pray. He meant to *do* something. Maybe Leslie would be at the office early today, too. Even if it cost him his job, he was going to come right out and ask for help. Someone of influence had to act. Papa's whole future lay in the pale, nervous hands of a madman.

◆　◆　◆

"I don't know," Leslie said, fingering a stick of sealing wax on his desk. "I just don't know what to say to you. Your father has been his Excellency's closest friend. His most trusted adviser."

"Then, how can there suddenly be nothing between them? Even if she agrees, how can we let my mother come, with—"

"With the man who has been your father's security not even speaking to him? I don't know that either." Leslie tossed the wax aside and folded his arms. "Would it help if I told you a little of what's been happening this past month?"

"Oh, yes, sir, it would! You see, I feel a terrible responsibility for—both my parents."

"I know you do. I'd never allow myself to get maudlin enough to tell you how much I admire you, John. Can I trust you not to tell any of this to your father? Just in case it might in some way further compromise his position with Quesada?"

John hesitated. "I won't tell him if you don't think I should."

"I don't know what I think except that, under the circumstances, you deserve to know. The governor called a *junta*—a conclave of all advisers—about three weeks ago. If you've noticed, I haven't been to see your father since. Nothing personal. I was just afraid he might have gotten wind of the *junta*, and I find him hard to resist."

"He didn't even know there'd been one. He still doesn't."

Leslie picked up the wax stick again, then threw it down. "Poor McQueen! Poor, well-intentioned, trusting John McQueen!"

"Mr. Leslie, is his Excellency—peculiar in his mind?"

His employer studied him, then said carefully, "These outbursts would indicate that, wouldn't they? And yet Quesada's brilliant, you know—a brilliant young man who came up rapidly through the Spanish Civil Service to the high office of governor. Too rapidly, perhaps."

"The *junta*, sir. What happened after my father gave

him the list of names? What's the governor going to do about the Georgians on the frontier?"

"He's already done it. Against the advice of every member of his official staff. Colonel Howard sent a letter of total disapproval of Quesada's wild scheme. Did no good whatever. Some twenty or thirty merely suspicious settlers are right out there now in the Castillo. Howard's Rural Militia's out hunting for more to arrest."

"What about McIntosh?"

"On a ship bound for Havana—and prison at Morro Castle. Along with Abner Hammond. I might as well tell you—his Excellency went mad! That list of names—all but Hammond, men who'd accepted the favor of Spain—turned loose his demons. Your father may have been his fist victim. He chanced to be the man who handed him the list. Has he told you what happened the day he fell?"

"No, sir. I finally stopped asking."

"Well, I've probably already said too much, so I might as well tell you the rest of what occurred at that meeting. Your father's holdings are still intact—one small but good sign—but his Excellency also ordered burnings between the two rivers."

"Burnings?"

"Nothing would do the governor but that all the settlers with plantations between the St. Mary's and the St. Johns, and west of the St. Johns, had to be moved. Either back to Georgia or closer to St. Augustine, where they could be watched. Clearing out the areas made some sense to us at the meeting that day, but what put all our backs up was his order to burn the homes of these people and their crops!"

"Even when you tell me, sir, I find that hard to believe!"

"Colonel Howard did too. He's the one who'll pay for it. Every burned-out settler will have the right to demand food and supplies and housing. You know how much we have on hand here—not enough for the city."

The young man jumped up. "But—to burn their homes!"

"Sounds like all the tales you've ever heard from your mother about Spaniards, doesn't it? I suppose his Excellency figured the burnings would serve as a warning to any other settler who might be tilting toward the French-American cause."

"Did Colonel Howard actually carry out the order?"

"He had to. We have no more defense line on the St. Mary's whatever. It's all moved down to the south bank of the St. Johns. It's crazy. After urging the Georgians to settle up there, Quesada's emptied most of the area of everything—and everybody."

"Mr. Leslie, what will happen now? What will happen to my father?"

The Scotsman scratched his head. "What will happen to us all? I think even the governor's scared at this point. At least, he sent agents again last week to visit all the main Creek towns. Unless by some miracle his insane tactics work, we're going to need Indian help. Just when the French seemed to be giving up."

"Do you think his Excellency is—really mad?"

"Who knows? He's had a bad tantrum or two in the past—one, I recall, right before your father settled here. The man never has time, you know, to regain his strength between fever attacks. But don't ask me why he took his fury out on your father, of all people, because I don't know."

John dragged the high stool out from his own small desk in the corner and pulled out a ledger. In a moment, he asked, "Do you suppose when he turned on my father—it was at the sight of McIntosh's name on that list?"

"Possibly. There's never been any love lost between the McIntosh family and Spain, in spite of all the land grants Quesada gave this particular member of the clan. That's never made any sense to me, either."

"The Georgians are going to hate His Majesty more than ever when they find out another McIntosh is in Morro Castle."

"Are you going to tell your father that?"

"Should I?"

"Maybe not yet. Let's just ride it out for a while and see what comes next."

◆　　◆　　◆

The schooner expected from Savannah did not appear that day, so John—with no cargo to check off—left work early. Since being alone with his father would now be more awkward than ever, he decided not to go directly home. If only the schooner had docked, there might have been a letter from the family to help occupy his father's mind, but there was no letter and, thanks to both Leslie and the señora, he now knew much more than his father did about what had been going on. He needed time alone to try to sort it all out.

Both hands thrust deep into his jacket pockets, he started down the waterfront past the guardhouse and the sheds and stalls where meat and vegetables and fruit were sold—when there were any. At the southern limits of the city, he stood looking out across Maria Sanchez Creek, still without a helpful thought in his head. His heart had also been set on the possibility of a visit from Mama and the children and Margaret. There could not be a worse time for them to come! Events at Government House in February of the year 1794 were confirming his mother's most exaggerated fears.

Unable to think, he tried to skip a flat piece of shell across the surface of the creek. It sank. He tried another. It sank too, as did every thought. Suddenly nothing mattered as much as getting back to the house to be with Papa.

Walking rapidly now, he cut across the Plaza, past the half-finished church, and into St. George Street. Without clanging his usual signal on the bell at the loggia gate, he shoved it open and hurried inside.

At the foot of the outside stairs stood his father—with Ysabel Perpal in his arms.

The boy ducked back into the street, closed the gate, and leaned against it, wondering what to do. For a moment he felt rage begin to rise. Then, almost as suddenly, it was gone. He waited.

No more than a minute passed when he heard the iron gate latch lift. The señora stepped into the street beside him.

Looking him straight in the eye, she said softly, "*Su padre*, he needs you."

John watched her walk up the street, her head high, almost regal. When she disappeared inside her own house, he reentered the open gate and faced his father.

Green and yellow traces of the ugly bruises still stained the broad face—boyish, even more helpless now, as the big man stood waiting.

"I'm—sorry I burst in without ringing."

"I'm glad. That is, if you're man enough to—forgive me."

John could only nod.

"Undoubtedly God sent you. In time." His father sank into a chair. "I've been most unlike myself of late, I know. I—I've felt so useless. As though no one on the face of the earth—needed me." He looked up. "The señora—appeared to need me."

John sat on the wide chair arm and embraced him. "Then I'm glad I rescued you, Papa," he said.

At the same instant, they both began to laugh. They were still laughing and clinging to each other when the bell jangled briefly and Juan Quesada strolled in, his pale, sharp features so wreathed in smiles that neither McQueen could think of a word to say.

For what seemed to John an endless time, his father stared at the governor as though he were a ghost.

"I have missed you, Don Juan," Quesada said at last, his head cocked quizzically to one side. "Is it not peculiar when the governor himself is forced to discover where his best friend has been hiding for so long a time?" Turning to John, he said, "And you, *hijo*—you hide from me too!"

"We—we've missed you, Excellency," McQueen said simply.

Before John could think of anything sensible to say, the governor was at the gate, ready to leave. There he turned back and, as though ordering a servant, clapped his hands and announced in a crisp voice, "Tonight, with no more delay, you will come, father and son, to Government House for family dinner!"

◆　　◆　　◆

Wide awake in his bed after the strange, almost shocking evening at Government House, John felt numb and a little cheated. Tonight, of all times, he and his father should have settled down for a long talk. Instead, euphoric over his restored friendship, Papa had returned to his own room almost as soon as they reached home.

John could hear the low rumble of Papa's voice now as he said his rosary with far more fervor than the boy had heard in weeks. Why? In gratitude for the grant of the Los Molinos de McQueen land, which Quesada had indeed promised tonight? Or from guilt because he'd been caught holding the señora in his arms this afternoon?

John tried to smile. Either way, Papa sounded more like himself, and even if Quesada had lied to them both, what mattered, he must believe, was not whether Quesada was insane but that his father appeared hopeful again.

He tried to drop off to sleep, as he had so many nights, lulled, often half amused at the length of his parent's prayers, but this time he could not dismiss the memory of the troubling evening. If, as his Excellency claimed, he had been too ill to send a message of sympathy to his injured friend, how could he have felt up to calling that *junta*? The question was, of course, ridiculous; Quesada had not been too ill! During almost every subject discussed at dinner he had deliberately lied to Papa. How was it possible that an intelligent man like Don Juan McQueen could pretend to believe those lies?

On impulse, John grabbed his dressing gown, put on his slippers, and knocked at the door of his father's room. "May I come in?"

The low, rumbling prayers quickened—to the end of a decade, he supposed—and then the door flew open.

"Come in, come in! I'm always ready for one of our good talks, son. At least, I am from this night on." The big man pulled up a chair for John by the brazier and crawled into bed to keep warm. "Too bad the servants are back in their quarters. This would be a fine time for hot tea, wouldn't it?"

John was not smiling. "Quesada lied when he told you Colonel Howard ordered those burnings. The governor ordered them. Howard and every member of the staff tried to talk him out of it. Leslie told me today. He attended the *junta*." When his father remained silent, John added: "Please don't count too much on what the governor says!"

"His Excellency and I have been—still are—fast friends."

"Then why weren't you invited to the *junta*?"

"I have no explanation for that." His father's voice was quiet, almost resigned. "Now that things are right again, I need none. I do need his Excellency. You heard him promise the Los Molinos land. I believe he'll keep that promise. He might not, you know, if I added to his burdens by indicating in the slightest manner that I doubted his word concerning Colonel Howard—and the burnings."

"You don't believe Howard ordered them, do you?"

"Violence of that nature has never been Howard's way. Nor has it been the governor's, at least in the past. I—intend to leave well enough alone."

"I see."

His father got out of bed and came to stand behind his chair. John felt the warmth of the strong hands on his head.

"Son, it's going to be all right. Leave his Excellency to me. The burnings were harsh, no matter who ordered them. But they may quiet some of the thunder on our frontier." He smoothed John's hair, as though comforting them both. "Now, about this afternoon. When I laughed after the señora left so hurriedly, I want you to know I wasn't laughing at her. Or at the seriousness of the moment. I laughed in—relief that my son did not condemn me."

"I know, Papa. I know lots of things I don't say."

"Good boy! Now, it's time for a fine night's sleep for us both." His father plunged back into bed and reached for his nightcap. "If my ears are warm, I sleep like a baby. Have a good rest, son."

"You too."

"By the way," Papa said, pulling on his cap, "it's been a long time since John McIntosh has made a business trip to St. Augustine. In view of what's happened, we must come up with a logical excuse as to why we can't entertain him here on his next trip, you know."

John's anger at Quesada rushed back. He stood in the middle of the room trying to decide if it would be cruel to tell him the truth tonight.

"Colonel McIntosh comes rather often. The man's long overdue."

"Papa?"

"Hm?"

"I kept waiting for Quesada to tell you," John blurted. "Colonel McIntosh has already been here and gone. He was arrested—right after your fall—and shipped out the next day."

"Shipped out?"

"Your friend the governor ordered McIntosh and Abner Hammond sent to Morro Castle."

McQueen fell back against his stack of pillows. "That's going to be hard to explain to your mother, isn't it?"

Chapter 21

✦✦✦ Early in May, Anne McQueen loaded the wagon with her three children, a crate of chickens, and enough clothing for a long visit at her mother's home in Savannah. Her sister Mary Cowper and her niece, Margaret, were due from Jamaica sometime toward the end of the month. "It's only proper," Grandmother Smith had written, "for all of you to stay here in the family home. Goodness knows, Anne, The Cottage is too small and anyway, a mother—along in years as I—likes to believe that her children and grandchildren love her enough to make her home their headquarters. Certainly, young Margaret would never feel adequately entertained out there in the country."

Several days before the Cowpers were due to arrive, Anne left the Smith house on the pretext of shopping and walked rapidly toward Aleck McQueen's office on Commerce Row.

So far, she had managed, in spite of her own anxiety, to keep from her mother rumors of food shortages in East Florida. Her own dread of anything Spanish warred against what appeared to be her mother's cunning way of twisting every event so that it became somehow Big John's fault. No one could ever convince Anne that her husband had had anything whatever to do with the burnings on the frontier. After all, many of the ruined plantations had belonged to family friends.

When the frontier trouble was mentioned, she simply tried to steer conversation to the one fairly hopeful area—

the planned French attack, which did seem to be petering out. Months ago, Georgians and South Carolinians in Anne's social class had sickened of the machinations of both Mangourit and Genêt. They had begun to suspect that French revolutionaries were not motivated only by sympathy toward the American republic. Erratic, pompous Citizen Genêt, now literally tossed out by President Washington, had helped bring about the change of heart among many planter families. Still, she knew that even if French efforts to capture the Floridas failed, M. Mangourit had stirred up a blaze among other Americans which could spread—with or without French aid. On that, her mother was right.

Americans like General Elijah Clark, Governor Moultrie, Georgia's new Governor Mathews, the Hammond brothers, and every McIntosh man meant some day to acquire the Floridas and Louisiana. As much as she'd enjoy not thinking about the whole confusing mess, she had to think. Her husband and son were there, and for the past few weeks, her own desire to visit them had become an obsession.

Anne's latest letter from the wife of Colonel John McIntosh reinforced her fears that many Americans who had accepted free Spanish land and had sworn allegiance to Spain had done so in order to be on the scene when the time came to overthrow the hated Spanish monarchy. Mrs. McIntosh feared for her husband's life each time he went to St. Augustine on business, even though he stayed in the house of John McQueen.

On this issue, Anne's inner warfare raged painfully. Mrs. McIntosh prayed that Big John's high standing with the Spanish might somehow prevent Governor Quesada from suspecting the colonel's desire to overthrow East Florida. For her friend's sake, Anne hoped so too, but at times that high standing of Big John's made her almost ill, since in order to gain and hold it he had had to become a loyal Spanish subject.

She tried, as she crossed Bay Street and started up Commerce Row, to enjoy the soft May morning. She did pause a moment to glance at the usually calming stretch of water beyond the busy wharves, but the inner warfare went on: if Spain lost East Florida, Big John would once more be at the mercy of the Georgia courts!

"I want the truth, Aleck," she said as soon as her brother-in-law had seated her beside his cluttered desk. "*Are* they short of food in St. Augustine? Has the planned French attack really begun to dwindle? Both my husband and young John write that it has. Neither mentions a food shortage. I've a reason for wanting your opinion." Aware of how Aleck loved the sound of his own voice, she added, "I haven't much time. Mother doesn't know I'm here."

"Well, dear lady, it so happens that only last night I was a guest in the home of the British consul, Mr. John Wallace. Splendid gentleman, really. Excellent poker player, although I managed to beat him."

"Did you discuss East Florida?"

"At length. Wallace corresponds regularly, you know, with my brother's treacherous friend, the Spanish governor."

"No, I wasn't aware of that."

"You might say that Wallace is the liaison between Quesada and Georgia Governor Mathews—and sometimes even our President. As is typical of Spanish inefficiency, they have a distinct shortage of consulates in this country. It's fortunate for Quesada that relations are, for the moment at least, rather good between Spain and England."

"That's interesting, Aleck, but Mama thinks I'm shopping. I'll have to take home a few bundles. Please do get to the food shortage—and the immediate French danger."

Aleck rubbed his balding head thoughtfully. "Well, concerning the food shortage, I can report that the brief American embargo was lifted last week."

"Oh? Now, don't go into an explanation of why there was an embargo, but will its disappearance be good for St. Augustine people?"

"John Wallace has already sent down a shipload of flour. More will follow from the British, I presume. But no matter what my brother fails to report, that fiendish governor burned out their food supply locally. I suppose more crops will be planted—by whom, I don't know. Quesada's cleared the area of all but a handful of settlers, those kow-towing to him." He glanced at her, then out at the river. "Don Juan McQueen's holdings were, of course, not de-stroyed."

Anne moved to the edge of her chair. "But do you agree that the French threat is over?"

"I do. That is, as far as the government of the new French republic is concerned. At the end of last month, I wouldn't have given you two pins for the safety of either your son or your husband. The attack from the sea was to have begun the end of April. They may still be expecting it down there—or, with so many French privateers captur-ing mail-bearing ships, they may not have known it was about to take place."

"Aleck, why didn't you tell me?"

"What could you have done, Anne, but worry? As things turned out, Samuel Hammond's plans collapsed. Not one promised French vessel turned up to support the attack." He shook his head. "Now, his poor brother, Abner, is in Morro Castle in Havana. He made the grievous error of entering East Florida in order to buy off some Semi-noles. Your husband's great friend, Quesada, had him arrested—and with no chance to defend himself, Hammond was shipped out the very next day."

Anne shuddered.

"Causes one's blood to run cold, doesn't it? My brother is devoted to a wicked and cruel man."

"What does Mr. Wallace think of Governor Quesada?"

"Wallace puzzles me. He seems to consider Quesada the same as any other official with whom he has dealings. Of course, with their two monarchs on friendly terms, I suppose he has little choice but to assume Quesada to be as honorable as any other Spaniard."

Anne decided to take the plunge. "Aleck, now that you feel the French danger is past, and as soon as I've spent a few weeks with my sister and niece, I'm—taking the chil-dren to St. Augustine."

He gaped at her, puffed his cheeks once, then splut-tered. "Why, Anne—I thought you'd been doing very well. Why the sudden decision?"

"It is not sudden! I've had to force myself to stay here every minute since he went away." To prevent Aleck's response, she hurried on in a lower tone of voice. "What of the men along the frontier who'd already enlisted with M. Mangourit? Will they calm down now that French support has collapsed?"

"Never!" Her brother-in-law's eyes narrowed. "The United States needs the Floridas—and Louisiana. Whether those brave fellows can do it, I have no way of knowing. But they'll try. We'll get all that Spanish land one day."

The last thing Anne wanted was an argument with this exasperating man who had been kind. She felt herself begin to tremble, but managed to ask, "Do you—really *want* Big John trapped again?"

Aleck's fat hand pounded the desk; his jowls shook. "I detest anything Catholic and Spanish—as deeply as any McIntosh alive! I'd rather see my brother dead than loyal to a Catholic monarchy." He stood up. "I forbid you to go!"

"You forbid me?"

"You and your children are living on funds borrowed against my holding, dear lady. You have, by the default of my brother, become my responsibility."

True, he had signed a note for young John, but so far every payment had been met. Too angry to trust what she might say, Anne started for the door.

"Now, this will never do! Come back, my dear. Sit down again." Aleck was wheezing in his effort to control his fury. "Let me tell you the real reason I forbid you to go. I think I've earned the right."

She came stiffly back to her chair.

Still short of breath, he perched awkwardly on the corner of the desk and started over in a somewhat quieter voice. "I grant you, things are better down there than a month ago. The madman Quesada has, according to Wallace, even received some additional troops from Havana. The major French attack has collapsed. *But*"—he wagged a thick finger—"General Elijah Clark's forces—including part of the company of Georgia Militia under his command—are still spread out for miles along the west bank of the Oconee River. Clark wasn't interested in helping France colonize Florida; he was making use of the French. Knowing the general as I do, losing their support will not deter him. He's itching to kill both Spaniards and Indians. The man's wanted trade in the Floridas since the British held them during our Revolution. Clark won't be stopped for long. Neither, my dear lady, will Georgia!"

"But Aleck—this year? Wouldn't I have time to take my children for a visit with their father?"

"Anne, listen to me, the Georgia Assembly is right now debating an act whereby the state will put on sale miles and miles of land claimed by both the Creeks and the Spaniards. Your husband knows none of this, but I happen to know that Elijah Clark means to buy up much of that land. Nothing short of the Georgia Militia can stop him—and he's a leader in that. Furthermore, the Georgians who have settled across the St. Mary's are not going to go on bending their necks to the Spanish yoke just because the French government has given up. They're working from inside the colony, right now, every minute." He laid his heavy hand on her shoulder. "This is not the time to go, Anne! My brother is known to have been a friend of Elijah Clark. Quesada has only John McQueen's word that he's not still Clark's friend. John is also congenial with many of the very settlers who want to overthrow the government he pretends to serve. One false move on his part and he'll end up rotting in Morro Castle with Abner Hammond—*and* Colonel McIntosh!"

Anne's hands flew to her mouth. "Aleck! Colonel John McIntosh too? In a—a Spanish prison?"

"I'd hoped to spare you that ugly news. Your stubborn insistence forced me to tell you." He stood up. "If you're still determined to go to him yourself, I have no power to stop you. But you must not take Eliza and William and Sallie. At least, not until we see what's happening a year from now. If your husband's hateful little colony survives this year—then we'll talk again. I *do* forbid you to take the children for another year."

15 May, 1794
Savannah

My Dearest Husband,

It is late at night, but since I have not written this week, I must, before I sleep. My silence has been due to the happy early arrival of our guests from Jamaica, whose voyage was far better than expected. The Cowpers are well, though tired. Tell young John that his Cousin is even more beautiful than I remembered. They both send warm regards to the two of you.

Dear, dear John—have my recent deeper longings to be with you reached across the miles? I will come to the point of this letter at once. With news of the fading French threat, I went to Aleck to discuss a visit to St. Augustine a few weeks from now. He forbids it. Please do not be angry with him. He knows firsthand, evidently, that General Elijah Clark poses a new danger. At least, he forbids me to bring the children. My woman heart longs to come on alone, but my mother heart dictates otherwise. I pray for your patience and understanding. I could not bear the children's heartbreak if they had to stay behind. It has helped having Mary Esther Huger, and now my sister and Margaret will in some measure ease my own impatience as I wait. Aleck feels that a year may change the situation, and so I promise you, beloved husband, that we will be there one year from now. Since my father's death, my loneliness for you has grown until at times I feel I will choke on it.

Mary Esther considers me a fool to permit anything to separate us, with the world so full of tragedy. She has had no word from her son in months, but did learn from a Paris friend that Mme Lafayette is in danger of the guillotine and that her husband is still in prison.

Aleck told me of the dreadful fate which befell Colonel John McIntosh. It is all so confusing and terrifying. I long to be with you, yet I am afraid to leave Georgia. Surely, I am a weak woman and do not know, except by God's grace, how I have lived so long away *from you, whom my heart loves as much as ever—if not more.*

Just think, in one year when, the Lord willing, I see you at last, I will be nearly forty-two and you will be forty-four. I must sleep, but at least this scrawl can be en route to you tomorrow by some means. We all send deep affection to young John and I send my heart to you.

Your faithful and loving wife,
Anne McQueen

PART 3

Chapter 22

✳✳✳ Sometimes, listening to night sounds—autumn insects, a horseman riding by, soldiers laughing or scuffling in the street below his window—young John let his thoughts roam back to the hot June day when he and Papa first read the memorable letter from Mother, written after her talk with Uncle Aleck. They had heard often since, of course, but that letter more than four months ago had changed life in the St. George Street house. There was still a long wait, but she had at last promised to come.

"Just think, son," Papa had said over and over, "I'm going to get acquainted with William the Stranger! Do you realize how little I know my younger son?"

The day the letter arrived, John had been sent on the run back to Leslie's office to fetch the largest sheets of paper in stock. Then, his father had worked for hours marking off each sheet with dates to cover the waiting time—from June of this year, 1794, to June of next year. Each evening, with a flourish, he had placed a large X across the day just ended. When Papa and Harry went on journeys, the current sheet was in his saddlebag. The page for August had even gone with him to Havana, where, as Father O'Reilly's agent, Papa went to request furnishings for the altar of the church and for bells.

It galled John that Uncle Aleck had undoubtedly been right to delay the visit. True, the summer months had been relatively quiet, but Quesada's Indian runners continued to report that more and more Americans were joining Elijah

Clark's forces. Rumors also reached the Plaza that an occasional band of Creeks was trading secretly with Samuel Hammond. At Papa's suggestion, Quesada had ordered new medals struck as gifts for the demanding Seminoles around St. Augustine. Small border forays still went on to the north. In the city itself, though, the days dragged by without event.

Only to Leslie did young John admit that, in the smothering summer heat, some of his own enthusiasm for life in St. Augustine had dimmed. Just knowing that Margaret Cowper was as nearby as Savannah—that he would not see her for months—brought new restlessness. Not that he wanted to live or work back in Georgia, but there were times when his father's perpetually hopeful speeches wore a bit thin.

The friendship with Quesada appeared stronger than ever, but in his heart, Papa seemed to count most on the common sense of President Washington. "He won't permit Governor Mathews to drag his feet much longer," Papa prophesied. "After all, Georgia is part of the union. I predict Washington will one day order Mathews to send the state Militia after Clark. Quesada's bombarding Philadelphia with complaints. The President wants an end to the border trouble too, son." Then his father would laugh. "I'm a loyal Spanish subject, but I still trust the American President!"

John had no reason to doubt his father's judgment concerning affairs of state. After all, in one way or another, he was a man of long and varied experience in such matters. But more and more frequently, John was beginning to understand his mother's fears.

Of course, he meant never to admit this to his father. Why upset him when he could talk to John Leslie? The Scotsman hated St. Augustine and lived there only because he had no choice. He also enjoyed complaining and confessed once that it was an enormous relief to him that Don Juan McQueen's son saw things as they really were. "Since you do," Leslie had said, "you just may be able to keep your father's feet touching the ground—at least once in a while."

In October, another shipload of troops arrived from

Havana, and Quesada, ill again with fever, ordered Acting Governor Bartolomé Morales to send Rural Militia Captain Don Juan McQueen to San Vicente as troop escort. San Vicente on the St. Johns was, of course, too near Los Molinos de McQueen for his father to resist an inspection trip to his new property. So, for a month, John lived alone in the St. George Street house.

After work, he passed the hours by helping Pedro and Harry with the massive task of housecleaning ordered by McQueen before he left. "I know we've months yet to wait," Papa had told Pedro, "but Doña Ana's eyes are not only beautiful—they're sharp. We'll start now. Every windowpane must sparkle. Every window sill must be clean enough to eat from. Fresh paint on the loggia gate and—oh, new cane seats in every chair in the house! Never mind that more dust will fall. Each winter month and into spring, we'll clean it all again!"

John and Pedro were painting the loggia gate one evening about two weeks after his father's departure when a young Government House servant raced through the garden and began to chatter at Pedro in the Minorcan dialect.

"His Excellency, he demand to see you at once," Pedro translated for John.

"But, I thought the governor was ill—in bed."

"Today he is well enough to be no longer in his bed. Go now," Pedro urged. "His Excellency struck this fellow once today. He does not want to be struck another time!"

His heart pounding, John hurried after the Minorcan boy through the garden and up the staircase to Quesada's office. When he knocked, the governor's own voice invited him in. Juan Quesada, his face as white as the pillows against which he was propped in his high-backed chair, appeared far from angry. He was smiling.

John's nervousness eased a little. "I'm sorry about my appearance, Excellency," he said, "I was painting the loggia gate. Your servant seemed to consider your request urgent."

"*Sí,* Juan—urgent." The governor gestured toward the nearest chair. "You will understand that I cannot rise to greet you."

"Of course, sir. I'm glad to see you at your desk." He

sat down, not knowing what to expect. "Nothing's happened to my father?"

Quesada laughed. "No, no, no! But when he learns of the glorious news, he may for joy fly on to Paradise!"

"It doesn't take much to make him happy."

"That eternal hope in his heart is a gift from God," the governor said, with reverence. "*Su padre* is—a man of greatness. He is my friend. *Mi amigo querido.* The one true friend of my heart."

"I hope you know how important that is to him, Excellency."

"And to me." Quesada shuffled through some papers on his desk, selected one. "Here—read. It is written *en inglés.* It was translated for me. I will watch your face as you read!"

Puzzled, John took the paper. The further he read, the more he smiled. His father's prediction had been right. Quesada's endless complaints to the President had turned the trick. Georgia Governor Mathews had finally obeyed Washington's order to send troops after Elijah Clark with full military assistance from Carlos Howard. The old general and all his troops were now back in Georgia.

"*¿Es muy bueno?*" The frail governor began to applaud, then to laugh. "Is this not the best of news?"

"It certainly is, Excellency! You're right. My father may take wings."

"I applaud that the devil Clark is no longer claiming our land," Quesada said warmly. "I applaud also, Juan, that with my own eyes, I now see you are one of us in your heart!" He pushed back his yellow hair. "I am still not strong enough for much talking. But I did not send for you only for the good news. There is another reason."

"At your service, Excellency."

"Spanish Indian Agent Señor Hambly reports the Creek towns remain loyal to His Majesty, Carlos the Fourth. The defensive military skill of Colonel Howard *and* the diplomatic skill of Juan Quesada have once more brought peace to East Florida." He ticked off the months. "March, April, May, June, July, August, September—and now October. No dangers to the residents of St. Augustine." He smiled warmly. "Will this good news not bring your mother here before June?"

Who could begin to guess, John wondered, what this erratic man might say or do next? "I don't quite know how to thank your Excellency for such concern. I hadn't realized you—understood my father's loneliness."

"Don Juan is my friend! The man has suffered too long. Why would I not want to see the suffering end?"

John's smile was tentative. "I wish I could express myself as—as I'm sure he would if he were here."

"Do not tire me with gratitude. Speak to me of your mother. Does she love him as he believes?"

"Oh, yes, Excellency," he said warmly. "She loves him with all her heart."

Then, without warning, his feeling of warmth gave way to a chill. The quixotic, almost womanly Spaniard looking at him now with such deep concern was not only the same man who had burned settlers' homes along the frontier; he was the man who had, a few months ago, shattered his father's spirit.

Quesada lifted his hand to end the interview. "So. Doña Ana McQueen loves him. That is all I need to understand. The pain is once more in my head. I must ask you to leave, *hijo*. I will go to my chapel to pray."

John stood up. "Of course, Excellency."

"I will pray your mother comes soon. Perhaps heaven will grant my desire to be well when she arrives." He laughed softly. "I suspect she believes me to be—an evil man. If God will answer my plea for health, I promise you she will learn not only to admire but—to trust Juan Nepomuceno de Quesada."

As John walked slowly back through Government House Gardens, a flat, leaden cloud slid across the sun. He was puzzled that a cloud had also settled over his enthusiasm of a few moments ago. Why? Quesada was right. With the threat from Elijah Clark past, Uncle Aleck would now have no valid reason to forbid the visit. There was still a food shortage, but Papa had ways of handling that. Their meals were monotonous but not scarce. He could picture his father pounding suave, unbending Colonel Howard on the back over the good news about Clark. If his mother came soon, Margaret would be with her. That alone should have sent him racing to the house to shout the good word to Harry, to Pedro, to Black Katrina—to anyone who would listen.

The cloud was passing from the sun, but not from his mind.

The coquina rim of his father's well had become a favorite place to think. He sat down now and stared into the wet, mossy depths of the well. Fragile maidenhair fern grew in St. Augustine wherever there was dampness and shade. The wall on which he sat was thick with the delicate, bright fronds. Mama had always loved maidenhair fern. She would like that much about the tiny city anyway, he thought, and realized that the cloud over his thoughts had somehow to do with his mother. Mama's ingrained fear of Spanish Catholics had always made it hard for him to imagine her actually there among them, but he believed almost as deeply as Papa that she had begun to change a little. At least, she wanted to come. Why was he disturbed?

From somewhere upstairs in the house, he could hear Pedro teaching Harry a Minorcan song. Neither boy knew that he wasn't still with the governor; he would not be missed if he were to be gone a few minutes longer.

Protecting Mama had become a habit. On impulse, he found himself hurrying to the house across the street, not at all sure what he meant to say, but compelled to talk to Señora Perpal.

"You will drink tea, Juan?"

"No, thank you. I can't stay long."

The señora nodded toward a chair, but remained standing. John sat uneasily.

"*¿Su padre?* You hear from your father? An accident to him?"

He shook his head.

"You frown. Why?"

"Señora?"

The woman responded with a slight lift of her head.

"You know, of course, that—my mother is coming for a visit."

Slowly, never taking her eyes from his face, Ysabel

lowered herself onto the edge of a straight chair. "*Sí*. She will come perhaps in the month of June. More than half a year from now."

"There's a good chance she might come—sooner," he said, unable to return her gaze. "I've just learned that General Clark's been driven out of the Oconee region. The last threat seems to have vanished—for the moment, anyway."

"Who tell you this?"

"His Excellency."

"Wh-ht!"

Too nervous to stay seated, John walked around. "It's true. I saw the report myself. In fact, the governor hopes my mother will come right away, while things are quiet."

"Why do you tell me?"

"I'm not sure."

The señora too was standing now. "Then I will tell you. You are here to find out about your father and me. So, you will be told—but only if you look at me. Voices can lie. Eyes—between friends—cannot." The intense, dark eyes were bright with tears, but she spoke slowly, evenly. "The young are cruel. You are young. Yet, you saw what you saw, that day. You deserve to know. I can speak only for Ysabel Perpal, not for your father. The census of St. Augustine declares me to be married to Antonio Perpal—absent. He is *absent*. From my life and from my heart. I hate him."

The lift of her chin, the straight back made John think of his mother.

"Only by the law of the Church is Ysabel Perpal the wife of Antonio!" She waited, then the husky voice grew tender. "By the truth, Ysabel Perpal loves Don Juan McQueen enough to want his wife here because—he desires her."

For a long moment, they faced each other, then she touched his shoulder. "Only the two of us? You will promise? Your father does not know. He must not."

Shaken, John could only nod in agreement.

Her hand dropped to her side. "If your mother robs me of the months remaining in this year, I can do nothing." She shrugged. "I *did* nothing but—live dull, flat days before he came to St. Augustine. I can as well do nothing again. *Buenas tardes, hijo.* Do not worry."

"Thank you, señora," he managed, just above a whisper.

She allowed him to go to the door alone, but called, "I love him—as my child too! Your father *is* a little boy. Even that stiff Irishman, Father Miguel O'Reilly, can find no sin in—in caring for a child!"

Chapter 23

✤✤✤ I had given you up for dead, Don Juan," Quesada called, as he crossed his office to welcome McQueen on a cloudy, gray November afternoon. "On such a day, you are a most cheering sight!"

"*Gracias*, Excellency," McQueen said, escorting the frail governor to his chair behind the desk. "Colonel Howard sends his respects and wants you to know our new troops are working out well."

"Do not lead me about as though I am still ill! Can you not see I am stronger?"

"Indeed! And I'm overjoyed. Young Juan told me how ill you've been during my absence. But with our fortunes improving, I predict your Excellency will now remain in health. You deserve to feel well enough to enjoy your success, *amigo*." Don Juan pulled up his favorite chair. "Believe me, there's real celebration on the St. Johns among the loyal settlers now that Elijah Clark's back in Georgia. I bring greetings and high commendation for your Excellency's masterful handling of an impossible situation. Captain Andrew Atkinson, Señor Timothy Hollingsworth, Don Francis Philip Fatio, Don George Fleming, Captain Peter Carne, and many others wish to be remembered."

The governor sat smiling. "I did not realize," he joked, "that we had so many citizens loyal to me. But do not stop talking. Your words of praise give me strength. Indeed, I share the success with Colonel Howard, but I intend to enjoy my own accomplishments as well. Do you not believe me to be a genius to order Don Carlos Howard to pull our defense line back from the troubled St. Mary's?"

"I do, and Howard has carried out those orders in every respect. After escorting our new troops safely to San Vicente, I visited my various holdings on the St. Johns." He beamed. "Especially the beautiful Los Molinos de McQueen—and wherever I stopped, I heard no bad reports of any kind."

"No sign of French privateers in our waters?"

"None. My son tells me even the pirates haunting us here around Anastasia Island have vanished too."

"Like a flame blown out. Young Juan has told you also, I am sure, that Señor Hambly reports loyalty among the savages?"

"Yes. The signs are all good. God has protected us—with your Excellency's help, of course. And with a bit of an assist from the Georgia Militia—the companies not under Clark's command."

They laughed. Then Quesada asked carefully, "How do you feel about the fate of your old friend, Elijah Clark?"

"I pity him, of course. But—good riddance."

"I am jealous even for one shred of pity. Still, since the old man is now stopped in his evil efforts to destroy us and our Indian allies, I forgive you." He paused, eyes twinkling. "Now, tell me, Doña Ana will come soon?"

"I wrote to her from San Vicente the instant we learned Clark was gone." His face clouded a little. "There is only one reason why she might not agree."

"What is that?"

"I beg your Excellency's forgiveness for mentioning him, but—my wife is devoted to the whole McIntosh family."

Quesada's eyes narrowed. "So?"

"You recall, I'm sure, my telling you once of my mother-in-law's domination over Doña Ana. The old lady knows Colonel John McIntosh is in prison."

The governor shook his head. "Poor Don Juan McQueen! I must remember to thank God to be married only to my wife—not to her mother, who is safely back in Spain." He sat up straight. "But—I will now impart a secret. My extraordinary success as governor of East Florida is owing, in part, to my adherence to a posture of defense, *not* attack. I sent McIntosh and Hammond to Morro Castle only in order to shock the other traitorous settlers. The effect has been as I expected." He smiled slyly. "Now, I have no need even for so small an offensive act toward the United States. You do not need to inform me that *el presidente* desires the release of Colonel McIntosh, even though he pretends to be a Spanish subject."

"In other words, since Washington helped us with Clark, you will not lift a finger to thwart the President's efforts to free McIntosh."

They sat for a moment in the altogether pleasant silence of mutual admiration and understanding. When McQueen stood to leave, Quesada whispered impishly, "You will promise to run all the way through my gardens to tell me—when the good news arrives from Doña Ana?"

"Never, Excellency! As my son teases—I'll be too happy to run—I'll fly!"

The prospect had seemed dull, going from shop to shop alone in the carriage with twelve-year-old William, but Margaret Cowper had been pleasantly surprised. The two had laughed their way in and out of almost every shop along the Bay and danced for joy when they found a large packet of letters waiting at Uncle Aleck's office. More than ever, Margaret looked forward to the visit to St. Augustine next June because William—away from Grandfather Smith's house—was as amusing and lighthearted and full of surprises as she remembered Uncle John McQueen.

"Has anyone told you how much you're like your father, William?"

He drove the carriage deftly around the corner into Bull Street. "I sure hope I'm like him. I get mad every time Grandmother says I look like Mama. Who wants to be—pretty?"

"I do."

"You are."

"John thinks I am. Do you know he vows he's going to marry me some day?"

William grinned at her. "My brother?"

"Your brother, John."

William turned off the street into a lane and reined the horse to a stop at the end of it, by the back door of the Smith house. "Do you think you'll ever marry him? Is old John the reason you want to go with us to Florida?"

She smiled her most mischievous smile. "Perhaps."

"Perhaps you'll marry him?"

"No, silly. Perhaps he's one of the reasons I want to go. Your father's another, though. I was just a little girl when I saw Uncle John last, but I remember him as the handsomest, most gallant, funniest man on earth!"

"Yeah," the boy said solemnly. "Course I don't know how he is by now. I was just eight when he went away. Four years can make a lot of difference in people. I've sort of—had to take his place."

"You've done a fine job too."

He sighed. "Aw, I dunno. I can't say I like it much. I hate work. Makes me tired to have folks depending on me. I think Papa has the right idea, even though it got him into all that trouble." He thought a moment, then added proudly: "My father didn't like to do anything but buy up land! All you have to do that way is sign a bunch of papers."

Margaret laughed. "I'll bet you don't tell your mother things like that."

"Naw. Grandmother either. They both believe in work." He sighed heavily again. "I sure wish we didn't have to wait six more months to visit Papa. I'm tired. I need a good, long rest."

Margaret had watched her Aunt Anne before when letters came. The sheer romance of it took her breath away. To think a woman past forty would still look so eagerly for word from a man even older than she! In the Smith kitchen, where they deposited their purchases, she watched her aunt flip hurriedly through the stack, then hide one letter in her apron pocket.

"Grandmother's been settled in the parlor for over an hour, Margaret, expecting each one of these to be read aloud. I happen to prefer to read my husband's letters alone."

"I think you have a perfect right," Margaret said. "You don't feel guilty about it, do you?"

Her aunt smiled. "Sometimes, yes, sometimes no."

"Don't let the old darling get by with that. Take full advantage of our being here!" Margaret took the stack of mail. "In fact, here's another one for you from Mrs. Huger. Go right up to your room now and read them both. William and I can perfectly well handle Grandmother."

Alone upstairs, the door to her room closed, Anne broke the seal on Mary Esther Huger's letter first and read it quickly. The news was all terrifying. Not only had Mary Esther learned from a French friend that her son, Frank, was deeply involved in a dangerous attempt to free the marquis from prison, still more tragedy had struck the pitiful life of Mme Lafayette. Mrs. Huger, writing from her home in South Carolina, had enclosed a translation of an article from a French newspaper, set down in such grisly detail, Anne thought she might faint as she read: Mme Lafayette's mother, grandmother, and sister had been hauled in the same tumbril to the guillotine!

Anne could only stare at the page and thank God that she had escaped reading any of it to her own mother and sister and the children.

She was able, finally, to finish Mary Esther's letter:

How I manage to live through these days not knowing that my son is safe in the midst of such horror, I do not know. My heart bleeds, as I'm sure does yours, for gentle, long-suffering little Mme Lafayette, but I can only take this opportunity to remind you, beloved Anne, that I have prayed once more that God will do whatever is necessary to drive you to East Florida! The world around us is rocking on its axis from bloodshed and tragedy. Why add to the chaos by keeping your own heart in turmoil when you could so easily go down to the wharf and board a ship to St. Augustine? Do it, Anne, I beg you—before it's too late!

Nervously, Anne refolded the pages and held Big John's letter—still unopened. Where was poor Mme Lafayette when the horror had struck three generations of her loved ones? Had she been forced, as had so many others, to watch? Or had she managed somehow to reach the marquis in prison, as she'd vowed to do? *Her children with her!*

As always, Anne kissed the seal on her husband's letter, then breathed a prayer for him before she broke it.

As she read the bold, familiar script—page after page—its message so positive, so surprising, so full of hope and joy—so welcome, she had to keep drying her eyes to go on.

> *I repeat, dearest Anne, that the danger here has passed. Elijah Clark has been soundly whipped and is no longer a threat to the peace of the colony. With my whole, eager heart, I plead with you to come to me at the earliest possible moment. There is now no reason to wait until June. None whatsoever. You have promised to come and I hold you to that promise. I need you and our children. And once you are in my arms again, we can live each glorious hour as though it will never, never end. . . .*

Still holding the letter, she fell to her knees beside the bed. "Dear Father in heaven," she whispered. "I need him too. Our children need him! Suddenly, Lord, the time has come. I've fought Mary Esther's advice long enough. I'm *not* waiting any longer. While my sister is here to stay with Mother, we're going. Just as soon as we can find a way to get there. The world *is* too—too full of horror to wait."

Numbly, she got to her feet and stood looking out at her mother's dying November garden.

If I sin by taking the children into that heathen country, I'll ask forgiveness—later. Later, Lord. . . .

After the others were asleep on the cold December night before they were to sail for St. Augustine, Eliza and Cousin Margaret lay in bed wide awake.

"You know, you've really grown up since I've been here," Margaret whispered. "Do you realize that even a month ago, you'd have trembled at the thought of giggling over Grand?"

"Really? But I do still respect her."

"So do I. She's like a handsome old brigantine in full sail." Her laugh tinkled. "I can still see the look on her face when she said with that careful smile, 'Anne, my dear, you know perfectly well your letter may not reach him. Big John could be miles away from St. Augustine if you sail so soon! Whatever would you and the children do if you got there only to find him off on one of his wild missions?' " Imitating her aunt now, Margaret went on, " 'Why, I'd wait, of course, until he got back.' Anne McQueen's changed too, believe me! And how romantic, Eliza—how terribly romantic that she still loves your father so much!"

Eliza didn't say anything for a while, then she whispered, "I think she must love him even more than ever— just lately. Does that make sense?"

"Ah, yes. Love is impossible to define, impossible to anticipate."

After another silence, Eliza said, "Then, maybe some day you'll find out you truly love John."

"Who knows? But right now, I'm excited about conquering St. Augustine. I've never turned a single charm on a Spanish officer in my whole life!"

"Do you think my father will be there? Has our letter really had time to reach him?"

"Of course! Captain Atkinson sent it by his son George's own hand, didn't he? Uncle John will be waiting for us with open arms."

Chapter 24

✳✳✳ The morning of December 23 could not have dawned more to Don Juan's liking. He was dressed and at his bedroom window in plenty of time to see first light. Smiling, he watched the dark fall slowly back and red-gold begin to spread across Matanzas Bay. He had said morning prayers by lamplight, but except for the Glory Be, his mind had been elsewhere. How, indeed, could even heaven expect a man to concentrate? After all, tomorrow—dear God, *tomorrow*—he would come awake in this room with Anne beside him!

He flicked a bit of dust off one carefully polished black slipper; then, not satisfied with the shine on the buckle, took off the shoe, blew his breath on the silver square, and rubbed it vigorously against his sleeve. On this day any small activity helped. The room, the whole house could not contain him much longer. No sound yet from Juan's room, even though Cousin Margaret was also on the ship bringing Anne. Too young, he thought, to know what love is. Well, let the boy sleep. His father is no longer lonely. . . .

At the looking glass for still another inspection of the closeness of his shave, he reminded himself that, since the ship from Savannah wasn't due until early afternoon, he could, if necessary, shave again—to please Anne.

"Anne. . . ." He spoke her name aloud. How would he look to her? Perhaps a bit thicker in the waist, but not one gray hair and no sign of baldness. He smiled at his reflection. "She always admired my smile. Thank God, no missing teeth yet." He jerked at his black woolen jacket, stood erect and tightened his stomach muscles.

I much prefer my Spanish captain's uniform, he thought, then laughed. It would be most unwise to meet her attired as a Spanish officer. He was going to be gentle with her on all those sensitive issues.

He glanced toward the windowless north end of the room, where stood his private altar with its crucifix. A tingle of dread prickled. For the first time in the hilarious week since he'd known she was coming, the gentle ghost of Padre Font invaded his thoughts. Every memory of the Franciscan priest brought not only the presence of the dying young man, but a sense of the very presence of God.

Better, he reminded himself, to make certain that the treasured Franciscan habit was well hidden. He strode to the black painted chest and opened the bottom drawer. The brown bundle lay in plain sight. He touched it briefly, then tucked other items of clothing over it.

The brown homespun habit had comforted him more than once. Especially during the agonizing weeks when Quesada had appeared to have forgotten that Don Juan McQueen was alive. Often, after young Juan was in bed, he had put it on and held it warmly about his body, seeming to receive comfort and some peace from the very texture of the garment itself. In his last will and testament, redrawn for him a year ago by Quesada's solemn *escribano*, Señor José Zubizarreta, he had specified that he wished to be buried in the robe of the holy young Franciscan who had called him "my son in Christ."

Well! What a time for solemn thoughts, he prodded himself. This day is for joy. He closed the drawer and listened, his ear against the wall of young Juan's room. The boy was up! Good. The day could begin. The day for which he had waited—nearly four long and lonely years.

Every step of the arrival plans had been rehearsed. Señora Perpal had lent him her two male servants, and Pedro had persuaded three of his relatives to help tote the trunks, boxes, and other baggage across the Plaza to the St. George Street house. Orange, lemons, and magnolia leaves were not to be cut and placed in vases in every room until noon. Anne was to be met with beauty the moment she set foot in his scrubbed and polished home.

At breakfast with John, he went over the plans once more. "Just before noon, Pedro will cut the greenery and stack it on the loggia, then—"

"Who's going to arrange it in all those bottles and jars and vases, Papa? Not I."

"Why, the señora! She offered yesterday. Only a woman knows how to do that."

"The señora—fixing bouquets for Mama's arrival?"

He took his son's question as a joke, then plunged back into rehearsing the plans. "Once the bouquets are in place, Pedro and Harry will inspect the house for any mote of remaining dust, and only then will Pedro run to the market for fresh fish. Tomorrow, Christmas Eve, we dine, of course, with his Excellency." He rubbed his hands with delight. "I'm still amazed at the elaborate plans the Quesadas have made for entertaining our visitors. Think of it! One week from tonight, a fancy-dress ball at Government House in honor of—*your mother*! Two family dinner parties between now and then, and after that, only heaven knows what his gracious Excellency may dream up."

"What time is it, Papa? How much longer do we have to wait?"

McQueen took out his gold timepiece. "Let me see, it's now half past nine. With the good wind today, I would estimate that we must find a way to pass roughly four more hours." He snapped his fingers. "I forgot to tell you—or did I? We've been invited to keep our last watch from the lookout tower on the roof of Government House."

"No, you didn't tell me! That's the best yet. We'll be able to see their ship out beyond Anastasia Island from up there."

"Precisely! While they're moving into the Bay, we'll have time to race across the Plaza, hop into our borrowed boat, and when they anchor, we'll be waiting alongside—with open arms."

"At least you know Mama will fall into your open arms."

"Cousin Margaret will do the same—mark my word.

This is going to be a time of—romance! Did you observe your sun-browned good looks this morning when you shaved?"

John laughed. "I'm afraid not."

"You should have. I did. It strengthens a man's confidence."

"I could use some."

"Nonsense. Be fully confident. Margaret's a fortunate young lady." He drained his cup and took out the watch again. "Upon my word, do you suppose my watch is broken? I could have sworn at least half an hour had passed."

Father and son had climbed to the balcony atop the second floor of Government House two hours before even McQueen could hope to sight the arrival of the ship. He had always reveled in the view from up there, and to pass the sluggish minutes he recalled for John the first time he'd climbed the steep stairs with old Governor Zéspedes, back in the year 1784, just after the boy's mother had taken him and the younger children to Europe.

Today, he declared the scene to be even more breathtaking. The skyline at the north end of the city was dominated by the massive Castillo de San Marcos. From their vantage point, they could see all of the defense lines—the Cubo redoubt and deep ditch extending from the fortress across the peninsula to the San Sebastian River, broken only by the City Gate; then, running south and guarding the western limits of St. Augustine, they could follow the irregular line of the Rosario redoubt all the way to Maria Sanchez Creek, the city's natural protection to the south.

They passed a little more time trying to pick out, from among the several garden plots and huts surrounding the earthen defense lines, which of them might be the crops of the enterprising señora. The best-tended ones, they decided, of course.

"Has it changed much since the first time you saw it, Papa?"

"Generally, no," he chuckled. "But I do have to conceded that the British, who had just left shortly before my visit to Zéspedes, were considerably more industrious than the Spaniards. I recall acres and acres of thriving orchards ten years ago. They appear to be a bit overgrown now. Can't even find them, to be truthful."

John focused the long glass they'd brought along and scanned the empty sea. "Not yet," he said.

"Juan . . . your mother will be here. She will actually *be here* in what suddenly seems a very short time. Should I—be afraid that she won't like my little Spanish shelter from the storm? Or should I be—confident?"

John laid down the glass and smiled at his father. "I guess you'd better be confident. That was your advice to me."

Juan Quesada had not felt equal to the steep tower stairs, but he was watching from his office window when the two bolted past.

Slowly, he returned to his desk and sat down to stare once more at the dispatch from the frontier which had arrived that morning. He crossed himself and vowed again to God that he would not tell McQueen that Lang, Plowden, and Wagnon were once more meeting with French stragglers at Coleraine across the St. Mary's in Georgia. He had hurt Don Juan once. With every ounce of his limited strength, he meant now to make it up to him. Even though Quesada was still able to recall only the explosion of anger in his head, he would always blame himself.

"God has forgiven me," he whispered into the high, empty room. "But I have not forgiven myself. So, with the help of heaven, I will find a way to keep the peace—at least as long as Doña Ana and his children are here."

Don Juan McQueen's friend and overseer, Captain Andrew Atkinson, stood on the leeward deck of the ship, watching the small boat scud toward him across the water. He had seldom dreaded a moment more. The ancient little cutter was just near enough for him to see that young John McQueen gripped the tiller with one hand, the sheet with the other, freeing his father to stand and wave. Atkinson's sympathy poured toward the amazing man who had not only proven his loyalty to Spain through four turbulent years, but whose fidelity to his wife had never been questioned even by the vilest of men. The aging captain felt in his pocket, making certain Anne McQueen's hastily scrawled note was there.

Her stricken face still haunted him. In Savannah they had all been happily aboard, with enough boxes, trunks, and barrels stowed to supply their needs for an indefinite stay in St. Augustine. Eliza McQueen had even brought her new pianoforte—because "my father loves music."

Atkinson had been standing beside Don Juan's wife and family, waving with them to their friends and relatives on shore, when little Sallie fell to the dock in a faint. The girl had felt hot and limp in his arms as Atkinson struggled with her into the boatswain's chair, which had lowered them over the ship's side and back onto the wharf. The sight of the mother's face, waiting out the long, anxious moments as she too had been lowered, would, he knew, never leave him. There had been far more in that face than concern for the unconscious child.

Just before Atkinson had climbed back into the boatswain's chair to be hoisted aboard again—the whistle piping for departure—Anne McQueen had clutched his arm. "Here—give this to my husband, please. And—tell him—*we were coming*! Be sure he knows we were all on board, Captain Atkinson! Reassure him that—when Sallie is well—I'll try again."

The woman could have made no other decision. If the child were as ill as she appeared, it was unlikely that she could have survived the voyage. Even if she had lived to reach St. Augustine, Travers, the only doctor, might well have been away.

Andrew Atkinson squared his shoulders. He was also the bearer of bad news for his Excellency: word of fresh plans for an expedition from South Carolina to move on Spanish-held Amelia Island. Loyal Captain Atkinson was devoted to the frail young governor. He dreaded to tell him, knowing full well that the tiny Spanish battery on Amelia at the mouth of the St. Mary's could never defend itself. But when the cutter had pulled near enough for him to see McQueen's face, Atkinson knew he would not find it half as difficult to deliver the bad news to Quesada as to tell Don Juan that his family was not coming.

Chapter 25

Ysabel Perpal smacked the puppy's rump affectionately and wiped dinner remains from its whiskers and ear. "You are the best in the litter. I long to keep you for myself." She tucked the dog under her shawl and headed through a cold drizzle for the McQueen house.

As soon as Pedro had been sent for warm milk for the puppy, the señora placed the dog in Don Juan's arms. "For you," she said. "He was too young to be a Christmas gift. Now—he is a gift. You need to smile again."

McQueen held out the pup—short legs flailing, one black and white ear drooping—and studied the square, stubby nose, the bright eyes. Ysabel watched closely for a sign of his pleasure. He was merely polite.

"You're kind, señora," he said. "He's a wiggle worm, isn't he?"

"You cause him to struggle!"

"I do?"

"He will fidget until you give him a name and let him give you many kisses on the face."

Pedro returned with milk and the three watched the dog's bowl empty and the little sides swell. When Pedro left, McQueen picked up the puppy, which in no time was fast asleep on his lap.

"You see? He has come home to you, Don Juan."

He said nothing.

"The pup, he has come home to you," she repeated.

"It would seem so. Do you think I need a pet, señora?"

"My bitch had five puppies. With the lack of food in St. Augustine, can I feed five?"

"Is this one really the choice of the litter?"

"He is the choice. So, he is yours."

McQueen stroked the dog's back. The pup snored.

"Juan will be sorry to have missed the presentation," he said after a silence. "He took my place at the checkerboard with Father O'Reilly tonight." McQueen glanced toward a large jar of drying magnolia leaves which the señora had arranged for Anne's arrival three weeks ago. "I—haven't been very courageous in my disappointment, have I?"

She crossed the room to where the jar stood, jerked out the stiff branches, and tossed them into the fire. Without comment, they watched them sizzle, curl, and turn to ashes.

"If you will not promise to empty every jar and vase of old leaves, I will go to all rooms of this house and rid you of them myself!" Perched again on her chair, she forced a smile. "Who knows? A better time for Doña Ana to come could be later, no? You want her to find out we are short of food?"

He sighed. "I—hadn't faced that. I was just too happy at the prospect."

"I tell you a secret. My son in New Providence has managed to ship flour and garden seeds to me. In my kitchen now, you could not find ten cups! So, if the British schooner escapes the French privateers, you will also have flour. And seeds for your garden."

He stared at her. "Your son? I didn't know you had a son in New Providence!"

"I have a son there," she said drily. "Like yours, his name is Juan. I have not seen him since the year 1784. He was the age of your Juan when he deserted his mother to go from East Florida with the British."

"But—it's impossible for you to have a son in his thirties!"

"I am older than you by nearly four years. He was born to me back in Minorca. But, this is not important."

Her voice softened. "What is important is that his flour and seeds reach us. And, if my boat bearing your St. Mary's timber docks also in England—we will be better in every way, no?"

Her face was radiant with concern and courage, but he could only nod and mutter, "Of course. All thanks to you."

"Wh-ht!" The tenderness in her eyes gave way to their more customary fire. "Had not his stupid Excellency burned every barn between the St. Mary's and the St. Johns, we would not now be hungry!"

McQueen had no desire to debate with her, but the woman was obviously trying so hard to take his mind off his heartache, he felt compelled to make an effort. "You forget," he said, "that the planned attack on St. Augustine was stopped without bloodshed. History may record that his Excellency's plan was not as brutal as it appeared."

"History! He has so angered the American settlers that in the remaining years of our lives, we will not be safe again!"

Ysabel was trying, but he could not enter in. He wanted her to leave.

The puppy squirmed in its sleep, and Don Juan felt the warm wetness spread across his thigh. He lifted the dog; looked down at his darkened trouser leg and up at the señora. Her eyes smiled first. Then, holding the dog in the air, he found himself joining her in the first spontaneous laugh of the evening.

"That settles it," he said. "I've just given him a name—Niño!"

"So, Niño! Boy!"

"He's all boy!" McQueen got up. "If you'll excuse me, I'll take him outside."

"Why? It is too late for that." She pointed to the pup. "Niño, he has done for you what your son and I could not do. He has caused you to laugh again. As Don Juan McQueen has always found a way to do."

He frowned. "Are you hinting that I've been feeling sorry for myself?"

"No. Not hinting. Declaring. You have been thrashing around in self-pity like a man trapped in a well!"

Had his guest been a man, he might have thought of an

adequate response. He could only glare at the woman . . . and she had not finished.

The señora was settled in a chair, one arm thrown across its low back. The look in her eyes was downright haughty, he thought, as though only a fool would need to be told what she was about to tell him.

"Do you not know your son's heart is heavy too that he is not now with the girl, Margaret? Do you not know that Doña Ana is also heavy in her spirit?" She shook her finger. "It is a help, Don Juan, to remember that no one suffers alone."

Still standing, the dog in his arms, McQueen struggled against a surprising temptation to bury his head in Ysabel's lap and beg for comfort—and an end to the scolding.

Abruptly, she stood up. "Do you fail to understand why young Juan is not now on the journey to Savannah to discover about the sick child? To see his cousin? I tell you why. He wants to go, but he is afraid to leave you! A man so sorry for himself is not safe alone."

The puppy, wide awake now, began to lick McQueen's face and bite at his ear. He smacked the fat little rump sharply. The dog yelped.

Hands on hips, the señora looked at him almost pityingly. Then she asked in a quiet voice, "So, you rid yourself of your shame by whipping Niño, huh?"

"No!" He held the trembling dog close to his face. "No! I—didn't mean to do that. Forgive me."

"We can all forgive everything, Don Juan," she said in the same soft voice, "if we know you are once more yourself."

"Out of the well?"

"Out of the well."

"And how can I prove that?"

She spread both hands. "Easy. Send your son to Savannah at once. Not only for his sake, for yours. You are a good father. Even absent. Do you not think I know you worry about the sick little girl?"

Niño was licking McQueen's face again. The best way to show his gratitude to the señora, he supposed, was to permit it. He had never fancied being kissed by a dog, but in a way he didn't yet comprehend, Ysabel Perpal had met another need tonight.

With the graceful movement he so admired, she slipped her shawl around her shoulders, lifted his chin briefly with her fist, and left before he could collect himself sufficiently to see her out.

Slowly, he returned to his chair, thankful for the distraction of the puppy in his arms—and for the ways of Señora Perpal.

Chapter 26

✤✤✤ Young John had been gone less than a week when a breathless Pedro caught up with McQueen crossing the Plaza. In a torrent of Spanish and English, the boy told him that a New Providence schooner had been seized three days ago off nearby Anastasia Island.

"Diego, the fisherman, he saw with his own eyes the crew from the pirate ship climb aboard the schooner!"

"Why didn't he report before now?"

"Diego, he is a good fisherman, but dumb in the head. He went on fishing. Only you have been told—and the señora." Pedro appeared about to cry. "The captured schooner surely held her flour. The flour we were to have too!"

"Which way did the two ships sail after the boarding?"

"To the north. The frontier."

Don Juan sighed. "Very well. Go back to your work. No question that was a French privateer. I thought we were rid of them. I'll go to the governor at once."

"You cannot. Diego's cousin, he say his Excellency is sick again. Colonel Bartolomé Morales is the governor today."

"How in blazes do you Minorcans find out everything first?"

"We listen."

"Then listen to me now. Before you go back to the house, run to Leslie's place for any letters I might have. Take them straight home. Not a word from my wife since my little daughter fell ill. Surely today. I'll be there as soon as I see Morales."

"Pedro bring you luck, maybe!"

McQueen smiled halfheartedly. "If the French are in our waters again, I'm not hopeful."

He found Acting Governor Morales, a helpless look on his long, flat face, staring at a sheaf of papers on Quesada's desk.

"Look, Don Juan—letters from Georgia Governor Mathews, Indian Agent Señor Hambly, the British consul in Savannah—all *en inglés*! None I can read. *Escribano* Zubizarreta, he too is ill with a cold in his nose. I have already more than I can handle as commandant of the Third Cuban Battalion! How am I to be acting governor too?"

"I'll read the letters, Colonel. But, tell me, how is his Excellency today?"

"Out of his head again with fever." Morales shuffled the stack of papers. "One look at his desk and I am also out of my head."

McQueen pulled up a chair and began to read. As he suspected, the two from Governor Mathews contained only empty promises to control the Georgians within their own borders. The lengthy report from Hambly was interesting. On his most recent tour of the Creek towns, Hambly had not only found them still mainly loyal, but had heard repeated rumors that McGillivray's war chief, Louis Milfort, had returned to France.

When Morales appeared puzzled that McQueen found this good, Don Juan explained only that he had never trusted the Frenchman Milfort to take McGillivray's place. He went on to the short letter from Wallace, the British consul in Savannah. "Good news here too," he said. "Wallace has sent us another shipment of flour."

"*¡Excelente!*"

"Maybe. If his ship gets through." Don Juan tossed back the dispatches. "I really came to inform you, Colonel, that the instant his Excellency is well enough to talk, you must tell him that a British schooner was seized three days ago off Anastasia Island. I believe the pirate ship to have been French. If so, we're in fresh trouble."

Morales' response was to groan and bury his head in his hands.

Don Juan got up to leave. "Someone from the Plaza must go at once to the frontier. My guess is that both schooners are right now docked at St. Mary's. When you can, tell his Excellency I'm going myself tomorrow."

At his door, McQueen was met by Niño yapping a welcome and Pedro waving a letter from young John. Nothing was said about the absence of word from Anne. He stooped for a brief romp with the dog, then handed him over.

"Get out now, both of you. I want to read this with no talking or tugging at my shoe buckles." When Pedro lingered, he repeated, "Go—everybody go!"

"But, Señora Perpal, she—"

"What about the señora?"

"You are invited to her house to eat *fromajardis* this evening."

"Thank her, but I've too much to do. I'm leaving tomorrow for the frontier. Anyway, she has no food to spare. Certainly not now that her flour was stolen." He brushed boy and dog away and strode into the parlor with John's letter.

> 5 *February 1795*
> *At St. Mary's en route Savannah*

Papa, Dear Sir,

> *I am writing in haste because the tide serves and I am waited for by a boat of sorts which, with luck, will take me all the way. Since Mr. Fatio offered to bring this by hand to his plantation, then by a trusted Negro to St. Augustine, I will write only facts of immediate interest to you and Quesada. By now, you may know that a French privateer seized a New Providence schooner with a cargo of cotton, flour, etc. off*

*Anastasia. Both ships docked two days ago at St.
Mary's estuary, ostensibly to sell off the captured cargo
to local merchants. The truth is, the crew of the privateer at once began to unload armament on the northern end of Amelia Island, where it is rumored that a
few scattered French supporters are still hiding. By
sheer luck, I also learned that the privateer is headed
back to patrol the St. Augustine waters to prevent your
receipt of any further food shipments from the British
Consul at Savannah. Because still another privateer
may join the one soon to return to your waters, travel
by sea will be even more hazardous. At the tavern last
night, I also learned that ten to twenty French agents
are said to have landed on the undefended coast south
of St. Augustine and five others are said to be headed
for Anastasia Island. The tiny Spanish battery there
should be warned. Of course, all this rumored activity
may come to nothing, as happened last year, but I
knew you would want the privilege of bearing his unhappy but vital news to his Excellency. I am well, but
cannot say the same for the old horse we obtained for
my overland ride to San Vicente. Colonel Howard
wishes to be remembered to you, as do I, my dear father. I will write The Cottage news upon my arrival in
case you have not yet heard from Mama. In haste, but
with a pat for Niño.*

Yr aff'ct son,
Juan McQueen, Jr.

Don Juan refolded the pages slowly and stuffed them
into his pocket, proud of the intelligent report, but somewhat let down that for the moment he need not make his
own trip to the frontier. John had verified his suspicions:
indeed, the two ships had put in at St. Mary's, and the privateer *was* French.

With Quesada too ill for conversation, he was at a loss
concerning his own next step. Like everyone else, he had
never understood why his excellency chose Morales to
govern during his fever attacks. Until Howard had been
sent to the frontier, there had been no problem when the

governor fell ill. Loyal Morales hated the assignment and, out of fear of making a wrong move, either acted too quickly or not at all. It might indeed be wise to hold the critical information in John's letter at least for a day or so, in the hope that he could confer with the governor himself. In the meantime, he would try to convince Morales that a search party, led by McQueen, should be dispatched to Anastasia Island. Even if his son's rumor of a French landing there turned out to be false, the time would not be wasted.

For days, his main interest had been in finding ways to pass the hours without John and no word whatever from Anne concerning Sallie. Even in bad weather, a ship could sail the sea route from Savannah in a week—or less. At least, now that he knew the French were in their waters again, he could be almost certain, knowing Anne, that letters had been sent and were captured. The last niggling fear—that she had not written at all—vanished. Only his worry over Sallie lingered. He had been away from home six years ago when little Alexander died. The thought of being away from Anne at the death of still another child was more than he could face.

He moved his favorite chair near the fire and sat down. Another long, lonely evening stretched ahead.

Out of nowhere, Niño skittered across the cold tabby floor and bit at his shoe. Delighted at the reminder that the señora had invited him to eat her delicious *fromajardis*, he scooped up the dog and tickled the pink belly. "You heard Pedro say she wants me to dine with her, didn't you, Niño?" The shrill bark hurt his ears. "Since I'm not heading north tomorrow, I'll accept. In fact, we'll both go."

Upstairs in his bedroom, he rescued a clean shirt from Niño's sharp teeth and slipped into it, feeling still more confident that he was right, not only to remain in St. Augustine until he could speak face to face with Quesada but to keep the other rumors in John's letter to himself for now. After all, events moved slowly at best, and Morales had no authority to reward him with a new land grant in exchange for the potentially valuable information.

He combed his hair before the looking glass and studied his reflection. Now and then, he told himself, a man has to consider his own best interests. For tonight, he would enjoy the señora's cheese pastries and try to put the whole matter out of his mind.

When his second knock at Ysabel's door went unanswered, he knocked again. For such a short walk, he had not bothered to wear a jacket. Niño, held against his chest, had begun to shiver. He shivered too, then whistled a little tune while he waited. Where *was* Ysabel?

He knocked again. His whistling stopped at the sound of a scuffle somewhere at the back and the unmistakable voice of the señora—cursing in Spanish. He could feel Niño's heart beat, and his own. Then the back door slammed and heavy, hurrying footsteps crossed her chicken yard, followed by a thud, as of a man landing on the ground after a jump—a leap, he was certain, over the wall alongside the church.

He rattled the door. When he found it bolted, he put Niño down and hurried to search the churchyard for the intruder. Finding no one, he hurdled Ysabel's wall and ran to her open lighted kitchen in time to see her grab her chest, stagger, and slump to the floor.

He knelt beside her. A trickle of blood oozed from her mouth. But more alarmingly, her eyes bulged with horror and pain. In the lamp light, he could see the color drain from her face.

He lifted her head a little and cradled it in his hand.

"Señora! Oh, señora!" He stopped her when she tried to speak. "No. Just move your head, yes or no. The servants are not here?"

She shook her head no.

"Then, I'll get Katrina and send Pedro for Dr. Travers!"

Ysabel clutched his hand. "Doctor can—do nothing. Twice before—my heart. When—I was—afraid."

He kept her quiet for a time, then poured a little brandy and held it for her to swallow.

Later, with his help, she managed to walk to a chair in her small, shadowy parlor. "Both other pains—many years ago," she said. "Not since. Until—tonight."

"Who was here? Did you know him?"

"*He*—was here. The absent one!" She spat the name: "Antonio Perpal!"

"I see."

"What you see?"

"Nothing. I—was just wondering if there's anything—anything at all I can do to—keep him from bothering you again."

"You can kill him! He's mixed up with the French now."

"The French?"

"He row across in a stolen boat—from Anastasia—to spy." Her head fell back against the chair. "So he said. His hatred—for me—it ruin his mission, I pray!" She snorted. "The fool—could not keep himself from this house. I—cut him—with my kitchen knife! He—cannot—spy while—dripping blood. No?"

Don Juan thought a moment. "So, the French are indeed after us again. Young Juan's rumors are true."

"Juan?"

"He wrote of rumors at Saint Mary's. I hoped they were false."

"The same as false." She leaned toward him. "Do not worry. The boy, Juan? He is all right?"

"Yes. So far as I know. He should be with his mother by now."

"Do not worry, Don Juan," she repeated. "This small flurry will be—as always. A gun fired here—a knife flashed there. Only a monarchy can conquer. I despise—but I do not fear—the French or the Americans! The men of a republic, they buzz—like bees. No damage but a sting. Do not forget my words. There will—be no big trouble. Only a sting on Monday—or Wednesday. Nothing more."

"You're talking too much," he stood to leave. "I order you to sit right there until Katrina can put you to bed."

"You come back? You eat my *fromajardis*? I make for you!"

"I'll try to drop by again if it isn't too late. I must tell Morales that the French are on Anastasia."

"Maybe yes, maybe no. Antonio Perpal is a liar. You come back. Eat my *fromajardis*. Do not waste my flour!"

He stopped by his house and dispatched Katrina. Then, bundled in a heavy jacket, he hurried toward Morales' house on the Calle de la Marina. The señora had been right before, when she took new threats lightly. He prayed she was right this time. He, too, had lived in East Florida long enough to expect most rumors to be false, or at least exaggerated. Never, of course, to be ignored; always to be reported as promptly as possible to Quesada. But not to be worried about too much in advance.

As he knocked on Morales' door, he felt certain that once the anxious acting governor heard that Ysabel's husband had rowed over from Anastasia from a French encampment there, he would agree immediately to a search of the island. Such a mission would cause Morales to feel a bit more competent, would pass some time for Don Juan, and would surely impress his Excellency once he was himself again.

Young John's trip by open boat from St. Mary's to Savannah—much of it in a cold rain—had been slow and miserable. He was relieved when the family, gathered to greet him at Grandmother's house, had insisted that he retire early. Margaret had actually kissed him of her own accord. For tonight, that was enough.

Besides, he missed his father and was writing to him to say that Sallie was getting better when he heard a light knock at his door. He opened it to admit his mother, her finger pressed to her lips.

She closed the door softly and without a word threw both arms around him and held him for a long time. "I know you're tired," she whispered. "I'm not going to stay."

He led her to his chair and sat down on the bed. "Don't you know that any man likes the surprise of an embrace like that, Mrs. McQueen?"

"You *are* a man now, John. And—you love your Cousin Margaret, don't you?"

He tried to joke. "It's that evident in one short evening?"

"To me, it is." The gray eyes studied him. "Margaret's still very young and frivolous. Can you be patient?"

"I've always loved her, Mama. I'm not quite sure why I haven't told you before. But, yes. I can be patient—for as long as I need to be."

"Did you tell your father?"

"Yes."

"You were writing to him, weren't you?"

"That's right. I know you've sent him three letters about Sallie but he hadn't heard when I left. I thought I'd try to get one through. He's been—terribly upset."

"The doctor says Sallie can travel as soon as the weather's warm. I—want us to leave no later than May." She got up. "John, I already know without your telling me that—you haven't been just visiting in St. Augustine. So, don't feel you need to explain that. Just tell me, will it be safe for us to go in May?"

His smile, he knew, was not convincing. "I—uh, was just asking Papa's opinion on that in this letter tonight. There are some rumors. But—things have been peaceful for months."

"You've been down there with him, John. Will he—tell us the truth about—conditions?"

"Yes. He'll tell the truth."

"All right, I believe you."

At the door, she whispered, "You won't mention those—rumors to your grandmother, of course."

He grinned. "As Sallie would say, 'Never'!"

She kissed him. "Can you wait here until she can travel?"

"Madame, I have orders from your husband to escort his son William and all his ladies—personally." He stopped smiling. "Will Margaret stay that long?"

"Yes. She's going with us. Don't worry for a minute about that."

"Then, don't you worry either, Mama. Just leave everything to Papa and me."

♦   ♦   ♦

It was too late when Don Juan left Morales to stop at the señora's. She was in good hands with Katrina, and his mood after such a long, unsatisfying talk with the acting governor was too troubled for a sick call. He went home instead and prayed for her recovery. He prayed, too, for the poor colony in the uncertain hands of anxious Colonel Morales, and begged for Quesada's return to health.

After petitioning the Almighty for the well-being of his family—especially Sallie—he pulled on his nightcap and crawled into bed. He shivered from the damp chill in his room, and at a terrifying question which had begun to form in his mind: Would he *want* to go on living in St. Augustine without his Excellency?

What if Ysabel's heart failed one day? What if Morales was right when he predicted tonight that if Quesada continued ill, Enrique White, the stern, austere governor of West Florida, would be sent to take his Excellency's place at the Plaza in St. Augustine?

I would have to stay, he told himself, hunching his body for a little warmth. I'm trapped. I would have to stay . . . but what would my life be like without Juan Quesada?

Chapter 27

✦✦✦ Erique White slammed the lengthy letter from Morales down on his desk at Pensacola's Government House and strode in disgust across the wide room. The office was stuffy—almost as stuffy, he thought, as the mind of Bartolomé Morales. He threw open a window and stared out over the Bay.

The governor of West Florida had long ago given up trying to understand why Juan Quesada—even in the throes of a fever attack—would permit Morales to govern. The rambling letter had been dictated by a rattled weakling!

Granted, East Florida's frontier was only the width of the St. Mary's River from the clamoring Georgians, but weren't they—along with Americans from other states—crossing the eastern mountains and pushing down the tributaries of the Ohio and the Mississippi to plague Louisiana and West Florida too? Ten years ago, there had been only about seventy-five thousand American settlers on western land that rightly belonged either to Spain or to the Indians. Now, their number was well in excess of one hundred thousand. Only a chronic complainer like Morales would dare write as though trouble from the United States stalked only the eastern province.

Both West Florida and Louisiana, geographically barring the aggressive United States from the Gulf of Mexico, were an abomination to Americans. The pompous motto of New Englander Josiah Quincy had surely reached the ears of all three Spanish governors: "We want West Florida!

We will have West Florida! By God, we will take West Florida!"

But what, White reasoned, could be accomplished by panic? Or by a steady stream of fawning letters to Havana, pleading for help? Even if Morales' rumors of French privateers in the East Florida waters were true, another plea for troops, ships, and ammunition would, without peace between Spain and France, fall on deaf ears. Diplomatic skill, judgment, and the right combination of political intrigue would more readily contain the Americans. Most of the Spanish colonies were empty of settlers. There was no way known to man to lock up an open field or a river—certainly not a river as wide as the Mississippi.

Juan Quesada, when he was well enough to govern, understood this. White admired Quesada's tactics. His latest letter from Quesada last year had reported that more than half of the official staff at the Plaza had turned against him when he burned out the traitorous settlers along the St. Mary's River, but so far, the strategy had worked.

Of course, East Florida did interest Enrique White. Months ago, word had reached him from Captain General Las Casas in Havana that, should Quesada fail to regain his health, White himself was being considered as his successor at the Plaza in St. Augustine. Such an eventuality was being kept from Juan Quesada, but White had responded at once with favor. He did not believe East Florida to be any more important geographically than his own colony, but life there would be more civilized. The appointment would constitute a definite step forward in his career.

Morales' garbled, nervous letter asking White to reinforce the plea for more troops had been so long en route that by now, undoubtedly, Juan Quesada had recovered enough to govern again. The letter, written early in February, had arrived only this morning—the third of April! How like Morales to have sent it by an unreliable messenger. Only a rider who stopped along the way for long periods of drunkenness could have required two months for a journey possible in two weeks.

According to Morales, a handful of French and French

sympathizers had reportedly encamped on Anastasia Island, in sight of St. Augustine, but a search party led by Don Juan McQueen had turned up nothing. If no further troubles had appeared in two months, why should White press his own fortunes with Havana by joining Morales in his futile request for more troops and guns? Beyond that, the West Florida governor was sure that once the war between Spain and France was entirely settled abroad, danger from Frenchmen still in the colonies would be sporadic at best.

He would decide later whether to ignore Morales or to respond to Quesada himself, assuming the East Florida governor's health was improved.

Back at his desk, the name of Don Juan McQueen—nearly overlooked as he had read Morales' letter—surfaced in his mind. He had met the American once at the home of William Panton. He recalled having rather liked McQueen and knew that Panton regarded him highly. Anyone in the three Spanish provinces was aware of McQueen's importance to Quesada, owing to his influence among the more prominent American settlers along the St. Mary's and the St. Johns. Most surprising and perhaps most important, though, was McQueen's apparent loyalty to Spain.

Enrique White sat erect in his chair, hands folded on the desk—his habit when an idea had begun to take form. If indeed he were one day to be appointed governor of East Florida, would it not be wise for him to have established a more direct line of communication with Don Juan McQueen? Loyal American settlers were scarce at best. With Colonel Carlos Howard away from the Plaza now, at San Vicente on the frontier, who was left in St. Augustine with more knowledge of the real workings of Quesada's province than Don Juan McQueen? Might it not at least be interesting to write by his own hand—not through his *escribano*—to McQueen himself? He could select at random any muddled, contradictory passage from Morales' letter and simply ask McQueen to clarify it for him. No harm could come of it. A man as ambitious as McQueen was reputed to be would surely be flattered by a handwritten letter from the governor of West Florida.

He stroked his strong, square chin with a quill, thinking . . . then began to write rapidly.

> 3 April, 1795
> Government House, Pensacola

Honorable Don Juan McQueen,

By the time you receive this, his Excellency, Governor Quesada, may be much improved and able once more to govern. I sincerely hope this is true, since today I am in receipt of a most perplexing letter from acting governor Morales. In view of your knowledge of East Florida affairs and your loyalty to Spain, as indicated to me through Wm. Panton, I hereby seek your opinion on one passage from Morales' letter.

In one instance, Colonel Morales begs me to urge Las Casas to send reinforcements—at least an eighteen-gun ship to drive away the French corsairs haunting the St. Augustine bar. In another instance, he appears to be contradicting that request by assuring me that it is his belief that the French mean to push no further south than the St. Mary's River area. Can you elaborate? And are you in possession of any fresh information concerning the Georgian threat from any person in your wide and valued acquaintance?

It is, my dear sir, my hope that the opportunity may present itself for our meeting in the near future. I regret my absence from Pensacola during your visit to Panton at the time of McGillivray's death. My respects to his Excellency and to John Leslie.

> *Y'r obed. serv't,*
> *Enrique White*
> *Governor West Florida*

Chapter 28

✷✷✷   Lengthening late spring days made a man more restless than short winter days, Don Juan thought, on his way one morning to Leslie's place. True, the señora was herself again, for which he thanked God. Her heart seizure, a light one, had evidently been caused by fear that Antonio Perpal might be forcing his way back into her life. The man had vanished that night, as had the French from Anastasia Island. If additional enemy troops had landed on the undefended coast south of St. Augustine, as John reported, they had caused no trouble in nearly three months. Neither had there been a French privateer in their waters for more than two weeks.

His Excellency was attempting to govern again, although Don Juan's frequent visits with him, while congenial, had been somewhat unsatisfactory. Quesada still held to his defensive military posture. Wise, perhaps, but dull. For Don Juan, the monotony of the uneasy peace caused time to hang heavily.

Still, there was much to be thankful for. Sallie was getting well, and Anne had assured him that in late May or early June, as soon as the child would be in less danger of catching a cold, she meant to try again to make the voyage.

Today was May the third. A Panton and Leslie brig was due to dock this very morning from Savannah. He should be ashamed to have felt restless over the monotonously uneventful days, when surely he would hear any time that Anne had settled on a sailing date.

Before he reached the Bay at the foot of Treasury Street, he could see what appeared to be an unfamiliar schooner—not the expected brig from Savannah—at anchor beyond the bar. Puzzled, he hurried into Leslie's office, to be greeted with a surprisingly cheerful smile.

"You're five minutes too late," the Scotsman said.

"Too late for what?"

"To hear for yourself that your wife is coming by mid-June! Fatio was just here. He's had Savannah visitors. Mrs. McQueen sent word to you. It's even brightened my day. Sit down, sit down."

Don Juan said thoughtfully, "I know you expect me to whoop for joy. In fact, I surprise myself. But I was hoping for May. Still!"—he began to beam—"that's only about six weeks to wait, isn't it?"

"Just about. Provided our luck holds with the French privateers. My brig didn't make it. But there was bad weather to the north, Fatio says."

"Say, what is that strange schooner out there in the Bay? Has Panton made a new investment? I thought your business was supposed to be dwindling away."

"It is. We took the boat on some otherwise bad debts. It's a rickety hull, but it got here—with this for you." He opened a drawer and handed McQueen a letter. "And—I do admit to a large chunk of curiosity. It's from his Excellency, Enrique White."

"Why would he be writing to me?"

"I'm waiting to hear."

Don Juan opened the letter and read it all aloud, his voice rising with interest. When he finished, he was smiling broadly. "I declare to you, Leslie, the Almighty is in full charge!"

"Of what?"

"His Excellency Enrique White plainly wishes to confer with me, wouldn't you say?"

"Obviously, he wants a reply."

"As long as there's the slightest chance that the French are still in our waters, I wouldn't consider risking a written reply. I plan to leave at once for Pensacola."

"With your wife coming? Man, you're crazy!"

"Not at all. The journey will redeem the time. Pedro

and Katrina can get the house in order, and with the good spring weather I'll be back by the first week in June." He banged his knee. "Confound it, Leslie, I'm too impatient just to walk the streets while I wait for her!"

Leslie's incredulous look had turned to silent laughter. "It couldn't be that you've also heard the rumor that White is next in line at the Plaza, could it?"

"I dare not hope to find such a friend as Juan Quesada again," McQueen said solemnly. "Still, I have no choice but to be prepared."

"I believe you're serious about that trip."

"Never more so. Harry and I will leave first thing tomorrow." He picked up his hat. "Should anyone inquire why I'm in Pensacola, you will, of course, indicate that my mission is—personal business? Especially in the event that Quesada should ask?"

Leslie shrugged. "What else could I say? It is most certainly personal, isn't it?"

McQueen had been gone less than two weeks when a thin letter from his wife reached Leslie's office. The Scotsman sat looking at it and admitted to himself that he had worried every day since McQueen left for fear his family might come early. Leslie loathed curiosity but, of course, a man frequently read an absent friend's mail.

He broke the seal and read the letter. As he had feared, they were now due to arrive early in June—at least two weeks before he could hope for McQueen's return. Young Juan had booked an earlier passage as far as St. Mary's, and Colonel Howard had arranged the remainder of the voyage on the Spanish gunboat, *Santo Tomás*, coming to St. Augustine for repairs.

Leslie put the letter in a drawer and paced his office, his irritation growing as he realized that none of McQueen's Spanish friends could be permitted to be on hand to meet the family—not even Father O'Reilly. He could picture Anne McQueen's face should a gray-robed Catholic priest be there to welcome her! Not funny, he decided. Swearing softly, he began to try to make some plans.

Easy enough, of course, to notify Pedro and Black Katrina. At least, he could be sure the house would be spotless—and food prepared. But he could by no means depend on his own wife's being sober enough to meet the boat with him—if he hid her rum she would only turn shrew and refuse to go—and so he was alone with the responsibility of making Anne McQueen welcome in a city she despised.

Why did he feel obligated to bother at all? He'd never trouble himself for anyone else.

"You're a sentimental son of a gun, Leslie," he muttered aloud, "and you know blamed well you bother because it's the family of John McQueen!"

Chapter 29

✱✱✱ When, on the evening of June 5, Black Katrina, holding Sallie by one hand and Eliza by the other, led the way to the parlor of the St. George Street house, young John waited back with Leslie to thank him for their welcome. A disturbing message given to John by Colonel Howard when they had stopped at San Vicente would have to wait. He was too tired to attempt to get it straight enough tonight to tell Leslie.

"I doubt that Father has a better friend anywhere than you, Mr. Leslie," he said. "I need to talk to you, but it will keep 'til morning, I think. And—I apologize for being gone so long."

"Forget it. Business has been rotten. Your mother's here at last. That's what matters, although your father may shoot himself for being away."

"In a way, it might be better for her to have a few days to get accustomed to—our little heathen city . . . well, I'd better get inside. After all, Katrina's happy to see them, but she can't explain much." They shook hands. "Good day, Mr. Leslie. We all thank you. I'll see you in the morning."

When John walked into the parlor, Pedro was talking to everyone at once, but as always when excited, his speech came out mostly in Minorcan dialect. John was sure even Eliza, with all her study of Spanish grammar, couldn't understand.

John thanked the two servants and sent them off with the children and Margaret to inspect their sleeping quarters.

Then he turned to his mother, who was sitting quietly in Papa's chair. "Do you like the house, Mama?"

She nodded. "Yes. It's fine. I'd think these tabby doors would be cold in winter." Then, softly, she began to weep.

"I know," he whispered. "I know; it's—bad he isn't here."

His mother dried her eyes. "But—he will be soon. I'm just tired, I guess. John, does—does he sit in this big chair?"

"Yes. Every day and every evening he's home."

"I thought so."

"Katrina is going to bring a tray to you upstairs. Want to go up now?"

"I suppose I'd better rest a while." Her chin lifted. "When he does get here, I don't want to look worn out. Did Mr. Leslie say it will be—two weeks?"

"Maybe not quite. Depends on the weather."

"Well, that won't be so hard. Not like four years."

His mother stopped a moment on the outside stairs to glance at the garden, then followed him in silence to his father's bedroom on the second floor.

Neither spoke while she stood just inside the door and looked around the room.

"Nice and airy," John said.

"Yes."

Her eyes moved slowly from the large bed with its high painted Spanish headboard to the chest of drawers, to the small desk where his father wrote letters. Standing beside her, John still held her cloak over his arm.

Finally, she began to move from one piece of furniture to another, touching each, as though alone in the room. Then her eyes fell on the blue, somewhat frayed officer's jacket hanging on its wall peg.

She looked at the empty jacket for a moment, then rushed to clasp it in her arms.

John hung her cloak beside the jacket and waited.

"This is—second best," she whispered and sent him away with a good-night kiss.

He knew she had seen the altar at the shadowy far end of the room, but she made no mention of it.

Early the next morning, before the others were up, John left for Leslie's office. Even if he had been less tired last night, he had been too concerned for his mother to think clearly about the troubling news which Howard had entrusted to him. Seeing her in St. Augustine had stirred a stronger, almost painful sense of responsibility for her. During the months back in Savannah, the two had experienced a new closeness. Being with her now in Florida somehow increased it. Oh, he still thought her wrong—dead wrong—to have stayed in Georgia, but she had seemed almost childlike last night, struggling to accept Papa's absence, the strange house, Katrina's eerie silence, Pedro's foreign chatter.

Leslie had assured him that this was as good a time as any for them to have come. But Leslie didn't yet know what John knew—that Elijah Clark was about to make new trouble. Of course, none of Howard's information meant that the peace in St. Augustine itself would be disturbed any time soon.

When he reached the Panton and Leslie store, his employer was outside checking off goods just arrived by a pitifully small pack train. John waved and went inside to wait. The change in the big front room shocked him. Just months ago, when he had left for Savannah, the room had been stacked almost to the ceiling with skins and furs and blankets and barrels of flour. Perhaps it was true that only a few sneaking Creeks had begun to trade with Americans, but the bare room indicated otherwise.

Howard had told him that Chief Mad Dog and four lesser chiefs had traveled to the Georgia capital at Augusta to sell the rights to tribal lands in the Oconee region. The colonel, of course, expected Elijah Clark to take full advantage of the move by purchasing the land. John needed Leslie's advice as to how to approach Quesada with the news. In his father's absence, should he make an appointment through Father O'Reilly? Or was the governor's mood these days such that he could go himself without an intermediary?

"Your guess on that is as good as mine," Leslie said, when John had told him the gist of Howard's intelligence. "Of course, there's no way of knowing whether you'll see Quesada or Morales. The governor is in and out of his bed." John waited while Leslie lit a cigar. "If your rumors turn out to be true this time," the Scotsman went on, "*and* if old Clark plans to buy up that Oconee land, his Excellency should know, even if it puts him back to bed. I wouldn't be a bit surprised to learn that the Georgia Militia stopped Elijah Clark only temporarily."

"Did you suspect that all along?"

"I did. And just last week, your father's overseer, Captain Atkinson, told me the old goat's been seen back on the Georgia border at Coleraine, plotting openly with the French. What's more, unless I'm getting senile before fifty, they're going after Amelia Island this time." He blew a smoke ring. "We've got a two-gun battery there. How long do you think we could hold out? Morales is a fool. If the governor doesn't get well soon and stay well, I wouldn't give a skinny Minorcan chicken for our chances. I, for one, don't count on one iota of help from the Creeks from now on. But then nobody ever asks my opinion any more."

"I'm asking it now. Shall I go right over to Government House? You see, the remainder of Howard's message indicates that it *is* Amelia Island that's in danger."

Leslie rubbed his forehead. "I wonder why I remain so modest. I could have told anyone that a month ago."

"How?"

"A feeling. Quesada has all but lost control of his province. I keep telling you, Morales is worse than no governor at all. Get out of here, son, and try to see somebody over there. Why not try his Excellency's *escribano*, Zubizarreta, if Quesada's in bed today? He's smarter than he appears. At times, I think the little man does carry the weight of government on his round shoulders—just as he believes he does."

"Do you think I dare give him Howard's message?"

"Why not? If you have to make a sworn statement,

he'll be the one to take it, won't he? Señor Zubizarreta has no humor, but he does have sense. That's more than you can say for Morales."

Pudgy, unsmiling Señor José de Zubizarreta met John on the stairs to the second floor of Government House. The two exchanged greetings, and the señor delivered a speech reporting on Quesada's slightly improved health, characteristically punctuating each statement with chops of his right hand like a man pounding a nail.

When he finished, John asked, "Do you suppose you'd be able to arrange an interview for me with his Excellency? I have important information from Colonel Howard at San Vicente." Recalling his father's way of flattering the señor, John added: "If anyone can manage this, I'm sure you can. And I'll be ever so grateful."

Zubizarreta bowed, drew down the corners of his mouth importantly, and said, "I will make every effort. Will you wait inside?"

"You mean you can arrange it right now?"

"It is my honor to have access to his Excellency through his wife, Doña María Josefa, who is with him."

John held the door for the bustling *escribano* and followed him into the governor's office. Zubizarreta bowed again, gestured toward a chair, and left on his mission.

At that moment, John missed his father more than ever. They had always enjoyed even the most casual meeting with the conscientious señor, whose genius McQueen declared was to make a momentous occasion out of nothing.

He was puzzled as to why his father had gone to Pensacola. Personal business, Leslie had said. Of course, in the four months John had been in Savannah, who could tell what new personal business the man had thought up? Most of the McQueen holdings, though, so far as he knew, were along the St. Johns River to the north.

He decided not to worry about it now and tried to rehearse the details of the information he hoped to give Quesada.

♦   ♦   ♦

In a few minutes, Doña María Josefa admitted John to the governor's bedroom, then sat down in her customary place in the anteroom while the two men talked. Her husband was pleased to learn that the McQueen family had come at last, and when he was happy, so was Doña María. Too often, she had listened to the governor's fretting over the loneliness of Don Juan McQueen. "It is wrong, María," he would say, "for a man to be forced to live without his wife. Her duty is to be at his side . . . to sleep, to eat, to pray."

María had met few Protestants aside from Don William Panton, Don Juan Leslie, and the few other British gentlemen permitted, for reasons she didn't understand, to remain in East Florida. She had met only one Protestant woman—Doña Belle Leslie, who frightened her because she was seldom sober. But María had promised her husband to do everything in her power to win the friendship of Doña Ana McQueen. With God's help, whatever brought happiness to the troubled life of her husband she would do.

The two men spoke in low voices. As far as she could tell, understanding little English, the talk was of new threats on the frontier.

"You will go now to make a sworn statement, *hijo?*" her husband asked in a voice that seemed to be ending the interview.

"Yes, Excellency. Señor Zubizarreta is undoubtedly waiting for me in your office—quill in hand."

María tiptoed to the door of the large bedroom. Her husband was smiling. Young McQueen stood up. Perhaps, she thought, now would be the proper time to ask about the boy's mother. He was coming toward her on his way out.

"*Gracias*, Doña María," he said. "My mother is well. I'm sure, had she known I'd see you, she would have sent her regards."

"Soon I will be strong again," Quesada called from his bed. "Your family will honor us by a visit to Government House?"

John hesitated. "To be honest, Excellency, my mother will probably want to wait for my father's return. Everything here is strange to her, you know."

María, not understanding all he said, looked from one to the other, a perplexed little smile on her pretty, round face. Quesada explained in Spanish, and she nodded.

"Do you know why your father went so unexpectedly to Pensacola?" the governor asked.

"No, sir. I'm as curious as you are."

Quesada smiled. "To pass the time, no doubt. Send him to me the moment he is home. If the bad news you bring from Colonel Howard is true, I will have need of him as captain of my Rural Militia."

María caught the word *militia*. "There is trouble?"

Quesada sank back against his pillows. "There is always trouble, María. But God will keep it far from St. Augustine while Doña Ana is here. I have prayed for that."

Chapter 30

✦✦✦   About midday June 8, on the west bank of St. Johns where they waited for Job Wiggens' ferry, Harry unsaddled their horses and began to rub them down. He was worried about his master today. They had stopped to rest only once all the way from Alachua to the river. Had McQueen not been so silent, the hard ride itself wouldn't have worried Harry. Miss Anne and the children were coming soon, and anyone who knew Don Juan would know that he was going to cover the distance back to St. Augustine in a hurry. But the man who filled Harry's world had said almost nothing since morning. Their journey to Pensacola and back to King Paine's village at Alachua had been pleasant, his master in good spirits all the way—until his talk with Paine.

Maybe, Harry thought, he's just worn out. After all, he's getting older. At seventeen, forty-four seemed ancient. No matter how hard Harry tried, he couldn't get him to take proper care of himself. Let the man get a new idea about something and off he'd go. The least Harry could do was go with him. Staying at his side was easier anyway, because being sure his master was all right was Harry's reason for waking up in the mornings.

"Time you stop walking up and down and stretch out, Don Juan," Harry called, as he unrolled a blanket and spread it on the ground. There was no response, not even a gesture to let the boy know he'd heard. Learning to call his master "Don Juan" had not been easy. He'd been Mausa John for all of Harry's early life in Georgia, but that would not do once they moved to St. Augustine. Whatever I calls him, Harry thought, he'll always be my master.

"You hear me?"

Without a word, McQueen walked back toward him and stretched his big, weary body on the blanket.

"You want I should put this other blanket under your head?"

"No, Harry. I'm fine. We surely won't have to wait long for Wiggens. Mustn't get too comfortable. Too much on my mind." After a moment, he added: "You'd better rest some too. We've come a long way."

Harry spread the other blanket and lay down nearby. "You like that governor we seen in Pensacola all right? You ain't said."

"Yes. His Excellency Enrique White was most cordial. I did all I could do to—protect our future."

"We going to get more free land in West Florida now?"

"No! Deliver us from that wilderness." McQueen lifted himself to one elbow and smiled. "I can see you're not going to shut up 'till I tell you. You've done fine up to now. I went to Pensacola because there's a chance, if Quesada doesn't fully recover, that White will become governor of East Florida. Does that answer your question?"

Harry grinned. "It sure do. All this time I been wondering."

A quick frown creased Don Juan's forehead. "White lacks Quesada's warmth and charm, but he could be strong enough to handle things in St. Augustine. If any man is that strong. But it isn't Governor White I'm worried about now. King Paine had some bad news. Worse because our family is coming."

Harry sat up, his eyes wide with alarm, but knowing when to keep silent, he waited for Don Juan to go on.

"Oh, there won't be any trouble in the city, I'm sure. I don't worry much any more about the blasted French and Georgians with their little jabs here and there. It's the disloyalty of the Indians I fear. You remember what I said when Chief McGillivray died. That our colonies would begin to crumble."

"I remember the words you use. You said the Indians was like a good fence holding back the Americans."

"Paine swears that some Creek chiefs have now signed a peace treaty with Georgia and agreed to cede all rights to their lands around the Altamaha River. If General Elijah Clark decides to buy those lands, he can march right through them to our frontier."

Harry thought a moment. "General Clark, he used to be your friend back in Georgia. Do we hate everybody up there in Georgia now—except our own folks?"

McQueen got up. "No, Harry. No. We don't hate them. I just try to forget they're there. All my old friends."

"You still like 'em?"

Don Juan laughed drily. "Yes. But I manage to keep those feelings snuffed out most of the time. Directed the other way, at least—toward Miss Anne and the children."

It was a little dark when they rode into the McQueen stable. Don Juan turned his horse over to Harry and walked wearily through the garden. He needed a bath and a shave. He was bone-tired and worried. Pedro and Katrina must have been looking for them. The house was glowing with light.

He had just picked two ripe, sticky figs from the tree by the well when the loggia door opened and out romped Niño. The happy dog under one arm, he stopped a moment to enjoy his welcoming house. A man can't be too worried when he owns a good house and a comical dog and is blessed with faithful servants. Niño kissed his stubbly chin again and again and bit at his boots when he set him on the ground. "You don't care that I need a shave, do you, pup?" He sat down on the loggia and began to unwind his leggings, a ritual now for Niño, who tugged and batted at the rough, muddy strips of cloth.

His traveling jacket over one shoulder, boots in hand, Don Juan trudged in his bare feet across the loggia, wondering idly where Pedro could be. Preparing his bath, he supposed, as he lifted the iron latch, kicked open the door, and stood face to face with Anne.

♦   ♦   ♦

She and Pedro had planned the moment. Anne had planned a hundred things to say. No words came.

He was older, a little heavier—muddy, tired, barefoot—but his face at the sight of her could have lighted a dark room.

She took a step toward him, then another. He stood, drinking her with his eyes. In the glow of the lamp, she could see tears glisten on his bearded cheeks. Nothing had changed. Even without a touch, there was at last no distance between them. . . .

"The children are at—Government House," she said. "I—prayed you'd come tonight."

His boots and jacket dropped unnoticed to the floor and she ran into the dear, familiar arms, grateful that their magic still held.

If only for this moment, she was no longer afraid.

Chapter 31

✦✦✦ The June days trooped by, filled to the brim for Don Juan McQueen. William pestered him to go fishing or hunting or exploring around the city, and Sallie, refusing to agree that William had a right to be alone with his father, pestered to go along. Their attention pleased him enormously.

He found Cousin Margaret as bewitching as young John had claimed, and his few conversations alone with Eliza had only strengthened the special bond between them. "I still can't decide," Eliza confided, "which makes me happier—being with you here in St. Augustine or hearing Mama laugh again!"

Quesada appeared almost fully recovered and had granted four hundred acres on Amelia Island to Don Juan for his firsthand information that the Creeks had ceded to Georgia new land along the Altamaha. Never mind that the French were rumored to be encamped on Amelia. Don Juan was once more convinced that trouble would pass. At least he owned today with his family, and he meant to live it.

Waking each morning to find Anne beside him was like a delicious dream. But he wasn't dreaming. She was there, sleepy-eyed, nestling against him as though to put off the moment when even the children might interfere, to say nothing of life in this alien city. She was being admirable—charming with all the Quesadas, gracious with his St. Augustine friends, all a wife should be. He was filled with pride in her and, since only he could know that her appearance of ease was costing her some effort and that the effort was entirely for his sake, he was filled with gratitude as well.

"You were always a sleepyhead," he teased on a bright morning after she had been there nearly three weeks. "I like you, Mrs. McQueen. Did you know?"

She pressed her face into his shoulder. "Yes. I know. I know I'm a sleepyhead too. But it's more than that. John? Am I selfish to wish we could have one day and one night alone?"

"Not at all. And young Juan and I have worked it all out. Next week, leaving Margaret and the children in his care, we leave—just the two of us—for a trip to the St. Johns!"

She sat up, her eyes troubled. "Are you sure the children will be all right?"

He laughed. "Of course! You'll have to think of a better excuse than that, madame."

"I don't want an excuse. I—*want* to be with you. But—"

"But—what?"

"You—won't press me to move to your new property, Los Molinos de McQueen, will you?"

He pulled her back down beside him. "Have I ever put undue pressure on you?"

The sound she made was half laughter, half groan. "Every day you've been gone! Every thought of you— every letter has been—almost unbearable pressure."

"But that's love!"

Her look struck fear into him. "Yes. But it's—the way you *are*, too. Don't—push me, John. I beg you."

Without a word, he got slowly out of the bed and stood looking down at her. In three glorious weeks, there had been no bad moments. Not one. He had even managed to bury his guilt at missing his daily prayers. So great was his happiness that he had worried not at all about the day when he would have to confess that he had lacked the courage to kneel at his altar before his crucifix—in Anne's presence. The altar had simply stood at the far end of the room, in the shadows, unmentioned by either of them. He had tried in every conceivable way not to push her. Now, afraid of an argument, he could only stand there.

She returned his look but made no effort to help him. At last, his need to know what she really meant overcame his fear.

"How have I put pressure on you, Anne? Tell me how and I'll stop at once."

She sat up in the bed and clutched the covers so tightly that her knuckles whitened. "Men don't know—the way women love! I love you more every day I live. That alone presses down on me, John. Sometimes—I think—I'll die. . . ."

In one movement, he swept her back into his arms. "Anne, Anne is it so bad here? Have I—forced you into any situation here to cause this? I—haven't even prayed!"

She clung to him, her fingers dug into his back. "Don't talk any more. You've been—perfect. I'm trying to be."

She had begun to weep, and for the first time he knew her pain. Until now, there had been no room in his heart for any but his own.

"Anne, I—thought everything was going so well." He felt her arms tighten.

"It is, John. You're showing us all a beautiful time! I'm just afraid that you've been dreaming—false dreams that I might some day live at—Los Molinos with you."

"I swear to you, I haven't," he lied, trying to get her to look at him. "It's simply an incredibly beautiful spot, and I do plan to build a fine house there on the noble St. Johns; less than three miles from Fort San Vicente—amply protected. You've always wanted me to settle down and plant. I'm going to do that at Los Molinos." He waited for her to say something—anything. She only clung to him. "A journey to the property will—give us time alone. That's my dream today. All we ever have is—*now*, Anne."

In his enthusiasm, he had almost forgotten his real reason for haste—the impending threat by Clark's men to the frontier, which he dared not share with her. He went on, "At dinner tonight with Leslie, young Juan may find out whether he wants to take the position Panton is offering. The boy could be leaving us for Pensacola in a month or so." He lifted her chin, forcing her to see that he was smiling. "This may be our only chance to go alone. Two lovers together, forgetting the future—just this once. Can you resist that? Next week, right after we attend the fancy-dress ball in your honor at Government House, we'll go. Agreed?"

Her eyes still swam with tears, but she smiled too. "John McQueen, I declare, you're married to—the weakest woman on earth!"

In a few minutes, he had gone whistling down the outside stairs, to douse himself in Pedro's bucket arrangement, leaving Anne to bathe in the warm water Harry had set by their door.

Why *not* go with him this once? she thought as she toweled herself and slipped into her smallclothes. She was tired of suffering alone; sick to death of the struggle to live up to a good mother's sense of responsibility. Sallie and William would be all right with young John, of course. She had done her best by her children for four long years, and she knew in her deepest heart that she would never really fail them. She owed it to Big John at least to *see* his land. If she hadn't learned by now not to give him false hope, she would never learn. And although she dared not hint at such a thing, who could say that some day a miracle might not happen for them?

She pulled a thin, flowered-voile dress over her head. As she tied the blue ribbon at its high waist, she began to dance slowly across the room, her heart suddenly so light that she felt dizzy. A dusty sunbeam lay along the wide board floor. Time to open the shutters, she thought, and let in the full light of what was surely going to be a happy day.

Flinging wide the shutter at the window nearest the north end of the room, she froze. In the blaze of light, the carved white crucifix above his altar leaped out at her. She stared at the stiff ivory Christ sagged in death, the poor head hanging. Each day she had avoided looking at the idol, but now the old fears coursed again through her veins like blood. She stood twisting her fingers, wondering frantically how to rid herself of the fear, so shadowy it overpowered the sunlight.

Then she knew. Perspiration broke over her body as she moved woodenly toward the altar. Her heart pounded. Before her, on the altar in a little heap, lay his rosary. Her hand reached to touch it, then drew back. The same twisted figure of the Christ hung at the end of the rosary beads. She stiffened. What if he came bounding up the stairs and found her there? Never mind, she had no choice now but to do what she had to do. She snatched up the rosary and thrust it into her dress pocket. But that was not enough. Desperate to break the hideous spell, she stepped up onto his thick tapestry prayer cushion and on tiptoes, reaching as high as she could stretch, she grasped the bottom of the ugly wooden cross and lifted it from its peg in the wall.

She could hear him laughing downstairs with the children as she hurried across the room and jerked open the bottom drawer of his wooden chest. Working as fast as she could, she tucked both the rosary and the crucifix inside the folds of a bundle of brown cloth. A blanket? What difference did it make what the cloth was? God had given her time and sense enough to put the heathen objects out of sight.

Now close the drawer! *Close the drawer!* She could not. Her hands trembling, she lifted out the hidden objects, laid them to one side and opened the brown cloth to its full length.

"A robe!" She stifled a cry. "A—monk's habit—in my husband's room!"

She was trembling so, her fingers were all thumbs as she refolded the robe swiftly, stuffed both the crucifix and the rosary deep into the brown bundle, pushed it well back in the drawer, then slammed it shut.

The loud noise helped. Slowly, she backed away from the chest and stood erect in the flood of sunlight. She smoothed her dress, tucked in a wisp of hair, lifted her chin, and smiled. . . .

Now in some sort of ridiculous peace she could go with him to his place on the St. Johns. Who cared if the peace *was* ridiculous? A tingle of almost wicked delight caused her to hug herself. Not only would they be alone on the St. Johns River—they would be *free*. There was no church at all up there in the wilderness. Neither hers nor his.

No frightening distance of any kind between them.

Chapter 32

✱✱✱ Her slippers barely skimming the floor of Government House ballroom, Eliza wondered how she would ever find a way to record the magic of the evening of June 30, 1795, in the pages of her diary. The night was almost unbearably hot and humid, but the music, played by Minorcans and Negroes, was familiar enough from her first visit to cause her to feel nostalgic, yet foreign enough to make her tingle with romance. The whole affair was like St. Augustine itself, she thought, as she executed the tiny steps of a proper Spanish dance with the laughing son of Papa's friend and business manager, Don Bartolomé de Castro. Everything in her father's city was a mixture of so many things. The rollicking hodge-podge of music—both Spanish and English—matched the fragments of conversation she overheard as couple after couple moved past.

For once, John appeared to have Margaret's full attention. Eliza had prayed for this, but the prayer, she noticed, had not prevented Margaret's quick inspection of each young Spanish and Irish officer in the bright blue jackets, red vests, and buff knee breeches of the St. Augustine regiments.

"You dance like an angel," young Castro said again in Spanish.

Thank heaven she had studied her Spanish grammer all those nights back in Thunderbolt. Papa was proud that on this visit his daughter could converse a little in their own tongue with his friends. But the brightest joy was seeing her mother and father—far and away the handsomest couple on the floor—dancing and laughing as though they were young again and living together like other parents. On their way through Government House Gardens earlier tonight, John had whispered, "I think we're making progress with them, don't you?" She had agreed, and seeing them now, she agreed still more.

Her escort guided her to a seat by a window for a moment's rest and left to bring cool drinks. She was watching her parents—especially her mother, smiling up at Papa's Spanish friends—when from outside she heard someone cough. It was not a signal for attention. The cough had a choking sound as though the person meant not to be heard. She turned and saw the tall, straight figure of Señora Perpal half hidden in the shadows of a large clump of bushes. Eliza smiled, but the señora's face was grim. Not knowing exactly what to do, the girl turned back to the noisy room. Ysabel Perpal, of course, would not have been invited to the governor's ball.

On a sympathetic impulse, Eliza jumped up and leaned out the window. "*Buenas noches*, señora. It's a lovely night, isn't it?" Their eyes locked, but the woman remained silent. "I imagine it's cooler out there," Eliza offered.

"*Sí*, señorita," Ysabel said in a low, hard voice. "It is cooler than you know." Then she vanished into the shadows of the courtyard.

Eliza's escort was coming toward her, and behind him she could see her parents making their way across the crowded floor. She would say nothing about the awkward moment with the señora. Papa would only laugh and accuse her of having a soft heart. He was fond of the Minorcan woman, but it would never occur to him to think it strange that she had to stand outside looking in at the festivities.

There was no need to explain anything, because halfway across the room her father was stopped by Señor José de Zubizarreta, a look of urgency on his round face. Papa excused himself and left the room abruptly, in the company of the governor, Mr. Leslie, Don Bartolomé Morales, and a half dozen other Spanish officials.

◆ ◆ ◆

His travel-soiled shirt wet with sweat, an almost scornful look on his bearded, honest face, Rural Militia Captain Peter Carne was waiting when the elegantly attired gentlemen filed hurriedly into Quesada's office. Don Juan knew that Carne, once a Georgian from Camden County, now a loyal Spanish subject, would waste no time on pleasantries. The expression on his face had already sounded an alarm.

"I regret the absence of chairs, gentlemen," Quesada said, sinking wearily into his own chair at the desk, "but we had no advance notice of this meeting." He rubbed his forehead, then looked directly at Carne. "This is an evening for merriment, Captain, so be brief. My head aches."

"Sorry to interrupt, Excellency, but our post at Juana has been captured." Ignoring the exclamations, Carne went on. "Last night. The attacking party of renegade Georgians out-numbered our pitiful force four to one. They had no chance to defend themselves or the post."

In spite of the heat, Don Juan felt the dampness on his body grow cold. The outpost at Juana was just nine miles north of St. Augustine, directly on the road over which he and Anne would have to travel if he accepted his Excellency's offer of the royal carriage for their trip.

There followed a babble of questions, but McQueen walked to a window and stood staring into the darkness, at first only half hearing the captain's report. But then the details began to penetrate his numbness: how the attackers had crossed the river under cover of darkness; how they had advanced through the palmetto swamps, overcome the one sentry with regrettable ease, and captured the garrison without firing a single shot. They had also rounded up over a hundred head of cattle belonging to George Fleming—meaning that much of St. Augustine's beef supply was gone.

"I do not want to know more," Quesada snapped. "Only that your news is from a reliable source."

"Does your Excellency think I'd have made the ride from San Vicente without the facts?"

"I do not know what I think. What is your source?"

"Militiaman Robert Burnett," Carne answered. "I put him under arrest for suspicious behavior. He betrayed the others who attacked Juana with him."

Quesada moaned. "How can I govern a province when my own militiamen cannot be trusted?"

"I reckon Colonel Howard would be interested in the answer to that question too, Excellency," Carne said. "A turncoat like Burnett can come in handy, though. If he can be believed, he wasn't the only one of our men who took part."

"Give to me the names of the leaders," the governor demanded.

"Lang and Plowden—with the aid of boats said to belong to Colonel John McIntosh."

"That is not possible! McIntosh is in Morro Castle in Havana!"

Carne shrugged. "Believe that if you like, Governor, I don't."

"Neither do I," John Leslie said. "We'd have no way of knowing here, but President Washington has been trying for weeks to use his influence with Las Casas to free McIntosh."

"You see, Excellency?" Morales broke in, wringing his hands. "You see? What have I told you? It is our luck that both McIntosh and Hammond are once more back in Florida!"

"I did not ask your opinion, Colonel Morales! When I am in need of it, I ask." Quesada tossed his hands. "*¡Marchense!* All of you—go! Dismissed until tomorrow. Only Don Juan McQueen will remain."

When the others had gone, McQueen sat down near the governor's desk. "I'm sure we'll find upon further investigation, Excellency, that Captain Carne's story is exaggerated."

"I am not sure. The captain is no liar. You are not as hopeful as you say, either, Don Juan. Do not pretend."

"Why not retire without going back to your guests? I'll gladly take your regrets. You look ill."

"Not too ill to say to you that, tomorrow, you must find a way to send Doña Ana and your children back to Georgia!"

He stared at him. "You're joking, of course. Doña Ana and I are planning to visit Los Molinos de McQueen."

Quesada slapped the desk. "With the devil Georgians raiding our outposts, you will take her into their line of fire?"

"No, of course not, but if it's true they've captured Juana, it isn't at all likely they'll strike again soon. Can't you see now is the best time for me to take her? More than that, we'll be stopping at San Vicente. They wouldn't dare attack our best-fortified position."

"I forbid you!"

Don Juan got up. "Forgive me, Excellency, but you know many of those Georgians are my friends. Acquaintances, at least. Doña Ana is safe in the presence of a McIntosh. Any McIntosh."

"You are too shocked to make sense, Don Juan! You will find a way, on my order, to get her out of Spanish East Florida at once!"

"Why, sir, is it so important to you? Am I understanding something you're trying to tell me? You know, I wouldn't endanger my family."

Quesada sighed. "You are misunderstanding my heart. You would never forgive yourself should danger come to Doña Ana and your children. I have watched you suffer all I can bear. Would you leave them here in St. Augustine when the enemy has struck so near by? You will not be here, you know. As Rural Militia captain, Colonel Howard will need you on the frontier."

Don Juan's shoulders sagged. "Of course. And I'll go should there be further trouble. But with Howard up there, I'm certain there's no immediate danger."

"You talk with the desire of your heart, not from your brain, Don Juan. Can Carlos Howard create new, loyal troops? Is he God?" He spread both hands helplessly. "Am I God? Can I do more than send another letter of protest to the stupid governor of Georgia, who will in the future—as in the past—take no action to prevent them from attacking again?"

The music had stopped. Undoubtedly Morales had declared the ball over. Don Juan clenched and unclenched his hands, then went to stand again by a window, his back to Quesada.

"I am sorry for you," his Excellency said softly. "I can—feel your struggle. But I am waiting for your obedience."

Back at the desk, McQueen whispered brokenly, "I—know you're right, but I can't let her go. I promise not to take her on—on the journey we'd planned, but—I can't let her go! Not yet."

Don Juan was hurrying, head down, through Government House courtyard, when Leslie stepped onto the path and took his arm firmly. "I saw your wife to the house. She's packing."

"Packing!"

"I hate to send a ship only half filled with cargo, but I made up my mind in the governor's office a while ago. No way to be certain the pack train bringing more skins from Oconee will get through now anyway. I'm ordering the *Deliberate* to sail tomorrow for Savannah. John's taking them home. Your family will have a safe journey."

"No!" He grabbed Leslie's lapel. "Why is everyone but me giving into fear?"

"She wants to go," Leslie said in a calm voice. "Don't be such a selfish son of a gun."

Don Juan's fist caught his friend's jaw and sent him sprawling backward into a clump of oleanders.

For what seemed a full minute, Leslie lay there motionless; then, his voice still calm, he said, "You *are* a selfish son of a gun!"

McQueen rushed to him, pulled him to his feet, and began to brush off his jacket.

"I thought only a cracker or a Georgia mule kicked like that," Leslie mumbled, pushing him away.

"I—wouldn't have done that for anything," Don Juan whispered. "I wasn't angry, Leslie, I was—*scared*." He started toward his house, then turned back. "You're right, of course. They must leave. But"—he held out his hands—"if she leaves me now, she may—never come back!"

♦   ♦   ♦

Young John waited on the loggia, dreading to see his father come home. Leslie had told him the bad news about Juana. With Eliza and Margaret helping, he and Mama had packed all their belongings in half an hour's time. The bundles and bags stood now in a row at the gate. The tide, if his estimate was correct, would serve no later than eight tomorrow morning. The dream was over. The old strain was back on his mother's face. There could be no worse ending to her visit. Whatever fragile bridge had been built between her and Papa's East Florida friends had been washed out by the wave of terror this night had brought.

Even if his father refused to face it—tonight or ever— John was certain that his mother was leaving St. Augustine for the last time.

"I won't begin to rest," she said only minutes ago, "until we're on Mr. Leslie's ship."

John had taken her in his arms, unable to keep back tears.

Mama, dry-eyed, straight-backed, had then begun to move about Papa's room as she had done that first night. "At times," she said woodenly, "I've rested here in this room beside your father. I may never really rest again, leaving him alone like this. But God will have to give me strength to accept that." She had then turned to look straight into his eyes. "I want you to know and remember, John, that if I had only myself to think of, I would somehow manage to live here. As things are, I dare not think of myself. Or—your father." Her voice trembled as she added, "If—only we could go now—while I'm still strong! Before he walks back in this room."

It was then John decided to wait downstairs for his father, to beg him not to plead with her to stay. He had no idea what Papa's mood might be, or why Quesada kept him after the others were dismissed.

The question struck him suddenly, as he stood waiting: *Why was it up to him to tell his own father how he should be with his mother?* Perhaps he shouldn't even be there when Papa came home. . . .

Still trying to decide, he heard the heavy, slow

footsteps—so unlike his father's—crunch toward him along the shell walk that led from the governor's gardens into the McQueen property. He listened as the steps came nearer, then stopped. His father was alone in the shadows, out of John's sight. Praying, he supposed . . . undoubtedly using the coquina well-rim as an altar. Papa always has to kneel somewhere. John would have found it impossible to pray tonight even if, as with Papa, it had become a habit. He could only stand stiffly in the darkness, convinced that a God who permitted the new storm that was tearing his mother and father apart again—this time maybe forever— would not be likely to listen.

He ran up the stairs to his room and closed the door. Only then did he let himself face the fact that Margaret was leaving too.

After a long time, he heard Papa climb the stairs, the step firm and steady. The door opened softly and his father whispered: "Go to sleep, son. Don't worry. I've—settled it all in my own mind."

"I'm—taking Mama home tomorrow."

"I know."

"Papa?"

"Hm?"

"I think you ought to know before you see her, she told me that if it weren't for the children—she'd stay with you."

"Thank you for telling me. I'm going to her now."

Anne scarcely heard him open the door to their room. He didn't look at her, lying motionless in the bed. She waited as he began to undress slowly. Neither spoke. Moments ago, she had claimed God's courage to face down the unrelenting child in this man whom she loved far more than her own life. He had always won if she cried. His arms around her to comfort her, to stop her tears—also stopped her will. But she was not prepared in any way for his surprising calm and silence.

Dressed for sleep, he walked out of the shadows at the far end of the room and sat beside her on the bed, holding his nightcap in his hands. "I saw your things at the door downstairs. You're all packed?"

"Yes."

"I'm coming to lie beside you in a minute," he said, his voice so quiet and strong that she moved the lamp for a better look at him. He looked old, determined. "But, Anne, there's something I have to say first. I'm coming to Savannah. Just as soon as we get things under control here. His Excellency and John Leslie convinced me that you and the children must leave tomorrow. But don't forget for one minute that, as soon as I can safely slip across the border, I'll be there—if only for a few days."

She reached for his hand. "John—they'll put you in prison!"

"I have no choice. I've—had you in my arms again."

He had made no move to touch her, but Anne clung to him as though to draw some of his unexpected, almost frightening strength into herself. Still embracing him her eyes fell on the dark, empty wall above his altar. "John," she whispered, "I—hid your—crucifix."

"I know. I forgive you."

"It's in the bottom drawer of the chest—tucked in that—brown garment."

"Thank you. Outside just now, I wondered where to start hunting."

"The rosary's there too."

He nodded, patted her head, holding it down against his shoulder . . . but the old distance had begun to open between them. . . .

She had begged God only for strength to stand up to his pleadings that she stay. But there he sat, stronger, quieter, more determined than she'd known him since the long-ago night back in South Carolina when he'd left her to fight for American freedom. They had both been young then—Anne too young to want him to be brave and determined and able to leave her. He'd promised then to come back when the war was over. He was promising now to make the dangerous trip to Savannah—but, as then, only *after* he'd fought again for his country.

"John," she said in a small, shrill voice. "John! If it weren't for the children, I'd stay. No matter what."

"You don't know what that means to me. I'm glad you told our son first, though. The boy suffers over us. Now, he and I will both be comforted."

He put out the lamp and got into bed beside her. He held out his arm, as always, to pillow her head . . . and kissed her. In every crisis moment, Anne had counted on her own spiritual strength. Only now, as these final, silent moments slipped by, did she realize that she had also counted on his spiritual weakness.

Beside her lay a tender stranger, possessed of a new and lonely courage which drew her to him even as it took him away from her. . . .

Chapter 33

✤✤✤ The heat from the sun, noon high, pressed down upon him as he walked numbly in the direction of his house, away from the St. Augustine waterfront.

They were gone.

At the corner of Treasury and St. George, he stood a moment, looking down the narrow lane at the clean lines of the half-completed parish church. If only it were finished. He needed its sanctuary, but he dared not stop to inspect the work under way again at last. Talkative Ysnardy the builder, would undoubtedly be there, full of questions about the sudden departure of his family and the fall of Juana. It would be far better to go straight home, to speak to no one but God, who never thought a man weak when tears flowed—as his flowed now, suddenly and without warning.

He walked rapidly down St. George Street, trying to comfort himself with the thought that as soon as he could safely cross the border he was going to her. There was small solace, though, in a journey which could be far, far in the future.

Forgetting that for her sake he had stopped carrying his rosary, he felt for it in his pocket. "Why do you need it, John?" she had asked. "Why must you have all these symbols of God? Isn't God himself enough?"

He walked faster, desperate for one token of holy comfort. A token he could see and touch . . . Christ's broken body on His cross . . . the familiar rosary in his hands.

God walked with him. God felt his sorrow . . . but he needed to feel the dear consolation of the holy objects Anne feared. He crossed himself as he walked, head down, pleading silently for God's mercy on them all and for courage to enter the empty house alone.

"Two bowls of garbanzo soup wait on my table, Don Juan!"

Startled, he looked into the hopeful face of Señora Perpal.

"Since early this sad morning for you, I cook. Thick and spicy. You will be strong from my garbanzo soup."

He stared at her, unable to think of anything to say, even when she deftly rubbed a tear from each of his cheeks with her thumb.

"I hear she is gone. I hear it before the roosters crow. So, I cook for you."

"Later, perhaps," he muttered, then pushed past her inside his loggia and latched the gate behind him.

Halfway up the outside stairs, he met Harry holding something white and lacy which he quickly hid behind him.

"What are you hiding, Harry?"

Tears of sympathy welled in the brown eyes as Harry reluctantly held out Anne's white lace collar. "Miss Anne," he whispered. "She forget to pack this."

Don Juan took the lace, hurried up the stairs to his room, and closed the door. The heat held under the low, dark-beamed ceiling seemed about to smother him as he hung his hat on a peg and moved like a man in a nightmare to the bed.

Pedro and Harry had been instructed not to change the linens. The bed was made up under its heavy red coverlet, but for this first lonely night without her, the pillows would still hold her fragrance. He turned back the coverlet and with the fingers of one hand touched the place where she had slept. Then he recovered the bed and sat down, still holding the lace collar.

Why do you need a symbol, John? Why?

"Because it's—all I have, Anne," he answered.

The servants did not disturb him. No one knew that after what may have been an hour or two hours, he still sat holding the piece of lace in both hands. . . .

Not until a clap of thunder roused him did he notice that the room had filled with yellow-gray light recognizable to any Augustinian as the sign of a sudden summer storm. From the open windows to the west, warm wind poured through the room and out into St. George Street, not refreshing him. A thunderclap so loud it shook the house caused him to jump stiffly to his feet.

It was not raining yet. The windows could be left open a bit longer. He could hear Harry scurrying about downstairs, closing doors against the downpour which would surely come to break the heat. He thought of Anne and the children on the ocean at the mercy of the storm! He reached his altar in three strides and fell to his knees. There was another crash of thunder and the next blaze of lightning illumined the white wall—empty of its crucifix.

He got up and crossed the room to where the chest stood. The heavy bottom drawer creaked as he opened it. From the back of the drawer, he carefully drew out Padre Font's habit. There, as Anne had said, tucked in its folds, lay his rosary and crucifix. Reverently, he placed the bundle on the bed and removed the beads, then the wooden cross with its agonized, dead Christ. At the altar, he kissed the tortured feet and hung the crucifix back in place.

He had not prayed here once while Anne was with him, but he now experienced no guilt. The welcome home from God was too sweet, too real . . . his rosary too comforting in his hands.

The heavy rains fell, soaked the sandy soil of the city for an hour or more, and then stopped. He got up from his knees and stood looking from the Christ to the crumbled lace collar on the bed beside Narciso Font's habit.

If anyone had asked, he could not have explained why he smiled. Little in his life was right. Governor Quesada, his human security, was undoubtedly ill again after the shocking news of last night. Anne was gone. His children were gone. The house was empty and silent. In a day or a week, he could be ordered into battle to kill Georgians who had once been his friends. Still he smiled, almost at peace because he had been free again to pray. . . .

He picked up the brown robe and held it. Once more, in spite of the wait ahead before he could expect to learn that his family was safe, he found a measure of comfort. Enough for now.

Rain still dripped from the eaves of his house and the air seemed less heavy, as did the silence.

After a while, he reached also for the white lace collar.

Chapter 34

✦✦✦ In the early evening of July 10, Don Juan welcomed the clang of his bell and went himself to open the loggia gate to a bowing Señor José de Zubizarreta, inkwell and quill in hand, his arms full of papers.

"I come, Don Juan, at the request of Colonel Morales, to ask help of you. You are alone?"

"Too much alone, señor. Come in, come in."

Leading the way to his parlor, he glanced over his shoulder at the *escribano*, who was obviously delighted with his first look at the interior of the McQueen house. He had always like the conscientious, unsmiling little official and was eager for them to be seated so that he wouldn't miss a single predictable expression on the round, rubbery face. He especially enjoyed the profound look of self-satisfaction which never failed to appear following each of Zubizarreta's statements, the lips tight, the corners of the mouth pulled down for emphasis.

Don Juan settled himself comfortably in his own big chair, to watch. The señor perched on the edge of another chair, cut his eyes again around the well-furnished room, and cleared his throat to begin. "As you know, his Excellency is again ill with fever, and Colonel Morales is in control of government." The mouth clamped shut as though a secret pronouncement had just been concluded.

"I'm sure having you in charge of all the paper work is a great comfort to the governor," McQueen said. "You are a man of long and faithful service, señor."

The *escribano* ducked his head in a small bow of acknowledgment. Then in a businesslike manner he set his inkwell and quill on a nearby table and adjusted the sheaf of paper on his lap. Still on the edge of his chair and using the knuckle of his right forefinger for emphasis, as a man knocks on a door, he began, "I am here in your impressive home because his Excellency ordered Morales to send me. I have here my written report of the *junta de guerra* called, as you know, by Morales on the fourth day of July. I might add that it is a full and complete report."

"Knowing your efficiency, I'm sure it is."

"*Sí*. But such a report must always be approved by a man of responsibility to the government. His Excellency, being too ill to study it, requests that you do so."

McQueen crossed his long legs comfortably. "I'd be delighted to have you read it to me, señor. I have all the time in the world."

The señor frowned. "If you will excuse me, I am not sure that any of us has much time. When a man has written down the actions of our council of war as I have done—in his own hand—the solemn facts leap from the page! We are in danger. Serious danger."

"Oh, I have no doubt of that whatever. But this evening, I can give you all the time you need."

Zubizarreta nodded, ending that section of their conversation. Then he shuffled his papers and coughed as though to begin, but instead stole another glance around the room.

"Shall I light a lamp, señor?"

"The light is good yet from the sun." He sighed softly. "It is—this house. For years, I have worked my fingers to the bone to have sufficient money to buy such a house. Of course, I was not important enough to have received his Excellency's permission at the time of your purchase, but—"

McQueen grinned at him. "And do you have enough money now?"

"*Sí*. I have enough. But his Excellency's joy in you as his neighbor is of more value than my desire for the house."

"Well, now, hold on a minute. I'm not offering to sell it."

"Even if you were," Zubizarreta went on earnestly, "I would grieve for Governor Quesada. I find it barely possible to function under Morales. It is his Excellency who holds my devotion." With a nod which now settled that, the señor selected a page and began, without further comment, to read. " 'Herewith a full account of St. Augustine *junta de guerra* called the fourth day of July in the year of our Lord, 1795, by Colonel Bartolomé Morales at the request of his Excellency Governor Juan Quesada, ill. In attendance at the meeting were these officials: Don Dimas Cortés, Don Gonzalo Zamorano, Don Bartolomé de Castro, Don Juan Leslie, Don Juan McQueen, and Captain José de Córdoba of the Third Cuban Regiment.' "

He looked up for McQueen's approval, received it, nodded, and went to the second page. " 'The *junta* was called for the reading of the most recent dispatch from Colonel Carlos Howard following the capture of the Spanish post of Juana; which dispatch enclosed several reports from Howard's agents scattered along the frontier. All reports stressed the need for utmost caution in offensive action against the rebels, as they are numerous and well armed. One report declared that Richard Lang, along with W. Plowden and R. Wagnon, commanded between forty and fifty armed men in his camp and expected two additional groups, one under the command of General Elijah Clark.' "

"The old rascal."

Zubizarreta nodded vigorously and went on: " 'Still another report contained the disastrous news that nearly all of His Majesty's garrison at Juana had expressed a desire to desert the Spanish Rural Militia and to join forces with Lang. Another report declared that Abner Hammond, out of prison and back in East Florida, was on the march with a force of fifty Frenchmen to join Lang, Plowden, and Wagnon with another five hundred supporters of Clark due to arrive soon.' "

McQueen was no longer amused at the *escribano's* comical mannerisms. The señor was right. Reading it from a paper brought the whole rotten mess to life. He thanked heaven that Anne and the children were now—barring bad luck—safely in Savannah. "Do you believe Abner Hammond *is* really back here again, señor? Or is that report, in your opinion, just another wild rumor?"

"It is not my place to express an opinion, but I believe Hammond to be in Florida." Nod.

"Which means my old acquaintance, Colonel John McIntosh, is probably here too."

Zubizarreta settled that with another brisk nod and turned to the next page. " 'In the dispatch read to the *junta* from Colonel Carlos Howard, several suggestions were set forth for the preparation of a defense line along the St. Johns River, including the erection of a small fort on the northern bank and a battery at the estuary. Colonel Howard also requested armed Negroes and a small number of trusted Indians to be used by him as scouts."

He here lifted one finger for McQueen's special attention. " 'Howard's recommendations were emphatically *defensive* moves. He urged *no offensive* action whatever at this time or in the future, due to the inadequacy of Spanish forces and armaments. Howard concluded with a copy of a report that Richard Lang had announced his desire to harm no one in East Florida, *if the whole province would yield to him in peace.*' "

McQueen began to pace the room. "What a lowdown skunk Lang is! What an audacious, bullheaded ingrate! If the whole province would yield to him indeed! The thought of the man makes my blood boil, señor."

"It is not my place to permit my blood to boil." The *escribano* cupped one hand at his mouth as though to funnel his whisper to McQueen's ears only. "*But* long ago—four years ago—I had to bite my tongue in order not to warn his Excellency concerning Richard Lang." Nod.

McQueen sat down again. "You were right, of course. Go on, señor."

" 'There then followed a heated debate among the members of the Council of War, the main controversy centering on the question of Colonel Morales' sudden desire to attack the rebels at once, before reinforcements could reach them from Georgia. The acting governor stood alone in this desire and, after some convincing statements from

Don Juan McQueen, agreed in the end to follow the plan of Colonel Howard to watch and wait.' "

"Then," McQueen said, "once we calmed Morales, as I recall, we set up a six-point plan for defense of the colony. Is that next? I'm eager to hear how the plan sounds to me now."

"And I am to make certain of your approval of my wording of the six points. 'One, to collect and arm all free Negroes and mulattoes who have fled from Georgia to Florida. Two, to solicit aid from neighboring Indians in return for the promise of supplies and arms.' "

"I'm not sure how we'll keep those promises, but go on."

" 'Three, to unite all available militia groups north of the St. Johns River, still loyal and above suspicion. Four, to send an additional eight men for reinforcement of the garrison of the battery at the bar of the St. Johns. Five, to request Havana to send at least two small armed vessels to aid in the defense of the province. Six, to approach the captain of the English privateer, now in port at St. Augustine in possession of a small prize schooner, and to ask to purchase this vessel.' " The señor clamped shut his lips to indicate that he had finished.

"You're to be congratulated," McQueen said. "At least, I can report that we've managed to execute point six of our plan. I dined yesterday with British Captain McCockburn, and the purchase was completed. We now own his little prize schooner. Father O'Reilly will rechristen her the *Santa Mónica*. Lieutenant Sebastian Verazaluze will command her. She'll be a fine little message boat, and she carries ten guns too. Well, is that the end of your report, señor?"

"All but the conclusion of the meeting, which I shall read quickly."

He had just cleared his throat to begin again when they were both startled by the clang of the loggia gate bell. McQueen excused himself and opened the gate to Ysabel Perpal.

"I must talk to you." She pushed past him. "There is more bad news! You are alone?"

"No. Señor Zubizarreta is here on business."

"Good."

Gesturing for McQueen to follow her, she hurried inside. "Señor." She greeted the *escribano* absently. "It is well you are here. What I say must be reported at once." Brushing aside McQueen's offer of a chair, she spoke rapidly, in both English and Spanish. "My nephew, he come tonight by horse from the outpost at Santa Ysabel, six miles downstream from the post, San Nicolas. His cousin, Minorcan Sergeant José Pellicer, he send him. The Georgians—speaking Spanish in order to fool the stupid garrison—they now capture San Nicolas too!"

"Wait just a minute, señora," McQueen tried to calm her. "Let me get this straight. Pellicer is in command of Santa Ysabel. Is that correct?"

"José Pellicer *was* in command! Santa Ysabel is now abandoned. How you expect Pellicer to stay with only fourteen men and hordes of rebels swarming the land not six miles away? Huh? How you think even a Minorcan soldier dare to try to hold Ysabel but six miles distant from captured San Nicolas?"

"I'm sure he did the right thing. Where did Sergeant Pellicer and his fourteen men go when they abandoned Santa Ysabel?"

"To Colonel Howard at San Vicente." Her eyes flashed with pride. "But—they spike the one cannon at Ysabel first!"

"Excellent. And you did the right thing to come here to me first, señora." Turning to Zubizarreta, McQueen said, "This means military action for us. Will you take the bad news to Morales, señor? Or shall I?"

"The acting governor will be at his home on the Calle de la Marina at this hour, Don Juan. I will bear the news to him, but it will have more effect if it comes from you."

McQueen thought for a moment. The señor was undoubtedly right. Should he bear the news, Morales might act in too much haste—or not at all. The members of the war council, after all, had barely managed to convince Morales not to attack when Juana fell. Indeed, only McQueen's powers of persuasion had called the usually timid acting governor.

He looked from the señora's flushed face to the round,

intense face of the *escribano*, his materials again in his arms, ready to take his leave.

"I'll go to Morales' house," McQueen said quietly. "He doesn't even know yet that I purchased the *Santa Mónica* from McCockburn yesterday. You've done well with the report of the *junta de guerra*, señor. You have also done well to come here to me, Señora Perpal. You're both welcome to enjoy my house as long as you like, but I'd better not wait to see Morales. With two more outposts gone, we have no fortifications left along the lower St. Johns except San Vicente and the little battery at the bar of the river. Morales must have all that straight in his mind."

The señora laughed. "What mind you mean?"

McQueen picked up his hat. "I'll be leaving early in the morning myself for San Vicente. Zubizarreta, you will go at once to Lieutenant Sebastian Verazaluze to tell him the *Santa Mónica* must be rechristened and ready to sail with the tide tomorrow."

The señor nodded.

McQueen held out his hand to Ysabel, smiling. "And—señora? If I do not see you again before I go off to war, I know I can trust you to watch over my house and my little dog."

As though Zubizarreta were not there, the señora, as steady as a tree, looked at McQueen with solemn eyes and said, "Would to God I could go with you—to watch over your *life*."

McQueen caught the look of puzzled surprise, then discreet comprehension on the face of José de Zubizarreta, but the chunky official only bowed, clamped his mouth shut and hurried out the door.

Chapter 35

✦✦✦   L̲ate the next afternoon, Don Juan climbed the bluff at San Vicente with his aging overseer, Captain Andrew Atkinson, whose small craft had come alongside the rechristened *Santa Mónica* just in time to take Don Juan and a half-dozen soldiers ashore.

"Let the younger ones go on ahead," Atkinson said, stopping to catch his breath. "I'm too old to climb fast any more. You've got fifteen years on me, McQueen, but you look all in too. Are you so worried about our chances to stop the rebels?"

"I'm trying not to be, Andrew. If I look old, it's my family. This new trouble at San Nicolas forced me to leave before I'd had time to hear that they'd reached Savannah. I had to send them away on short notice, you know, when Juana fell."

Atkinson brightened. "Why, I can ease your worries! They arrived safely, in spite of that bad storm. My son, George, was just there. He got back to Fort George Island as I was leaving today."

Don Juan threw both arms around the old man, then banged him on the back. "Oh, thank you! Thank you, Andrew! Now I can turn my full attention to what's ahead of us here. You've no idea what this means to me. You've just knocked ten years off my age."

Atkinson chuckled. "I've known you too long to doubt that. There are some folks in Savannah who wouldn't agree, but I *know* what your family means to you. And they're safe and sound." He paused. "Do you suppose we could sit down for a few minutes? I need to talk to you before we get into the middle of whatever Howard has planned for us."

"By all means. I'm sure he won't call a meeting until Lieutenant Verazaluze comes ashore."

The older man settled himself against the trunk of a live oak, and Don Juan, too excited to sit down, squatted on his heels nearby. "Anything wrong at my place on Fort George, Andrew?"

"No. Considering we've had too much rain, the cotton crop isn't bad. It's your overseer—me. Don't have my usual get-up-and-go any more. Have you made up your mind to build a house at Los Molinos? You mentioned putting me in charge there too. I don't think I'm able."

Don Juan laid his hand affectionately on his old friend's shoulder. "No one else will do the job you've done, Andrew, but don't worry about it. Yes, I am building a fine house for my wife at Los Molinos. Maybe your son, George, can help me out until I know when I'll be moving there myself."

"He might be interested, all right. I'll talk to him." Atkinson looked at him for a long time, then asked, half teasing, "You're honestly going to build a house there? With money so scarce?"

"That's my dream. When we're finished here, I'm going straight to Los Molinos to select a house site."

"Has Mrs. McQueen actually agreed to live in Florida?"

"No. But I live in hope."

"You'd be a long way from the parish church."

"Eight hours at the most. No problem at all."

Atkinson shook his head. "You never say die, do you?"

"Never!"

"Well, I guess I've held us up long enough."

McQueen helped him to his feet and they walked on toward the fort. "Before we see Howard, Andrew, there's something I want you to promise me. Whatever action we take at San Nicolas, you must not try to go with us. Our foray could amount to nothing, but it could also be rough going."

"Forget it. I'm as much a Spaniard as you. Everything I own in the world is in East Florida. I'm taking my place with the rest of you."

When they reached level ground, Atkinson squared his shoulders and quickened his stride. "Looks like Howard's rounded up a lot of men. You don't suppose he plans to go on the offensive for once, do you?"

The parade ground below the cluster of wooden buildings was milling with Negroes, a few Indians, and a motley gathering of rural militiamen, many with their own horses.

"We could be in for some hot work," McQueen said, slowing his pace a little to look around. "Andrew, what's your opinion about Colonel John McIntosh? Do you think he's out of Morro Castle, stirring up all this trouble for us?"

The older man shrugged. "Who knows? If we'd lost only Juana, I'd say Lang was behind that. But McIntosh hates Spaniards a lot worse than Lang does. A year in prison didn't lessen that hatred, either. I hope you've said your prayers, McQueen."

Don Juan and Atkinson barely had time to finish a light meal when, along with Captain José de Córdoba, Lieutenant Verazaluze, and Sergeant Pellicer, they were summoned to Howard's quarters.

"Two days ago, gentlemen," the colonel said, "I would not have given you one puny fig for the value of our entire defense line along the St. Johns. It seemed on the verge of collapse. It still may be. For that reason I have now put into motion an *offensive* plan I've had drawn for a long time." Howard smiled slightly. "Our mighty armada has been made ready for action. We are all here, such as we are, and my scouting reports of the past two days are in. Our agents—two of them—managed to penetrate the rebel lines at San Nicolas and creep inside the fort. They found the Georgians drunk and celebrating their exploits. As of yesterday, at least, they were all too drunk to fight. This time, His Majesty's militia is going on the offensive. Any objections?"

The five men looked at each other, then at Howard.

"We're surprised," McQueen said quietly, "but we're at your command, Colonel. The reinforcements I brought on the *Santa Mónica* don't appear to warrant attack, but I doubt that there's a man among us who doesn't trust your judgment on the matter."

The others signaled agreement.

"I quite understand your remarks, Captain McQueen," Howard said. "You've known me to resist Morales' stupid demands for any offensive maneuver. We've lacked both men and guns. We still do. But circumstances alter conditions. In view of our scouting intelligence, we have no choice but to make an attempt to flush out the drunken Georgians at San Nicolas. Our little battery at the bar of the river is not worth trying to hold. So, we abandon that and combine our forces to regain San Nicolas. Once that's accomplished, Sergeant Pellicer and his men will be free to return to Santa Ysabel with some safety."

Howard turned to Andrew Atkinson. "Now, before I lay out my plan for your approval, gentlemen, I feel compelled to ask you, Captain Atkinson, if you're well enough to command the thirteen St. Augustine militiamen I've assigned to you. We all know of your courage, but how is your health?"

"I plan to command my men, sir."

"Very well. Our assault on San Nicolas will be direct and water-borne. I will command from the *Santo Tomás*, with half the Negroes and Indians, along with Captain Atkinson and his men. The schooner *Santa Mónica*, under the command of Lieutenant Verazaluze, will carry Captain McQueen and thirty soldiers. Finally, the remaining Negroes, Indians, and militiamen, supplies and ammunition will be carried by the launch, *St. Augustín del Patrón*. We will set sail with the tide tomorrow morning. My belief is that we have a chance to succeed. There is, of course, a rumor that Colonel John McIntosh is back in East Florida. If so, our chances lessen. But, I have never commanded on rumor and I do not intend to begin now."

The tide served just at dawn. Don Juan, after a sound sleep, bounded up from his mat-covered pallet in the tiny officer's quarters, ready for whatever the day might bring.

But Howard's manner, as they saluted before boarding their separate ships, sent prickles up his spine. The cautious colonel was commanding a risky action, no one doubted that, but McQueen saw no value in sending men to fight with their nerves on edge. Alert, on guard, with orders firmly in mind, yes, but half the reward for a military man lay in the good stimulation that must precede action. Howard, grim-faced, spoke to no one beyond reiterating his orders. The men straggled in silence aboard their assigned ships, minus the needed zest for such an undertaking.

He had considered requesting that Howard permit Atkinson to board the *Santa Mónica* with him. The older man appeared more tired than yesterday. But the colonel's icy manner forced the idea from his mind. Best to leave well enough alone. He was relieved when Howard ordered the gunboat, *Santo Tomás*, to sail alongside his own vessel. At least he could keep an eye on Andrew.

A cool breeze off the wide river lifted his spirits as the tiny armada slipped quietly away from the San Vicente dock and headed in the direction of San Nicolas. Their course was set midway between the river's banks as they stood upstream. Don Juan took his station aft, behind and to starboard of Lieutenant Verazaluze, where he could watch the skillful mariner, hear his orders, enjoy the sight of the coming day and the feel of the following breeze, and still keep tab on Atkinson. The deck rolled under his feet as the little fleet of boats moved at a fair clip.

San Nicolas, he knew, had been one of the few decently fortified Spanish outposts. No one had any idea how much extra firepower the rebels had added in the two weeks since they had occupied it. Militarily, he understood Howard's cautious, chilling manner, but he fully intended to keep his own hopes high that their plan would succeed. Within a few days it could be all over and he would be camping out at Los Molinos, his head full of plans for the new house. Anne and the children were safe, his Excellency would reward him abundantly for this dangerous mission, and a man needed the stimulation of attack once in a while. He meant to make the most of the entire adventure.

The sandy beaches gave way to stands of scrub palmetto and undergrowth along the river's banks, then to pines and live oaks; and in what seemed a short time they had rounded the big bend in the river and were executing the wide invisible arc for the maneuver necessary to bring them steadily, carefully near enough to the San Nicolas dock for firing.

San Nicolas, with its big square moat and surrounding settlement and barracks, was at last in sight—set back about three hundred yards. The sun had climbed high enough in the sky for the rebels to be up and stirring. He could leave the positioning of the schooner to its captain. McQueen's duty was to command his men—to keep the ten small carronades loaded and primed, should their fire be returned. The little armada's one cannon was carried on the bow of Howard's gunboat.

In his mind, McQueen went quickly over his orders: Howard's first command—one cannon ball and a round of small arms from the *Santo Tomás*—would be Don Juan's signal for two timed rounds of carronade fire from the *Santa Mónica*. He paced a short pattern up and down the crowded deck and waited.

Howard's boat had already moved ahead and was now bearing toward the riverbank. McQueen focused his long glass, hoping to see Atkinson at his post aft. He was not there. He refocused the glass.

The old man was lying prone on the deck.

Carlos Howard's piercing order split the silent air, and the cannon ball, with its explosion of powder still ringing, lobbed toward the land. Almost before it landed, the *Santo Tomás'* round of small arms began. Don Juan counted to ten and ordered his own fire.

In the silence that followed, not a shot was returned from the fort, and before his second round had ended, he could see through his glass that fifty or sixty rebels were leaping into canoes and heading into the thick salt marshes that bordered the St. Johns.

McQueen ordered his men to reload and kept the glass trained on the colonel's slight, erect figure in the boat ahead. Howard stood motionless for about five long minutes; then, one hand raised, ordering McQueen to hold his fire, he signaled another round of small arms from his own boat. Still no shot nor other movement from what appeared to be the suddenly deserted outpost. After another long, cautious wait, Howard maneuvered the *Santo Tomás* alongside the *Santa Mónica*.

"Lower two small boats and land them to the south," he ordered. "Four men in each boat and McQueen!"

McQueen had no need to be told why the colonel had ordered him to join the scouting party. Uppermost in Howard's mind, as in his, was the whereabouts of John McIntosh. McQueen knew McIntosh well enough to be able to recognize his boats and his guns or other possessions, should any have been left behind. If McIntosh was indeed back in the vicinity of the St. Johns with the rebels, only heaven knew what lay ahead for the province.

Don Juan and eight of his men let themselves down hand over hand by a rope into their skiffs, then took the colonel off the *Santo Tomás*. The two boats rowed silently for land. The colonel ordered the eight men to spread out and approach the fort from the outer perimeters. He and Don Juan would move carefully toward it in a direct line.

When the skiffs were tied at the dock and the eight men had fanned out, Howard and Don Juan began to creep up the silent, tangled riverbank.

"What of Atkinson—is he dead?" Don Juan whispered.

"No. He fainted. He's too old for work like this. No way to keep him out of the heat, either, until we find out if they've really gone. I'll have him brought into the fort for the night when we're sure it's safe."

For several minutes the two men moved cautiously from tree to tree up the long approach to the fort.

"What do you think, Colonel?" Don Juan asked when they paused behind a giant oak. "Are they tricking us?"

"Quite possibly. They certainly made no effort to hide their flight when we fired."

The two ran across an open stretch and stopped again in the shelter of a myrtle grove to listen.

"We could be heading directly into a trap, Captain McQueen. I don't have a family. Are you willing to risk it?"

"Do we have a choice?"

"Not with replacements on the way from Georgia. We've either retaken San Nicolas or we haven't. I can hear our men moving in. We'll soon know."

"I'm with you, Colonel."

Every few yards they stopped to listen. The offices and quarters were in plain view now. There was no movement, no sound but the warning screams of blue jays in a tree overhead. Perhaps a snake was nearby. Or a hawk. Don Juan scanned the hot, clear sky, saw a hawk swoop down from a pine tree, the jays in pursuit, and breathed easier. There was no alternative to creeping through the tangle of bushes. Both Don Juan and Howard instinctively circled fallen logs, wary of rattlers.

A soft whistle swept across the stillness.

"There's our signal," Howard whispered. "The men have found no sign of life either. Let's run for it!"

They met the eight men at the barracks, then made a quick inspection of the quarters and offices through the entire settlement surrounding the fort. All buildings were empty, but most bore signs of the rebels' hasty departure—salt pork was still frying over a fire in the barracks kitchen, and a barrel of flour stood open beside a tin bowl of half-mixed batter. The men reported finding ammunition and food supplies in the quarters and a pile of discarded saddles—evidence of the haste with which the Georgians had fled on foot to their canoes. So far as anyone could tell, the brief enemy occupancy of the post had done no damage.

After helping to settle Atkinson in the San Nicolas officers' quarters, Don Juan joined a small party sent out to search the creeks and nearby inlets. The only sign that the rebels had been there was a pair of rowboats—evidently those used in the capture—tied near the dock.

"I hate to report this, Colonel," Don Juan said when he returned to the fort, "but those boats belong to John McIntosh. I have no doubt whatever. I used a bit of influence to help him purchase one of them when he first settled in Florida."

Howard looked at him a moment, then asked, "And now that you're certain McIntosh is back leading the forces against us, how do you find your loyalty to his Excellency?"

Don Juan smiled. "As firm as ever. In fact, as soon as I take Captain Atkinson back to his home on Fort George Island, I'll remain on the frontier as long as you need me."

Chapter 36

My Dear Son Juan,

I returned to the city yesterday, after more than two months on the frontier, to learn the exciting but heart-breaking news that you had been here and are now in Pensacola with Panton. You will find him a good employer, but I longed to hear from your own lips every small bit of news from Savannah. I had planned to return here within a week following our recapture of San Nicolas, but after spending time at Los Molinos selecting my house site, fresh trouble developed on Amelia Island. Early in the morning of 2 August, I crossed the bar of the St. Mary's in command of our refurbished gunboat, *Titiritera*, with Howard in command of the *Santo Tomás*. We moved in toward the Amelia beach, where the Georgians were constructing fortifications. I will not write details, but we were hilariously successful—although we all felt foolish at the end. You see, we ran aground, our boats headed the wrong way—out to sea—so that when the rebels fled in the direction of the Georgia shore, we were forced to lie silent—without firing a shot. Needless to say, Howard was not amused but, in dire times like these, I chose to be, especially since we did rout the lunkers.

There seems to be no end to their continuing efforts

to sting us, but Howard is wise and his clever maneuvers, mainly defensive, striking only at the right moments, have succeeded in driving the rebels back over the St. Johns. We abandoned Amelia Island for the present, but one day I will gain possession of my grant there.

I returned to the Plaza to find his Excellency somewhat improved in health, though weak. As always, he has rewarded me, not only with an additional five hundred acres at Molinos, but with a royal recommendation for my military services at both San Nicolas and Amelia. I am glad to be home with my faithful servants and little dog (growing fast), but after such excitement (I led scouting patrols for four weeks following the Amelia foray), I dread the long, lonely winter ahead and must pray for patience to endure until it appears wise and safe for me to attempt a visit, however brief, at The Cottage.

Do write a long letter about them all. Find the time to tell me in detail of your grandmother's attitude. Did you and your mother decide to tell her that the family had to flee what appeared to be danger here? If so, what did the old lady say? What is your mother like without me now? Does she speak of me? Are the children well? Has Cousin Margaret come to her senses yet? I have known little comfort since my family left me—either in body or spirit. The activities to the north were hard, but at least they occupied me.

Word has reached us that at long last, Spain and France have ended their struggle abroad. The Treaty of Basle was signed late in July. Unless the still angry Frenchmen here continue to harass us, we may now have a period of relative peace.

I urge you to meet and show deference to West Florida's Governor Enrique White, a strong and able man, though not particularly engaging or warm. I send my sincere regards to him and to Panton.

Since you and I are friends as well as father and son, I will report that Señora Perpal is well and attentive. In fact, too attentive at times. She has spoiled my fun by dropping her litigation to regain the house. The woman tends to tire me a little unless she is gay or crotchety. Believe me, I am careful. She is, at times, still a temptation, but by grace, a fleeting one. Her pampering gives me some discomfort, since I enjoy fencing with her and find her eyes more beautiful when flashing than when adoring. Oh, well. Your mother fills my thoughts and my heart as always. I long to hear from you.

> *Your truly affectionate Father,*
> *Don Juan McQueen*

John had strolled away from the bustling Panton and Leslie complex on Pensacola Bay to read his father's letter in privacy. He missed him. Work in Panton's office was absorbing, but the town of Pensacola was far drearier than St. Augustine, and he felt more remote from both parents than at any time in Europe as a boy.

His own disappointment at finding his father absent from St. Augustine was still sharp. Had he traveled by the rivers and overland from Savannah, instead of by sea, he would surely have met him somewhere along the frontier. But when the offer from Panton came only a week after he took the family home, his only thought had been to get to St. Augustine as quickly as possible and talk it over with his father.

To escape the cold wind off the water, he turned away from the Bay and walked in the shelter of the eight-foot-board stockade which surrounded the government buildings. Until he could move into a private room in the new Panton mansion, he could find little time alone for writing or reading. The three other clerks with whom he shared a cabin cared for neither. He thought them amicable, but had no doubt that they would all remain merely clerks. There would be dancing tonight at a Creole's house. If he were lucky, his three cabinmates would attend and he could write at length to his father. Somehow, he must convince him that he dare not risk a trip to Savannah until next year. Perhaps not even then, since new laws were slow to pass the state Assembly, and if Don Juan McQueen were caught in Georgia now, he would surely be imprisoned.

At the wharf the day John sailed, Uncle Aleck had told him of the new, more liberal debtor's law in the making. "But your father should be warned," his uncle had said, "that it would be dangerous for him to show his face in Savannah until the law is passed. The firm of Mein and Mackay have been putting strong pressure on me of late over his large indebtedness to them. Young Robert Mackay, in my opinion, has his eye on Eliza, but the lad's a businessman above all else."

He must write his father, too, of Frank Huger's futile but brave attempt to free Lafayette from prison. After nearly a year in a dungeon himself for his efforts, Frank was back in Savannah. Their reunion had been the high point of John's short stay. Wanting, as always, to spare his father heartache, he had not yet decided to tell him that plucky little Mme Lafayette had managed to gain entrance to the dungeon where her husband was confined and was now living there with her children.

The question still twisted in John's mind: Did his mother love his father less than Mme Lafayette loved the marquis? Most of the time, he chose to believe that there were no grounds for comparison. His mother was Anne McQueen—a separate person from Mme Lafayette. Only an immature boy drew such unfair comparisons. He had seen with his own eyes that the woman Anne McQueen loved John McQueen as deeply as a woman could love. A man of almost twenty-three years had no right to judge even his mother, as though he were still a child.

On a night in mid-November, the gate bell startled Don Juan from a deep sleep. He jumped out of bed, surprised to find the wind howling and torrents of rain rushing from the eaves of his house. The sky had been bright with stars when he retired early, with a new book just arrived from England.

He grabbed a dressing gown and hurried downstairs, sure that something drastic must have happened. No one in his right mind would be out visiting on a night like this.

The bell jangled again and he swung open the loggia

gate to Father O'Reilly, water streaming from his round felt hat.

In the parlor, McQueen threw a handful of pine chips on the fireplace embers and poured two glasses of Madeira.

"I don't apologize for rousing you," the priest said. "My mission is urgent. Anyway, you went to bed too early."

McQueen lifted his glass. "To his Excellency," he said from habit.

"Well said. His Excellency is in need of any help we can give him right now. I've just left him. The man is distraught. He's given up—at last."

"Given up?"

"He's leaving us." O'Reilly touched his forehead. "His mind, I'm sure. A brilliant mind to have withstood the fever for such a long time. He received his release today from Las Casas in Havana."

Stunned, Don Juan shook his head. "He must have requested it weeks ago—without a word to any of us!"

"He did. Only Doña María knew. He wants to see you tonight. He's so riddled with fear of another fever attack, he's convinced tomorrow could be too late. I promised him you'd come."

"I will indeed, Father! I can be ready in five minutes. Will you go with me?"

"No. His Excellency wants to see you alone. He's all dressed and waiting now—in his office. Wearing his uniform to honor your visit." O'Reilly downed his wine. "Just go to him as soon as you can get there."

When Don Juan let himself quietly into the governor's office, Quesada was sitting propped against pillows in his high-backed chair, his face chalky white. He smiled, lifted one hand in greeting, and said, "You came, Don Juan."

"Yes, Excellency. As always, I'm honored that you wanted to see me."

A lock of yellow hair fell unnoticed over the governor's forehead. McQueen thought he had never seen him look so young, so frail, so helpless. He pulled up a chair near the desk and sat down, but all he could say was, "Excellency! Oh, Excellency!"

"I am ill in my heart and in my mind, Don Juan. I am going home to my native city of Jaén. Father O'Reilly told you?"

"Yes."

"I am going home—to die among my family."

"Not to die!"

Quesada tossed one hand in the old familiar gesture. "We do not speak of that tonight. We speak only of our friendship in the years of my life here. *Tú eres mi amigo querido*. You have served me well—as a friend and as His Majesty's official. To express my gratitude I have sent for you now."

Tears had begun to slip down McQueen's cheeks. He made no effort to conceal them. "Serving you has been all joy, but without you, Excellency, the joy will be gone."

Quesada rested his head against the chair back. "My great dream has been to govern this province well. My heart will not leave this place when I am gone. And you must go on with your energy and courage to preserve East Florida." He closed his eyes. "If the despised Georgians succeed in defeating us at last, I pray I will have died first." The eyes opened slowly, to stare, not at McQueen, but beyond him. "Tell me, Don Juan, how you were able to—leave behind your native land of America? I could not do that. Even in my weakness, love for Spain consumes me."

Shocked by the question, McQueen had no idea how to respond.

"You have—not pretended allegiance to Spain, have you, Don Juan? If you have feigned love for the colony in order to—keep my favor and esteem—do not tell me!"

After another silence, McQueen answered, "I had no choice when I arrived, but—*you* have taught me love and loyalty for the province, Excellency."

"That is enough to say. Doña María and I have spoken many times of your heartbreak for Doña Ana and your children. We have thought, too, that such heartbreak might—be also for your native land."

"How can I thank you for such understanding, Excellency?"

"I loathe your country! If I sin, God must forgive me. But I hate the United States of America!" He sighed. "Still, by heaven's grace and mercy, it is good for you to know that my heart has many times ached for *you*—so near its border, but locked here in what must at times appear to you as a—a foreign land."

McQueen could find no words. His gratitude for such unexpected sympathy was almost an agony.

"We will never meet again on this earth, once I am gone," Quesada went on. "So I must know one thing. If, in the future, the law is changed in Georgia, or should you find a way to repay your debts, will you desert East Florida and go back?"

McQueen's hands dropped to his knees. For a long time, he sat staring at the floor. God knew how he longed to repay his debts, to amass another fortune to leave to his children when he died. God knew how he longed to live again with Anne. God knew also of his attachment to St. Augustine—of his pride in his rich, productive lands— Spanish lands he had grown to love. But, if God knew the answer to his Excellency's probing question, He did not impart it.

"I am waiting for your answer, Don Juan. . . ."

"If I'm honest, Excellency, I'll have to confess that—I don't know what I'd do. I've—always only dreamed of my family joining me here."

Quesada slapped the desk. "I will pray for God to strike you dead if that is not true, Don Juan McQueen!"

McQueen recalled Father O'Reilly's bony finger tapping his own forehead when he spoke of the governor's illness. He stood up. "I can only be truthful with you, Excellency," he said. "If you're no longer here, I—honestly don't know what I'd do, should I ever find myself free to return to Georgia to live."

Chapter 37

✥✥✥ The walk from Government House to the waterfront was not a long one, but on the bright, cold winter morning when the Quesadas sailed for Havana, the governor was too sad and weak to make the effort. At his request, only Don Juan rode beside him up St. George Street in the ancient royal carriage, followed on foot by the entire official staff, the governor's family, John Leslie, and a straggling crowd of Minorcans and Negroes.

Not until the carriage reached the corner of Treasury Street and turned toward the Bay did Quesada speak. Then he said in a choked voice, "Your first prayer in the parish church, when it is finished at last, will be for me, Don Juan?"

"I promise, Excellency. I promise."

"Very well." His tone changed abruptly to business. "Now then, one last official action. Aboard the ship on which I sail will be my recommendation that you, Don Juan McQueen, be made Commander of the River Banks of the St. Mary's and the St. Johns."

"Excellency!"

"You are free to travel about the province," he went on, looking straight ahead. "Your military judgment is to my liking. You will answer to no one along the frontier but Colonel Howard. You alone will make decisions when the need arises for excursions of the Rural Militia. You will assemble and command troops." The official manner aside, he turned to look at McQueen. "Your appointment will not come through at once"—he smiled—"if the future continues in Havana as the past, but it is official—by my hand, *amigo*. Heaven keep you safe."

"Excellency, I can never thank you enough. I'll—never have a chance, now, to show my gratitude."

Quesada brushed this off and, once more in his official tone, said, "Also, I have sent to your house by messenger the papers granting to you two thousand choice acres of land at Cape Florida." He laid a hand on McQueen's knee. "For that, do not thank me! It is my farewell gift to you. A large one because I will never have the chance to give you—another."

When the sun-whitened sails of the Havana-bound brigantine were out of sight at last, the people walked slowly, almost in silence, back to their homes and places of work.

Don Juan had nothing to do. He was now Commander of the Banks of the two important rivers, and at his house were papers to the richest grant yet, but Quesada's last acts of kindness had left him more sorrowful than stimulated. He could only try to realize that his Excellency was gone. That nothing would ever be the same.

Even his once enjoyable strolls along the narrow St. Augustine streets could never again lift his spirits. Halfway down St. George Street—always his favorite—he now saw only shabbiness and crumbling walls and poverty. He took out his watch. One o'clock. Who needed Don Juan McQueen at one o'clock of a bright winter afternoon? Oh, Harry would make him welcome at home. Pedro would stop his work to chatter at the drop of a hat, but he had no heart for chatter, and faithful Harry would surely be too sympathetic.

How good it would be when at last he could find sanctuary inside the finished church on the days when his loneliness was too heavy to bear. Such solace was barred to him now by crews of workmen, back at their jobs after waving his Excellency away forever.

A trip to the St. Johns or to Ortega or to his comfortable place on Fort George Island would pass a month or so, but he had promised Quesada to stay close by Acting

Governor Morales until Enrique White arrived sometime next summer. Of course, there were letters to write, but what he might set down in his present state of mind, he could never post.

A cheerful *"¡Hola!"* broke his reverie. There stood the señora, a warm smile on her face.

"¡Buenas tardes, señora! How did you know I was hungry? I didn't. I suddenly find I am."

Why had he not thought of the señora before, when all avenues of companionship seemed closed to him on this sorrowful afternoon? At any rate, she had appeared out of nowhere, and his spirits rose a bit.

There was mischief in her smile when she said, unlocking her door, "So, his Excellency is gone. Did you see that I too went to say farewell?"

He hadn't noticed her in the crowd, but he was genuinely glad. He followed her inside and put his hat into her outstretched hand. "That pleases me greatly." He sat down in her parlor. "I'm very lonely today, señora. And full of sadness."

"Why do you think I made shrimp *pilau*?"

"Because you're a good neighbor." He sighed. "I have one good neighbor left, at least."

"Sí. You have me. Come, I feed you."

His stomach full, McQueen tilted back contentedly in the señora's kitchen chair.

"It is an insult to be fed in the kitchen of a working woman, Don Juan?"

"Never. For *pilau* like that, I'd dine in a stable."

She pulled at the sleeve of his uniform jacket. "That is uniform of captain of Rural Militia? Shame! Take if off. A button is missing. I sew for you."

"Nonsense. Harry sews better than most women."

"Not better than Ysabel Perpal. Take it off."

He handed her the somewhat worn blue jacket and sat back down to watch as her flying fingers stitched on a new button.

"I had no idea you were a seamstress as well as a cook, a ship owner, and a merchant," he said absently.

She bit off the thread and held up the shabby jacket. "Wh-ht! Looks bad for a gentlemen to wear. I make you a new one."

McQueen laughed. "You'll do no such thing! I can perfectly well afford to have a jacket made. As a matter of fact, I think I will do just that. No one knows yet but you that the governor—in the carriage on our way to his ship—appointed me Commander of the River Banks of the St. Mary's and the St. Johns. I may indeed design myself a new uniform. One befitting the new appointment."

She handed back the coat. "I am glad for you! I am—*proud*."

"Thank you," he said, suddenly solemn. "But losing his Excellency at such a troubled time for the colony drains some of the happiness from the honor. We're peaceful now, but without Quesada, how long can it last?"

"Colonel Howard has been in charge of the province for years! We will be the same as before. What kind of uniform do you want?"

"I believe you're serious."

"I am going to make a new uniform for the Commander of the Banks. How you like it? With gold lace?"

He sat up, interested. "Gold lace, eh? How about a scarlet jacket trimmed with wide gold lace? For that matter, since there is no precedent—no official uniform for this high office—what would be wrong with scarlet breeches too?"

"Nothing wrong. I make it."

"You're teasing, of course. And I refuse to agree. We've a perfectly good tailor I can afford."

"When I tease, you know. I have not done so for months."

"And I've missed it." He slipped back into the jacket. "Thank you for a delicious meal, señora. I really must go."

"To sit alone with your sorrow?"

He tried to lighten his voice. "Don't tell me you accept my sadness that his Excellency is gone!"

She stood up. "I believe whatever you tell me."

"I know," he said carefully. "A very foolish thing to do, too, I might say." He managed a brief smile.

The dark, penetrating eyes were fixed on his. He tried to look away. He could not.

"I go to the farewell for Quesada only for *you*," she said, her voice tight with emotion. "I love you, Don Juan McQueen. Do we not deserve *something* from this ugly life?"

He stood staring at her, but said nothing.

Ysabel drew a deep, uneven breath. "If you will lie with me upon my bed, I will pray God to place your sin upon my soul. *Who but God will know?*"

He took one step toward her, then turned and ran out, across the street and up the stairs to his room. He locked the door.

"Anne!" His voice sounded like someone else. Surely there could not be another fool on the face of the earth the equal of Don Juan McQueen!

Winter sunset was staining the white walls of his room a deep rose when a knock sounded at the door. Forgetting he had latched it from the inside, he said, "Come in!"

"I can't. It's locked," Harry called.

He got heavily to his feet, leaving the Franciscan habit and Anne's lace collar crumpled on the bed. He unlatched the door. "What is it?"

A tentative smile on his face, Harry handed him three letters from young John. "Mister Leslie, he bring them just now. Surprise!"

"Thank you. It is a surprise indeed. The rascal hasn't written to me since he got to Pensacola."

"Look like he did. Mister Leslie, he say 'til today they ain't no ships got through. Didn't I hand you three at once?"

McQueen opened one letter and scanned it. "I see what you mean," he said. "Juan wrote this one back in October. This is January! Three months on the way. The lad must have wondered why my letters made no reference to his."

"If he got 'em at all."

"Exactly. All right. You may go."

When Harry still stood, McQueen looked up. The boy's eyes were riveted on the bed. "Oh," Don Juan laughed, embarrassed. "I—uh, forgot to clear off my bed, didn't I?"

"What *is* that brown robe of a thing, sir? I seen it there before."

He felt less and less need to pretend with Harry about anything, but all he said was, "Oh, it's nothing. Nothing at all."

"You want I should put it away for you?"

"No! I want you to get out of here and let me read my letters in peace." The sharp tone shocked him. "Sorry. Sit down. I'll tell you what it is."

Harry perched on a footstool, and McQueen sat again on his bed, one hand on the rough brown cloth. "This is Padre Narciso Font's habit. You remember young Father Font, don't you?"

"Yes, sir. He's the one that die right there in your bed."

McQueen nodded. "In a way I still don't understand, I—met God almost face to face that night with the young priest. This was a new habit he'd been waiting for. He left it to me—through Father O'Reilly." He paused. "If you think I'm crazy, Harry, don't say so—but when life gets hard, I find some sort of comfort just holding it."

"Yes, sir. That be good."

"Are you saying that in your usual way just to please me?"

"No, sir. I be glad you got it."

"I guess I expected you to be or I wouldn't have told you. And since we're on the subject, I might as well say this too. When I die, don't let them bury me in my military uniform."

The young man frowned. "But—you like your uniform!"

"I know. In fact, I'm thinking of having Barca, the tailor, make me a new one. You see, just before we said good-by today, his Excellency appointed me the new Commander of the Banks of the two rivers."

"That be good!"

"But I want your solemn promise that you'll dress me in this robe when I die. No uniform. This."

"Yes, sir. I promise."

Don Juan refolded the habit carefully and went to the

chest of drawers to put it away. "Whatever I do to displease or please the Almighty for the remaining years of my life, I want Him to see me first in—the gift from the young priest."

The boy stood up. "Father Font, he be glad to see you first in it, too!"

McQueen smiled. "Funny, I hadn't thought of that. You simply take life in the next world for granted, don't you?"

"Oh, yes, sir!"

He whacked Harry on the bottom and dismissed him. When the door had closed again, he picked up Anne's collar and kissed it, then put it away in the same drawer. It was like Harry not to have appeared to notice the bit of lace.

The first of John's letters he opened—the earliest written—warned him against returning to Georgia any time soon. Well, he couldn't go anyway until White arrived. He would serve himself to give full attention to the new governor, at least until their relationship was established. But the prospect of John's hope for the easing of the debtor's law in Georgia left him cold. He wanted Anne in St. Augustine with him—where a wife should be—looking after him, guarding him against *himself*.

He could not blame the señora for her offer today. Surely God had given him the strength to run from her house—as well as respect for her new vulnerability. He thought too much of her to want to hurt her, and it gave him a pang to think that he might have.

The remaining two letters from John would help fill the lonely evening ahead. Better to keep them unopened for now. He reread the first one.

> *Mother is my friend now, in a different way. I don't anticipate any future serious misunderstandings between us. She seems to be closed again to East Florida after her hasty departure, but the visit to you had some softening effect I can't explain. I hope it will last. I believe it will. Even Grandmother Smith doesn't ruffle*

her much any more when she lectures in her usual
way, bless her. Maybe I have changed too. Grown up.
Just hold steady, Papa, because the next year or so
can make a great difference all around. Of course, I
think I would be relieved if the change in the law
would make it possible for us all to live in Georgia
again. Pensacola is undoubtedly the dullest spot on
earth. I am learning the business against obstacles,
with the Indians sneaking off to trade more and more
with the Americans, but learning is my sole reason for
being here. Uncle Aleck has a good man operating
Oatland, so you and I must just hold our separate forts
and wait for what the future has in store for us—with
both our women.

Unable to postpone at least a look at the second letter,
Don Juan lighted the lamp by his bed and broke the seal,
promising himself to read only one page. But this one was
about Enrique White, who would be leaving sometime
early in June to take up his duties in St. Augustine. "He
is assisting new Governor Folch here now in the transfer
of government business, and I must say I believe you in
East Florida are getting the best of the two governors.
White is somewhat formidable—nothing like your often
charming Quesada—but Folch is, to my thinking, a downright unpleasant man."

He stole a glance at the third letter and read it too: all
about Eliza and her first serious suitor, the merchant Robert Mackey, whose Savannah firm of Mein and Mackay
held McQueen's largest debt. "My sister is trying to be casual about him, but I know her well enough to read between the lines. He is, according to her, breath-takingly
handsome, just enough older and very rich and promising.
I'm glad I have your humor. I am sure Mother is finding
all sorts of reason for embarrassment in such a potentially
confusing family situation as your debt to Mackay allows."

McQueen, pacing the room, felt suddenly excited. Not
only for his beloved daughter, because Mackay was a real
catch, but for the challenge of finding a way to form what
might well be a most profitable arrangement with Eliza's

suitor. At this point, ridding himself of that one large debt would certainly please Anne more than anything he could do.

His son's letters had given him much to think about, but the need to share this particular piece of news sent him hurrying for his hat and jacket. A brisk walk would be just the thing, and once outside, he could determine whether to impart the potentially good news to his new business manager, Don Bartolomé de Castro, to John Leslie, or to Father O'Reilly.

No matter. Any one of them would surely offer him tea, and he would eventually tell them all anyway. For a while, he would walk under the darkening St. Augustine sky, thankful that, in spite of the loss of Quesada, he still had friends—and prospects.

In good spirits, he headed up St. George Street.

Chapter 38

✳✳✳ Don Juan passed the short, often dark winter days of the year 1796 by reading, visiting, and writing letters. In April, he inspected his holdings on the St. Johns. As always, he made San Vicente his headquarters, and when he returned, he was the bearer to St. Augustine of jolting news. Colonel Carlos Howard was to be transferred, as soon as White arrived, to the Louisiana Regiment to serve as director of Upper Louisiana.

By the Treaty of San Lorenzo, signed last year, the United States had at last secured the long-disputed Natchez District as well as the right to free navigation of the Mississippi. Another large chunk of Spanish and Indian land would soon become the new state of Tennessee.

In a long conversation with Colonel Howard on McQueen's last night at San Vicente, the colonel agreed that His Majesty's holdings on the North American continent had indeed begun to crumble with the death of McGillivray.

"Still, you and I must continue to believe," Howard had said, "that right will triumph. True, the Americans have cut enormous gashes in our trade. Panton and Leslie must be in deplorable condition financially. Yet the Spanish colonies have never pursued an offensive policy in our lifetime, McQueen. It's an old wives' tale that we're aggressive. Only the land-hungry Americans block the peace."

Back in St. Augustine in May, Don Juan dreaded telling the excitable Morales that Howard would no longer be the guardian of the East Florida frontier. As he expected, the acting governor buried his head in his hands and muttered, "There is no help for us now but God!" Then, as the truth dawned on him, he asked, "Do you know what this means? I will be sent to replace Colonel Howard on the frontier—and I am not man enough for the task, Don Juan! I have done my best, but my best is not good enough to hold back the Georgians. East Florida will surely fall! Perhaps before White arrives next month."

McQueen would not agree because he dared not. His own fortunes were too tightly linked with those of East Florida. To cheer Morales, he did agree eagerly to assume full responsibility for planning the city's festivities of welcome for Enrique White. He could at least free Morales to govern up to his capacity during the time of transition.

St. Augustine, McQueen decided, would make a gala affair of his Excellency's arrival. Night after night, he wrote out detailed plans covering everything from a thorough refurbishing of Government House to suggestions to Father O'Reilly for special religious services. The señora would supervise the cleaning and redecorating of Government House and, with her deft needle, could make suitable costumes for the comedy which McQueen would order the Havana Regiment to perform on the Plaza. His warmhearted business manager, Don Bartolomé de Castro, would be a splendid choice to handle arrangements for official dinners in White's honor.

So he passed the remainder of May and the first two weeks of June. The señora, hard at work for him at Government House, appeared also to have put aside the incident in her kitchen. Nor had she mentioned again the offer to create a new uniform. He was relieved. Wiser, he thought, not to increase his obligation to her. But he would need the uniform for the coming festivities, so he instructed Pedro one June morning to fetch his best militia jacket and run with it down the street to Señor Barca, the tailor.

"Tell him to cut some scarlet cloth the size of that jacket and that I'll be by his shop soon to explain how I want it trimmed. Better take my good breeches too, to be used as a pattern for a new pair—also of the same scarlet material."

Pedro left the room for about one minute, then raced back, his eyes wide. "The jacket is not there, Don Juan! It is stolen!"

On questioning, Pedro faltered, stammered, and then, bent double with laughter, ran again from the room. In no time at all, he marched back into the parlor carrying a magnificent scarlet uniform—the jacket trimmed with not only gold lace but gold buttons as well.

"Pedro! Where did you find that?"

The boy stood holding the uniform as high as he could reach, his face hidden behind it. "I am not a servant in your house, Don Juan McQueen," he boomed in a mysterious voice, "I am a—magician!"

McQueen grabbed the suit. "You're a rascal, Pedro Llufrio! Where has this been? Not in my house!"

"In my room behind this house. The señora and I, we commit the scheme together. You are to wear it as the most handsome gentleman in the whole festival to welcome the new governor. It is a surprise from the señora and me!"

"I see," he said, suddenly subdued. *"Gracias."*

"You are—sad, Don Juan?"

"No. Not sad. Dumfounded."

"That is bad?"

"To be dumfounded? Not always." He mussed the boy's hair. "I'm touched, Pedro. By you and—by the señora. You Minorcans are sometimes too kind."

"That is good!"

"It is? I suppose so." He started toward the stairs.

"You will dress up now?" Pedro called.

"Not on your life! I'm saving this masterpiece for the festival."

"But, Don Juan. . . ."

"What now?"

"The señora, she deserve to see how it fit! Señora Perpal is not so good. Her head whirl all the time she sew. You dress up now and go to her house?"

McQueen grinned. "Is that a command?"

"Sí."

"From you or from the señora?"

Pedro held up two fingers. "Both. Two."

He dressed carefully in the splendid uniform, brushed up his best tricorn, and headed for the señora's house.

So as not to spoil the impact of his first public appearance as Commander of the St. Johns and the St. Mary's, he hurried across the street, vaulted the wall into Ysabel Perpal's chicken yard, and knocked a playful rat-a-tat on her kitchen door.

He waited, settling the jacket just so, arranging the wide lace cuffs. There was only silence from inside the house. At the sound of a light thud behind him, he turned barely in time to see Pedro duck behind the Perpal fig tree. Pretending not to have noticed, he knocked again, admiring the look of his hand beneath the fold of gold lace.

A mockingbird ran a cadenza from somewhere in her garden, but not a sound from the señora or Pedro. He knocked loudly once more, then tried the latch. The door swung open and he stepped grandly inside the smoky, whitewashed kitchen.

An iron pot of garbanzo soup—his favorite—bubbled over the recently tended fire. But on the floor, a wooden ladle still clutched in her hand, the señora lay dead.

PART 4

Chapter 39

✦✦✦   A tolerable relationship had developed with Enrique White during the first months of his tenure in St. Augustine, but Don Juan no longer felt attached to his St. George Street house. In the fall of 1796, when it appeared courteous to leave, he began to gather a crew of stonemasons and carpenters for the long-planned trip to Los Molinos de McQueen. As soon as the house was staked out there, he would go on to Georgia.

For months, he had worked long hours at White's side, assisting in the troublesome task of questioning and disposing of the rebels who had since Quesada's time been confined in the Castillo de San Marcos. The monotonous, often painful work had left him exhausted in body and spirit. Some of the prisoners who filed before him and the governor had been his friends, fellow revolutionaries with whom he had fought in the American War for Independence.

With Colonel John McIntosh at least, he had done what he knew he must if he hoped to retain even a scrap of his own mother-in-law's good will. He felt that because most of the men he questioned had sworn allegiance to Spain they deserved no mercy. But in the case of McIntosh, Enrique White was persuaded to meet McQueen's proposition for leniency: he would cancel the 50,000 pesos owed him by the government of East Florida in exchange for special consideration for McIntosh—retention of his citizenship, freedom to come and go on the border, and the return of his holdings. When Lang, Plowden, Wagnon, and the others came before his Excellency, all their goods, lands, and crops were confiscated, although the men themselves were allowed to return to Georgia.

"You have served me well," White said when McQueen called at Government House on the evening of November 15 to report his departure. "We'll keep our personal judgments of Morales to ourselves where his work as acting governor was concerned, but I've just made him Colonel Howard's replacement on the frontier at San Vicente. I trust you agree he can handle that post."

"I hope so, your Excellency. Anyway, I foresee no more uprisings—no major rebellions along the St. Johns in the near future!"

White chuckled drily. "Stripped of their lands and houses, they'll need time to move against us again, eh?"

"Exactly. Some are bound to go farther west, too, now that we no longer hold shipping rights on the Mississippi. There, of course, the troublesome gentlemen will again run head on into Colonel Carlos Howard." He rose to leave. "By the way, Governor, I would consider it a favor should you find time to write a short commendation to the daughter of a deceased Minorcan woman who served me well in the rather extensive job of making ready for your arrival. Her name was Señora Ysabel Perpal."

"The Minorcan wench who lived across the street from you?"

"She was a Minorcan, yes. But, in my judgment, a lady. Her daughter, Juana, would treasure your commendation."

"I'll try to remember to do that. Safe journey, Don Juan."

"Thank you, Excellency. Should you need my services, mail will reach me at San Vicente for the next two weeks or so; then, during December, address any letters to my son at The Cottage, Thunderbolt, Savannah."

White nodded, his mind already on other matters, and McQueen walked slowly, dispiritedly down the familiar outside stairs of Government House. Juan Quesada would have bidden him a warm good-by—and warned of the dangers which could await him in Georgia.

That night, with Pedro trotting beside him, he walked

by lantern light across his Treasury Street lot toward Campo Santo Cemetery on the Street of the Swamp. He had promised the boy this short, painful journey for a long time, but had had no heart for it. Tonight, he found himself unable not to go—unable to leave St. Augustine without a proper good-bye to the señora.

When McQueen, Harry, and the crew of workmen reached Los Molinos, they were greeted by a far healthier-appearing Andrew Atkinson—not his son as expected. To Don Juan, an excellent omen. Even he had not dared to hope that the old man would be well enough to make the trip from Fort George Island.

"After your letter," Andrew said, "I had to come myself to find out exactly what you're up to. Judging from the crowd you brought along, I believe you're really going to build a house."

Laughing, McQueen threw an arm around Atkinson's shoulders, as they walked up the bluff toward the caretaker's cabin. "What's more, as soon as I've staked out the house and ordered my sawyers to start cutting timber, I'm off to Georgia to visit my family."

"You're taking a chance. I don't know how long they could keep you in jail as a Spanish subject, but who can decipher the law these days—in either country? Maybe not the younger partner, Mackay, but old Mein is itching for his money. At least, that was the talk the last time I was up there."

"I'm going with my eyes wide open, Andrew. I promise not to set foot in Savannah. My men and I are traveling by small boat so we can land at my dock at Thunderbolt, in fitting stealth. This is not a business trip, you know. I won't stay long. But, I—I need to see my family."

"Building a big house here?"

"Indeed I am. The finest in East Florida, and I include the Fatio place on the St. Johns when I make that claim. I've enjoyed the smaller Fort George house, so I thought I'd just enlarge those plans. There's a fine situation on that rise of land up ahead for a two-storied edifice with a balcony all the way around the second floor. At least a mile from my sawmill. Anne and the children will never be bothered by noise or rowdy millhands. I'm sure such a sweeping view of marsh and forest and water will delight my wife."

Atkinson took a deep breath and exhaled noisily. "Oh, John McQueen, I pray your hopes are not too high. I'm acquainted with her mother too, you know. Would your wife ever agree to come without the old lady?"

"I would hope so, but if not, I'll even build a wing onto my house—to Mother Smith's specifications!"

At the door of the cabin, the shorter Atkinson looked up at him. "If you can persuade Elizabeth Smith to move to Spanish Florida, you might just as well go ahead and try to persuade the Lord to let Lucifer back into heaven. You'd have a far easier job of it."

On the morning of November 22, with Atkinson's promise to stay on at Los Molinos until the house was under way, Don Juan and Harry, along with three of his Fort George Negroes, set out for Thunderbolt. The fine weather—cool, sunny, free from summer deer flies and gnats—shortened the journey and kept the men from tiring at their oars. Don Juan thought he had never heard human voices sing so well; felt that he himself had never been in better voice. Past Talbot and Amelia Islands, through Cumberland Sound, and along the stretch of blue-gray water rolling between Cumberland Island and the mainland, they filled the air with song. Don Juan shouted and waved in the direction of Kitty Green's new Cumberland house, Dungeness, still under construction, and reminded Harry that some day they must surely bring Mrs. McQueen for a long stay with the charming widow of his late friend, Nathanael Greene.

They slept well on the shore at night, and he found himself enjoying the company of black men in a new way. Their capacity for joy at the smallest event—a good catch of fish, a fire which flamed up quickly—matched his own. Together, they gobbled their fried fish and boiled cabbage-palm hearts, standing or sprawled on the sandy riverbanks, the servants caught up in their master's anticipation of what lay ahead.

Anne was alone in The Cottage, dusting the parlor, when she saw a boat head for the dock. Curious to know who might be arriving by water, she straightened her house cap a little and hurried to the porch. Four Negroes were bringing the boat alongside, and standing in the stern, a tall man in a scarlet uniform waved both arms high in the air and shouted her name.

When, without waiting for the boat to be tied, the man leaped to the dock and began to run up the path, she ran too—both arms outstretched—her heart bursting.

Neither had any idea how long they stood embracing. Between kisses, Anne tried to explain that the children were in Savannah seeing the Cowpers off to Europe and that if she had known he was coming, she would surely have changed into a pretty dress. But touching mattered most, and time stopped. Finally, he looked back down the path and laughed; the oarsmen and Harry were nowhere in sight, and the secured boat had been quietly unloaded and lay rocking peacefully in the quiet river.

"I'm not one bit ashamed to tell you, dear Anne, that I'm relieved to find you alone," he whispered as they went on up the path arm in arm. He all but carried her onto the porch. "The people rowed hard and well—but my heart brought me."

"Your face, John," she murmured, touching his cheeks, the strong chin, smoothing the broad forehead—pushing back the heavy auburn hair. "Your face, John . . . I'll make sense in a minute, but—oh, your face! Close enough to touch. . . ."

In the parlor, he pulled her down on his lap. "Did you know you left your white lace collar at my house?"

"I certainly did know. I hope you brought it."

He laughed. "I did not. It's mine now."

Anne was trying to decide how to comment on the outlandish red uniform. Her fingers toyed with the trim on the jacket. "Do you need my lace collar—with all this?"

He roared with laughter and hugged her. "That's good, Mrs. McQueen! A splendid joke. I must say—a splendid joke."

She knew it wasn't all that funny and felt a twinge of familiar guilt that she'd never been able to cope with his humor. In his dearness, he was still trying to encourage her.

"How do you like my new uniform, madame?" He flicked a lace cuff under her nose.

"I—was just going to ask where you got it," she said, hoping her voice sounded light.

His smiled vanished. "It's a touching story, my dear. Do you remember my neighbor, Señora Ysabel Perpal?"

"Yes. A rather handsome woman. You introduced us once when you and I were taking a walk. Did—the señora *make* this uniform for you?"

"She did indeed. As a surprise—worked out with Pedro. When I went to thank her, I found her dead on her kitchen floor. She was kind to me."

Anne felt her body stiffen. "I suppose you—miss her."

His big, warm hand brought her head down on his shoulder. "Yes, I miss the señora. In fact, with both Ysabel Perpal and Governor Quesada gone, I don't feel at home in St. Augustine any longer."

And then he had begun to tell about Los Molinos de McQueen, describing the house he was building, the setting, the view from the balcony where they would sit together for all the remaining years of their lives, looking out over the bright, quiet waters of the St. Johns—"the most beautiful river God ever created anywhere on the face of His earth!" Desperately, she tried to think of a way to stop him, but only grew more helpless because she didn't want him to stop—ever. He would, he went on, settle down as she'd always wanted, to become a successful planter and mill owner, loving father and husband. He would never fight her again for freedom to race around the country in search of more land. They were growing older, and his need for her mounted with the passing of every day and every lonely night. . . .

"John, stop!" She stood up. "Don't say another word about—any of this. Promise me!"

"Why, Anne? Why?"

He followed her to the window, where she stared unseeing across the river toward Oatland. A pair of white egrets soared slowly, contentedly past, their wing tips almost touching.

"Why?"

"Because, more than anything in life, I *want* to live there—with you!"

He turned her around almost roughly and held her to him. "Don't *you* say another word, either. Not now. I need to have that to remember."

"But, John—"

"Sh-sh! I'm hungry. I don't need to clean up. We stopped down the river to let me bathe and dress in my gold lace for you. Let's eat. When will the children be home?"

"This evening sometime." She tried to smile. "I'll see what's cooked. Lessie went along to help Mama's Hannah stuff some pillows. We had splendid goose feathers this year."

"I remember sitting here with our son John like this," she said after supper, when they'd settled on the piazza to wait for the children. "It was almost the same time of the year. His first night home from school. He made me think so much of you. It—wasn't a very happy evening, I'm afraid."

"You've been brave."

"No, I haven't. I've been rigid as iron. I've had to be. Otherwise, I'd have put you first. I don't learn at all how to be away from you. I wonder if I ever will."

She fully expected him to begin the unbearably sweet persuasion. Instead, he reached for her hand and said nothing. The only times she'd known him to remain silent in the face of such a good opportunity were during moments of guilt. He must not feel guilty tonight! He'd risked too much to come. If the new law passed, he would be free to return to The Cottage—as a prisoner. Her instinct told her this was not the moment to mention that. The law had not yet passed. This, her heart prodded, was the time to be together in peace—to live these treasured few hours before the children came back from Savannah. Hours for remembering when he was gone again.

The marsh and the river were darkening, the red afterglow turning the grasses bronze. A soft, thick, almost comfortable hush held them both silent, leaving small noises to the sleepy marsh hens at the water's edge and the flying squirrels in the pines behind the house.

Her hand nestled in his, Anne closed her eyes, trying to imagine what it would be like never to fear the return of the distance between them.

The children should have been back by now. Perhaps they'd decided to stay the night at her mother's house. She said nothing to him, but secretly felt that if they could have this one night alone she would be glad.

Suddenly, he got to his feet and strode to the end of the porch. The red glow across the horizon was deepening and moving . . .

"John!" Anne sat rooted in her chair. "Is that—*fire*?"

He came quickly back to her. "Yes. It's fire, all right. Somebody got careless burning off a patch of woods today, I suppose."

"Can you see flames?"

"No. Just that waving red glare. Don't worry. It's a good distance away."

Her heart stopped. "As—far away as Savannah?"

For two hours, they walked helplessly back and forth from the house to a vantage point at the barn where a carriage lantern could be seen a mile down the road.

But there was no sign of a lantern . . . there was also no doubt in either of their minds that Savannah was burning.

Wrapped in blankets, they watched through the long, terrifying night, even Big John silent for minutes at a time, Anne alternately loving and cross. Cross when he kept repeating, until she thought she would scream, that undoubtedly the children had stayed behind to be sure their grandmother was safe.

What, her heart cried, *could anyone do to help a heavy,*

rheumatic old woman if fire was roaring through the square where the Smith house stood?

If the children had already started the drive home when the fire broke out, how could they manage to get back to her?

When, cold with anxiety, she fell silent for too long a period, he would turn from his maddening optimism and threaten to make the ride into the city alone. "No one's likely to arrest me in the midst of a holocaust like that! I can't just—sit here!"

And then her exasperation would swell with a new alarm, until her impassioned demands that he stay beside her gave way to tender pleas.

After a reassuring embrace, he would settle back in the old rocker once more, and the silence would engulf them again. If only they could pray aloud together, she might find comfort! Had he been praying inside himself as she had through the agony of this night? Neither had mentioned the word. How could a man and a woman be one except in *shared* faith—whatever the faith? The thought knifed again and again, sharp, cleaving what had only hours ago seemed to her to be a new and stronger bond between them. She had never been so afraid. Wherever her mind darted, there was fear ... After such a long separation, how did two people find a way to be close when they were both so afraid?

"I'm here, Anne," he said helplessly again, just before dawn. His arm was firmly about her on still another plodding walk to the barn to strain their eyes for sight of a carriage lantern. "I'm here, Anne ... you don't need to be afraid. Everything will be all right. You'll see."

She had stopped trying to respond.

By the time the sun began to fade the hideous red in the sky, billows of black smoke could be seen drifting all the way to Thunderbolt. Panic choked her. *He was there.* His arm *was* around her, but that did not mean that her children, her mother, were not dead!

He had been away too long ... his own children were strangers to him. He had no way of knowing how helpless her mother had become ...

"William's a big boy now. He'll be able to help your mother. And don't forget Eliza's good, level head . . ."

Dear God, she breathed, if he says one more word, I'll scream! Keep him quiet—keep my husband quiet!

About midmorning, they dragged themselves once more to the barn to stare off down the road.

There was no carriage in sight, but Anne caught Sallie's voice first, calling, "Mother! Mother!" a long way off.

She broke away from him and ran as hard as she could in the direction of the child's frightened cries and the rattle of the carriage—now close enough to hear.

When the carriage rounded the big curve in the road, Anne could see that everyone in it was crying, even Grandmother Smith and the two neighbor ladies who were crowded into the cramped space with Lessie and Hannah and the children.

Weak with relief, she called their names, each one, as she ran stumbling alongside the old carriage that William seemed determined to keep rolling all the way to the barn.

From one and then another, she gleaned shouted fragments of how it had been. Almost the entire city of Savannah lay in ruins. Many buildings were still burning. Only her mother's Dresden vase and the portrait of Anne's father had been saved from the Smith home. Nothing stood now of her mother's house but the brick shell of its walls.

Anne reached for first one outstretched hand and then another, muttering thanks to God that they were safe.

Only after she had touched each one did she realize that Big John still stood on The Cottage path—alone.

Then she heard William whoop; saw Sallie and Eliza jump from the carriage. All three of the children ran past her to throw themselves into their father's arms.

Chapter 40

✦✦✦ McQueen did all he could to make the visiting ladies comfortable, but by the third day he had faced the hard truth that the most he could do for Anne was to leave.

After the noon meal, driven by the need to talk to someone, he managed a walk alone with Eliza in the pine grove back of the house. He would, he was sure, find it far easier to be honest with Eliza than with her mother just now.

"I do indeed feel sorry for your grandmother," he said carefully in response to the girl's question. "For her and for her neighbors. How long do you suppose they'll stay?"

"Grandmother will have to live with us now, of course," Eliza said. "Mrs. Morgan and Mrs. Finley will be here until their houses can be repaired. The ruins of Grandmother's house will just have to be hauled away."

"I know. The old lady made it very clear to me last night—before her friends—that she'd planned to leave it to your unfortunate mother, too." He held his thumb and finger an inch apart. "I felt so high."

"Oh, Papa!"

The look of incredible sadness on Eliza's face pained him. "I'm sorry. I didn't mean to sound bitter. Your mother could certainly have made good use of a fine house in the city some day. At least until my pleas for her to join me in Florida stop falling on deaf ears." He took her hand. "See here now, not so glum, young lady. You can't imagine how clever I had to be to get you off alone like this.

Let's have one of our good talks. How about returning with me for the holidays? I'm building a fine house in Los Molinos. We could stop there en route to St. Augustine."

"You mean—you're *leaving before Christmas*?"

"Yes. Tomorrow. I should have known better than to come. The last thing I want to do is make things any harder for your mother."

Tears stood in Eliza's eyes. "You know I can't go now. Of all times, I have to help Mama—with company in the house. Please don't leave yet! Does Mama know?"

He gave a dry laugh. "My dear girl, I don't see your mother alone except for a few minutes in the morning, when she stops off in William's room before her duties as hostess begin for the day. We're alone then only if your brother happens to be still asleep. I'm devoted to William, but I didn't come all this way to share a room with him, you know. Look here, you'll understand, once you're married, that—uh, the circumstances of my visit are not the best." She looked so troubled, he lifted her chin with his finger. "Tell me, do you love this handsome, rich gentleman? This Robert Mackay to whom your shameful old father is so deeply in debt?"

"Yes. I love him. We've talked about your debts. He understands. He respects you. I couldn't love him if he didn't."

"Good girl." He hugged her, and they started slowly back toward the house. "No one is dearer to me than you, Eliza, and you mustn't worry. I'm going to handle everything—somehow. I mean to go on making every effort—within my awkward limitations—to convince you that your father loves you with all his heart. And longs for you to visit him again."

"Oh, Papa, it's terrible to grow up! I did love St. Augustine—I really did."

"I know. Well, maybe William will go back with me."

"I don't believe I'd mention that to Mother if I were you. I'm sure she wouldn't want him or Sallie to stop their studies now."

"I suppose not."

"Please stay for Christmas!"

"I can't. So—don't ask again. You see, I don't know

how to be with your mother here in Georgia any more. She's lost with me, too. There's no place for us here together." His voice sounded bitter again, but he suddenly didn't care. "No place for me—even in your mother's bed. As everywhere else—your grandmother holds forth there too."

"She can't help it that her house burned!"

He laughed a little. "No, even I don't suspect the old lady of starting the fire." He embraced her again and held her to him a long time. "Keep your hopes high, Eliza. Your old papa will find a way. Mama and I will surely some day build a new life together—the kind only she and I can build—at Los Molinos. We love each other. She'll be happy when she can be alone with me again where we can shape our own world."

"Will you tell her tonight that you're leaving?"

"No. I'll leave a note. I—find I can't face another good-by."

"Where will you go for Christmas?"

"There won't be time to get back to St. Augustine. I thought I might stop at Pierce Butler's place on St. Simons Island. He's usually there from Charleston at this time of year. He's a sour fellow, but at least he won't report my illegal presence in Georgia."

Anne's voice from The Cottage called for Eliza.

"I have to go, Papa." She hugged him. "I love you so much!"

"I love you, child. Don't forget. Don't ever forget."

The next morning in The Cottage parlor, after he had gone, Elizabeth Smith dabbed at her eyes with a lavender-scented handkerchief as she dipped a quill to write the letter she could no longer postpone.

Thunderbolt
4 December, 1796

My dear Grandson, John, Jr.,

  I am too distraught to write newsy drivel. I have tried with every ounce of my strength to remain cheer-

ful, in spite of the tragedy of the Savannah fire about which your mother wrote. I cannot, however, bear the burden of this household a moment longer alone. Your father was here, as you may know, for a few days, but left this morning without so much as a handshake. I did manage to pry from your mother that he slipped out before daybreak—leaving her only a note. She would answer no further questions and has taken to her bed.

You must come home at once, John. Planting is a respected occupation, but if you so despise it, why not find a profitable position in a trading firm here? Mein and Mackay are flourishing. Robery Mackay will surely one day be in our family. You are not even in the same colony with your father, so why bury yourself in horrid Pensacola among foreigners? I fear your mother will fall ill grieving over your father and you. Besides, how can you learn the mercantile business under such primitive conditions? And do you expect for one moment that your Cousin Margaret would ever agree to live there? I promise you will fare far better in that young lady's graces as a clerk in a reputable American firm. We need you, son, at once.

Your dev'td Grandmother,
Elizabeth Smith

Chapter 41

✦✦✦ His traveling desk propped on his knees, Don Juan sat in the March sun on the veranda of Pierce Butler's new house overlooking the Hampton River on the north end of St. Simons Island, Georgia. He had been safe from the Georgia courts on the remote island and, inwardly lonely though he was, his natural sociability had enabled him to spend a fairly enjoyable Christmas and New Year's with his old South Carolina friend, Senator Butler. With no pressing reason to return to St. Augustine, he had lingered these last few weeks on the pleasant island—luckily, it now seemed.

One could never really tell about the dour, opinionated senator, but he had appeared to welcome Don Juan and had given a sumptuous dinner party last night attended by John Couper, master of Cannon's Point, the adjoining plantation, and a Yankee named James Gould. Young Gould, who had come to St. Simons to oversee the cutting of the timber for the U.S. frigate *Constitution*, might well turn out to be Don Juan's salvation where the need for ready cash was concerned. In an hour, he was to meet Gould and Couper at Cannon's Point to close a deal whereby James Gould would assume the operation of his St. Mary's lease at Mills Ferry.

The news was too good to keep until he returned to Florida, and so he had dressed early in order to have time to write at least a short letter to Juan, whose relief would surely match his own—especially when he told him that Mrs. Drayson's son had been murdered and all income stopped from the valuable Mills Ferry timberland. He must let Juan know, too, why he'd left Thunderbolt so abruptly.

He wrote rapidly, apologizing for his long silence and giving his positive impressions of serious young James Gould from New England. "Through him," he wrote, "I expect to amass a small fortune—far more than when poor Drayson was operating the mill.

"I must leave by boat in minutes, for the signing with Couper and Gould, but I did want you to know why I found it necessary to depart The Cottage before Christmas. Someone from there has undoubtedly written you of it, so I want my own oar in the water too." He expressed his sorrow at the tragic loss of the old Smith home, but what he longed for Juan to understand was his own feeling of intrusion now that Grandmother had moved to Thunderbolt to stay. "Until then, I found your mother warm and loving, downright happy to be with me again. Then, alas, the ladies descended upon us! I am devoted to your brother, William, but not as a bed partner. He kicks. More than that, your mother's attitude of welcome seemed to dry up. She tried, but I found it no longer endurable, knowing the strain my very presence caused her."

He ended the letter by urging John to continue in his resolve to please Panton. "At least," he wrote, "with my son in the other Florida, where I am respected, I can be sure that I will be welcome there."

Young John stood in his room in William Panton's new residence and looked out over the Bay, reviewing his latest letter from Papa. The one-sided picture presented in his grandmother's letter of last December had been rounded out by Papa, but more or less as he had already imagined. Meantime, he had not taken too seriously the wail from Thunderbolt.

He was sure of one thing—he would not go back to Georgia any time soon. He was doing too well in Pensacola, in spite of his boredom with the town, and had no more desire than Papa to live in such close quarters with Grandmother Smith. His father's news that he'd found an ambitious young man to operate the St. Mary's lease was heartening. With the señora and her merchant ships gone, John could now work out a mutually profitable arrangement for a Panton and Leslie boat to transport the squared timber to England. Gould could raft it down the St. Mary's, and as long as Spain held the port, there should be no problems. With the Florida-Georgia frontier quiet, at least for the time being, it would be safe for a Panton and Leslie ship to handle the McQueen timber. William Panton had not been well of late. He would be happy to take his employer a bit of good news.

His grandmother's little device about his heightened chances with Margaret, should he return to Savannah and work for an American mercantile firm, had not moved him. He was lonely, but only he knew how much he was learning in the office of the steady, far-sighted Panton. And, in Pensacola, he was free to be himself. He could wait for Margaret, who must some day come to love him for what he was, not for what Savannah connections could make him. She showed no serious interest in any other young man. He could wait. He could be patient for years, if necessary, before he'd risk the kind of interference his father had always faced in Grandmother Smith. Poor Papa . . . poor Mama.

The dinner bell clanged, and he wondered, as he washed to go downstairs, if his father had anyone with whom to eat tonight.

On a balmy May evening, Don Juan latched his loggia gate and walked slowly into the parlor, the purchase paper and money in his hand. Señor José de Zubizarreta now owned the St. George Street house. The little *escribano* had paid down a sizable sum and was good for the remainder in the years ahead. The house which had held McQueen's dream for Anne would now hold another man's dream. The señor's excitement had been so evident when he was offered the place that Don Juan had signed his name to the papers without too much sadness.

The Los Molinos house was progressing; in another two or three months and for the remainder of his life, it would be the home of Don Juan McQueen.

Of course, he would need a St. Augustine residence, too. No man in his right mind would risk absence from the Plaza for long. He had a good tenant in the Treasury Street house, and so, before closing the agreement with Zubizarreta, he arranged to rent the second floor of a small house on the Lane That Leads to the Marina, not fifty steps from Father O'Reilly's place. To this apartment he would soon transfer just enough furnishings for comfort from the St. George Street house, to which he had promised Zubizarreta possession in sixty days. The rest of the house's contents would travel with him to Los Molinos.

He hoped that Pedro, whose mother refused to permit him to leave St. Augustine, would be available to serve him when he stayed in the city. He would miss Pedro at Los Molinos, but Harry would surely buoy his spirits when the day came to move out of the St. George Street house, and Katrina, of course, was going to Los Molinos too. However lonely or cheerful the days of his old age might be, Harry and Katrina would be in them, and they were his friends.

The señora's dog, Niño, grown older and more sedate, got up slowly when he did, stretched, yawned, and followed him upstairs. "You and Harry and Katrina and I are going to be just fine, pup," he said. "Just wait 'til you see Los Molinos de McQueen on the St. Johns! You'll feel like the master of all you survey—as will I."

After prayers, he undressed and sat on the side of his bed, smoking. The dog sat contentedly on his foot, only moving to sneeze when the smoke tickled his nose.

"I've just had an idea, Niño! I believe I'll journey to visit Juan in Pensacola before we move to Los Molinos. The round trip plus a month with my son would pass almost the entire time until our new home is finished. Anyway, I'm less lonely for his mother when I'm traveling."

Chapter 42

✦✦✦ During the first two years in his new house on the wide St. Johns, he made the long journey to Pensacola nine times.

The Los Molinos house could not have pleased him more. It was an almost exact replica of the Fort George place, but far more spacious. Nowhere in his mind was there a single doubt that, if only Anne would visit him, she too would fall under the charm of the mansion which, timber by timber, had been built for her. He had received no new grants from Enrique White, but the governor had bestowed another honor—Don Juan McQueen was now not only military Commander, but Judge of the Banks of the St. Mary's and the St. Johns. He could serve his Excellency by settling property disputes and other legal matters among the scattered settlers, and also pick up a few extra pesos for himself in fees.

When not traveling, he sat every evening on his ample balcony, watching the sky change over the vast river and nurturing his dreams by frequent speeches aloud to Anne. "This is living, my beloved," he would say to the trees and the wide river. Niño, always at his feet, would respond by settling his square head more firmly on one boot. "It won't matter, wife, that we're growing old, so long as we have this view of the land I love—and own. As long as we're together, I will welcome old age. Harry's still young, you know. Only about twenty or so. He'll long outlive us and care for us in our every need. Perhaps, when you're here too, Anne, I should get a good girl to look after you. Who knows? I might find one beautiful and good enough for Harry! Of course, I'm dreaming! Isn't life meant to be dreamed?"

But, as the months at Los Molinos wore on, at some point in his lonely evening vigil his head would fall into his hands and tears would drop on Niño's back. He began leaving the balcony earlier and earlier, even in good weather, to go inside and pray at his altar. To pray and then to write his dreams to Anne, keeping them alive for himself.

In the summer of 1799, he prayed for forgiveness the day Anne's letter came with the news that her mother had suffered a stroke. Forgiveness, he suspected, was withheld, because he had not felt one twinge of guilt that his own spirit soared at the thought that Elizabeth Smith might be about to join her husband in the next life. He should have felt guilt for Anne's sake, but the old lady had lived a long, full life while he and Anne still starved for the sight of each other.

By now, he was firm in his conviction that his wife stayed away only because of her mother's total dependence upon her. The years had convinced him that their separation could not be blamed only on the occasional uprisings in East Florida *or* on his religion. Certainly not on his religion! He loved God too much. God is love and love does not separate. Love draws together. He prayed daily that Anne would one day turn to the true Church, but he had no doubt that she, too, loved Jesus Christ as he did. No, the Lord could never be blamed for their tragedy. Especially not here in the vast, lonely beauty of the St. Johns. God was too much with him to be blamed for anything.

Years ago, he had taught Harry to read, and nothing soothed his troubled spirit now as much as Harry's voice speaking the words of Christ—a low, velvet voice that was never singsong, but rich and strengthening, as though the Lord Himself spoke the message alive for Don Juan so long ago by dying Padre Font. . . .

"Come unto me, all ye that labor and are heavy laden, and I will give you rest. . . . For my yoke is easy, and my burden is light."

•   •   •

On occasion he entertained Colonel Morales, stationed for the past three years at San Vicente, only a three-mile ride from Los Molinos de McQueen, but he still did not find Morales the best of company. Except for Manuel Romero, the storekeeper at San Vicente, who always brought fruit or fish, his most welcome visitor was his business manager, Don Bartolomé de Castro. Castro was now overseer of the Royal Treasury, but he still looked after McQueen's holdings and seemed to enjoy making a monthly journey from St. Augustine whether business demanded it or not. Don Bartolomé remembered Ysabel Perpal from the days of her litigation over the St. George Street house and, in his loneliness, Don Juan enjoyed their reminiscences of the fiery señora.

"Do you believe I *never* touched her, Don Bartolomé?"

"No! Am I a fool?"

"But it's true. I swear to you. That is, I took her in my arms once. Just once—in broad daylight on my loggia. Even then, my son walked in and caught us!"

Castro, grinning, asked, "And did you confess to Father O'Reilly?"

"No need to—my son saved me!"

Their friendship continued to grow, in spite of the fact that managing the McQueen business interests required patience, not exactly a natural endowment with Castro. The quick-witted young official had more than once saved McQueen's neck in the courts—proving devotion. Still, their companionship consisted mainly of laughter and the exchange of risqué stories. No one could tell a story with more finesse and color than Don Bartolomé, but, growing older, McQueen sometimes missed having a more thoughtful friend. There was no one but Harry with whom he could share his need for God.

Of course, a man needed to laugh too, so he made every effort to arrange his travels to be back at Los Molinos in time for Castro's monthly visit.

"Tell me about Pedro Llufrio," he asked, when Don Bartolomé came in September 1799. "Is the boy glad he went to work at Government House?"

"I doubt that he is glad at all. His Excellency is a governor of superior ability, but a beast as an employer."

"Sorry to hear that. Pedro's a fine lad. Is White cruel?"

Castro shrugged. "Cold. Pedro is frightened of him. Also, his Excellency does not pay. In two years, his chief servant, Don Santiago Gonzales, has received ten pesos!"

"Is our Royal Treasury so empty?"

"Almost. But Enrique White is not Juan Quesada. I say no more. Don Miguel Ysnardy will go to his grave with only half the monies due him for building the church."

"Tell me, how is the attendance at the new church? Still up?"

"Down. And threatens to be almost as low as before. A mystery, with the Plaza so much improved in appearance."

"I haven't been to St. Augustine, you know, for over four months. I'm hungry for news. What of Father O'Reilly?"

"The same. That is to say, growing richer in properties, skinnier, more bald in the head—and better at checkers. One real piece of news—Don Juan Leslie is finally rid of his wife. You have heard that?"

McQueen nodded. "I saw the woman on my last trip to Fort George Island. She's staying with the Atkinsons. I rejoice for Leslie but pity Andrew. He's an old man. His wife and Belle Leslie don't draw one sober breath between them."

The two men sat for a time in silence; then McQueen said, "This is 1799, Don Bartolomé. One year short of a new century. What do you think will happen to us in East Florida a decade from now?"

"Who can know that? At least, for this day, the province is quiet." Castro sighed. "So quiet, I am curious at times to know if, in Havana, they believe we are still here."

In early October, young John, en route back to Pensacola from a business trip for Panton in Charleston, surprised his father with a visit at Los Molinos. The boy's shoulders were heavier, he sported a new mustache and, when they talked these days, it was truly man to man. John knew instinctively, McQueen felt, how much to tell him concerning the family—and how much not to tell.

On this visit, their main topic of conversation was Eliza.

"You wouldn't know her, Papa, except for that quiet, contained manner. She's radiant with happiness, but even in her present romantic haze, I could still go to her if I needed help. Robert Mackay's a lucky man."

"Tell me about him. Is he really good enough for her? Oh, the child's written at length—I'm perfectly aware that in her eyes he's too handsome to be true—but I want a man's viewpoint."

"Mackay and I talked only a short time, but I liked him. He has a way of coming right to the heart of a matter. He says he wants to help you."

Don Juan flushed and forced a short, somewhat embarrassed laugh. But he could not resist asking how young Mackay could help him short of canceling his enormous debt to his firm.

"Oh, no chance the debt will be marked off," John said quickly. "Old Mein would never stand for that. Neither would my father." He lifted an eyebrow. "Or would he?"

Don Juan looked at his son for a long time, unsmiling. "I don't know. It's all so long ago and far away now, I honestly don't know. But what if I said yes, I'd relish having a debt of some thirty thousand dollars wiped out? What if I said I'd accept such gratuity on my daughter's behalf? What would you think?"

John smoked a while in silence. "I'd say you had your reasons. You've always granted me mine." He tapped the long ash. "I don't anticipate your having to decide, though. I didn't press him for his ideas because I felt you should do that. He's coming down here to see you next month."

Don Juan brightened. "So he is—your mother wrote me. It's good of him, and I'm eager to meet him." He paused. "Mama likes him, doesn't she?"

"Yes. And having a nearby man in the family is going to ease both our worries where she's concerned. We have left her pretty much alone, you know." He looked away. "Papa?"

"Hm?"

"Do you still believe she'll come some day?"

Don Juan waited a moment before replying. "Yes, son. I believe she'll come. I have to believe it. I have no choice."

Chapter 43

✦✦✦ I've never seen a more beautifully situated house, sir," Robert Mackay said as they walked out onto the second-floor balcony at Los Molinos.

"It's my dream," McQueen said simply.

The shorter, more compactly built Mackay looked up into the face of the big man whose gentle brown eyes scanned the vast stretch of marsh, sky, and water. He thought him a true gentleman, and one of the handsomest. Nearing fifty, Mackay reckoned, but—as Eliza had said— still a boy in his heart.

"Well," Don Juan said suddenly brisk, "I'll make us comfortable, young man."

Mackay watched him energetically drag well-made wooden chairs toward the part of the balcony where the view was best at sunset. McQueen had seldom stopped talking since they'd met at San Vicente in the early afternoon. The reason for Mackay's trip to East Florida had been dispensed with almost at once. There was no doubt that the couple had the blessings of the bride's father. For the remainder of the evening, they could spend the time becoming better acquainted.

Robert Mackay knew well some of the outstanding men of the day in both America and Europe, but he already realized he was in the company of a person of distinction. How, he wondered, had John McQueen managed to remain so polished and articulate after nearly nine years in rough, uncouth, poverty-ridden East Florida? As far as Mackay knew, McQueen had not been out of the Spanish colonies during all that time except for a few official voyages to Havana and the one visit to Thunderbolt at the time of the fire.

Yet he was able to converse knowingly and colorfully about many things and people. He had undoubtedly lived every year of his life to the full and knew how to retain the experiences. Through the delicious dinner, he'd regaled Mackay with little-known stories about Thomas Jefferson, the Marquis de Lafayette, Count d'Estaing, Benjamin Franklin—even President George Washington.

I've fallen in love with the daughter of a magnificent man, he thought. No wonder Eliza all but worships him. No wonder Mrs. McQueen appears to be wasting away, if she loves her husband as Eliza believes.

Settled in their chairs with glasses of choice Madeira and cigars, McQueen went back to Lafayette and the tragedy of the great man's life, with so many years lost in a dungeon.

"Men suddenly freed from long confinement, as was the marquis two years ago," his future father-in-law was saying, "tend to find freedom too vast, distances too frightening. Unless Lafayette has changed more than I would imagine, I don't believe that to be true of him. I suspect he finds the new France too narrow and confining, peopled by dwarfs like Napoleon—men without faith or real enthusiasm for their fellow human beings. To think of the marquis—a full general at twenty, a world-famous hero at twenty-four, overshadowed now at only forty by the ugly little Corsican conqueror!"

"Your son's friend, Frank Huger, received a letter of gratitude from Lafayette for his daring attempt to free him from prison. I'm sure John has told you that Huger's become an idol now that he's back in America."

"Indeed he has told me, at length." McQueen was silent, then said quietly, "He's told me, too, of the years the good Mme Lafayette spent with the marquis—in a prison cell—with their children. I'm sure she was criticized cruelly for her sacrifice."

Eliza had, with great difficulty, confided to Robert Mackay her own perplexity on this very subject. "Does Madame Lafayette love the marquis," she once asked, "more than my mother loves my father?" He had reflected a moment and then asked her if she thought her mother could have subjected her children to such an ordeal.

"Never," she had said at once. She went on, more slowly, "What a dreadful choice for a woman to have to make—her love for her husband versus the good of her children."

Although they both knew that this was not all that had kept the McQueens apart, Eliza had been comforted; but Mackay found himself wishing at this moment for a way to change the subject. The tragedy of Anne and John McQueen had come to be almost more than he could bear, now that he had at last met this man. Until now, he'd felt deep sorrow for Eliza, had, for her sake, offered to try to help her father, and had thought her mother kind and rather beautiful, though old for her years. As for McQueen himself, Savannah gossip had depicted him as a lovable but irresponsible rascal who, though well-born, brilliant, and able, had deserted his wife and family in order to protect himself, had shocked Georgia and South Carolina patriots by turning his back on America, and—most despicable of all—had become, for expediency's sake, a Roman Catholic.

"You're quiet, Mackay. I don't blame you. But I want you to know, whether you believe it or not, that my wife loves me as deeply as Mme Lafayette loves the marquis." The low, vibrant voice grew tender. "When you marry my daughter, you'll become a member of a family that is fractured only outwardly. In our hearts, we've never been apart."

"I—understand, sir," Mackay said, too surprised by such frankness at their first meeting to think of a more appropriate response.

"You'll see more of Eliza's mother than of me. Our—tragedy is all my fault. I want you to know that at the outset. But, I'm trying to make amends. I believe I will in time. You can help, if you find it in your heart to do so."

Surely, Mackay thought, the disarming man was not going to bring up the indebtedness to his firm too! "I—I want to help. I love Eliza. I'm not sure what I can do, though."

"Your best way of helping would be to put in a good word for me when you see my wife again. I built this house for her, you know."

Robert only nodded.

"My mother-in-law will be called to her eternal reward some day," McQueen went on, without rancor. "I believe her influence on my wife to be far stronger than mine. Not stronger than Anne's love for me, mind you." He exhaled smoke into the quiet air. "I can wait. I have to wait. When a man goes on loving a woman with only two brief visits in eight and a half years—he loves. Wouldn't you agree?"

Don Juan lifted his glass. "Welcome to the McQueen family, Robert Mackay! I will pray that your children will one fine day play and romp in the sheer beauty and freedom of their grandparents' home—Los Molinos de McQueen." He smiled wistfully. "If not, I shall do my utmost to be a good and attentive grandfather—at a distance. I see no hope that I will ever go back to Georgia, except perhaps as a prisoner, should your government succeed in taking over our province."

"But with the new law in effect, sir, you can satisfy the courts by confinement at either The Cottage or at my house in Savannah."

"I know about that, but *I want my family here with me.* Could you force yourself to crawl back like a whipped pup with its tail between its legs—to be jailed in your own house until some dried-up judge decided you could step outside?"

When Mackay only smiled, Don Juan put his head back and gazed at the darkening sky. "No, the conquering American government will have to take me *here*, where I've rebuilt my life. Ironic, but I fully expect my old dinner partner, Thomas Jefferson, to become your next president after Adams. Jefferson and I have butted heads in philosophical arguments. In the past, I've won over him often. I won't again, because Thomas wants the Floridas. If he wins, all my years here will have been wasted. Even this house—built for Anne. And I'll be once more at the questionable mercy of the Georgia courts." He stretched his long legs. "The grasping Georgia courts—where I was for a short time a judge myself."

◆   ◆   ◆

The new century began with Eliza's wedding to Robert Mackay at The Cottage on January 30; for Don Juan, unable to attend, a day of both happiness and sorrow. As month followed month in the year 1800, his restlessness grew. Los Molinos was his home but, unable to be still for long, he kept traveling. By September, his next destination was his favorite city.

"Don't unpack everything, Harry," he ordered after their return from Fort George Island. "We leave soon for St. Augustine. I'm sure our quarters there need dusting, and I need time with Father O'Reilly. I need to attend Mass." He tried to smile. "Do you suppose I'm growing old, Harry? Do you imagine that old age causes a man to feel hollow inside?"

Miguel O'Reilly saw them ride up the lane and hurried to his balcony to wave. "*Buenos días*, Don Juan," he shouted. "Checkers tonight by all means!"

"By all means, Father," McQueen called out, dismounting. "It's good to be back in the city. I'm in need of a priest."

O'Reilly laughed. "Perhaps I can arrange for one. Have you managed to convert that heathen, Harry, yet?"

"Not yet, but wonders never cease." McQueen laughed, too, waved again, and disappeared inside his rented quarters.

He seems as buoyant as ever, O'Reilly thought. Evidently Bowles and his Seminoles had not yet struck in the vicinity of Los Molinos. But how had he dared leave his house? Surely McQueen knew that William Augustus Bowles had escaped from prison and was now back stirring up more trouble in Florida. Of course, news traveled erratically those days.

Inside his house again, Father O'Reilly began to doubt that McQueen did know of the new danger. It wasn't like him to have left his beloved Los Molinos, with Bowles and the Seminoles firing plantations along the St. Mary's. Well, he would find out. Certainly, no man should try to anticipate McQueen.

The priest looked forward to the evening. He was

holding two letters for his guest—one from the bride, Eliza Mackay, and one from her calm but disturbing mother. Both had ended up in St. Augustine, and O'Reilly had planned to send them on to Los Molinos by the first conveyance. Mail services were worsening, no doubt about that. Everything in the province was worse. Miguel O'Reilly had lived in a vacuum since White had taken over. He could have given McQueen the freshest possible news of Bowles had Quesada still been governor. But even at confession, he found Enrique White a cold, uncommunicative man.

Had McQueen been joking when he said he had need of a priest? This both pleased and distressed O'Reilly, to whom McQueen's lonely life had been a far greater burden than O'Reilly had ever been able to express. Their relationship, one of male camaraderie, was the only such friendship he had ever permitted himself. Oh, he'd heard McQueen's confessions year after year; had given him the Most Blessed Sacrament of the Altar. Those moments he remembered often with the kind of unself-conscious pleasure he seldom experienced in working among such a diverse lot of parishioners.

Perhaps tonight, he thought, they could at last speak of God together. He brushed dust from the game table and smiled. What kind of priest was he, to *hope* that the name of the Almighty might come up? Well, no matter. Just being with his old friend was an experience of God which he'd never quite understood.

He went to his desk, took out the two letters, and sat looking at them. Too late, of course, to pray, but with all his heart he hoped they both contained good news.

Later that night, after his evening with Father O'Reilly, Don Juan walked alone under a bright autumn moon, along the familiar, narrow St. Augustine streets, his heart filled with quiet joy. He reached into his pocket and touched both his letters. The one from Anne was brief but warmer than of late, her heart as full of gladness as his own would be, she said, that in just two months, perhaps by December, they were going to be grandparents.

"At Mama's insistence," Eliza had written, "we did not tell you before that I expected a child. Mama thought you'd suffer enough, not being here. But now, the doctor thinks all will be well for me, and so Robert and I want you to know."

Anne, still fretting over him! Still caring that he suffered. No wonder the moon shone so brightly. He performed a little jig down the middle of St. George Street. God hung the moon! God was giving him a grandchild . . .

The church gleamed in the stark white moonlight. It would be locked, but he walked slowly up to the entrance, crossed himself, and laid both hands against the doors, more certain than he had been for years that some day—perhaps sooner than he believed—his life would no longer be lonely. Surely, when the new child was old enough to travel, it would be brought to visit him. Maybe Anne would come too. And when she saw his house, she would surely stay.

He felt he had been able to quiet O'Reilly's fears that Bowles would dare to cause any serious trouble on the St. Johns. The fool was not suitably armed, and King Paine had convinced Don Juan that only a few of his Seminoles would ever turn against the Plaza to follow Bowles.

For the first time in all the years of their acquaintance, Father O'Reilly had blessed him as they said good night. "A good omen," he said aloud. "An excellent omen for the future!"

After two weeks in St. Augustine, he grew restless again and eager to know how the new water gin he'd had built on Fort George Island had turned out. He said good-by to O'Reilly and Bartolomé de Castro—White had not even invited him to Government House—and on a dull, cloudy October morning, he and Harry again rode away from the city. They made the journey by land, and even with frequent delays to rest their horses, arrived in a little more than eight hours at San Vicente, where a boat could be had for the water trip out to Fort George Island. Before they reached the McQueen dock on the island, he recognized the tall, graceful man on the shore, waving both arms. Young John was paying his father a surprise visit.

They embraced and pummeled each other, McQueen complaining that he was far too old and feeble to contain so much happiness all at once.

"Do you know I'm going to be a grandfather?" he demanded.

"Of course I know. I'm going to be an uncle too. My letter from Eliza came the very day I said good-by to Pensacola. Congratulations to us all!"

McQueen stopped smiling. "*Good-by* to—Pensacola? What happened, son?"

"Nothing new. That's one reason I left."

"But you didn't write to me about any plan to leave."

"I'd have beaten the letter here. Robert Mackay suddenly offered a far better position with his firm in Savannah. I'd gone as high as I could with Panton, not being a member of the family." He smiled ruefully. "In one way, I suppose Mama and Grandmother have won out."

"I see."

"Look here, Papa, it won't change anything between us."

"Except to see each other far less often in the years ahead."

"Why, I can come to Florida as often as—"

"As often as a new employer who will properly be expecting you to prove yourself will allow?"

"But Mackay's my brother-in-law!"

"Just as you once said, though, he's first of all a businessman. A good one." He grinned crookedly. "By the way, I didn't have to decide whether or not I'd accept charity from him on that debt. He didn't offer. Oh, I don't condemn him. He's right. I wear the beggar's rags. Not he." Hooking his arm in John's, they walked up the path toward the house. "Well, I wish you success with the ladies of Georgia, son. You're here with me now, though, and we'll take advantage of every minute."

John patted his hand. "As always."

"As always."

Los Molinos de McQueen
3 July, 1801

Robert, my Dearest Husband,

How will I ever thank you for letting me visit my father here on the St. Johns? He spends his days playing with the baby, or pacing the floor waiting for Robbie to wake up. This time alone with Papa is both blessing and breaking my heart. His hunger for family love is almost more than I can bear. He is a strange mixture of boy and man and seems to hold no grudges. Considering the trouble caused in East Florida by Colonel John McIntosh (by whom my last letter to you was delivered), I should think Father would despise him. He does not and is even attempting to persuade the other John (Houstoun) McIntosh to move here. It would not surprise me if Papa has in the back of his mind the idea of selling Fort George Island to him. He laughs when I suggest it, but my woman's instinct tells me the old darling is harboring (if only now and then) an almost serious longing to return to Georgia himself. Since you will not receive this in Mother's presence, I am confiding in you, due to your dear willingness to help him. He still insists that God has assured him that Mother will some day come to Florida to live. This, above all, he would prefer. But life in East Florida is no longer as pleasant for him, I fear, as when Quesada was Governor.

You must quiet your heart where the danger of a Seminole raid is concerned. My father's business manager, Don Bartolomé de Castro, during his monthly visit, did confirm the rumors that Bowles is raiding some plantations, but no one expects him to come this close to Fort San Vicente. Castro feels Papa's plantation, San Juan de Nepomuceno, at Ortega, may be in danger. Father only laughs. But, should Bowles become a real threat, it could be the means persuading Papa to return to Georgia. If only there might be a way to settle his debts! I am dreaming, I know, because I so want him home with poor Mama. My father loves *the Spanish colony, but it is crumbling. He loves his family, but they are far away. He both laughs and grieves. Only a greathearted man could survive as he does.*

The sad news of William Panton's death at sea has eased some of Papa's sorrow that John is no longer with the Pensacola firm, but he is somehow affronted that my brother is not still a resident of his adopted land. He believes that the recent completion of the Ellicott line, setting a boundary at last between Georgia and Florida, can bring some peace, but mourns the loss of Spanish territory. I do not try to understand the poor dear's turmoil, just to love him and that is easy.

We will give him consolation by adding grandchildren to his lonely life.

I am sorry that you are lonely, too, but womanlike, I also rejoice that your "bachelor's hall, after having had a Mistress for so long, will never do again for Robert Mackay." Your latest letter is read to tatters, and I am half a person without you. I bring our son home as soon as I can without too much pain for Father, who joins me in sending love to all. Again, you are kind, my dearest friend, to have let me come.

Your ever affectionate wife,
Eliza McQueen Mackay

Chapter 44

✤✤✤ On a windy, blustery November afternoon, John Leslie looked up from his almost blank account ledger for the year 1801 to see Don Juan standing in the doorway.

"McQueen, you son of a gun!" He rushed to greet him. "I'd sound downright maudlin if I told you how glad I am to see you again. Sit down, sit down. Still like your mansion on the St. Johns?"

"Indeed, yes. A bit—uh, large at times, but I'm happy as a chipping sparrow."

Leslie climbed back on his stool. "Liar."

"Yes, I'm lying." The men looked past each other for a moment, in silence. Then Don Juan asked, "Is it all coming to an end for us, Leslie?"

"It began to end the day McGillivray died, as you've always claimed. The end moved nearer when Howard left. Now that we've ceded Louisiana to France, I predict your old friend Thomas Jefferson will take it and finish us off. *If* Bowles and his savages don't beat him to it."

Don Juan's laugh was dispirited. "I'd hoped you'd convince me my fears are groundless. Perhaps I should try to convince you that Bowles and a handful of Seminoles simply *can't* finish us off."

"You don't believe that any more than I do. I just heard he's getting fresh British supplies every month or so. Of course, Bowles' savages are only committing tribal suicide. The Americans will eventually gobble up all their gains." John Leslie swept a hand over an almost empty page of accounts. "It's all right there. No trade—imminent collapse."

After a long silence, McQueen said, "I'm fifty-one years old today, Leslie. Things certainly aren't the way I'd hoped they'd be—at fifty-one."

"You came to the wrong man to be cheered, but I'll try. You don't look fifty."

Don Juan grinned. "If I do say so, I believe I could still charm a lady. Of course, I haven't seen one since my daughter left me six years ago."

"Panton was only fifty-six."

"I tried to write you my condolences."

"I got the letter. Thank you. You and I are among the last of the old breed." He slammed shut his ledger. "I may sell out my interest in the firm before it caves in along with the province."

"That bad?"

"When Ellicott ran his line, he cut off every Indian tribe that owed us money! I don't even have any bad debts left to mourn." He laughed drily. "Sorry to use a vulgar word like 'debts.' "

"Quite all right. I've grown accustomed."

"Anything new on the subject? Changed your mind yet about that new loophole in the Georgia law?"

"You mean, am I considering imprisonment in my own house—or Mackay's house until I've served my time? Never! Going to prison—even one where the jailer would be my beloved wife or daughter—is no way for an honorable man to repay his debts." He slid his chair nearer Leslie's desk. "I've been thinking . . ."

"Don't you mean scheming?"

"Judge for yourself. But John Houstoun McIntosh wants to buy Fort George Island."

"Do you want to sell to him? Do we need another McIntosh in the province?"

"The answer is no to both questions, but McIntosh *could* pay for it in Georgia—on my debts. Now that Eliza is married to one of my largest accounts there, I—I find it hard to live with my own humiliation."

"Yours or Mrs. McQueen's?"

"I'm not sure." He spread his hands in a helpless gesture. "Suddenly, at fifty-one, I'm not sure of anything—but God and my infernal loneliness!"

"I'm not even sure of God."

"What do you hear from Governor White? He's cut me off."

"Nonsense. We all feel that way, living right here under his Excellency's haughty nose. You're at least picking up some cash because he made you Judge of the Banks."

"I'm picking up *promises* of cash. Who has any? Don Bartolomé tells me the Royal Treasury is swept clean."

"I hate money."

"Are you still able to supply his Excellency with gifts for the Indians?"

"None. Spain owes the firm too much now. How can we go on supplying new merchandise on bad credit?"

"But with Bowles back, his Excellency *has* to have gifts—for the Seminoles at least."

Leslie only grunted.

"Did the governor receive any arms or munitions for Morales up on the frontier?"

"What do you think?"

"They're desperately needed!"

"I must be slipping in my mind, McQueen. I could have sworn I heard you say Bowles *wasn't* properly armed."

"He isn't. But neither is Morales. I base my hopes for safety at San Vicente on the fact that Bowles doesn't *know* the deplorable condition the fort is in. What's more, the rebels are digging in again on Amelia Island—on land I own and can't claim because the Georgians won't stay on the other side of the St. Mary's River where they belong."

John Leslie laughed. "Never thought I'd hear you sound quite so out of sorts with your wife's people. Oh, you fight 'em, but I never heard you criticize them before."

Don Juan did not laugh. "I—think one way and talk another. Then I reverse myself." He slumped in his chair. "Leslie, I don't know anyone else to ask but you. *Do* you believe—Anne will ever come now?"

John Leslie, always uncomfortable with pity, got up

and strode to the window. "No. No, I've never thought she'd come. Not to stay. I'm getting old too. I tell the truth these days—at least, most of the time." He turned back to Don Juan. "You *can't* be still hoping! Even you can't still be hoping for that."

"Oh, but I do hope. In fact, my periods of doubt—like today—are rare."

"Don't you think she's heard that Bowles and his red men burned two loyal settlers' plantations on the St. Mary's just a month ago?"

Don Juan said nothing.

"Of course, Chief Mad Dog and one or two other good Indians are determined to kill Bowles, but they're probably not going to make it. McGillivray couldn't. McQueen, you asked me. I didn't bring it up. If you want my advice, you'll lock up your house at Los Molinos and stay here until Bowles shows his hand one way or another along the St. Johns."

"You're not serious!"

"Never more so. You could go back there tomorrow and find your fine mansion in ashes. Don't think Bowles doesn't know it's yours, and don't think he's forgotten that it was Don Juan McQueen commissioned to capture him back in ninety-one." Leslie shook his head. "You're no fool, man."

"No, except where Anne is concerned," Don Juan said hoarsely.

Leslie thought for a moment, weighing the value of what he felt compelled to say. "Your wife has won in most ways, you know. It might help to admit it—just once."

"But we haven't been fighting each other!"

"Only you know about that. She has the family around her, even young John's doing her bidding now. He wrote me last week about planting again at Oatland—to please his mother."

Don Juan stared at him. "I wasn't told that. . . ."

"Sorry. I assumed you had been."

"Oh, that's a bad decision, Leslie. He shouldn't give up work he loves! But I'm not at all sure he did it only to please his mother." The heavy shoulders sagged. "He probably did it to—attempt to make up for the failures of his father."

John had also told Leslie about the new scheme he and Robert Mackay were hatching. It sounded irrational but, like his father today, young John had been more or less asking for advice. Leslie hated the role. It was a McQueen family affair, not his.

John had written that he and Mackay wanted to sneak most of McQueen's Negroes across the St. Mary's as payment on part of the indebtedness. By now, he had acquired more than seventy, and they were the only negotiable securities the man had. He was land rich in East Florida, of course, but, as a Spanish subject, he could sell land right and left and not be able to send a peso back to Georgia. Leslie could well understand why a man like Don Juan would refuse to take the easy way: imprisonment under the new law in his own house. That could kill a proud man by inches and still not pay his debts—except to society, whatever that meant.

Leslie asked, "Do you—uh, want to go back to Georgia?"

"No," he answered quickly. "No. I want my family here!"

"Then why did you mention selling Fort George Island to McIntosh? You're raising cotton there and cutting timber."

After a long silence, Don Juan said, "I may *have* to go back, if I'm ever to be with my wife again."

"You still care that much about her, eh? After all this time."

He nodded. "And my children and my grandchildren." He brightened a little. "Young Robbie is quite a boy."

"I'd help if I knew how."

"I know you would. I feel some better since we talked, anyway. A man's troubles mount in solitude." He settled his tricorn on his heavy hair and popped its crown with the palm of one hand. "It's hard to discuss faith with you, you old heretic, but faith *isn't* as nebulous as you think. Somehow God will help me."

"How long will you be in town?"

"Who can tell? I take a day at a time." They shook

hands. "I want you to know, Leslie, that in spite of my life as a wretched recluse, I would never permit Anne to move to Los Molinos until conditions are perfectly safe." He smiled broadly. "That's where my faith comes in. I have to believe our lot will improve. Especially do I have to believe it—on my fifty-first birthday."

At Father O'Reilly's insistence, Don Juan remained in St. Augustine until early in the troubled new year of 1802. On January 20, Enrique White called a *junta de guerra*, to which McQueen was invited, and announced that William Augustus Bowles had declared his Muskogee Nation to be at war with Spain.

"You will leave at once, Captain McQueen, to make known the danger to Colonel Morales at San Vicente?"

"At your service, Excellency."

"En route," White went on, "you will stop at New Switzerland, the Fatio place, and report back to me concerning the rumors that Bowles' so-called army has stolen Fatio's Negroes. I must know whether or not the savages are indeed in the vicinity of the Plaza. We need all of the New Switzerland Negroes fully armed as they have been for the past two years. Fatio is nearby. The safety of St. Augustine could well depend upon them. You will also make a tour of both the St. Mary's and the St. Johns. I need a full report of all damage to date."

Don Juan left the meeting at Government House with Bartolomé de Castro. "The time has come," Castro said as they parted. "You must find a way to arm your own Negroes at your plantation at Ortega. You have neglected the place. If the Muskogees move along the St. Johns, they could strike there first."

"But, I have no arms! No arms and no money. I do have securities, as you know, Don Bartolomé. Is there no way you can arrange at least a small loan for me from the Royal Treasury?"

Castro laughed. "You will not believe this, but as his Excellency spoke a moment ago, I formed the plan in my head to tease *you* by asking for a loan in behalf of the colony from Don Juan McQueen—as of old!"

Chapter 45

✳✳✳ At the end of February, about mid-point in the inspection of his and other holdings along the St. Johns, Don Juan stood on the low bluff above the rickety dock at San Juan de Nepomuceno at Ortega near Cowford and looked back at the still smoldering outbuildings.

So far, he had found no other damage on the St. Johns. White's rumors about Fatio's troubles at New Switzerland had evidently been false; but Bowles, the self-styled director general of the Muskogee Nation, had indeed fired what few buildings McQueen had put up at Ortega and had stolen the four McQueen Negroes who were there, Savannah Strephon among them. The day was gray, the sky heavy, the wind cold. His emotions lay close to the surface. The tears flowed.

Numbly, he watched blackjack oak leaves blow about him and tried not to be nervous because he had not yet caught Harry's low whistle, their signal that the boat was still tied in the creek where they had hidden it.

After more than ten years, he had almost had his first glimpse of William Augustus Bowles. He had not gone first to Pablo Creek, Los Molinos, and his Saw Mill Tract, he and Bowles might well have met face to face. The savages must have left only hours before he and Harry docked, because on the half-burned chicken house, the director general of the Muskogees had nailed a scrap of paper on which was scrawled, *Best wishes, Don Juan McQueen—W.A. Bowles. God save Muskogee!*

He would keep the brash note. As did every loyal Spanish subject, he despised the handsome rascal Bowles, who had pirated His Majesty's waters too long in his black schooner, but the legends that followed the man intrigued him. The note might amuse Father O'Reilly too, after one or two glasses of *aguardiente* on the next trip to St. Augustine.

Harry's soft, low whistle reached him then on the blustery wind, and in minutes, the boy was maneuvering their boat into the dock. Don Juan turned once more to look at the land Quesada had granted him so long ago. Without doubt, he would never set foot on San Juan de Nepomuceno again. It too would be offered for sale to John Houstoun McIntosh along with Fort George Island.

He started slowly down the path and stepped aside so as not to crush an early brave violet—a long-stemmed one, as purple as a king's robe.

Could something so small as a violet lift his heart? It had. Harry smiled encouragement. Neither spoke. It was not safe. There was no way to be certain that the Seminoles and Bowles were not still nearby. He smiled back at Harry, eased himself into the boat, and shoved off.

Back at San Vicente, Manuel Romero, the storekeeper, had more bad news.

"You should not find the elder Fatio so hopeful now as on your visit last month, Don Juan. Bowles' savages burned three of his outbuildings and stole forty-nine Negroes—last week! Fatio's son went after them and only managed to escape with his life. For his efforts, he lost four horses." Romero groaned. "If this store was not all I own in the world, I would return tomorrow to St. Augustine. On the frontier, we are in the midst of war with the Indians. Why you do not get out while there is time, I do not know."

Don Juan had always been ready for the change in the seasons. He felt ready for autumn now that the red-spotted dogwood leaves had begun falling in his yard at Los

Molinos. The spring and summer had seemed long and uncertain, but no trouble had come closer to him than Ortega, and he thought the green-eyed sunflowers lovelier than ever.

Late in November, Eliza wrote that he had another grandchild—a girl. Such a surprise normally sent him running for Harry or anyone close at hand who would listen. He must be changing too, he thought, as without a word he slipped into a coat and left the house alone.

He thanked God for the new life—a part of his own through Eliza. But with the joy, he could feel a cold, unfamiliar resistance building within him. Was change coming too fast—too suddenly? Or had it been coming all along without his owning up to it? Did he resist his family's being changed naturally by events such as the birth of a new generation? Events that would go on happening without him? Halfway along the path that ran by the marsh, he stopped to look across into his favorite stand of trees, where lingered a few patches of yellow Spanish needles. In the other direction, lavender asters spread like a pale mist across the dry marsh beyond the path. Winter was near.

A skein of wood ducks headed swiftly toward their roosting place in his cypress swamp a mile or so to the west. There would be no sunset along the low-hanging horizon. The sun lay buried under thick, leaden clouds, as impenetrable as his growing gloom.

The birth of his second grandchild had lowered, not buoyed his spirits, causing him to feel foreign to himself. He might be another man standing there on the path. Surely tomorrow, perhaps even later this evening, he would run shouting to Harry that he had another grandchild. Then he would ride into San Vicente and invite any available person to his house to celebrate.

The light lowered still more in the flat gray sky. A mounting sadness, that everyone in the family but John McQueen knew what the baby looked like, left little room for the joy he wanted to feel. And had he really thought of himself as *John* McQueen? How long since he had done that? Why now?

For the odd, unaccustomed despondency of this moment, he had neither explanation nor remedy.

His hands thrust into his pockets, he hurried back to the familiar house, vowing to tell no one ever—not even Harry—how much he longed this night to be at Thunderbolt. . . . How *afraid* he was—not to be.

Early in the new year, a letter came from Anne in which she enclosed silhouettes of little Robbie, Sallie, now twenty, and herself. "Raphaelle Peale and his brother, Rembrandt, have just left Savannah after making many profiles," she wrote. "My heart, which should be light now that we have two grandchildren, is often strangely heavy for you these days, dear John, but I did think of how you would laugh at the names given the Peale brothers by their prophetic mother. How humiliated she would have been had they grown up to be sailors or carpenters and not painters!"

Nothing cheered him as much as a small joke from Anne. He explained the joke to Harry, his only companion for weeks at a time since the Indian uprisings had made travel dangerous.

"I wonder might the artist brothers come to St. Mary's, Don Juan? You could get a picture made too." Harry's face brightened. "That way the grands, they could see what a fine-looking gentleman their grandfather be!"

McQueen was not listening. He was studying the silhouettes, one at a time. "Poor Sallie has my mark upon her. Look at that strong chin, Harry. Always thought it became me very well, but a girl shouldn't have a chin like that, do you think?"

Harry chuckled. "You sure would look good in one of them pictures, sir. Spring be coming round again soon. No danger if we was to travel to St. Mary's by boat."

"We'll see. Take a good look at my profile. Do I have a double chin yet?"

Harry examined him from several angles. "No, sir! You don't begin to look fifty-two."

"I'm not—not for quite a while yet! Maybe we can find out if the Messrs. Rembrandt and Raphaelle Peale are going to stop in St. Mary's. I've wondered what to send Mrs. McQueen in April, to let her know I remember our wedding day." He laid aside the silhouettes. "Let's see, this is 1803. Thirty-one years ago the second of April, Miss Anne Smith became the bride of Mr. John McQueen. I've never gotten over the wonder of it."

Harry picked up Anne's silhouette and studied it.

"Her letter is unusually cheerful this time," McQueen went on. "No complaints about being short of funds. I suppose our son-in-law sees to that, bless him. And Juan. Too bad Sallie didn't take after her mother, though. Neither of our daughters inherited Miss Anne's lovely straight nose—or her gray eyes. Sallie's and Eliza's are brown, like mine. Say, I wonder what that sturdy little Robbie looks like by now?"

"Running all over the place, I bet, on them fat legs. The new baby she got a name yet?"

"Mary Anne. After her Aunt Cowper and her mother, I suppose. I'd have named her Margaret, I think. Might have brought her some of Cousin Margaret's beauty and verve."

"Don't reckon Miss Anne she have nothing to say about Mr. John and Miss Margaret, do she?"

"Not a word. I must remember to pray more about that, Harry. My son needs a wife."

"Yes, sir. I know he do. He going to be faithful like you, Don Juan. Only one woman."

Talk with Harry, the only person in his life who remembered his family from the old days, usually helped. Not this time. On the verge of unexpected tears, he shouted. "Get out, Harry! I'm so lonesome for them, I want you to shut up and get out!"

In letter after letter, during the remaining winter months and into the spring, using both humor and pleading, Don Juan urged Eliza to bring his new granddaughter and young Robbie for a visit. Harry kept telling him he seemed more like his old self, especially since John Houstoun McIntosh appeared to be interested in the purchase of both Fort George and Nepomuceno, but his longing to look at his grandchildren, to hold them in his arms—to know them—was eating away at his soul. The more so when Eliza wrote that Robbie looked more like his grandfather every day—even to a head of dark red hair. She did write often, as did Anne, but made no mention of a visit.

Not since early autumn had there been even a rumor of another Indian raid. He felt vindicated. Why *did* everyone in the colony but Don Juan McQueen expect the worst always? The sift, mild spring days found him spending long hours outside—riding or taking walks along the river and through his vast stands of timber. He much preferred his woods to regular inspections of the planting in his fields. Like father, like son, he mused. Poor Juan, forced to plant the dreary fields at Oatland.

Often, he walked to San Vicente because it took longer to walk. He had little business at the settlement, but there were people to talk to. Dull as he found Colonel Morales, he could at least buy the man a drink at a tavern, and Morales was a good listener.

In mid-April, he picked up a letter from Eliza at Romero's store, in which she told him at last why she hadn't brought the children to Los Molinos. Robbie had been ill. "One childhood disease after another," she wrote, "and they have left him pale and weak." She felt the boy was somewhat improved, but McQueen's distress over the little fellow sent him hunting for Morales, who commiserated in the worst possible way—by telling of a nephew back in Madrid who had finally died from too many childhood diseases. In self-protection, McQueen abruptly changed the subject.

"How soon do you think we'll know if President Jefferson actually bought Louisiana?"

The colonel downed his brandy. "The evil deed could be done now, for all we hear at San Vicente."

"Has his Excellency received the new troops and arms yet from Havana?"

"*Sí*. But no money. My troops have not been paid in three years! The Court at Madrid owes East Florida above three hundred thousand pesos."

"Any recent word of Bowles' whereabouts?"

Morales beamed. "Ah! You do not know? *You have not heard?*"

"No. How would I hear, sitting alone on my balcony at Los Molinos?"

"William Augustus Bowles is—in hell, where he should have been long ago!"

"Dead? Are you sure?"

Morales nodded briskly. "St. Augustine troops captured him three months ago. He died in Morro Castle."

McQueen smiled. "I'll miss him."

"I will not." The humorless Morales spat. "Even with Bowles gone, his savages will not give up! The recent quiet is false. I look for nothing but trouble through every remaining year of my duty here! If I could find an *escribano* I would plead with His Majesty to give me another post."

"Where?"

"I do not care. Just away from East Florida."

Don Juan tossed coins on the table, then got up. "Have yourself another brandy, Colonel. If you'll excuse me, I must start my long walk home."

He had not left so abruptly because Morales bored him, but because this very night he must write three letters. One to Eliza, promising his prayers for the full recovery of his grandchild; one to McIntosh, offering a still better deal on the new water gin, hoping to hasten the man's decision; and the third, most important of all, to Robert Mackay, setting forth the plan which had been forming in his mind for weeks. With Bowles still a threat, he had not dared write it. Now, he was free to take the chance. Once Jefferson did purchase Louisiana, conditions could worsen. He felt an urgency to write an open, honest plea for help from his son-in-law. Not asking for money or the cancellation of his debt—and surely not offering to become a prisoner in his own house. But, if McIntosh bought Fort George Island and Nepomuceno, McQueen would put in writing that all funds would be paid directly to Mackay.

With that pledge of good faith on record, he was certain that he could persuade either Mackay or Juan to move to East Florida for the two years required to establish residence. He could then deed to them what other properties the debts demanded. As American citizens, they could send the proceeds from their sale back to Georgia. Don Juan would, of course, remain a Spanish subject, keeping residence at Los Molinos, but free to visit Georgia. Then ... surely, with his debts a thing of the past, Anne would see that he meant to make a good life for her in East Florida. Bowles was dead. They would be relatively free from Indian attacks. With the debts paid, how could even his mother-in-law look down on him?

Whistling a little tune as he walked rapidly through the moist spring woods, he was cheered by the further thought that should it be Robert Mackay who consented to establish residence in East Florida and settle the McQueen affairs, his daughter and grandchildren would live with him at Los Molinos for the required years.

A cardinal began to sing nearby. He slowed his pace to look for it. He'd always tried to write some bit of beauty to Eliza. To describe the red bird would be perfect. Carefully, he stepped through beds of scarlet pine lilies and more varieties of fern than he remembered from any other spring. Then he saw the bird. A male, as brilliant as the lilies—stretching its throat in song from the white-blossomed branches of a wild plum tree. . . .

He listened and watched until the bird flew, then hurried home to write his letters.

Chapter 46

✳✳✳ Three weeks later, McQueen's letter reached Robert Mackay at his Savannah office. He read it twice, left word that he would not return that day, and hurried to his home on Reynolds Square.

"I'm leaving at once for Oatland, Eliza. Don't ask any questions now, please, but I have to talk with John. I've had an important letter from your father."

"Papa isn't ill?"

"No. I'd say he's very well." He kissed her forehead. "In fact, if John and I can figure out his plan and find a way to put it into effect, it could mean your father might some day be coming home a free man."

Instantly, he wished he hadn't told her, the hope in her eyes was so sudden. He took her in his arms. "We can't be sure, my darling. Not yet. The Old Gentleman's been known to hatch wild schemes, you know."

She clung to him. "Oh, Robert, do you suppose he's really given up down there?"

"It seems so, but I forbid you to say one word to your mother. Until we see if something can be worked out, you and John and I must keep it among the three of us. Promise?"

"Yes, but you'll have to see Mama on your way to Oatland. How can you bear *not* to tell her?"

He held her at arm's length. "Your mother's been through enough. This is a complicated plan. One that would require sacrifice for all of us. And time. It may not work. I'll think of something on the ride to Thunderbolt. She's the last one who should know—yet."

About midafternoon, Robert Mackay and John sat on the steps of the sagging front porch of the old house on Oatland Island, directly across Thunderbolt River from The Cottage.

"Read it again before you say anything," Mackay advised. "Read it again, carefully. The first time through, you must have been too shocked to think. I was."

He watched his brother-in-law's taut, handsome face, browned from weeks of spring planting. John read through page after page, his expressive eyebrows pulled together in concentration. Now and then he shook his head, smiled a little, or frowned.

Then, after staring a while at the river, John said softly, "I didn't think he'd ever give up."

"He's getting older."

"I suppose that's it. I can see Mama's age, but it's harder to believe about my father. He's always been lonely down there, but most of the time he made jokes about it. As long as he did that, I knew he had no thought of— giving in to my mother."

Sensing that John needed time to order his emotions before they could speak of the business involved, Robert said nothing.

"I once believed, too, she'd weaken some day and move there. That's what I wanted." John's eyes still on the river, he smiled ruefully. "As soon as Mama and Grandmother Smith maneuvered me back to Georgia—and Oatland—I knew I'd been wrong to think she'd ever go."

"Did you tell your father?"

"No. I suppose I should have, but I didn't."

Mackay felt a surge of pity for what his brother-in-law must have endured over the eleven years since he had returned from Europe, his own life torn between his parents. Anne McQueen did appear to have won with her bachelor son, although how could anyone *win* in a family tragedy like this one?

"Eliza and I kept hoping for a miracle," John said at

last. "Maybe the seeds of a miracle are here, in these pages. But I confess his plan makes very little sense to me so far."

Mackay got up. "It's so long, I didn't take time to have someone copy it before I left this morning. I wish I had. I need to study it too. But you keep it. Think it over tonight, then come in to my office in the morning. Just tell your mother I want to discuss some business with you." He smiled. "I do. We'll need legal counsel. As I understand the letter, one or both of us would have to move to East Florida as temporary settlers. Not Spanish subjects, of course. He would then deed to us whatever holdings are required to settle his Georgia debts. We would sell and, not being Spanish subjects, would be free to send the proceeds back here to wipe out the debts."

"It might work, provided Governor Enrique White hasn't tightened the Spanish law. I lived in East and West Florida as an American citizen for over five years. I sent money to Mother when I had it. Under Quesada, Papa could have deeded any amount of property to me. But he isn't as close to White."

"That two years' residence is the problem. I'm not at all sure I can leave my business that long."

"I think Mother would agree to my going if she thought he'd be coming home at the end of two years. I know why he suggested you and Eliza, though. Except to have Mother move there, I've never known him to want anything as much as he wants to be with his grandchildren."

"He's thought of everything, hasn't he?" Mackay said. "Your father is a remarkable man."

They went slowly down the front steps and out to the dock where Robert would take the skiff across to The Cottage.

"How about telling Mother for me that I'll be going into Savannah for a few days?"

"Fine. I'll be glad to. Easier for me than for you, eh?"

The two men shook hands.

♦   ♦   ♦

Every day through the months of June and July, Don Juan had ridden or walked to San Vicente, hoping for a reply from Mackay. There were frequent letters from Savannah—even a poorly scrawled note from William, begging to visit him. He detected in William, now twenty-one, an isolate from the rest of the family—to Don Juan, understandable; at least, if his younger son had grown to be anything like his father in the past years. They had not been together since the boy was fourteen. He longed to know him, but could not agree to the visit until his own plans were firm. Writing to tell William that he must wait would not be easy. One sentence in the note—"Lately, it seems as though I can't do anything right around here"—had whetted Don Juan's desire to be with him. William would undoubtedly be excellent company.

Toward the end of the second week of August, Harry fussed when Don Juan headed for the barn to make his daily ride to the outpost. "Sometimes I tell you what to do, Don Juan, and this be one time. You ain't riding nowhere today! Not full of that bad cold. You cough all night. Ain't no boats docking today anyway. Colonel Morales, he told you yesterday."

"Neither Colonel Morales nor anyone else—including you—knows when a traveler from Georgia may appear at San Vicente." He grinned. "All right. If I can't go, then you will."

By noon, Harry was back with a letter, but not from Robert Mackay; from John Houstoun McIntosh. The added offer of his water gin thrown into the Fort George transaction had perhaps turned the trick. The sale of his properties to McIntosh would be at least the first step in the execution of his plan. His heart pounded as he broke the heavy McIntosh seal and began to read:

> *Camden County, Georgia*
> *31 July, 1803*

My dear Sir, John McQueen,

> *The illness of Mrs. McIntosh has delayed my decision concerning the purchase of Fort George Island*

*and the place at Ortega you call San Juan de
Nepomuceno. My wife is up and around again and although at one time she resisted leaving Georgia, I have
not pressed my fortune by demanding to know why she
has now changed her mind. I accept the change and
hereby agree to pay you over a year and a half, 28,000
doll^rs for both tracts and their houses and outlying
buildings. I agree also to rent until this date in 1804,
your working Negroes at 120 doll^rs the head. Upon receipt of like agreement from you, I will meet you in St.
Augustine with half the amount in cash, at which time
papers will be signed.*

*I will not be establishing myself in Florida with
much enthusiasm for its government, but with confidence that the U.S. will govern it in the not too distant
future, since President Jefferson has (I have just
learned) authorized, and France agreed, to the outright purchase of the vast colony known as Louisiana.
I dare to risk imparting my lack of enthusiasm for
Spain knowing you will, in order to protect your business dealings with me, tell no one at the Plaza.*

> *Yr. very obed. servant,*
> *John Houstoun McIntosh, Esq.*

Incensed at the impudence, Don Juan slammed down
the letter and left the house without a word of response to
Harry's warning that a sprinkle of rain was falling outside.

He strode angrily down the path to the woods, fighting
the impulse to call off the whole deal with McIntosh.
More than the impudence, he minded being told by a
Georgian that Jefferson had indeed bought Louisiana! The
gaping American mouth, no matter who succeeded Jefferson next year, would surely go on taking bites of Indian
and Spanish land until the struggling Floridas were one
day also devoured.

Entering the damp, fragrant forest, he followed a favorite fresh-water creek for a quarter of a mile or so, then
stopped, scarcely realizing that the big drops of summer
rain which had pelted him since he left the house had
stopped too. He clenched his fists, needing to hold on to

his anger—fearing it would turn to grief for East Florida. Anger was more strengthening. He dared not grieve. *Were* the greedy Americans, even well-born gentlemen like J. Houstoun McIntosh, going to pour across the St. Mary's now in such droves that the day would come when he would find no more refuge in his beloved province? McIntosh had made no bones about it. Once, at least, Georgia settlers had been graceful enough to *pretend* loyalty to Spain.

"I'm aware I've hatched a scheme to go back to Georgia," he muttered aloud to the dripping trees. "I *want* to lie with my wife again before I'm too old to know I'm a man! I *want* to see my grandchildren! I've lived a hermit's life for twelve years. I need to be loved, but in the name of heaven, I don't want East Florida to fall!"

The anger had already turned to grief. He slumped against a rough, wet trunk of a giant pine. On the ground at his feet, a drooping blossom of a pitcher plant caught and held his eye. He watched as a long-legged insect crawled deliberately up the leafless stem into the blossom's hollow trumpet trap and lay gripped in the sticky fluid until digested—the pitcher plant's way of nourishing itself.

He turned away. Worse than the death of the Spanish Floridas so that the voracious United States could be nourished would be his own inevitable end in the Georgian courts, if Robert Mackay rejected his plan while Spain was still in control of this land.

Slowly, he retraced his steps. Before he reached his house, he had decided to write to Juan, Jr., for an accounting of the entire amount he owed. Waiting, with no action at all, was unendurable. As was the grinding contradiction within him: grief over East Florida *and* longing for Anne. If some decision could be made soon, surely, for a few years at least, he would be free to visit her for long periods of time, while keeping his beloved house at Los Molinos. What could be so wrong with that?

He hurried up his front steps, making more plans. He would ask Juan to reply at St. Augustine and leave for the sad little city tomorrow. Señor Zubizarreta would gladly assist in drawing up the papers for McIntosh. And who could say that the ambitious, frugal little *escribano* might not have saved enough money by now to buy another of the many McQueen holdings?

At his desk, he managed a brief, hopeful smile. If his Georgia debts and accrued interest were not too high a figure, he might just make it back to Anne with honor— *before* his own pride fell along with his adopted colony.

He took out a sheet of writing paper. Fresh trouble can sometimes stir a man into fruitful action, he thought, noticing that the quixotic August rain was falling again—in full sunshine.

Chapter 47

✤✤✤ The second-floor quarters in the house on the Lane That Leads to the Marina were airless, smelling of mildew when he and Harry arrived hot and exhausted from the day's ride overland. Don Juan left Harry to settle in and walked down the lane to give Father O'Reilly a report on his new plans for freeing himself once and for all of the old debts. He would make his report in detail first; then, if the priest hadn't heard, he would break the bad news that Jefferson had bought Louisiana.

After a cordial greeting, they took chairs on the balcony. Miguel O'Reilly listened without comment to the end of his story, the pale blue eyes looking off down the lane toward the Bay and the watch tower on Anastasia Island.

"I can see you've been busy, Don Juan," he said quietly when McQueen had finished. "Only one thing bothers me. Should your son-in-law *and* Governor White agree to your plan, would I—after the two years of your family's residence here—ever see you again? Most of my parishioners are bad company, you know."

McQueen studied the angular face, still in profile, the skinny freckled hands motionless, fingertips together as they had been throughout the lengthy account. "I'll always be a foreigner in Georgia, Father. I suppose, in a sense, a foreigner even with my family. The years here, I now realize, have been—will always be—the real years of my life."

"A pretty speech, but all nonsense, of course. If not, why on earth would you be making such a gigantic effort to get away? I've been a far better checkers partner than priest to you, but at times I've suffered your loneliness, experienced your body's pain at night on my own bed. My vows to God strengthen me. Your vows were made to a woman. A woman who should have been beside you. Your *real* life has always been—there, with her. Let's keep that straight."

O'Reilly crossed thin legs under the folds of his cassock and looked directly at him. "At the risk of lessening your humility, I must tell you that your faithfulness to her has been hard to believe."

"Father, you *do* believe it?"

"Yes. But I'd be still more remiss than usual as your priest, if I didn't insist that you be truthful about your reasons for concocting this plan. You've been a shadow man down here. Oh, a charming, amusing, and highly influential shadow, but a shadow." He laid his hand on McQueen's arm. "I will pray for the success of your plan. You belong there. But I do demand an answer to my question of a moment ago. Do you really think you would ever come back—to visit me?"

"Of course, Father! You misunderstand. I only want to be able to spend as much time in Georgia as my family needs—as I need. I fully intend to keep residence in East Florida. To remain a Spanish subject."

"And—a Catholic?"

McQueen smiled. "I didn't think you'd have to ask."

"Young Padre Font saw to that, didn't he?"

Aware that priests were human, therefore subject to jealousy as were all men, McQueen searched for a suitable response. Padre Font *had*, in one brief, light-filled instant, brought him face to face with the living God—the God of forgiveness. But Father O'Reilly had been his faithful friend and comrade, had helped fill his lonely hours; had given him God in the Blessed Sacrament. He must make O'Reilly understand that what he had done in a daily way had nurtured what Padre Font had begun. The thought of leaving, even two years from now, with any barrier between himself and Miguel O'Reilly was unbearable.

The priest interrupted his thoughts. "You're seldom so slow to launch into the answer to a question. Was it Padre Font's ministry to you that makes you so sure you'll never leave the Church?"

"You were present at my Baptism, Father. You know I became a Catholic—a Christian then—for life."

O'Reilly shook his head, chuckling. "That was diplomatic. Your tongue grows more golden with the years." He was suddenly serious. "Yes, I was present at your Baptism, but since young Font died in your arms, I've had to plead with God to keep me from—envy."

"Of Padre Font?"

"I thought all along you were missing my point. No. Not of Font. Of you. My life is far simpler than yours. Being a priest is, in many ways, an enormous simplifier of life. One labors, one forces back normal desires, but there are fewer temptations. I've envied you because since the Franciscan died, you've somehow known how to let God handle your life—your conduct—far better than I've ever known."

Don Juan looked at him in surprise. "That can't be possible! I've always felt—inadequate."

"Did someone else convince you of that?"

He supposed O'Reilly referred to Anne or to her mother, so let it go. "I'd say I've just observed myself off and on."

"There was a special experience with God the night the young priest died, wasn't there?"

"Yes. But, don't forget, there is one glory of the sun and another of the moon, Father. You have been my steady friend in Christ. And as long as His Majesty's colony is here, I will visit you."

"Thank you. Well said. You've quieted a few of the old priest's uncertainties. Now, tell me, when do you expect to hear from your son-in-law? And do you suppose he has a clearer concept of what it is you're trying to bring about than I? What if your native lands take us over before the two years are up?"

"In that case, I simply find out at last what it's like to be on the—the prisoner's side of a judge's bench."

"You know, don't you, that Jefferson has managed to buy Louisiana from Napoleon?"

"Yes. I thought perhaps you hadn't heard."

"White did condescend to tell me that. It frightened him enough to call on me for a bit of bolstering. I doubt that I gave it; I'm scared myself. I'd think the American President could eventually get the starving Floridas for far less."

"I'm counting on His Majesty's stubborn streak. He doesn't want to lose out altogether in North America."

"I suppose not, when he stops following the hounds long enough to remember we're here. Do you think Señor Zubizarreta does have funds to buy another of your properties?"

"Tonight, here with you and with that somewhat cooling breeze blowing up the lane, I'm quite happily counting on that too. He's a frugal man."

"How much do you owe in Georgia?"

"I've honestly never figured it up. My son's making an accounting. At least, I've asked for one."

"Do you plan to see his Excellency on this trip?"

"Indeed I do. If he sends for me."

"Then I'd better warn you. Enrique White, already a stern man, has hardened still more. His hatred for Georgians is now almost beyond the power of God to forgive!"

McQueen missed John Leslie, who was in London attempting to salvage the crumbling interests of the once powerful firm of Panton and Leslie. But when he dropped by Leslie's office to pick up his mail two weeks after reaching St. Augustine, there was a letter from young John. He perched on Leslie's stool to read:

25 August, 1803
Savannah, Georgia

Papa, my Dear Sir,

I'm sure you wondered if you'd ever receive a reply from Mackay or me, but expert legal counsel has been

hard to come by. Even lawyers don't understand Span-
ish laws. But for now, let me just say that, with some
alterations, we are hopeful that your plan can succeed.
Surprisingly, Robert has received the consent of his
partner, Mr. Mein, to establish residence in Florida for
the required two years, if Spanish law still permits.
Mama is curious, but we have said nothing yet, not
wanting to dash her hopes should the plan for some
reason fail. So, be careful in your letters. Eliza knows
and will move down gladly with the children in the
face of what will surely be a strong protest from
Grandmother Smith.

You must now learn from White about the status of
Spanish regulations involved in such a transaction.
Gossip here is that White is tough. How tough? At any
rate, nothing can happen for a year. If he is to leave
his interests here intact, Robert Mackay must first
make a lengthy visit to London.

The total amount of your indebtedness, I'm sorry to
report, is $60,000 plus interest. Write details of the
McIntosh deals and we'll see how we stand then. We
all send love.

> *Yr affec't son,*
> *John McQueen, Jr.*

"Sixty thousand dollars, eh?" Don Juan spoke aloud
into the empty office. "Well, with the rental of my Negroes, plus the McIntosh purchase money of twenty-eight
thousand, half of my indebtedness will be wiped away.
And—I'll still own five hundred acres on Pellicer's Creek,
four hundred on Amelia Island, the entire two thousand
acres of the Saw Mill Tract on the St. Johns, nearly twelve
hundred on Pablo Creek, plus my splendid large holdings
at Cape Florida and at Tampa Bay." He pocketed the letter
and started from the office. "And of course, I will also still
own my home—Los Molinos de McQueen."

Out under the baking September sun, he took a moment to revel in the blue water of Matanzas Bay, only a
shade darker than the St. Augustine sky. Why wait for
Enrique White to invite him to Government House as

though he, Don Juan McQueen, were not still a man of means and influence? Had he permitted himself to grow so heavyhearted that he imagined he was no longer of value to the governor of East Florida? Ridiculous!

He had intended to stop by the Royal Treasury to discuss an important new idea with Bartolomé de Castro, but why not take the idea directly to White?

His idea was not exactly new. Years ago, he had tried it on Quesada and failed. "Wrecking is not honorable, Don Juan!" He had only smiled then at the young governor's shock at his proposal that Spain should do as England and France had done for years—lay hold of some ready cash by going to the rescue of wrecked ships and reselling their cargo at enormous profit. He had never seen anything dishonorable in the wrecking business. Other nations had grown rich from it. Why not Spain? Especially now that the Royal Treasury was empty. Don Juan McQueen, with his naval experience in the American Revolution, would, of course, be the right man to head such a business for His Majesty. He certainly did not like White as he'd liked Quesada, but he found the older man more pragmatic.

Striding, shoulders erect, up Treasury Street toward St. George, he counted heavily on that pragmatism. At the foot of the familiar outside staircase at Government House, he paused a moment to think through an angle which had occurred to him. It would be better, perhaps, considering White's stubborn will, just to pay his respects now and hope for a dinner invitation soon in the company of other St. Augustine officials. Then, if White demurred at wrecking, there would be others present to help convince him.

He bounded up the stairs, wondering why he'd stayed away from the city so long when his mind worked so much better there.

Dinner the next evening at Government House with White, Don Dimas Cortés, and Don Bartolomé de Castro had not been as formidable as he'd expected. White was a cultivated gentleman and an informed conversationalist, and had indeed appeared mildly interested in Don Juan's wrecking proposal. At least, he had asked innumerable pertinent questions.

"You must be patient," Castro had said with a sly wink when he bade Don Juan good night at the end of the evening. "You planted the seed. But do not expect to hear soon that his Excellency will make the offer to you. Enrique White does not take another man's idea so swiftly. He waits until it appears to be his own. Be patient and do not worry."

The early autumn night was too hot for worry. At his quarters on the lane, Don Juan undressed and stretched himself on the bed. He could wait. Hadn't he spent the past twelve years of his life waiting for Anne? He loathed waiting, but his health, for a man of fifty-two, was excellent. There was still time to live. . . .

He pounded the pillows, circled them with his arms, and let himself grow drowsy. Zubizarreta would have the papers ready tomorrow for the sale of Fort George Island and Nepomuceno, and then any day, John Houstoun McIntosh would arrive for the closing. He would also speak to Señor Zubizarreta concerning the Saw Mill Tract or another of his holdings. It was good to be active again.

In spite of the heat, he slept.

He was still in St. Augustine when the year 1804 began. Dining with official friends, playing checkers with Father O'Reilly, and the blessed comfort of Mass kept his spirits high. He had missed it all far more than he dared admit, even to God. No reassuring friendship grew between him and Enrique White, but he dined with his Excellency, he observed, more frequently than did any other St. Augustine official. Now and then White spoke obliquely of the potential of a wrecking enterprise, but the license to begin operations did not come. This time, McQueen vowed, he would not press his luck.

Robert Mackay would be leaving early in the new year for London. Without asking outright, Don Juan had perceived no change in White's liberal observance of the law—Americans could evidently settle in East Florida and send money back to the United States without swearing allegiance to the Crown. Georgians were still crossing the border, accepting free Spanish land grants. His Excellency had begun a more rigid examination of their reasons for settling there, but land-hungry men lied convincingly, and they were needed.

One evening at Government House, Don Juan had casually mentioned that he had every reason to expect at least some of his family to settle there. White had appeared to accept the news calmly, with only proper best wishes. No questions.

As late as last week, McQueen had dined at a local tavern with Captain Peter Carne from San Vicente. In spite of Morales' continuing plea for troops and guns, Carne vowed that for months no one had seen a marauding Indian anywhere on the frontier.

His days rocked along like tight crafts on a gentle sea. Zubizarreta, who seemed at times to be the only man in St. Augustine who could lay his hands on money, after careful figuring, decided that he would be able to buy the Saw Mill Tract in a year and a half.

There was only one continuing heartache: so far as he knew, Anne still had not been told of his resolve to clear all the Georgia debts. Oh, she did know that the down payment from McIntosh had been sent directly to Savannah. Her letters had, from that point on, been even more affectionate. He was amused. "The way to a woman's heart," he told Harry, "is by the payment of a man's debts."

He felt certain that he knew Anne better, though, than ever before. Now that he was older, he understood, at least in part, how he must have appeared to her through the long years—as stubbornly choosing his own way of handling their tragedy. She had appeared stubborn to him too.

"You is both pitiful," Harry would say in his gentle voice.

They *had* been pitiful, he supposed, but not for long now. Not for long.

Chapter 48

✳✳✳ He couldn't recall a more hopeful period than the spring and summer of the year 1804. On two occasions, he made the journey to Cape Florida to see the proper cutting of the excellent timber there and found himself wondering—since he enjoyed it now—why he had been lax about such supervision in the past. Havana purchased, on credit, every shipload he could supply from Tampa Bay; and thanks to Leslie's London connections, squared timber from the St. Mary's lease, under the skillful management of James Gould, was bringing regular cash payments.

For the present at least, McQueen had even been able to quiet Gould's fears that he and his new wife might be burned out. Sporadic bands of Seminoles still haunted the St. Mary's, but a trip to Alachua had brought a promise from King Paine that McQueen's Mills Ferry lease would be protected. The promise was a comfort, if not a guarantee.

Between journeys, he worked more diligently than ever before to produce a good crop at Los Molinos. Anne's letters fanned his new determination to become a successful planter. Newsy letters from Eliza kept him up on the growth and amusing antics of his two grandchildren. The days no longer stretched endlessly ahead; as soon as he could settle down for the winter at Los Molinos, William would arrive to stay until the Mackays settled in the big house with him for the required two years. Robert Mackay, fully carrying out his part of the plan, wrote from England that he hoped to return to Savannah at the end of the year.

These were his last days as a hermit. Except for pains in his legs and shoulders now and then after a hard ride, his health and vitality were those of a much younger man. Even the deepening longing for Anne did not depress him. He'd always heard that a man's desires flamed higher in later life. He believed it now, but the longing was endurable. They would one day be together again. He was waiting with a purpose, not merely enduring absence which might never end.

A walk across a hammock of his Los Molinos property late in September bolstered his returning faith in change. The waiting time would end. His days would change for the better as, indeed, he had changed. Always, he had delighted in the tall summer spikes of orange-red buckeye. Now he found their reddish brown seeds—round and plump—as fascinating as the blossoms they had been and would become again next year. Even the scents on the air had changed. In the wind blowing out of the woods, he could smell the blend of green leaves drying and the salty winter dampness from the marsh.

His grandchildren would revel in this place, but would have to be taught not to run alone into a marsh—even a dry one—after handfuls of red- and green-beaded salicornia. He would take them, any time they liked, to explore what he called his marsh garden. They could pick wild delights to their hearts' content, but their grandfather would be there to keep an eye out for snakes. In the spring, the children could pick sweet, wild azaleas along the creeks for their mother and some day, he prayed, for their Grandmother Anne.

He was returning one day from such a pleasant walk when old Andrew Atkinson rode up his lane.

The men exchanged greetings, turned the horse over to Harry, and sat down on McQueen's spacious veranda. Atkinson looked frail, as always, too frail and old, Don Juan thought, to be riding anywhere alone.

"I left Mrs. Atkinson and Leslie's wife drunk as two coots to make the trip," he said, still winded from his ride. "But I didn't trust anyone else with what I have to tell you. Are you still expecting your daughter and her family to move here?"

"Indeed I am! I imagine they'll spend the Christmas holidays in Savannah, but I look for them by early spring anyway. Why?"

"They won't be able to come."

He opened his mouth to speak, but could not.

"Hate to be the one to tell you, but Governor White's closed the border to settlers. Closed it tight. Reckon he's had more than enough of Georgians pouring in here, feigning loyalty when all the time they're plotting rebellion. Whatever his reason, they can't come. You'll have to find another way to settle those Georgia debts."

That night, McQueen sat alone in his room, the brown Franciscan habit in his arms, praying for courage to face the sunrise tomorrow with a guest in his house—and his dream shattered. God would have to do something; McQueen could not. Without a drastic release from the new despair that enveloped him, he could not even manage hospitable conduct toward his faithful old friend.

When he was sure Atkinson had retired, he crept downstairs in his stocking feet and onto the veranda, leaving the parlor door unlatched because Harry awakened at the slightest sound. Even Harry would grate on his nerves tonight. He could bear the presence of no one but God.

He paced up and down the length of the veranda, dreading what he had to do before dawn. The letter to Robert Mackay must be ready when Atkinson left tomorrow morning. At this moment, in the face of his family's hatred of everything Spanish, to tell them that the Spanish governor had thwarted his plans was unthinkable. That it had to be done did not help. By some means, God would give him the strength to write it, but how could even God enable him to endure the weeks he would have to wait for Mackay's reply, setting forth the only alternate plan—the imprisonment of Don Juan McQueen in his own house in Georgia, until he had served out his time in stark humiliation under the self-righteous gaze of the McQueen family's long-time jailer, Elizabeth Smith?

He stopped pacing and looked into the full moon which hung like a carved metal disc over the St. Johns. "I won't do that! I'll find another way," he whispered hoarsely. "Pray, Padre Font, that God will show me another, more honorable way!"

Whether or not it was a sign from God, suddenly he decided to go to St. Augustine. Perhaps, on his knees in the church, the more honorable way would come to him. "A man's troubles *do* mount in solitude," he said aloud. He needed to talk to his friends, to be a part of the noisy little city, perhaps even to see Enrique White. Why rush the writing of Mackay's letter when there was the slightest possibility that another way might be found? News of the border's closing would not reach Savannah for a month or so, at least there was a chance that it might not. Even if Mackay's next letter disclosed that he knew, there was no certain way that Don Juan could have known. There was room for maneuvering. For finding another way.

In his bed, his mind seemed to come alive for the first time since Atkinson had given him the shocking news. Indeed he *would* see Enrique White. If his Excellency had closed the border to the much-needed American settlers, he must have hit upon another plan to increase the colony's income. And what other means was at hand but fitting out ships for wrecking?

He hurried in his nightshirt and cap to inform Harry that as soon as they had bidden Captain Atkinson good-by tomorrow morning, they were leaving for St. Augustine.

For two weeks he walked the streets of the city, waiting. In his sternest manner, Father O'Reilly had urged him not to try to see Governor White.

"I don't need to tell you that he's an unrelenting man," the priest said. "But it's worse than that now. My guess is that his Excellency feels more trapped every day and is—in his hardheaded way—fighting back at everything American. If you, an ex-Georgian, run in on him when he's of this mind, your plans for the wrecking business are ended. When he's ready, he'll send for you. Then, if the subject of Spanish wrecking comes up, he can take credit."

"I take it you don't agree with Quesada, Father, that wrecking is dishonorable?"

"If I agreed"—O'Reilly shrugged his thin shoulders—
"would I be advising you as I did? Ships wreck from poor
navigation, storms, coral reefs. You won't be asked to
cause their bad luck. Only to be there—on hand—to make
the necessary rescues of both men and cargo. The cargo, I
should think, would be considered rightly yours to sell. Of
course, you'd have to smuggle the money across the border, if it's to be applied on your debts, but there are areas
in all of life, Don Juan, where a thing is neither black nor
white, but gray. This is undoubtedly a gray area."

McQueen sighed. "I had guessed that you didn't disap-
prove, but I'm relieved to have you express it so reason-
ably."

"Would it matter to you if I had disapproved?"

"It would matter, yes."

"Would you refuse to enter into the scheme—provided
it never comes to pass—if I forbade it?"

McQueen smiled. "We don't have to decide that, do
we?"

He waited in his quarters on the Lane That Leads to
the Marina for a month before Enrique White invited him
to Government House. They dined, drank rather poor
wine, and spoke in generalities; then McQueen went de-
spondently back to his rooms. In a few days, on his way
to a second dinner with White, he picked up a letter from
Anne.

> *10 October, 1804*
> *The Cottage*

Beloved John,

  *I can scarcely write for my tears which fall almost
constantly and so must ask you to forgive such a short
note. Our beautiful grandson, Robbie, died at 11
o'clock at night, 7 October. Eliza is brave, but greatly
in need of her husband, who is still abroad and does
not yet know. My hand trembles too much to write
more, but please be assured that my heart is close*

against yours in what I am certain will be unbearably lonely grief.

> *Your loving wife,*
> *Anne McQueen*

At Government House that evening White, though sympathetic to his sorrow, again did not mention the wrecking license.

Early the next morning, he and Harry began the journey back to Los Molinos. Even Harry could not comfort him, although upon their arrival home he began at once to do the only thing a friend could do to help. As swiftly as possible, without a word, he tore down the fine playhouse which he had built for the grandchildren, stowed every plank away out of sight, and planted clumps of wild button bushes where the little whitewashed house had stood.

Robert Mackay did not return from England until early June of the next year, and on a warm June evening, Don Juan sat down on his parlor at Los Molinos holding his first letter from his son-in-law since the border had been closed. The empty, despondent days of winter and spring had somehow passed. Young Juan, he knew, had written Mackay that their plan had failed. All further plans had been held in abeyance until Mackay was home again. There seemed no hurry now to read what would surely be a difficult letter. Difficult to have written, difficult to read.

The button bushes were blooming, their fluffy, round white blossoms nodding in the late evening breeze. He looked at them for a long time, then broke the seal and began to read.

> *17 June 1805*
> *Savannah*

My Dear Sir,

> *I have been home for a few days, but my mind and heart have been slow to adjust to the silence of our house, now that Robbie is dead. My pain at having to*

*remain in London far beyond my intention will be with
me forever, since I longed so to be with my adorable
Eliza in her grief, and in mine. I stayed, sir, in the
hope of helping Mr. Leslie raise money for his failing
firm. Eliza insisted, since Leslie has been kind to you.
My efforts only partially succeeded.*

*John has, of course, informed me that our plan to
settle temporarily in East Florida fell short of success
too, thanks to Governor White's new law closing the
border to all Americans. After mature consideration,
John and I submit the following arrangement for your
opinion.*

*Even when smuggled across the border, exchange of
Spanish money is so inferior here, we believe a full
discharge from your creditors cannot now be obtained
short of swearing out a warrant for your arrest immediately upon your arrival in Savannah, should you
agree. You may then, according to the new law, be confined for the required time (or until the debts are somehow paid) at The Cottage or in my house, after which
every difficulty will finally end. Neither Eliza nor I intended to make Florida a permanent address, as you
know, and I now believe this plan to be superior. We
will be able to handle your problems here where Spanish and American political disputes cannot disturb you.
You may or may not have heard that Spain has refused
to accept the acquisition of Louisiana by the U.S.
Therefore, the President has ordered a body of troops
to take possession of it. In view of this dark prospect
for the Floridas, your family and I beg you to agree to
the above plan.*

*When I hear favorably, as I pray I will, further de-
tails concerning your Negroes, the disposition of crops,
etc., can be settled between us. Dear Sir,*

*Your Obed. son-in-law,
Robert Mackay*

*P.S. Your son John is in complete agreement. By ac-
cepting confinement as above, you will retain your
Spanish standing and lands until such time as your*

conscience dictates otherwise. We are all well. Even Grandmother Smith, though partially paralyzed, survives our vicissitudes.

He read the postscript again: *By accepting confinement as above, you will retain your Spanish standing and lands until such time as your conscience dictates otherwise.*

A humorless laugh surfaced. He crumpled the letter and threw it into a corner. "Elizabeth Smith survives," he whispered. "My grandson is dead!" As was his last hope now that anyone was going to help him shed the burden of his Georgia debts. It had even remained to his successful son-in-law to inform him that Spain—his own country—was taking military action in Louisiana.

"Your face be so sad, Don Juan," Harry startled him from the doorway. "You want I should read to you out of the Holy Book?"

He turned numbly to look at his servant. "What?"

"I said, you want I should read to you—to help you?"

"Oh. Yes. All right. Whatever you say, Harry."

Harry picked up the Bible from a nearby table. "What do you want me to read?"

"Doesn't matter. It won't help, I daresay."

The spacious room, so empty a moment ago, seemed less so because of the quiet presence of the only person who always sensed his every need. He only half heard the rustle of the thin pages as Harry searched for a Scripture. Let the boy read, he thought, resting his hand against the chair back. It can do no harm. The harm has been done—all of it.

But quickly, the rustling pages began to annoy him. "Hurry up, Harry!" His voice was gruff. "If you must read, then read. I can tell you now, it won't help. They've left us stranded. Our folks in Georgia have turned against us."

"Not Miss Anne," Harry said.

He sighed heavily. "No. Miss Anne still doesn't know about the plan. And that angers me too! She should have been told that I'm at least making an effort to—to—"

"To—make things right? So we can go back?"

He raised his head to look at the boy. "Well, to—

arrange things so you and I can come and go as we please, at least."

Harry returned his gaze for a moment, then said, "I found the place to read."

"All right, then! *Read.*"

" 'And Jesus answered them, saying, The hour is come, that the Son of man should be glorified. Verily, verily, I say unto you, Except a corn of wheat fall into the ground and die, it abideth alone: but if it die, it bringeth forth much fruit. He that loveth his life shall lose it; and he that hateth his life—' "

"That's enough!" He jumped to his feet glaring at Harry. "Get out! I need words of comfort—not words of dying and hate! I'm sick of dying by inches. Sick of abiding alone!"

The pages rustled softly again. "I believe this mean the same thing, sir," Harry said softly, "but maybe you like it better."

Don Juan paced the long room, back and forth, running his hands through his hair.

Harry began again to read. "Come unto me, all ye that labor and are heavy laden, and I will give you rest. Take my yoke upon you, and learn of me; for I am meek and lowly in heart: and ye shall find rest unto your souls. For my yoke is easy, and my burden is light.' "

Slowly, McQueen returned to his chair. This young black man *was* the only real friend he had in the world. "No priest ever read that as beautifully as you read it, Harry," he said.

"I believe it, sir, but I couldn't never read it except for you teaching me how."

"Do you pray, Harry?"

"Every morning and every night—for you."

"Don't you pray for yourself?"

"I guess so, but just that I'd be willing to—die if it was to make you—stop worrying."

"Nonsense. I couldn't do without you! There you go with talk of dying again. Stop it, do you hear me?" Harry said nothing. McQueen found the silence unbearable. He lightened his voice and went on. "Say, since you're already a believer, don't you think it's time you were baptized? Nothing would please Father O'Reilly more, you know."

Harry was silent again, then said, "If it make you happy."

"Well, now, indeed it would. I want to know we'll be together always, don't you?"

"Oh, we will be. Miss Anne and all of us."

He studied the quiet, expressive face. "You—sound awfully sure. When did you begin to believe all this?"

"Maum Lessie, she tell me when I was a boy in Savannah."

"Lessie just—told you? That was enough?"

"Yes, sir."

"But you've never gone to church."

"You can't go neither, living up here on the St. John's."

"So I can't."

"Don't mean you stop believing."

"Nevertheless, think about being baptized the next time we go to St. Augustine. I'd feel better if you were."

The cheering smile flashed. "I do it for you. Jesus, He love me either way."

"You wouldn't be afraid to die—tonight? In your sleep?"

"No, sir! I'd just hate to leave you."

He brushed him off affectionately. "You're the limit to anything I ever saw! It's dark outside. Go on to bed. And—say one of your heathen prayers for me, will you? I've got a lot to do before I can sleep."

His anger was gone. Harry had seen to that, but the big house at Los Molinos was too small to contain the perplexing struggle which had begun almost as soon as the young man left the room. Why the struggle? Robert Mackay had offered a way to satisfy the Georgia courts and still keep at least some of his Spanish holdings. Once, he *might* have considered such an arrangement, had the law been in effect before Mother Smith moved in to live at The Cottage. He could not endure it now. So, why the struggle?

Outside in the soft, humid night, he stood looking up at the sky, then out toward the river, his marshes and woods. The darkness was so dense that he could see nothing. Not even the shadowy outlines of his pines in the distance. Not a single star in the heavens. Nothing came into sight. His eyes did not grow accustomed to *anything*. He owned what lay within the darkness, but the pine woods, the fields, the cypress swamp—all were there only because he *knew* them to be. Knew them to be there—and to be *his*.

There isn't a man in East Florida with ready cash, he was thinking. I'm not alone in my need for money. In St. Augustine men and women and children often lack food for their tables. Even my last meal at Government House required Enrique White's sour wine to wash it down. His Excellency and I ate chicken that tasted like fish because these days the poor chickens, with no grain, eat only crabs scratched up along the waterfront! I own some cattle, I have a vegetable garden, a fine house, and the best of servants. "In Spanish Florida, compared to many, I'm rich," he said aloud into the humid, bleak night. "I'm rich!"

His words of bravado hung on the motionless air, suspended for him to examine. Then, other words moved silently into his mind beside them: *Except a corn of wheat fall into the ground and die, it abideth alone....*

He cursed Harry; then felt ashamed. But why in the name of heaven had the boy read such a passage when his master's soul cried out for comfort? What, indeed, did it mean for a man to die—like an ordinary corn of wheat? Man, made in God's image?

His hands clenched, he stared into the darkness. Hadn't he died a million deaths already? Hadn't he given up all he held dear for more than fourteen years? The pleasure of knowing his children? The older man's delight in his grandchildren? *Anne?* What more could God require of a man than to give up a wife he loved?

His eyes still unable to penetrate the thick darkness, he blinked, then rubbed them with his knuckles—and saw pale, tender sprouts burst through the hard shell of a brown seed to send tendril roots deep into still more darkness. But his eyes were closed!

He felt in the darkness for a veranda chair and eased into it. "Because Narciso Font died—*I live*," he whispered.

Had the sick young priest not made the effort to go to a strange man in trouble that long-ago night, he might have lived a bit longer. But he *had* made the effort. He had died.

As had the young Christ on His cross. . . .

He sat for a long time in the darkness that did not clear, but the struggle ceased. Don Juan McQueen had *never*, until this moment, thought of dying to himself. Had he died to his own willfulness now?

No joy came. Not even hope. But when at last he got up slowly and walked inside his house, his body moved like a man directed.

At his desk in the parlor, he took out paper, dipped a quill and began to write—not to Robert Mackay. To Anne. . . .

> *For all these long years, dear wife, I see only now that I have forced upon you the intolerable burden of my own selfishness. But the long years are gone and I can but trust God to make your forgiveness possible. I know now that the agony of our separation has been no more painful for me than for you, but in my ignorance of myself, I swear to you I did not know that I had willfully chosen to protect John McQueen at the expense of his family. My pity ran first to myself, even as I believed I was acting in the right, exerting every ounce of energy toward rebuilding a fortune which I would leave to our children and grandchildren. Which, in life, I could share with you.*
>
> *My hand moves stiffly over this page, because only minutes have passed since blind despair gave way to this weary peace. Alone, in the blackest of nights, I endured the realization of how unalterably I have lived these years in exact opposition to the life of Christ, who died that we might live forever. I cannot change the years. I can only hope that you will believe that at last, I see by a Light I pray will never dim for me.*

Our sons, Robert Mackay and John, now urge me to accept confinement at The Cottage for my debts. The law allows this, but I cannot agree to an arrangement which would not actually repay my debts; on which would merely satisfy the courts by my punishment, even though, as your prisoner I would know some degree of happiness. My heart and my mind and my body still cry out for you, but tonight—only minutes ago—I became that corn of wheat which fell into the ground and died. In short, dear Anne, to the best of my knowledge, I have relinquished you to God—come what may. If you live with me or if you do not, this house I built for you will only grow dearer because, wise or unwise, I did build it for you.

Evolving as I write these lines is a determination to pay the Georgia debts so that I may meet God with a clear conscience. Heretofore, any such plans sprang only from my desire to be with you.

I am suddenly too weary for details, but believe me, it is not another scheme, but a full commitment to the wiping out of my sins.

Harry told me earlier tonight, with the innocence and certainty of a child who trusts a Parent, that he fully expects us all to spend Eternity together with God. Harry is a communicant of no church—neither yours nor mine. God, in His mercy, will decide for us all. In one way, as I close this letter, I feel bereft—as though I have just learned of your death or mine.

Relinquishing you into His hands was agony. And yet, there is the peace and the hope that God loves us all as deeply and as infinitely as I tend to believe at this moment. I still pray for a visit from you some day, but if I never see your haunting gray eyes again on this earth, by some means, you must go on believing that I will love you beyond the temporary pause at the grave. Please remember me to our sweet children. Oddly, I feel closer to you than it is within my poor power to understand. As though now I know why, for the more than thirty years of our married life, you have feared distance between us. You need not fear the distance ever again. There is only Light ahead and the darkness cannot put it out. There is also no end to my love, or to my longing to see your smile. I am so strong now, beloved Anne, that I dare to sign myself (trusting you to smile as you read!) ever your adoring husband,

Don Juan *McQueen*

Chapter 49

✻✻✻ Just after dawn, John and William said good-by to their mother and grandmother at The Cottage and began to ride through the autumn woods toward Savannah. William's boat for St. Augustine was scheduled to sail in the afternoon with the tide, but John wanted time for a talk with Robert Mackay at his office. John drove the horse in silence, aware that he was annoying William, but unable to make small talk with so much on his mind.

"Mama's all right," William said, bouncing along beside him on the seat of the phaeton. "I'm tired worrying about her. She's where she wants to be or she'd have gone to Florida long ago. And don't tell me you care more about Mama than I do, because you don't."

"Don't you believe her when she says she really wants to go now?"

"Not exactly. It's still that one letter he wrote last summer." William laughed. "Must have been quite a letter—even for the Old Gentleman. But women are like that."

"Like what?"

"Funny. One day they want one thing, the next day something else. Papa's in the driver's seat now. I'm proud of him for not taking the easy way out of the mess. How would he feel being a prisoner in his own house? Anyway, he'd still owe all that money."

"I'm proud of him too. But I'm thinking about Mama."

John reminded himself that William had lived his life with the family trouble. He'd never known anything else.

There would be no way for him to see their parents as John saw them—lonely, needing each other, growing older—still trapped. William might never have realized that their mother, too, had hoped through all those years. Surely, he'd been too young to grasp the meaning of her near exuberance for the short weeks they'd visited in St. Augustine so long ago. He understood William's impatience with her, but he was two years past his own thirtieth birthday now and could no longer tolerate in himself the youthful rebellion he saw in William. Still, understanding his brother did not shift his concern from what appeared to be their mother's growing determination to go to Florida. Sallie was married and in a home of her own. Who could say that the gradual loss of family responsibility had not begun to free Mama at last? Women aged more quickly than men. Had his mother begun to fear being fifty-two?

As soon as they hitched their phaeton on Bay Street in front of Mackay's office, William hurried off to see to getting his trunk aboard the ship. John, walking alone into the firm of Mein and Mackay, wondered why he expected his brother-in-law to understand Mama's sudden impulse to go any more than he understood it. Robert knew, of course, about that one magnificent letter. Papa had surprised them all by seeming to relinquish any hope that Mama would ever come to be with him. He'd also shown himself to be too honorable to take the easy way of imprisonment in his own home. To his elder son, Don Juan McQueen was standing tall these days.

There was a chance, of course, that William was right about their mother. Once the memory of that one letter dimmed, she could, he supposed, fall right back into her old ways.

Grandmother Smith, he was sure, counted on that.

William had been gone only a few weeks when Sallie's newborn baby died. The evening of the funeral, Anne McQueen, Eliza, and Grandmother Smith sat around Sallie's bed in her Savannah home.

"There will be another child," Grandmother said for the third or fourth time.

"Yes," Sallie answered and turned her face to the wall.

"I know this is small comfort, sister," Eliza whispered, "but death is even harder after you've loved the child for a few years."

"Yes," Sallie said again and wished they'd all leave her alone to cry as much as she needed to.

"Sallie?"

"What, Mama?"

"This may seem a peculiar time to tell you this, but—I'm leaving soon to spend a long time with your father."

Sallie waited for Grandmother Smith's protest. There was silence. She turned her head slowly to look at her mother. The gray eyes were reddened from weeping for another grandchild, but she had never seen such peace in Mama's face.

"My mind is made up, Sallie. I don't know exactly when I'll go. Not until William's had his visit out—just the two of them alone. But somehow I thought it might—raise your spirits a little today, if I told you."

Tears streamed from Sallie's eyes, but she managed a smile and nodded vigorously. "It does, Mama. Oh, it *does* help!"

William and his father had read Eliza's letter about Sallie's baby at Leslie's office and were now walking arm in arm toward their St. Augustine quarters. Papa had said only, "Poor little brave Sallie." But William saw that his eyes were still full of tears, so said nothing as they walked along the narrow street. Tonight was the long-awaited occasion of dinner at Government House. He felt a twinge of guilt for hoping his father wouldn't cancel the engagement.

What could William say to comfort this man whom he admired more than ever? Maybe just being quiet for a change would be best. But he needed some response, and as they crossed the Plaza, he said, "I remember when my brother Alexander died, Papa."

"I still carry that grief, although I don't talk about it. Alexander was a funny little fellow—a charmer, really.

Poorly named, of course, still nothing would do Mama but that we name him for my brother." He smiled. "Our Alexander would have grown into a far more delightful gentleman, I'm sure."

Had he been younger, William would have hugged his father there in full view of everybody. Papa's heart was broken too, but he wasn't going to spoil their evening by sniffling or saying sad things. William could imagine how gloomy it was in Savannah now. He felt awfully sorry for Sallie too. She'd always been a convenient, pleasant sister. Brave, as Papa said. She'd have died before admitting William had hurt her in a wrestling match when they were children. He'd write to Sallie and tell her how sorry he felt, but it was surely better to be here with Papa, who was strong and believed as much in laughter and good times and small jokes—even when his heart was breaking—as he believed in a man being true to himself. He could be himself with his father, with no fear of criticism or scolding.

They'd been having the best of times in Florida, traveling for most of his visit from one of the McQueen properties to another. They had swapped stories and laughed, and also, although Papa didn't care much for either, to please William they'd hunted and fished. They had done a lot of serious talking, too, and he knew he'd been right all his life to believe that Don Juan McQueen was the greatest man on earth.

When the time came to go back to Savannah, he would certainly see Mama with different eyes. His father had asked him to think of her always as a lovely, lonely, courageous woman who needed all the help and cheer she could come by in order to live her days away from the husband she loved. William had seldom thought of her that way. He would from now on, and the first thing he meant to do when he returned was to put Mama on a boat to Florida.

He waited outside when his father decided to walk over to the church to pray for Sallie. Even Papa's religion didn't spoil him. He came back out in a few minutes, smiling like the sun coming up.

"All right, son, here we go—to my humble quarters to

transform our handsome selves into gentlemen. I'm more delighted than ever with Robert's gift of new silver buckles for my shoes. Especially since we're dining tonight with his Excellency. Enrique White is not my favorite person, but the old goat's eyes will pop when he sees those new buckles!"

As the schooner headed toward the Savannah wharf on February 11, 1806, William was on deck, looking hard for his mother among the noisy, cheering crowd on the waterfront. They would all surely be there to meet him—Sallie, John, Robert, Eliza, and little Mary Anne. Eliza might even bring her new baby. But it was his mother's face he searched for.

The creaking ship inched so slowly into its berth, he thought he might burst with excitement before he could tell Mama that his father had sent more than enough money for her fare to St. Augustine. He hadn't the remotest idea how he'd be able to keep Papa's big secret, but he'd promised not to breathe a word about the new appointment made right in his presence by Enrique White—"Old Sobersides," as Papa called him. In his pocket was the letter to John and Robert in which details of the new windfall were laid out by Don Juan McQueen himself, each phrase ringing with new confidence and hope.

His father had left it unsealed so that William could read and reread it on the voyage up. To pass the time now, while the maddeningly slow docking proceeded, he scanned it again:

> *I have the pleasure to inform you, my dear Messers Mackay and McQueen, that the King has been graciously pleased to grant me the exclusive privilege of fitting out vessels to wreck on the Florida Keys and all the coast of Florida, with powers to appoint any of His Majesty's subjects under me that I might choose to call in. I will be occupied in supporting the commerce and saving the vessels and lives of the unfortunate of any nation that may from time to time be lost on the Coast. This appointment, my dear sirs, will be no less honor-*

able than profitable. Twenty-eight to thirty British ves-
sels from Providence have annually been supported
from such wrecking and fishing, but until my humble
suggestion, the Eyes of Spain have never been opened
to view the advantages lost. Rest assured that the as-
signment is of the first magnitude in importance and
since, after a few years' labor, my rights can be sold
for a heavy sum, the days of my later years and those
of my beloved wife, can, if she so decides, be spent to-
gether in debt-free luxury. As you know, our border is
now closed to more U.S. settlers, but my son William
can attest (in case my word is doubted) that in his
presence was granted by His Excellency, Enrique
White, special freedom of entrance by Anne McQueen
at any time convenient to her. She may not, however,
take the Spanish oath of allegiance which fact, if I
know my wife, will cause her no anguish. (Smile.)

In the pushing, waving throng of people, William saw
both John and Robert, but there was no sign of his mother.
Oh, well, he thought, she's waiting in the Mackay
carriage—out of the crowd.

William was third in line for the boatswain's chair, and
as he swung out over the side of the schooner, he could
see John and Robert pressing through the knots of people.
They greeted him warmly, but he knew before he asked
that something was wrong.

"Grandmother had another stroke last week," John
said. "Mama's with her, of course, at The Cottage. She
wanted so much to come."

"Eliza and Sallie took the children to Thunderbolt
too," Robert said. "Otherwise, you know they'd be right
here to welcome you."

William looked from one to the other, trying but failing
miserably to hide his rage. When Mackay began to assure
him that Grandmother was not dying, that the stroke had
only increased her paralysis, he exploded: "I'm sorry, of
course, but it's enough to—spoil everything! You both
know as well as I that Mama won't visit Papa as long as
the old lady's that sick!"

He pushed ahead of them through the crowd toward

the area where his trunk, loaded with presents, would be lowered from the ship. Then, swiping at his tears, he whirled around: "Just when everything is going so well for Papa! The old witch must have known!"

"William! That's enough," John said, grabbing his arm.

"No, it isn't enough! Nothing will ever be enough—until she dies!" He held out both hands, pleading for understanding. "I—I'm sorry. I shouldn't have said that. I—care about Grandmother too. But she's old! And Mama and Papa are getting older all the time. They—don't have forever—any more. . . ."

Chapter 50

✼✼✼   On a hot, dry August afternoon in the next year, 1807, Harry was polishing silver in the kitchen at Los Molinos when he heard Don Juan ride in from St. Augustine, three days earlier than expected.

"All right, Niño," Harry shouted to the old dog, already jumping at the door to be let out. "I guess you and me eat again now that he done come home, huh?"

Dog and servant bounded across the backyard, Niño barking his welcome, Harry waving both arms and thanking God that his master had made the trip safely without him. In a good mood too, Harry could tell, because he'd galloped in, scattering chickens and ducks.

"Magnificent news, Harry," he shouted, dismounting like a young man. "The greatest news you've ever heard!"

"Miss Anne?"

McQueen laughed. "No. The old lady's still got Miss Anne beside her, but my news is excellent just the same. The governor has requested, not just five new schooners to begin my wrecking enterprise—but ten!"

"Oh, that be good," Harry said, unsaddling the horse. "And all this time you done wondered how you stand with the governor. Ain't you ashame?"

"Stop fussing around with that infernal saddle and listen to me," McQueen ordered. "With the request for my new ships, White also sent along instructions to the intendant in Havana for one thousand American dollars payable to Don Juan McQueen!"

Harry whistled. "All at once?"

"All at once! And I've requested Don Bartolomé to send it, immediately upon its arrival, to Robert Mackay. You know what for?"

"Them debts we owes up there?"

"Not at all. I'm handling those myself, now that my future is secured again. The money is to be a beginning toward William's education abroad! Receivable *only*—and his Excellency will specify this for me—if Mackay sees to it that the boy learns Spanish." He whacked Harry on the back. "William is one of us, Harry. Mark my word, he'll head straight for East Florida the instant his education is finished!"

Harry stood beaming at him. "We thought Mausa John was going to be the one, didn't we?"

"Yes. Yes, we did. But Miss Anne needs him. God in His mercy has given us William." He rushed on, "The boy's livelier anyway. A man of action, like his father."

"They's something new in the house," Harry said. "Spread out on Katrina's kitchen table."

"By the way, how is Katrina? After all, I made the trip alone so you could take care of her."

"She be better. Wouldn't surprise me none to find her out of bed. Them sharp ears couldn't miss you galloping in like you did."

"Tell me, what's all spread out on Katrina's kitchen table? The new silver from Jamaica? It came!"

"Yes, sir. Yesterday. I was polishing it when you rode up."

"Is it beautiful? Is my initial engraved on it?"

"It be beautiful, all right. And they's a fancy M on the spoon handles. Nothing got here yet but a big silver pitcher and fourteen tablespoons."

"Well, no matter. Until the rest arrives, our old knives and forks will go with it nicely." Don Juan started for the house, then turned back. "A good omen, Harry. The arrival of that silver, I've just realized, is an excellent omen that by some means, Miss Anne might get away one day soon to have dinner with us!"

Harry watched his master stride up the path. That be some gentleman, he thought. Keeps his cheer higher than a pine tree! I know it done break his heart when Miss

Anne, she couldn't come, specially after she done make up her own mind. He patted the horse's flanks. "You bring him home safe, though. Good horse. But I ain't letting you take him no more without me. I come near worrying myself to death."

It would be at least a year before the new schooners could be built and sailed to St. Augustine, but Don Juan redeemed the time by setting his mind to being, as he wrote Mackay, "a very steady and industrious planter."

Don Bartolomé de Castro continued to handle his business in St. Augustine, seeing to the rental and repairs of the small house on Treasury Street and successfully bringing off the sale of the Saw Mill Tract to Zubizarreta. The monies received would be, by a new arrangement with John Leslie, converted into British pounds and sent back to Georgia on his debts. The thought of Anne's face when she learned of that buoyed his spirits more than he could explain. With Fort George Island and Ortega now the problems of John Houstoun McIntosh, he could devote his time and energies to making Los Molinos de McQueen one of the finest, most productive plantations in Florida.

Deep inside, he had become reconciled to the fact that when and if Anne did manage to come, it would only be for a long visit. Still, he saw no harm in tempting her with life as the mistress of the kind of well-ordered plantation she had always dreamed of having.

Surely, he had been slow to see that through all the years, he had not been trusting her to heaven, but since he had let go—relinquished their future into the hands of God—he walked a new road. "I can wait now," he wrote to John early in September, "without too much pain and with no bitterness toward Grandmother Smith. At times, I even find it rather easy to pray for the return of her health. (Smile.) Owing, I suppose, to the knowledge that surely then, your mother would be free to come."

He wrote frequently that fall to his son-in-law concerning business matters, the crops at Los Molinos, and his mounting optimism about the years ahead.

*Not many of us believe that your Congress will suc-
ceed in acquiring the Floridas any time soon, and
Spain now has a few British settlers even among the
Keys. I do not doubt that one day, if my life be spared,
I will establish coffee and sugar estates along the
Coast. I also see great hope for profitable Indian River
fishing, with a view toward the sale of fish oil as well
as salt fish. Many, including John Leslie, still despair
over the fate of the Floridas under Spain. Once again,
Don Juan McQueen does not.*

To Eliza, he wrote, as always, from his heart.

*My faith never wavers in respect to your promise to
bring my grandchildren to visit me, beloved daughter.
I can honestly say that most days my faith does not
waver in any serious manner whatever. Oh, I am still
a faulty man, full of conceit and at times given to impossible dreams, I can collect enough money to pay my
debts before I go to my long home and leave something
to my dear children, I shall one day depart in peace.*

*If you should change your mind about accompany-
ing your husband to London this October, I pray you,
come to Los Molinos. Nothing in life would afford me
so much pleasure, but I leave you free to decide. One
brief visit for love of me, and longing for my company,
is far dearer than an extended stay for the sake of duty
to your old father, who loves you more than you can
imagine.*

At the end of September, he wrote to Anne:

*All is somehow different between us. The old stress
and strain have gone. That you will come when you
can, I have no doubt. Each morning and night, kneeling at my altar to pray before the same crucifix you
hid (smile), I ask the Almighty to reassure you where I
am concerned. Can a rosary or a crucifix ever come
between us again, dear Anne, when the God of all love
and comfort binds us together? Harry has promised
that when my life is finished on earth, he will dress me*

in the Franciscan habit which so repulsed and fright-
ened you long ago. Wise, I think, to speak of death
now, while we are both in excellent health. So, should
you, one future day, see me in my brown habit, it will
mean only that I have died in God, in order to live for-
ever with Him. That brown robe has often been my
comfort so far from your arms. I beg of you, do not de-
spise it.

I am waiting with the keenest possible anticipation
for your visit to me. Until we are together again, by
whatever means, you may trust me. Have you hinted
you did not trust me? Never. But at times, I have
known. . . .

Anne pushed the door open with her elbow and set her
mother's supper tray on the table beside the bed. "Sorry to
be a little late with this, but young John just rode in from
Savannah. You've been lying here in the dark, haven't
you?"

"No matter, my dear," Elizabeth Smith said. "Good
thoughts often come to a peaceful heart at dusk. The days
are shorter, now that November's here."

Anne lighted a candle from another burning in the hallway outside the bedroom and placed it near the bed. "It's
a mild evening, though. John's waiting for me on the
porch. I don't believe I've ever seen him look so tired
and—drawn. It's too much for him, managing Oatland
along with his position at Mein and Mackay."

She took her mother's good hand and lifted her enough
to plump the pillows, then spread a large linen napkin
across her breast. "There, now. Lessie's made chicken fric-
assee. Doesn't it look good?"

"Oh, as good as anything else, my dear. I don't get
hungry any more."

Anne hid a smile. Her mother seldom left a bite of any
meal she'd brought. Yet, every day for all the months
she'd been lying there, the old lady had complained about
her dwindling appetite—every serving was "way too
much."

"That's way too much chicken, Anne! And I'll never
eat all that rice."

Only the right side of her mother's body was paralyzed, but more and more often of late, the flabby left arm
had lain motionless too, so that Anne would feed her.

"I'm sure John will be in to see you after a while. Poor
boy seemed so distracted. He had almost nothing to say,
except that he did see William off to Europe today. Sallie
was at the dock too, with Eliza and the children. The
Mackays will be leaving for London in a week or so. Do
you remember?"

"Of course I remember! There's nothing whatever
wrong with my mind, Anne. How often do I have to tell
you that your mother's mind is as sharp as ever?"

Anne put a large forkful of chicken and rice into her
mouth. "There—how does that taste?"

"It's all right. Commend Lessie for me."

"She'll be in to bathe you later on. You can tell her
yourself then. It'll please her far more."

"Oh," the old woman said, chewing. "*You're* not bath-
ing me tonight?"

"Not tonight. I'm sure you want me to spend as much
time as possible with John." She loaded the fork again and
held it to her mother's mouth. "I hope nothing's wrong for
him at work."

"John will be all right. He's one of *us*."

"Maybe I just imagined he seemed nervous."

"Poor Anne. Poor Anne. God in His mercy will have
to give you peace."

Anne smiled. "Come now! Do I sound all that
wretched?" She mopped up the gravy with a piece of bis-
cuit and fed it to her mother. "There! Every bite gone. I
thought you weren't hungry."

Still chewing, Elizabeth Smith shook her head. "I eat
to please you, my dear. You're so good to your helpless
mother. You've had such little pleasure in your life, the
least I can do—is eat for you. I'm glad your father doesn't
know you're—still suffering."

"Nonsense." Anne removed the napkin, wiped the
wrinkled mouth, and held a glass of cool tea for her to
drink. "I'm not suffering at all tonight! Can't you tell?"

"Very hard to know about you these days. In spite of

your concern over John's being tired, you do seem—a little excited. Tell Mama."

"John brought a letter just now from Mary Esther Huger—the best friend anyone ever had. I stopped long enough to take a quick peek at it. She's coming to stay with you for as long as I'm in Florida with Big John!"

"I—see."

Anne stood up. "I know how you feel about my going, Mama, but things are quiet there now. Anyway, I have to go. There'll be no discussion this time."

"Very well," Mrs. Smith turned her head away. "Don't give me a thought. Mary Esther and I will be just fine—here alone. Just fine. She's our kind. My supper was excellent. Thank you. And tell young John I'm waiting to see him. I'll do my best, of course, to cheer the boy."

The river and the marsh were darkening swiftly when Anne joined her son on The Cottage porch. "Your grandmother cleaned up every bite again," she said wearily. John said nothing. "I told her I'm going to Florida."

It was too dark to see his face clearly, but his long sigh, which came in jerks, heavy—almost sobs—struck fear into her. "John! Are you ill?"

"No, Mama."

"Something's happened then! You're keeping back something dreadful. You weren't like yourself when you got home, but I thought you were—just tired." Her head began to shake from side to side and she couldn't stop it. *"John!"*

He fell to his knees beside her chair, weeping, with the dry, wracking sounds of a man fighting for control of himself. Setting erect, she held his head in both her hands. Her mind hurled back to the only time she had ever heard his father cry like that . . . the night their little boy, Alexander, died. The same terror stabbed now.

Helpless sobs from a man meant that it was already too late—that nothing could be done.

Mechanically, her fingers moved in his thick hair, their pressure unyielding, for giving comfort—grasping for it. "Is it—Papa?"

She felt his head move up and down. Wordlessly, he was saying yes. Yes. It's Papa. Papa's—*dead*. He hadn't spoken the word, but he needn't. His shoulders sagged, his strength draining away just as hers was.

If they could only lie down somewhere—both of them—she thought senselessly. But John was on his knees and she was sitting up in a chair.

"How do you know?" she demanded. "Who told you? Maybe it's all a mistake. He's so far away—it could be only a rumor!"

"It's—true," he said, reaching for a crumpled letter in his pocket. "Father O'Reilly wrote about—everything."

"But I'm going to Florida! I just told your grandmother—*I'm going to Florida!*" She pushed him aside and jumped to her feet. "I'm going to be with him for Christmas . . . and a long time after!"

"He's gone, Mama."

Backing away from him as though to escape what he'd said, she heard another woman's voice rasp, "He can't be! I'm—going to him!"

John drew her back to the chair and pushed her firmly into it. Now, he was smoothing her hair—holding her head between his hands, trying to *make* her accept it. She would *not*.

"Let's just be together for a while . . ." he whispered. "Then, if you like, I'll read you the letter."

"No!"

"Father O'Reilly cared about him. He wrote all the details . . . typhus fever . . . Harry watched over him for the one week he was sick. Harry was holding him in his arms when he died. It was on Sunday, October eleventh."

"No!"

"Because he had typhus fever," her son went on relentlessly, "they buried him in his yard beside the button bushes for three days. Until word reached St. Augustine. . . . The governor then ordered Don Bartolomé de Castro to fetch him. Papa's Negroes carried him on a fine litter over the forty-two miles to the city."

Except that her head was shaking again from side to side, Anne sat motionless, wanting desperately to get far, far away from her son.

"Papa had his own escort of dragoons, Mama," John said proudly. "Sent by the governor."

The pathetic pride reached her. She stopped shaking her head and sat straighter in the chair.

"He's in the Campo Santo Cemetery, right back of his Treasury Street lot—a little way down the Street of the Swamp. I can picture it. . . ."

She could picture it too, even after twelve years. The Treasury Street lot, the cemetery itself under the big trees. It helped. A strange voice, not her own, asked, "Those people—loved and respected him, didn't they?"

"Yes."

"Have you—told anyone else?"

"No."

"Poor boy," she whispered. "Poor John. . . ."

After some span of time unknown to her, John asked if he wanted him to get a candelabra from inside in order to read the priest's letter.

"Not yet. Later. But there is another letter I would like you to read to me." The voice was nearly her own. "In the lefthand top drawer of my bedroom cupboard—on top of the bundle of his letters. Right on top."

John kissed her hair and went inside. The marsh and the river were gone now . . . under a solid lid of darkness. A clapper rail cried out from the tall grasses down by their dock. Another answered a long way off. Odd for November. Something must have frightened them. . . .

The lighted candelabra in John's hand moved his shadow ahead of him across the porch. Then her son was in the rocker beside her, the letter from the top of the bundle in his hand. . . .

"It's the last paragraph on the last page I want to hear," she said quietly. "I've marked it. Do you see where I've marked it?"

The darkness was thicker now that John had brought a light.

"I've read it so many times," she whispered. "Can you see where I've marked it?"

"I see, Mama."

"Oh, wait—you *have* read all the priest's letter?"

"Yes."

"And—was Papa—buried in that warm brown robe? Did he say?"

It seemed to her that John waited a long time to answer. At last, he said, "Yes. Harry dressed him in it."

"And—did Harry remember—his nightcap too? Or didn't the priest think to mention that?"

"He mentioned it. Yes. It wouldn't be Papa without his nightcap."

She took a deep breath and lifted her chin. "Now, that paragraph from your father's letter, please."

As he read, her son's trembling voice became Big John's. Line flowed upon line and solace came, as strong and warm as her husband's arms. . . .

" 'Relinquishing you into His hands was agony. And yet, there is the peace and the hope that God loves us all as deeply and as infinitely as I tend to believe at this moment. I still pray for a visit from you some day, but if I never see your haunting gray eyes again on this earth, by some means, you must go on believing that I will love you beyond the temporary pause at the grave. Please remember me to our sweet children. Oddly, I feel closer to you than it is within my poor power to understand. As though now I know why, for the more than thirty years of our married life, *you have feared distance between us*. You need not fear the distance ever again. There is only Light ahead and the darkness cannot put it out. There is also no end to my love, or to my longing to see your smile. I am so strong now, beloved Anne, that I dare to sign myself (trusting you to smile as you read!) ever your adoring husband, Don Juan McQueen.' "

At long last, the distance dropped away.

Afterword

✱✱✱ On March 24, 1809, less than two years after Don Juan's death, Anne joined him forever. She died at Thunderbolt and is buried in Colonial Cemetery, Savannah. Grandmother Smith survived Anne by a few months and is presumed to be buried there also, beside Grandfather Smith, although her stone has been obliterated by time. Eliza, who lived until 1852, is buried at Laurel Grove; Colonial Cemetery was then closed. Her husband, Robert Mackay, died at the age of forty-four while on a business trip to New York and is buried there in the historic cemetery at Trinity Church. There is no recorded date of William's death, but Margaret Cowper, who did finally marry John McQueen, Jr. is thought to have died in the 1860's, long surviving John, who worked at settling his father's complicated Spanish estate until his own death in 1822. He lies near his mother in Colonial Cemetery, Savannah. Sallie (Sarah Postell Williamson) died in 1819, the year Spain ceded the Floridas to the United States under President James Monroe, by the Treaty of Adams-Onís.

Don Juan lies in what is now called Tolomato Cemetery (Campo Santo) in St. Augustine. The years have also destroyed his marker. But thanks to the skillful and dedicated efforts of the Historic St. Augustine Preservation Board, one can today experience parts of the old city Don Juan McQueen loved much as it must have been when he walked its picturesque, narrow streets. The Plaza is still there, and the building housing the offices of the Preserva-

tion Board stands where Government House once stood—
the site of the first seat of Government on the North American continent. Intricate and accurate drawings for future
reconstruction of old Government House have been made
by Dr. Carleton I. Calkin, until recently the Curator for the
Preservation Board. I am deeply indebted to Dr. Calkin for
the privilege of examining his excellent work and for his
informative assistance with many details.

The old coquina residence of Father Miguel O'Reilly
is still at the head of the Lane That Leads to the Marina—
now called Bravo Lane. The parish church of McQueen's
time is a part of the rebuilt, towered Cathedral on the
Plaza, and across St. George Street, the site of Don Juan's
house is vacant and—one can hope—awaiting the reconstruction of his residence.

Any view of the St. Johns River is surely one
McQueen loved. A section of the great river which I particularly like can be seen near St. Augustine at the terminus of the Picolata Road about fifteen miles due west of
the city, the same route over which McQueen rode on
horseback to take Job Wiggens' ferry across to the
Alachua Plain. One of the most scenic drives in Florida is
on Fort George Island, just north of the Mayport Ferry on
Florida route A1A, and at the end of that drive, in excellent repair and housing the offices of the Kingsley Plantation State Park, is Don Juan's little Fort George residence.
In fact, much of the land McQueen was granted is now
public land. His vast holdings at Cape Florida on the
southern tip of Key Biscayne are incorporated into Cape
Florida State Park. His acreage on Amelia Island is Fort
Clinch State Park, offering a magnificent view of the wa-
terways over which he traveled. His large plantation at
Ortega, San Juan de Nepomuceno, is one of Jacksonville's
finest residential areas.

In Savannah, McQueen's Island is part of Fort Pulaski
National Monument. Thunderbolt, outside Savannah on
the Wilmington River (once called the Thunderbolt River)
is a fishing village, and I have stood at the site of The Cottage and looked across at Oatland Island, attempting to reconstruct the surrounds for Don Bender and George
Sottung, my sensitive jacket designer and artist. One

reaches Thunderbolt on Skidaway Road, the same route the McQueen family traveled to visit Savannah, then a shell lane winding through forests of live oak and pine, widened from an ancient Indian foot trail which led from the Piedmont regions of Georgia to the sea island called Skidaway.

To thank everyone who helped me during my research in both Georgia and Florida would be impossible, but the book could not have been written without constant enthusiastic help, over a period of three years, from my valued friend, historian Walter C. Hartridge of Savannah. His two books, *The Letters of Don Juan McQueen to his Family* and *The Letters of Robert Mackay to His Wife*, have been indispensable. And as with my work on the St. Simons trilogy, he and Susan, young Walter, Gloria Green—and Elizabeth, the family dog—have supplied the warm, encouraging dimension an author needs during the anxious periods of trying to sort out complex and often obscure material. I am still searching for a way to say thank you.

My search goes on also for a means of adequate thanks to Eugenia Arana of the excellent St. Augustine Historical Society Library. I have not only learned from her the correct Spanish pronunciation for our shared name, I have benefited endlessly from her expertise as a linguist and as one of the most imaginative and original research historians it has been my good fortune to know. More than all that, Eugenia has become *mi amiga querida*, as well as my straight line to her busy and knowledgeable husband, Luis Arana, historian, National Park Service, Castillo de San Marcos. From my heart, I thank them both.

As with the Spanish East Florida research for *Lighthouse*, I am once more deeply indebted to another delightful friend, Dena Snodgrass of Jacksonville, one of Florida's most astute historical researchers, who not only assisted me with much authoritative information, but who managed to persuade James R. Ward, City Editor of the *Florida Times-Union*, and James H. Lipscomb, Jr., to read and criticize the manuscript. Thank you, Dena. Thank you, Mr. Ward, and thank you, Mr. Lipscomb.

I must mention my special friends, Pat Wickman and Ruth Kent of St. Augustine, in one happy sentence because Pat, as a Minorcan descendant, and Ruth, during her tenure at St. Augustine Historical Society Library, gave generously, not only of their knowledge of old St. Augustine, but of their own sensitivities to the often peculiar needs of this novelist. Most days, you can find Pat Wickman in charge of the reconstructed Gallego House on St. George Street—dressed in Minorcan garb and cooking Minorcan dishes over a wood fire.

St. Augustine's J. Evelyn Braddock, naturalist and writer, gave me invaluable source material on indigenous plants in old Florida, and if you are able to picture its natural beauty, it is because of her knowledge and joy in it. I am equally indebted to Captain Joseph Gould, USN, retired, for sharing his expertise on nautical matters in Don Juan's time.

My gratitude also to Mary Jane Kuhl, University of South Florida Library in Tampa, and to one of my closest and most loyal friends, Theo Hotch of Brunswick, Georgia. Elizabeth Rountree, Director, and Harriet Hammond, reference librarian, along with the staff of Brunswick Public Library have again served me well as did Virginia Shields until her death during the early stages of the writing. Lilla Hawes, Director of the Georgia Historical Society Library in Savannah, Fraser Ledbetter and Lillian Knight of the St. Simons Library, Pat Bryant, Deputy Surveyor General of the State of Georgia in Atlanta, Marion Green, Park Ranger at Kingsley Plantation State Park, Bernard Berg of the Ocmulgee National Monument, Macon, my erudite neighbor, Harry Parker, John Wilson, and Monroe Wilson of St. Simons Island, Mary Porter and Betty Jo Feltz of Lima, Ohio, Lorrie Carlson of Chicago, and Jacqueline Bearden of the St. Augustine Historical Society Library all gave far more specific help than they realized. Throughout the writing I made constant use of two invaluable books, *The Georgia-Florida Frontier* by Richard K. Murdoch and *Zéspedes in East Florida* by Helen Hornbeck Tanner.

Relative to the scenes laid in old Pensacola, my niece, Cindy Price of Nashville, and Mr. and Mrs. Paul Caro of Pensacola did special and perceptive research. For his assistance to them, I also thank Norman Simons, Curator of the Pensacola Historical Museum.

My mother's neighbor, Nancy Goshorn, has through still another book, given me not only hours of research and manuscript reading time but, along with my mother and Lady Jane Goshorn, far more deep-down encouragement than I can ever express. In the irrepressible Brother Pius of Holy Spirit Monastery, Conyers, Georgia, and in Sister Mary Assumpta Ahles OSF of St. Francis Convent, Little Falls, Minnesota, I have found two more treasured friends, both of whom helped me freely and with great good humor.

Once more I am faced with the happy but hopeless task of attempting to communicate my gratitude to my best friend and fellow author, Joyce Blackburn, and to my skillful typist, Elsie Goodwillie, for hourly understanding, good cheer, and concrete support in far more ways than met the printer's eye in the pages of the finished typescript. Words grow stubborn here, but Joyce and Elsie both know my heart. I must also thank Frances Stankiewicz, Lilly Higgins, and Frances Pitts for proofreading and valued criticism.

I am both personally and professionally indebted to Edward L. Burlingame, Editor-in-Chief of the Trade Division of J. B. Lippincott Company, and to Peggy Cronlund, my gifted copy editor, for their friendship as well as for their expert attention to the manuscript. This same gratitude goes warmly to everyone at Lippincott, who worked with what seemed unusual love and care through each stage of the book's publication.

My friend Carolyn Blakemore will understand, I hope, at least some of the many ways in which I am also indebted to her.

Don Juan McQueen would not have been thought of as a novel without my long-time editor, Tay Hohoff, the magnificent lady who guided me through the entire St. Simons trilogy and who came to mean far more to me as a human being than is usual in these days of often cursory author-editor relationships. Don Juan, who appeared briefly in *Lighthouse*, was a favorite of Tay's. In spite of failing health and eyesight, she "gave me" not only the beginning and ending for this book, but the particular kind of tough-tender guidance and faith in myself for which she was known throughout the publishing world. Tay was above all my beloved friend and, in a way I can't explain, she will go on giving me no choice but to believe that *I* can go on. She worked her magic through Parts One and Two of the manuscript, then died in her sleep during the final rewrite of Chapter 41. I hope she approves. When Tay Hohoff was still here, she railed if I used the phrase I am using now—but she *was* one of the world's great editors.

EUGENIA PRICE

St. Simons Island, Georgia
March, 1974

ABOUT THE AUTHOR

◆

EUGENIA PRICE is known the world over for her nonfiction as well as for her bestselling historical novels based on the lives of people in the southeastern United States. The first novel of her popular St. Simon's Trilogy, was published in 1965. For this trilogy she was awarded the National Endowment for the Arts Governor's Award and the Distinguished Service Award from Georgia College. In addition, she is known for her Florida trilogy and bestselling Savannah quartet. A resident of St. Simon's Island, Georgia, Ms. Price is currently working on a new Georgia trilogy which includes her most recent novels, *Bright Captivity* and *Where Shadows Go.*